THE PRACTICE EFFECT

The
Practice Effect

David Brin

BANTAM BOOKS
TORONTO · NEW YORK · LONDON · SYDNEY

Published simultaneously in the United States and Canada

Bantam Books are published by Bantam Books, Inc. Its trademark con-
sisting of the words "Bantam Books" and the portrayal of a rooster, is
Registered in U.S. Patent and Trademark Office and in other countries.
Marca Registrada. Bantam Books, Inc., 666 Fifth Avenue, New York,
New York 10103.

PRINTED IN THE UNITED STATES OF AMERICA

"To the 'Friday' crowd,
To Carol and Nora,
And to lovers of
    Other worlds—"

1

Sooee Generis

1

The lecture was *really* boring.

At the front of the dimly lit conference room, the portly, gray-haired director of the Sahara Institute of Technology paced back and forth—staring at the ceiling with his hands clasped behind his back—while he pontificated ponderously on a subject he clearly barely understood.

At least that's how Dennis Nuel saw it, suffering in silence in one of the back rows.

Once upon a time, Marcel Flaster might have been one of the shining lights of physics. But that had been long ago, before any of the younger scientists present had ever considered careers in reality physics. Dennis wondered what could ever have converted a once-talented mind into a boring, tendentious administrator. He swore he would jump off of Mt. Feynman before it ever happened to him.

The sonorous voice droned on.

"And so we see, people, that by using zievatronics alternate realities appear to be almost within our reach, presenting possibilities for bypassing both space and time. . . ."

Dennis nursed his hangover near the back of the crowded conference room, and wondered what power on Earth could have dragged him out of bed on a Monday morning to come down here and listen to Marcel Flaster expound about zievatronics.

His eyelids drooped. He began to slump in his seat.

"Dennis!" Gabriella Versgo elbowed him in the ribs, whispering sharply. "*Will* you straighten up and pay attention?"

Dennis sat up quickly, blinking. *Now* he recalled what power on Earth had dragged him here.

At seven a.m. Gabbie had kicked open the door to his room and hauled him by his ear into the shower, ignoring his howling protests and his modesty. She had kept her formidable grip on his arm until they both were planted here in the Sahara Tech conference room.

Dennis rubbed his arm just above the elbow. One of these days, he decided, he was going to sneak into Gabbie's room and throw away all the little rubber balls the redhead liked to squeeze while she studied.

She nudged him again. "Will you sit still? You have the attention span of a cranky otter! Do you want to find yourself exiled even farther from the zievatronics experiment?"

As usual, Gabbie hit close to home. He shook his head silently and made an effort to be attentive.

Dr. Flaster finished drawing a vague figure in the holo tank at the front of the seminar room. The psychophysicist put his light-pen down on the podium and unconsciously wiped his hands on his pants, though the last piece of blackboard chalk had been outlawed more than thirty years before.

"*That* is a zievatron," he announced proudly.

Dennis looked at the light-drawing unbelievingly. He whispered, "If that's a zievatron, I'm a teetotaler. Flaster's got the poles reversed, and the field's inside out!"

Gabriella's blush almost matched the shade of her fiery hair. Her fingernails lanced into his thigh.

Dennis winced, but managed an expression of lamblike innocence when Flaster looked up myopically. After a moment the director cleared his throat.

"As I was saying earlier, all bodies possess centers of mass. The centroid of an object is the balance point, where all net forces can be said to come to play . . . where its *reality* can be ascribed."

"You, my boy," he said, pointing to Dennis. "Can you tell me where *your* centroid is?"

"Umm," Dennis considered foggily. He hadn't really been listening all that carefully. "I guess I must have left it at home, sir."

Snickers came from some of the other postdocs seated around the back of the room. Gabbie's blush deepened. She sank into her seat, obviously wishing she were elsewhere.

The Chief Scientist smiled vaguely. "Ah, Nuel, isn't it? Dr. Dennis Nuel?"

Across the aisle, Dennis caught a glimpse of Bernald Brady grinning at his predicament. The tall, beagle-eyed young man had once been his chief rival until managing to have Dennis completely removed from the activity in the main zievatronics laboratory. Brady gave Dennis a smile of pure spite.

Dennis shrugged. After what had happened in the past few months, he felt he had little left to lose.

"Uh, yessir, Dr. Flaster. It's kind of you to remember me. I used to be assistant director of Lab One, you might recall."

Gabriella continued her descent into the upholstery, trying very much to look as if she had never seen Dennis before in her life.

Flaster nodded. "Ah, yes. Now I recollect. As a matter of fact, your name has crossed my desk very recently."

Bernald Brady's face lit up. Clearly, nothing would please Brady more than if Dennis were sent on a far-away sample-collecting mission . . . say, to Greenland or Mars. So long as he remained, Dennis presented a threat to Brady's relentless drive to curry favor and climb the bureaucratic ladder. Also, without really wishing to be, Dennis seemed to be an obstacle to Brady's romantic ambitions for Gabriella.

"In any event, Dr. Nuel," Flaster continued, "you certainly cannot have 'left' your centroid anywhere. I believe if you check you'll find it somewhere near your navel."

Dennis looked down at his belt buckle, then beamed back at the Director.

Why, so it is! You can be sure I'll keep better track of it in the future!

"It's disappointing to learn," Flaster said, affecting a hearty tone, "that someone so adept with a makeshift sling knows so little about center of mass!"

He was clearly referring to the incident a week ago, at the staff formal dance, when a nasty little flying creature had come streaking in through a window, terrorizing the crowd around the punch bowl. Dennis had removed his cummerbund, folded it into a sling, and flung a shot glass to bring down the batlike creature before it could hurt someone seriously with its razor-sharp beak.

The improvisation had made him an instant hero among the postdocs and techs and got Gabbie started on her present campaign to "save his career." But at the time all he had really wanted was to get a closer look at the little creature. The brief glimpse he caught had set his mind spinning with possibilities.

Most of those present at the dance had assumed that it was an escaped experiment from the Gene-craft Center, at the opposite end of the Institute. But Dennis had other ideas.

One look had told him that the thing had clearly not come from Earth!

Taciturn men from Security had quickly arrived and crated the stunned animal away. Still, Dennis was certain it had come from Lab One . . . *his* old lab, where the main zievatron was kept . . . now off limits to everyone but Flaster's handpicked cronies.

"Well, Dr. Flaster," Dennis ventured, "since you bring up the subject, I'm sure we're all interested in the centroid of that vicious little varmint that buzzed the party. Can you tell us what it was, at last?"

Suddenly it was very quiet in the conference room. It was an unconventional thing to do, challenging the Chief Scientist in front of everybody. But Dennis didn't care anymore. Without any apparent reason the man had already reassigned him away from his life's work. What more could Flaster do to him?

Flaster regarded Dennis expressionlessly. Finally he nodded. "Come to my office an hour after the seminar, Dr. Nuel. I promise I will answer all of your questions then."

Dennis blinked, surprised. Did the fellow really mean it?

He nodded, indicating he would be there, and Flaster turned back to his holosketch.

"As I was saying," Flaster resumed, "a psychosomatic reality anomaly has its start when we surround a center of mass by a field of improbability which . . ."

When attention had shifted fully away from them, Gabriella whispered once more in Dennis's ear. "*Now* you've done it!" she said.

"Hmm? Done what?" He looked back at her innocently.

"As if you don't know!" she bit. "He's going to send you to the Qattara Depression to count sand grains! You watch!"

On those rare occasions when he remembered to correct his posture, Dennis Nuel stood a little above average in height. He dressed casually . . . some might say sloppily. His hair was slightly too long for the current style—more out of a vague obstinacy than out of any real conviction.

Dennis's face sometimes took on that dreamy expression often associated either with genius or an inspired aptitude for practical jokes. In reality he was just a little too lazy to qualify for the former, and just a bit too goodhearted for the latter. He had curly brown hair and brown eyes that were right now just a little reddened from a poker game that had gone on too late the night before.

After the lecture, as the crowd of sleepy junior scientists dispersed to find secret corners in which to nap, Dennis paused by the department bulletin board, hoping to see an advertisement for another research center working in zievatronics.

Of course, there weren't any. Sahara Tech was the only place doing really advanced work with the ziev effect. Dennis should know. He had been responsible for many of those advances. Until six months ago.

As the conference room emptied, Dennis saw Gabriella leave, chattering with her hand on Bernald Brady's arm. Brady looked pumped up, as if he had just conquered Mt. Everest. Clearly he was crazy in love.

Dennis wished the fellow luck. It would be nice to have Gabriella's attentions focused elsewhere for a while. Gabbie was a competent scientist in her own right, of course. But she was just a bit too tenacious for Dennis to relax with.

He looked at his watch. It was time to go see what Flaster wanted. Dennis brought his shoulders back. He had decided he wouldn't put up with any further put-offs. Flaster was going to answer some questions, or Dennis was going to quit!

2

"Ah, Nuel! Come in!"

Silver-haired and slightly paunched, Marcel Flaster rose from behind the gleamingly empty expanse of his desk. "Take a seat, my boy. Have a cigar? They're fresh from New Havana, on Venus." He motioned Dennis to a plush chair next to a floor-to-ceiling lavalamp.

"So tell me, young man, how is it going with that artificial-intelligence project you've been working on?"

Dennis had spent the past six months directing a small AI program mandated by an unbreakable old endowment—even though it had been proved back in 2024 that true artificial intelligence was a dead end field.

He still had no idea why Flaster had asked him here. He didn't want to be gratuitously impolite, so he reported on the recent, modest advances his small group had made.

"Well, there's been some progress. Recently we've developed a new, high-quality mimicry program. In telephone tests it conversed with randomly selected individuals for an average of six point three minutes before they suspect that they're actually talking to a machine. Rich Schwall and I think . . ."

"Six and a half minutes!" Flaster interrupted. "Well, you've certainly broken the old record, by over a minute, I believe! I'm impressed!"

Then Flaster smiled condescendingly. "But honestly, Nuel, you don't think I assigned a young scientist of your obvious talents to a project with so little long-range potential for no reason, do you?"

Dennis shook his head. He had long ago concluded that the Chief Scientist had shoved him into a corner of Sahara Tech in order to put his own cronies into the zievatronics lab.

Until the death of Dennis's old mentor, Dr. Guinasso, Dennis had been at the very center of the exciting field of reality analysis.

Then, within weeks of the tragedy, Flaster had moved his own people in and Guinasso's inexorably out. Thinking about it still made Dennis bitter. He had felt sure they were just about to make tremendous discoveries when he was exiled from the work he loved.

"I couldn't really guess why you transferred me," Dennis said. "Umm, could it be you were grooming me for better things?"

Oblivious to the sarcasm, Flaster grinned. "Exactly, my boy! You do show remarkable insight. Tell me, Nuel. Now that you've had experience running a small department, how would you like to take charge of the zievatronics project here at Sahara Tech?"

Dennis blinked, taken completely by surprise.

"Uh," he said concisely.

Flaster got up and went to an intricate espresso urn on a sideboard. He poured two demitasses of thick Atlas Mountains coffee and offered one to Dennis. Dennis took the small cup numbly. He barely tasted the heavy, sweet brew.

Flaster returned to his desk and sipped delicately from his demitasse.

"Now, you didn't think we'd let our best expert on the ziev effect molder in a backwater forever, did you? Of course not! I was planning to move you back into Lab One in a matter of weeks, anyway. And now that the subministry position has opened up . . ."

"The what?"

"The subministry! Mediterranea's government has shifted again, and my old friend Boona Calumny is slotted for the Minister of Science portfolio. So when he called me just the other day to ask for help . . ."

Flaster spread his hands as if to say the rest was obvious.

Dennis couldn't believe he was hearing this. He had been certain the older man disliked him. What in the world would motivate him to turn to Dennis when it came to choosing a replacement?

Dennis wondered if his dislike for Flaster had blinded him to some nobler side of the man.

"I take it you're interested?"

Dennis nodded. He didn't care what Flaster's motives were, so long as he could get his hands on the zievatron again.

"Excellent!" Flaster raised his cup again. "Of course, there is one small detail to overcome first—only a minor matter, really. Just the sort of thing that would show the lab your leadership ability and guarantee your universal acceptance by all."

"Ah," Dennis said. *I knew it! Here it comes! The catch!*

Flaster reached under the desk and pulled out a glass box. Within it was a furry-winged, razor-toothed monstrosity, rigid and lifeless.

"After you helped us recapture it last Saturday night, I decided it was more trouble than it was worth. I handed it over to our taxidermist. . . ."

Dennis tried to breathe normally. The small black eyes stared back at him glassily. Right now they seemed filled less with malevolence than with deep mystery.

"You wanted to know more about this thing," Flaster said. "As my heir apparent, you have a right to find out."

"The others think it's from the Gene-craft Center," Dennis said.

Flaster chuckled. "But you knew better all along, right? The lifemakers aren't good enough at their new art to make anything quite so unique," he said with savor. "So very savage.

"No. As you guessed, our little friend here is not from the genetics labs, nor from anywhere in the solar system, for that matter. It came from Lab One—from one of the anomaly worlds we've latched onto with the zievatron."

Dennis stood. "You got it to work! You latched onto something better than vacuum, or purple mist!"

His mind whirled. "It breathed Earth air! It gobbled down a dozen canapes, along with a corner of Brian Yen's ear, and kept going! The thing's biochemistry must be . . ."

"*Is* . . . it is almost precisely Terran." Flaster nodded.

Dennis shook his head. He sat down heavily. "When did you find this place?"

"We found it during a zievatronics anomaly search three weeks ago. After five months of failure, I'll freely admit that we finally achieved success only after returning to the search routine you first designed, Nuel."

Flaster took off his glasses and wiped them with a silk handkerchief. "Your routines worked almost at once. And turned up the most amazingly Earthlike world. The biologists are ecstatic, to say the least."

Dennis stared at the dead creature in the glass. *A whole world! We did it!*

Dr. Guinasso's dream had come true. The zievatron was the key to the stars! Dennis's personal resentment had disappeared. He was genuinely thrilled by Flaster's accomplishment.

The Director rose and returned to the coffee urn for a refill. "There's only one problem," he said nonchalantly, his back to the younger man.

Dennis looked up, his thoughts still spinning. "Sir? A problem?"

"Well, yes." Flaster turned around, stirring his coffee. "Actually, it has to do with the zievatron itself."

Dennis frowned.

"What about the zievatron?"

Flaster raised his demitasse with two fingers. "Well," he sighed between sips. "It seems we can't get the darned thing to work anymore."

3

Flaster wasn't kidding. The zievatron was busted.

After most of a day spent poking through the guts of the machine, Dennis was still getting used to the changes that had been made in Laboratory One since his banishment.

The main generators were the same, as were the old reality probes he and Dr. Guinasso had laboriously handtuned back in the early days. Flaster and Brady hadn't dared tamper with those.

But they had brought in so much new equipment that even the cavernous main lab was almost filled to bursting. There were enough electrophoresis columns, for instance, to analyze a Bordeaux bouillabaisse.

The zievatron itself took up most of the chamber. White-coated technicians moved across catwalks along its broad face, making adjustments.

Most of the techs had come down to greet Dennis when he came in. They were obviously relieved to have him back. The backslapping reunion had kept him away from his beloved machine for almost an hour and had irritated the hell out of Bernald Brady.

When, finally, Dennis had been able to get to work, he concentrated on the two huge reality probes. Where they met, deep within the machine, there was a spot in space that was neither exactly here nor quite elsewhere. The anomalous point could be flipped between Earth and Somewhere Else, depending on which probe dominated.

Six months ago there had been a small port through which samples could be taken of the purple mists and strange dust clouds he and Dr. Guinasso had found. But since then it had been replaced by a large, armored airlock.

Working near the heavy hatch, Dennis realized that all a person had to do was walk through that door to be on another world! It was a strange feeling.

"Stumped yet, Nuel?"

Dennis looked up. Bernald Brady's small mouth always seemed to be slightly pursed in disapproval. The fellow was under instructions to cooperate, but that apparently didn't extend to being civil.

Dennis shrugged. "I've narrowed the problem down. Something's cockeyed about the part of the zievatron that's been pushed into the anomaly world—the return mechanism. It may be that the only way to fix it is from the other end."

He had come to realize that Marcel Flaster would exact a price for putting him in charge of the lab. If Dennis wasn't able to figure out a way to repair it from this end, he might have to go through and fix the return mechanism in person.

He hadn't yet decided whether to be thrilled by the idea, or petrified.

"Flasteria," Brady said.

"I beg your pardon?" Dennis said, blinking.

"We've named the planet Flasteria, Nuel."

Dennis tried to work his mouth around the word, then gave up. *The hell you say.*

"Anyway," Brady went on, "that's no great discovery. I'd already figured out it was the return mechanism that had broken down."

Dennis was starting to get irritated with the fellow's attitude. He shrugged. "Sure you knew it already. But how long did it take you?"

He knew he had struck home when Brady's face reddened.

"Never mind," Dennis said as he stood up, brushing off his hands. "Come on, Brady. Take me on a tour of your zoo. If I'm expected to go through and visit this place, I want to know more about it."

Mammals! The captive animals were air-breathing, four-legged, hairy mammals!

He looked over one that resembled a small ferret, going through a short mental checklist. There were two nostrils above the mouth and below forward-facing hunter's eyes. There were five clawed toes on each paw, and a long, furry tail. A tomography chart in front of the cage showed a four-chambered heart, a rather Earthly-looking skeleton, and apparently all the right sorts of viscera in all the right places.

Yet it was alien!

The creature stared back at Dennis for a moment, then yawned and turned away.

"The biologists have checked for bad germs and such," Brady said, answering Dennis's next question. "The guinea pigs they sent through aboard one of the exploring robots lived on Flasteria for several days and came back perfectly healthy."

"What about the biochemistry? Are the amino acids the same, for instance?"

Brady picked up a large binder, about five inches thick. "Doc Nelson was called away to Palermo yesterday. Part of the government shake-up, I suppose. But here's his report." He dropped the heavy tome into Dennis's hands. "Study it!"

Dennis was about to tell Brady where he could put the report for the time being. But just then a sharp, snapping sound came from the far end of the row of cages. Both men turned to witness a stout wooden crate begin shaking and rattling.

Brady cursed loudly. "Hot damn! It's getting out again!" He ran to one wall and slapped an alarm button. At once a siren began to wail.

"What's getting out?" Dennis backed up. The panic in Brady's voice had affected him. "What *is* it?"

"The *creature!"* Brady shouted into the intercom, hardly encouraging Dennis. "The one we recaptured and put in that temporary box . . . *yes,* the tricky one! It's getting out again!"

There was the sound of splintering wood, and a slat fell out of the side of the crate. From the blackness within, a pair of tiny green reflections gleamed at Dennis.

Dennis could only presume they were eyes, small and spaced no more than an inch apart. The green sparks seemed to lock onto him, and he could not look away. They stared at each other—Earthman and alien.

Brady was shouting as a work gang hurried into the room. "Quick! Get the nets in here in case it jumps! Make sure it doesn't let the other animals loose, like the last time!"

Dennis was growing increasingly uneasy. The green-eyed stare was disconcerting. He looked for a place to put down the heavy book in his hands.

The creature seemed to come to a decision. It squeezed through the narrow gap between the slats, then leaped just in time to escape a descending net.

In a glimpse Dennis saw that it looked like a tiny, flatnosed pig. But this pig was one of a kind! In midleap its legs spread wide, snapping open a pair of membranes, creating two gliding wings!

"Block it, Nuel!" Brady shouted.

Dennis didn't have much choice. The alien creature flew right at him! He tried to duck, but too late. The "flying pig" landed on his head and clung to his hair, squeaking frantically.

As Dennis let go of the biochemistry tome in surprise, the heavy volume landed on his foot.

"Ow!" He hopped, reaching up to grab at his unwelcome passenger.

But the little creature peeped loudly, plaintively. It sounded more frightened than angry. At the last moment, Dennis restrained himself from using force to tear it off. Instead, he managed to peel one webbed paw away from his eye—just in time to duck beneath a wrench swung by Bernald Brady! Dennis cursed and the "piglet" squealed as the bludgeon whistled just overhead.

"Hold still, Nuel! I almost had him!"

"And almost took my head off, too!" Dennis backed away. "Idiot! Are you trying to kill me?"

Brady seemed to contemplate the proposition syllogistically. Finally, he shrugged. "All right, then, Nuel. Come out slowly and we'll grab him."

Dennis started forward. But as he approached the other men, the creature squeaked pathetically and tightened its grip.

"Hold off," Dennis said. "It's just frightened, that's all. Give me a minute. I may be able to get it down myself."

Dennis backed over to a crate and sat down. He reached up tentatively to touch the alien again.

To Dennis's surprise the shuddering creature seemed to calm under his touch. He spoke softly as he stroked the thin, soft fur that covered its pink skin. Gradually its panicked grip eased. Finally he was able to lift the creature with both hands and bring it down to his lap.

The men and women in the work gang cheered. Dennis smiled back with more confidence than he felt.

It was just the sort of thing that could become a legend. ". . . *Yes, boy. I was there the day ol' Director Nuel tamed a savage alien critter that had him by the eyeballs. . . ."*

Dennis looked down at the thing he had "captured." The creature looked back at him with an expression he was sure he had seen somewhere before. But where?

Then he remembered. For his sixth birthday his parents had given him an illustrated book of Finnish fairy tales. He recalled many of the drawings to this day. And this creature had the sharp-toothed, green-eyed, devilish grin of a pixie.

"A pixolet," he announced softly as he petted the little creature. "A cross between piglet and pixie. Does the name suit?"

It didn't appear to understand the words. He doubted it was actually sentient. But something seemed to tell Dennis that it understood *him*. It grinned back with tiny, needle-sharp teeth.

Brady approached with a gunny sack. "Quick, Nuel. While it's passive, get it into this!"

Dennis stared at the man. The suggestion wasn't worthy of a reply. He arose with the pixolet in the crook of his left arm. The creature purred.

"Come on, Brady," he said, "let's finish the tour so I can get my equipment list together. Then I've got some preparations to make.

"You may thank our extraterrestrial friend here for making up my mind for me. I'll go through the zievatron and visit his homeworld for you."

4

The zievatron had become a one-way road. Anything shoved through the airlock would arrive on the anomaly world, as planned. Robots could still be sent through, as had been done for almost a month. But nothing came back.

Enough faint telemetry came back to show that the machine was still linked to the same anomaly world—the place the flying piglet creature had been taken from.

But the zievatron was incapable of sending even a feather back to Earth.

All machines fail sooner or later, Dennis realized. Undoubtedly the problem could be solved simply by replacing a burned-out module—

maybe two minutes' work. The rub was that it would have to be done in person. Somebody would have to go through the zievatron to do it by hand.

Of course, a manned expedition had been planned anyway. These weren't exactly the best circumstances for such a first visit, but somebody would have to do it, or the world they had found would be lost forever. Dennis had seen pictures taken by the exploring robots before the failure. They might search for a hundred years before stumbling onto another place so compatible with human life.

Anyway, he had made up his mind.

The equipment Dennis had asked for lay in stacks just outside the airlock door. The speed with which the list had been filled showed how anxious Dr. Flaster was to have results soon. Sending Brady after the supplies had also kept the fellow out of his hair while he triple-checked his calculations.

He had insisted on a long list of survival supplies, not that he expected to need them on this first outing. Even replacing every module in the return mechanism shouldn't take more than an hour, but he wasn't taking any chances. There were even cases of vitamins in case he was stranded for a while, and the biology report had missed a decimal point in its compatibility rating of the anomaly world.

"Okay, Nuel," Brady said. He addressed Dennis from the left side. The pixolet rode Dennis's other shoulder, surveying the preparations grandly, hissing whenever Brady approached.

"You've got almost enough gear to build another damned zievatron when you arrive on Flasteria. You should be able to fix it in five minutes. You'd think you were the Admirable Bird, lugging all that survival junk around, too. But that's your business."

The fellow actually sounded jealous. Still, Dennis hadn't noticed him volunteering to go.

"Just remember to fix the machine first!" Brady went on. "Then it won't matter if something eats you while you're trying to talk to all the local animals."

Richard Schwall, one of the techs who had worked with Dennis back in the early days, looked up from checking a schematic and shared a look of commiseration with Dennis. Everyone at S.I.T. appreciated Brady's sunny attitude.

"Dennis!"

Gabriella Versgo's valkyrian figure wove toward them through the crowd of technicians. When one tech was slow to get out of the way, he was swept aside by a well-swung pelvis.

Brady beamed as she approached, looking much like a lovestruck puppy. Gabbie gave him a brilliant smile and then took Dennis's right arm in a grip that partly interrupted the blood supply to his hand.

"Well, Dennis," she said, sighing happily, "I'm glad you and Bernie are talking to each other again! I always thought it was silly of you two to feud so."

Actually, she sounded as if she thought it was delightful. Dennis realized that Gabbie was under the mistaken belief that his enmity with Brady was over her. If that really were the case Dennis would have run up a white flag and surrendered long ago!

"I just came ahead to warn you two boys that Dr. Flaster's on his way down to see Dennis off. And he's bringing Boona Calumny with him!"

Dennis looked blank for a moment.

"The new Science Minister for Mediterranea!" Gabbie cried. She tugged his elbow sharply, accidentally thumbing his ulnar nerve in the process. Dennis gasped, but Gabbie went on, oblivious to his momentary agony.

"Isn't it wonderful?" She exclaimed. "Such an eminent man coming down to watch the first human set foot on an anomaly world!" In her final sweeping gesture she released her grip. Dennis stifled a sigh and massaged his arm.

Gabriella cooed at the pixolet, trying to chuck its diminutive chin. The little creature bore it for a few moments, then erupted into a tremendous yawn, revealing twin rows of needle-sharp teeth. She quickly withdrew her hand.

She went around to Dennis's other side and leaned up to kiss him primly on the cheek. "Gotta run now. I have an important crystal in a float-zone. Have a good trip. Come back a hero and we'll celebrate special, I promise." She winked and nudged him with her hip, almost knocking the pixolet from its perch.

The scowling Brady brightened suddenly when Gabriella gave him a peck as well, for equality. Then she sauntered away, doubtless aware that half the men in the lab were watching.

Richard Schwall shook his head and muttered. ". . . woman could upstage Lady Macbeth . . ." was all Dennis made out.

Brady snorted indignantly and stalked off.

As Dennis returned to his calculations, checking one last time to make sure he had made no mistakes, the pixolet launched itself into a low glide to land on a perch overlooking Richard Schwall. It peered over the balding tech's shoulder, watching as he adjusted a portable electronic drafting tool for Dennis to take along.

For two days, ever since Dennis had declared the creature tame, the technicians had routinely looked up to find those tiny green eyes staring down at them. Uncannily, the pixolet always seemed to choose the trickiest adjustments to oversee.

As the preparations progressed smoothly, the creature became a status symbol of sorts. The techs used bits of candy to attract it over to their stations. It had become a good luck charm—a company mascot.

When Schwall looked up and saw the pixolet, he grinned and picked up the little alien so it could get a better look. Dennis put down his notes and watched the two interact.

The pixolet appeared less enthralled with what Schwall did than how the tech *felt* about it. When his face showed pleasure, the creature looked back and forth quickly, from Schwall to the sketch pad and back again.

Although it was clearly not a sentient being, Dennis wondered just how intelligent the little alien really was.

"Hey, Dennis!" Schwall grew excited. "Look at this! I've made a real neat picture of the launch tower in Ecuador! You know, the Vanilla Needle? I've never really noticed how good I am at this! Your little friend here really *is* lucky!"

There was a commotion at the back of the lab. Dennis nudged his associate. "Come on, Rich," he said. "Get up. They're here at last."

Escorted by Bernald Brady, the lab Director approached the zievatron. With Flaster walked a short, stubby man with dark, intense features, who Dennis realized must be the new Science Minister of Mediterranea.

As he was introduced, Boona Calumny seemed to look right through Dennis. His voice was very high.

"So this is the brave young fellow who's going to take over your wonderful work here, Marcel? And he's starting right off by stepping through into that wonderful new place you've found?"

Flaster beamed. "Yes, sir! And we certainly are proud of him!" He winked conspiratorially at Dennis. Dennis was starting to realize just how badly Flaster wanted a success to show for his tenure at S.I.T.

"You'll be careful in there, won't you, my boy?" Calumny's finger pointed at the airlock. Dennis wondered if the man really understood what was going on.

"Yessir, I will."

"Good. We want you to return hale and hearty!"

Dennis nodded pleasantly, automatically translating the politician's remarks from Executivese to English. *He means that if I don't come back there'll be some nasty paperwork to fill out.*

"I promise, sir."

"Excellent. You know, bright young men like you are hard to find these days!" *(Actually, you squirts are a dime a dozen, but you're helping my buddy out of a jam.)*

"Yessir," Dennis agreed again.

"We have a real shortage of daring, adventurous types, and I'm sure you'll go far," Calumny went on. *(We're a bit low on meatheads this month. Maybe we can use you for a few more suicide missions if you come back from this one.)*

"I expect so, sir."

Calumny gave Dennis a very democratic handshake, then turned to whisper something to Flaster. The director pointed to a door, and the minister waddled out of the lab. Probably to wash his hands, Dennis thought.

"All right, Dr. Nuel," Flaster said cheerfully, "hoist your little alien friend and let's be off with you. I expect you back in under two hours . . . less if you can control your inclination to explore. We'll have champagne chilled by the time you return."

Dennis caught the pixolet in a midair glide from Rich Schwall's hands. The little creature chirped excitedly. After all the crates were loaded ahead of him, Dennis stepped over the airlock's combing.

"Beginning closure procedure," one of the techs announced. "Good luck, Dr. Nuel!"

Schwall gave him thumbs up.

Bernald Brady came forward to guide the heavy door. "Well, Nuel," he said lowly as the gears slowly turned, "you checked everything, didn't you? You poked through the machine from top to bottom, read the biology report, and didn't need to consult me at all, did you?"

Dennis didn't like the fellow's tone. "What are you getting at?"

Brady smiled, speaking softly so only Dennis could hear him. "I never mentioned it to the others, since it seemed so absurd. But it's only fair to tell you."

"Tell me about what?"

"Oh, it could be nothing at all, Nuel. Or maybe something pretty unusual . . . like the possibility that this anomaly world has a different set of physical laws than hold sway on Earth!"

By now the hatch had half closed. The timer was running.

This was ridiculous. Dennis wasn't going to let Brady get to him.

"Stuff it, Bernie," he said with a laugh. "I don't believe a word of your blarney."

"Oh? Remember those purple mists you found last year, where gravity repelled?"

"Those were different entirely. No major difference in physical law could endanger me on Pix's world—not when the biology is so compatible.

"But if there's something *minor* you haven't told me about," Dennis continued, stepping forward, "you'd better spill it now or I swear I'll . . ."

Strangely, Brady's antagonism seemed to fall away, replaced by apparently genuine puzzlement.

"I don't *know* what it is, Nuel. It had to do with the instruments we sent through. Their efficiencies seemed to change the longer they were there! It was almost as if one of the thermodynamic laws was subtly different."

Too late, Dennis realized that Brady wasn't *just* egging him. He really *had* discovered something that honestly perplexed him. But by now the hatch had closed almost all the way.

"Which law, Brady? Dammit, stop this process until you tell me! *What* law?"

Through the bare crack that remained, Brady whispered, "Guess."

With a sigh the seals fell into place and the hatch became vacuum tight.

In the zievatronics lab, Dr. Marcel Flaster watched Brady turn away from the closed hatch of the anomaly machine. "What was that all about?"

Brady started. Flaster could have sworn the fellow grew even paler than normal.

"Oh, it was nothing. We were talking. Just something to pass the time while the hatch closed."

Flaster frowned. "Well, I hope there won't be any surprises at this late stage. I'm counting on Nuel to succeed. I need Flasteria badly with my confirmation hearings coming up next month."

"Maybe he'll manage to pull it off." Brady shrugged.

Flaster laughed. "Indeed. From what I've seen around here, he's sure to succeed. In the last few days he's really got this place humming. I should have brought that young fellow back into this lab months ago!"

Brady shrugged. "Nuel might succeed. Then again, maybe he won't."

Flaster smiled archly. "Ah, well. If he fails, we'll just have to send somebody else, won't we?"

Brady swallowed and nodded. He watched the lab Director turn and walk away.

I wonder if I did the right thing? Brady thought, *giving Nuel the wrong modules for fixing the return mechanism.*

Oh, he'll figure it out eventually and fix them up. All he has to do is swap the right chips around. I made it look like a factory error so they'll never trace it to me—though he'll probably suspect.

By the time he's fixed the modules, I'll have had time to work on Flaster. And Nuel's stock won't be so high when the delay stretches into weeks, whatever his excuse!

Brady felt a little guilty about the stunt. It was kind of a nasty trick to play. But all indications showed that Flasteria was a pretty tame place. The robots hadn't seen any big animals, and anyway, Nuel was always talking about what a champion Boy Scout he had been. Let him camp out in the wild for a while, then!

Maybe he'd even figure out what had been happening to the robots, too . . . that strange alteration in their efficiency profiles.

Oh, Nuel would come back in lather, all right. But by then he, Brady, would have had a chance to win his way back into the Director's good graces. He knew, by now, what buttons to push.

Brady looked at his watch. Gabriella had made a luncheon date with him, and he didn't want to be late.

He straightened his tie and hurried out of the lab. Soon he was whistling.

5

"*Which law?* you sonova—" Dennis pounded on the door.

He stopped. It was useless. By now the sending probe had activated. He was already *on* the anomaly world—already on . . .

Dennis stared at the blank door. He felt behind himself and sat heavily on one of the crates. Then, as his situation soaked in, he suddenly found himself beginning to laugh! He couldn't stop. His eyes filled as he gave in to the giddy feeling.

No one had ever been as cut off as he was, cast from Earth to a faraway world.

People might read about adventures in faraway places, but the truth was that most, at the first hint of anything *truly* dangerous, would dig a hole and cry out for Mother.

As an initial reaction, then, perhaps laughter wasn't bad. At least he felt more relaxed afterward.

From a crate nearby, the pixolet watched, apparently fascinated.

I'm going to have to come up with a new name for this place, Dennis thought as he wiped his eyes. *Flasteria just won't do.*

The initial crisis of isolation had passed. He was able to look to his left, to the other door, the only one that would now open—onto another world.

Brady's talk of a "different set of physical laws" continued to bother Dennis. Brady had probably just been trying to get to him. Even if he *was* telling the truth, it would have to be something pretty subtle, since biological processes were so compatible on both worlds.

Dennis remembered a science-fiction story he had once read in which a minute change in electrical conductivity resulted in a tenfold increase in human intelligence. Could it be something like that?

Dennis sighed. He didn't *feel* any smarter. The fact that he couldn't remember the story's title sort of refuted that possibility.

The pixolet glided from its perch to land on his lap. It purred, looking up at him with emerald eyes.

"Now *I'm* the alien," Dennis said. He picked up the little native. "How about it, Pix? Am I welcome? Want to show me around your place?"

Pix squeaked. It sounded eager to be off.

"Okay," Dennis said. "Let's go."

He strapped on his tool belt, with the needlegun holstered to one side. Then, taking an appropriate "explorerlike" stance, he pulled the lever to unlock the far door. There was a hiss of equalizing pressure, and his ears popped briefly. Then the hatch swung open to let in the sunshine of another world.

2

Cogito, Ergo Tutti Fruitti.

1

The airlock rested on a gentle slope of dry, yellow grass. The meadow fell away toward a green-rimmed watercourse a quarter mile away. Beyond the stream, rows of long, narrow hills rose toward whitecapped mountains. Swards of yellow interspersed unevenly with carpets of varitone green.

Trees.

Yes, they looked like real trees, and the sky was blue. White cirrus clouds laced across the almost cyan vault overhead.

For a long moment it was eerily, unnaturally quiet. He realized he had been holding his breath since opening the door. It made him feel lightheaded.

Inhaling, he tasted the crisp, clean air. The breeze brought sounds of brushing grass and creaking branches. It also brought odors . . . the unmistakable mustiness of chlorophyll and humus, of dry grass and what smelled like oak.

Dennis stood in the airlock's combing and looked at the trees. They sure *looked* like oak. The countryside reminded him of northern California.

Could this place actually *be* Earth? Dennis wondered. Had the ziev effect played another trick on them all and given them teleportation rather than an interstellar drive?

It would be amusing to hitchhike to a pay phone and call Flaster with the news. Collect, of course.

Dennis felt a sharp stab as tiny claws bit into his shoulder. The pixolet's wing membranes snapped wide with a sound like a shot, and the creature soared off over the meadow, toward the line of trees.

"Hey . . . Pix! Where are you . . ."

Dennis's voice caught in his throat as he realized this *couldn't* be Earth. This was where Pix came from.

He began noticing little things—the shape of the leaves of grass, a huge, fernlike plant by the riverside, a feeling in the air.

Dennis made sure his holstered sidearm was unencumbered, and his boot cuffs well covered by his gaiters. The dry grass crunched beneath his feet as he stepped out. Tiny, whining insect sounds filled the air.

"Pix!" he called, but the little creature had flown from sight.

Dennis moved cautiously, all senses alert. He guessed the first few moments on an alien world could be the most dangerous of all.

Trying to watch the sky, the forest, and the nearby insects all at once, he didn't even notice the squat little robot until he tripped over it and fell sprawling to the ground.

Dennis instinctively rolled away into a crouch, the needler suddenly in his hand, his pulse pounding in his ears.

He sighed as he recognized the little Sahara Tech exploration drone. The 'bot's cameras tracked him with a barely discernible whir. Its observing turret slowly turned. Dennis lowered the needler. "Come here," he commanded.

The robot seemed to consider the order for a moment. Then it approached on spinning treads to halt a meter away.

"What have you got there?" Dennis pointed.

The robot held something in one of its manipulator grips. It was a shiny bit of metal, with a clawed pincer at one end.

"Isn't that a piece of another robot?" Dennis asked, hoping he was wrong.

Compared with some of the sophisticated machines Dennis had worked with, the exploration 'bot wasn't very bright. But it understood a basic vocabulary. A green light on its turret flashed, indicating assent.

"Where did you get it?"

The little machine paused, then swiveled and pointed with one of its other sampling arms.

Dennis got up and looked, but he saw nothing in that direction. He moved cautiously through the tall grass until, at last, he came to a flat area partly hidden by the weeds. There he stopped and stared.

The clearing looked like a wilderness parts store . . . a Grizzly Adams wrecking yard . . . a rustic electronics swap meet.

One—no, *two*—S.I.T. robots had been rather tactlessly disassembled; their parts lay in neat rows among the clumps of grass, apparently ordered and sorted by size and shape.

Dennis knelt and picked up a camera turret. It had been ripped out of its housing, and the pieces had been laid out on the ground, like merchandise for sale.

The trampled mud was strewn with scattered bits of straw, wire, and glass. Dennis looked closer. Here and there, mixed in among the tread marks and the torn pieces of plastic machinery, were faint but unmistakable footprints.

Dennis looked down at the neat rows of gears, wheels, panels, and circuit boards—at the faint marks in the clay—and all he could think of was an epitaph he had once read in a New England cemetery.

I knew this would happen someday.

Dennis had always felt he was somehow destined to encounter something really unusual during his life. Well, here it was in front of him—tangible evidence of alien intelligence.

The comforting Earthlike *Gestalt* finished evaporating around him. He looked at the "grass" and saw it wasn't like any grass he had ever seen. The line of trees was now a dark, unknown forest filled with malign forces. Dennis felt a crawling sensation on the nape of his neck.

A clicking sound made him whirl, the needler in his hand. But it was only the surviving robot again, poking through the pieces of its disassembled fellows.

Dennis picked up an electronics board from the ground. It had been *pried* out of its housing by main force. It could easily have been separated with just a twist, but it had been roughly sheared away, as if the entity doing the dissection had never heard of threaded sleeves or bolts.

Was this the work of primitives, then? Or someone from a race so advanced that they'd forgotten about such simple things as screws?

One thing was certain. The being or beings responsible didn't have a high regard for other people's property.

The robots had been made mostly of plastic. He noted that most of the bigger metal pieces seemed to be missing entirely.

Dennis suddenly had a very unpleasant thought. "Oh, no," he murmured. "Please, don't let it be!" He rose with feeling of numb dread in the pit of his stomach.

Dennis walked back to the airlock. He rounded the corner and stopped suddenly, groaning out loud.

The access panel to the zievatron return mechanism lay ajar. The electronics cabinet was empty; its delicate components lay on the ground, like pieces on display on a store shelf. Most were clearly broken beyond repair.

With an eloquence borne of irony, Dennis simply said "Argh!" and sagged back against the wall of the airlock.

Another epigram floated around in the despair that seemed to fill his brain—something a friend had once said to him about the phenomenology of life.

"I think, therefore I scream."

2

The robot "peeped" and played the sequence over again. Dennis concentrated on the three-day-old images displayed on the machine's tiny video plate. Something very strange was going on here.

The small screen showed shapes that looked like blurry humanoid figures moving around the zievatron airlock. The beings walked on two legs and appeared to be accompanied by at least two kinds of quadrupeds. Beyond that, Dennis could hardly make out any detail from the noisy enlargement.

The miracle was that he could see anything at all. According to its inertial recorder, the robot had been on a distant ridge, several kilometers away, when it detected activity back at the airlock and turned to photograph the shapes clustered about the zievatron portal. At that distance, the robot shouldn't have been able to see anything at all. Dennis suspected something was wrong with the 'bot's internal tracker. It must have been closer than it thought it was at the time.

Unfortunately, this tape was almost his only source of direct information. The records of the other 'bots had been ruined when they were so rudely disassembled.

He skimmed over the robot's record to a point about three days ago, when it all seemed to have begun.

The first to arrive at the airlock was a small figure in white. It rode up upon the back of something like a very shaggy pony—or a very large sheepdog. Dennis couldn't decide which simile was more appropriate.

All he could make out about the humanoid was that it was slender and moved gracefully as it inspected the zievatron from all angles, hardly touching it at all.

The figure in white sat before the airlock and appeared to begin a long period of meditation. Several hours passed. Dennis skimmed the record at high speed.

Suddenly, from the forest verge, there erupted a troop of mounted natives charging toward the airlock on shaggy beasts. In spite of the blurriness of the image, Dennis could sense the first intruder's panic as it bounded to its feet, then hurriedly mounted and rode off, bare meters ahead of its pursuers.

Dennis saw no more of the figure in white. But as one detachment of the newcomers gave chase, the rest came to a halt by the airlock.

Most of these humanoids seemed to have large, furry heads, distended high above the shoulders. In their midst there dismounted a smaller, more rotund biped in red wrappings, who approached the airlock purposefully.

Try as he might, Dennis couldn't make the images resolve any clearer.

By this time, the robot had apparently decided that all this activity merited closer attention. It began descending the hill to return to base and get a closer look. In moments it had dropped down to the level of the trees, and the action at the zievatron was lost from view.

Unfortunately—or perhaps fortunately—the little 'bot moved slowly over the rugged terrain. By the time it got back, the creatures had already finished their dissection of the Earth machines and departed.

Perhaps they were in a hurry to help pursue the figure in white.

Dennis let the recording play itself out again. He sighed in frustration.

It had been so tempting, on looking at those blurry shapes, to interpret them as humans. Yet he knew he had better not go into things with any preconceived notions. They had to be alien creatures, more closely akin to the pixolet than to himself.

He slipped the record disk out of the robot and replaced it with a blank one.

"You're going to have to be my scout," he ruminated aloud in front of the little drone. "I guess I'll want to send you ahead to find out about the inhabitants of this world for me. Only this time I'll want you to put a high priority on stealth and your own survival. You hear? I don't want you taken apart like your brothers!"

The little green assent light on the probe's turret lit up. Of course, the 'bot couldn't really have understood all that. Dennis had been mostly talking to himself, to gather his own thoughts. He would parse the instructions in carefully phrased Robot-English later, when he had worked out exactly what he wanted the little machine to do.

He faced a real problem, and he still wasn't quite sure what he could do about it.

Sure, Brady had given him ". . . almost enough gear to build another damned zievatron . . ." But practicality was quite another thing. No one had imagined he would need to bring along spare *power cables,* for heaven's sake! Both of the big, high-voltage copper busses had been shredded out at the roots, along with most of the detachable metal in the electronics bay.

Even if he did try to build and calibrate another return mechanism, would Flaster keep the zievatron tied up long enough to let him finish? Dennis felt he understood the S.I.T. chief pretty well. The fellow was anxious for a success to further his ambitions. Dennis might even be cast loose so Lab One could be put to work searching for another anomaly world!

And even if he tried to reassemble the device, would he be left alone by the natives long enough to finish?

Dennis picked up the one alien artifact he had found—a sharp, curve-bladed knife that had fallen into the high grass and apparently been lost by the vandals.

The long, tapered blade had the smooth sharpness of a fine razor, yet it was almost as flexible as hard rubber. The grip was designed for a hand smaller than his, but it was obviously meant to be comfortable and provide a firm grasp.

The butt was carved in what appeared to be the shape of a dragon's head. Dennis hoped that wasn't what the natives actually looked like.

He couldn't fathom what the thing was made of. It was certainly doubtful a better knife could be manufactured on Earth. It seemed to belie the idea that the natives were primitives.

Perhaps the vandals were the local equivalent of criminals or careless children. (Could the chase he had observed have been some sort of *game,* like hide-and-go-seek?)

What had happened here might be atypical of their society as a whole. Dennis tried to be optimistic. All he really needed was some metal stock and a couple of days in a good machine shop to fix and calibrate some of the larger ruined parts. The knife seemed to indicate the natives had a high enough technology.

They might even know many things men of Earth did not. He tried to be optimistic, and imagined being the first Earthling to make friendly contact with an advanced extraterrestrial culture.

"I might be able to trade my pocket nailclipper-stop-watch for a genuine *gompwriszt* or a *K'k'kglamtring*," he mused. "I could be wealthy in no time! . . . Ambassador Nuel. Entrepreneur Nuel!"

His morale lifted just a little. Who could tell?

The sun was setting in a direction Dennis decided to call west. A tall range of mountains covered that horizon, stretching around to the south and then eastward around this high valley. Sunlight glanced off numerous small glaciers. There were bright highlights from a winding river that weaved through the southeastern mountains.

Dennis watched the reflections from the distant river. The beauty of this alien twilight took some of the sting out of being stranded on a strange world.

Then he frowned.

Something was wrong with the way the river ran through the hills. It seemed to rise and fall . . . rise and fall. . . .

It's not a river, he realized at last.

It's a road.

3

Nothing could bring home the tangibility of a world better than trying to dig a hole in it. Exertion, the clank of metal against earth, sweat smell and the musty, dry dust of abandoned insect nests all verified the reality of the place like nothing else ever could.

Dennis leaned on his spade and wiped perspiration. Hard work had broken his numb reaction to the shocks of the day before. It was good to be active, doing something about his situation.

He scattered dirt around the flat mound, patting it down, then covered the cairn with a scattering of grass.

He couldn't take most of his supplies with him on his journey. But locking them in the airlock wouldn't do either. Leaving as much as a gram inside would prevent the people back at Lab One from sending another envoy.

He had used electrical tape to write a message on the side of the lock, telling where his detailed report was buried with the equipment.

Still, if he knew Flaster and Brady, they would dither a long time before deciding on a follow-up mission. Realistically, Dennis knew if anyone was going to fix the return mechanism it would be himself. He couldn't afford anymore slip-ups.

He had already made one big mistake. This morning, when he had opened the airlock and stepped out into the misty dawn, he found that the robot was gone. After an hour of worried searching, he realized that the little drone had departed during the night. He found its tracks leading westward.

It must have set out on the trail of the humanoids—apparently to find out all it could about them, pursuant to his instructions.

Dennis cursed himself for thinking aloud in the robot's presence the day before. But honestly, who would have expected the machine to accept orders in anything but prim Robot-English? It should have rejected the commands as too flexible and inspecific!

He hadn't even given the robot a time limit. It would probably stay out until its tapes were full!

The 'bot must have a wire loose somewhere. Brady wasn't kidding when he said something had gone flaky with the machines they had sent here.

Now Dennis had lost two companions since coming to this world. He wondered what had become of the pixolet.

Probably it was back in its own element, glad to be away from the crazy aliens who had captured it.

As the golden-white sun rose above the eastern treeline, Dennis made ready to go. He would make do alone.

He had to tie knots in the straps of his backpack to keep them from slipping. Apparently Brady had bought the cheapest equipment possible. Dennis muttered comments on his rival's probable parentage as he hoisted the pack and set off southeastward toward the road he had seen the day before.

4

Dennis hiked along narrow game paths, always watching out for possible dangers. But the forest was peaceful. In spite of the squeaky noises from his awkward pack, he found himself enjoying the sunshine and the fresh air.

He took bearings as well as he could with the cheap compass Brady had provided. When he took breaks by the banks of small streams he kept up a notebook on the ways this world differed from home. So far the list was brief.

The vegetation *was* very Earthlike. The predominant trees in this area looked a lot like beech, for instance.

It could be a sign of parallel evolution. Or the zievatron might open onto alternate versions of Earth itself. Dennis knew as much about the ziev effect as anybody back home did. But he admitted that that wasn't all that much. It was a very new field.

He kept reminding himself to move with caution. Still, as the forest became more familiar, he found himself passing the time playing with the anomaly equations in his head, trying to find some explanation.

The animals of the forest watched suspiciously from cover as a preoccupied Earthman hiked their narrow paths in the direction of morning.

When evening finally came, Dennis camped under the trees by a brook. Not wanting to risk a fire, he tinkered with the rickety little gas stove Brady had provided. A weak flame finally sputtered to life and he was able to stir up a lukewarm batch of freeze-dried stew.

I'll have to start hunting soon, he realized. The favorable biochemistry report notwithstanding, Dennis was still uncomfortable with the idea of shooting any local creatures. What if the "rabbits" here were philosophers? Could he be so sure *anything* he aimed at wasn't intelligent?

When the tepid meal was done, Dennis activated his camp-watch alarm. It was no bigger than a deck of cards, with a small display screen and a tiny rotating antenna. He had to tap it several times to get it started.

Apparently Brady had been saving Sahara Tech money again. "It may give me two seconds' warning if something the size of an elephant comes rooting through my pack," Dennis sighed.

With the needler by his side, he laid back in his sleeping bag and watched through the gaps in the branches overhead as the constellations came out. The configurations were utterly alien.

That finished off the parallel Earth theory once and for all. Dennis scratched three lines of equations from his mental chalkboard.

While waiting for sleep to come, he watched the sky and named the constellations.

Toward the southern mountains, Alfresco the Mighty wrestled with the great snake, Stethoscope. The hero's piercing eyes shone unevenly, one red and twinkling, the other bright green and steady. The green eye might be a planet, Dennis decided. If it moved over the next few nights, he would give it a name of its own.

Above Alfresco and Stethoscope, the Chorus of Twelve Virgins sang backup to Cosell the Loquacious as he chanted a monotonous description of Alfresco's mighty struggle. It didn't matter that the combatants hadn't budged in millennia. The announcer found color to fill out the time.

Overhead, the Robot rolled, squat and imperturbable upon a highway made up of a billion tiny numbers, pursuing the Man of Grass . . . the Alien.

Dennis stirred. He wanted to look at the destination the Man of Grass so doggedly sought. He wanted to turn his head. But he finally realized, with the complacency that comes in dreams, that he had been asleep for some time.

5

He came to the road late on the afternoon of his fourth day.

His journal bulged with notes on everything from trees to insects, from rock formations to the local varieties of birds and snakes. He had even tried to drop rocks from a cliff, to time their fall and measure the local force of gravity. Everything seemed to support the idea that this place was not Earth but was an awful lot like it.

About half of the animals seemed to have close cousins back home. The other half were unlike anything he had ever seen.

Already Dennis felt he was becoming a seasoned explorer—like Darwin or Wallace or Goodall. And best of all, his boots were beginning to wear in.

He had hated them at first. But after the initial painful blisters, they seemed to become more comfortable day by day. The rest of his equipment still caused him aggravation, but he seemed to be getting used to the stuff, gradually.

The camp-watch still awakened him several times every night, but he apparently was getting the hang of its tiny controls. It no longer went off every time a leaf blew through his camp.

Last night, though, he had started awake to see a troop of hairy-hoofed quadrupeds skirting the edge of his camp. They stared into the beam of his flashlight while his heart pounded. Then they scampered off.

On reflection they had seemed harmless enough, but why hadn't the alarm warned him?

Dennis's equipment worries dropped from his mind as he eagerly skidded down the last gravelly slope to the highway. He dropped his pack and approached to kneel by the shallow curb.

It was an odd road, barely wide enough for a small Earth landcar to pass. Uneven and twisty, it followed the contours of the land instead of cutting straight through, as a highway on Earth would have done. And its edges were ragged, as if no one had bothered to trim them when the bed was laid.

The shiny pavement felt smooth and yet tough. Dennis scuffed it and walked a few paces. He tried to scratch it with a metal buckle and dribbled water from his canteen. It seemed skidproof and weatherproof, and offered resilient traction.

Two narrow grooves—exactly one point four two meters apart—ran down its center, following every twist and turn. Dennis knelt to peer into one of the thin channels, its cross section a near-perfect semicircle. The inside surface was almost slippery smooth to the touch.

Dennis sat down on a nearby stump, whistling softly to himself.

This road was a very advanced artifact. He doubted a surface like it could be made on Earth.

But why the ragged edges? Why the grooves, or the twisty, inefficient path?

It was perplexing, like the illogical way in which the return mechanism and the robots had been taken apart. The locals seemed to think differently than men.

Back at the airlock, Dennis had found most of the metal parts taken away from the zievatron. He thought this might mean he had arrived on a metal-poor world. But in the past few days he had seen at least three areas where iron and copper ores lay open and available.

It was a mystery. And there was only one way to find out more.

To the west, the road climbed higher into the mountains. Eastward, it seemed to descend into a broad watershed. Dennis picked up his pack and started off along the road, away from the afternoon sun—toward what he hoped would be civilization.

6

It wasn't an easy idea to get used to, but Dennis was coming to the conclusion that he had misjudged Bernald Brady.

The night after encountering the highway, Dennis thought about it as he stirred a pot of soup over his little stove. Perhaps he *had* been unfair to his old S.I.T. nemesis. During his first few days on this new world, he had complained a lot about the quality of his equipment, blaming Brady for his blisters, his chafed shoulders, and his tepid meals. But those problems had all abated with time. Obviously he had needed time to adapt. Brady and the equipment must have merely been a convenient set of scapegoats for his initial misery.

Now that he had apparently found the knack, the little stove seemed to work just fine. Its first fuel canister had been used up in a day. But the second had lasted much longer and heated his food better. All it seemed to have taken was a bit of practice. That, he confessed a bit immodestly, and a little mechanical aptitude.

While the soup cooked, Dennis examined the little camp-watch alarm with new respect. It had taken him days, but he had finally found out that the colors of the little lights on its screen corresponded roughly with the carnivority of the creatures nearby. The correlation had been made clear when he witnessed a pack of foxlike creatures stalking a covey of small birds and watched the counterparts on the screen. Maybe it had to do with body temperature, but somehow the alarm had distinguished the two separate groups clearly into red and yellow dots on the screen.

It bothered Dennis a little that it had taken him so long to notice all this. Perhaps he had spent too much of the journey playing with equations in his head.

Anyway, the trip would be over soon. All this day he had passed signs of quarrying in the surrounding hills. And the road had broadened somewhat. Soon, perhaps tomorrow, he knew he would come upon the creatures who ruled this world.

The camp-watch hummed in his hands, and its little antenna suddenly swung about to point westward. The pale screen came alight and an alarm began to buzz softly.

Dennis cut off the sound and reached over to draw the needler from its holster. He turned off the stove. When its faint sigh died away, Dennis could hear only the soft, rustling wind in the branches.

The forest night was a thick maze of black shadows. Only a few wan stars winked overhead through a thickening overcast.

A small cluster of tiny dots appeared in the lower left corner of the camp-watch screen. They formed a twisting band, snaking slowly toward the center of the screen.

Finally he heard faint creakings, and soft snorting sounds in the distance.

The points on the screen sorted themselves into colors. Over a dozen large yellow dots moved along in a procession, apparently following the path of the highway.

Yellow was the color he had learned was assigned for herbivores. Interspersed among the yellow points were a large number that glowed pink, and even bright red. And in the center of the procession were two tiny green lights. Dennis had no idea what those meant.

Trailing some distance behind the end of the procession, there followed another small green pinpoint.

His camp was uphill from the road a bit. He laid the watch-alarm aside and moved carefully downslope. The night seemed to amplify the snap of every twig as he tried to move silently toward a better vantage point.

After a brief wait, a faint glow appeared to his left. It brightened, then became a painful, piercing white light, spearing through the trees by the road.

Headlights! Dennis blinked. *Now, why does that surprise me? Did I think the makers of a road like this one wouldn't be able to illuminate it?*

Hidden by the undergrowth, he squinted against the bright beam. Vague figures marched behind it, bipedal, with swinging arms.

The procession passed below his blind. He heard the low, chuffing snorts of beasts. Shading his eyes, he made out giant quadrupeds pulling hulking vehicles that slid soundlessly along the road. Each conveyance sent a bright beam spearing ahead of it into the gloom.

Behind each came a formation of striding bipeds. Dennis caught glimpses of heavy, coweled clothing and what seemed to be sharp, glinting weapons, held at high port.

But each time his night vision began to return, another giant sled came around the corner to the west, its bright beam dazzling him and sending him flat against the ground again. It was frustrating, but there didn't seem to be any way to get a better look!

More of the swaggering, coweled figures passed, then more quadrupeds, pulling hulking, eerily silent wagons. Dennis tried to make out how they moved. He neither heard nor saw any turning wheels. Yet hovercraft would give out blasts of compressed air, wouldn't they?

Antigravity? Nothing else seemed to fit. But if that was so, why were they using animal power?

Could these be descendants of some fallen civilization, patching their commerce together with rude fragments of their forefathers' science? It seemed to fit what he observed.

The idea of antigravity excited Dennis. Might that be the difference in physical laws Brady had talked about during those last moments on Earth?

A last troop of the hooded "warriors" passed below. These rode rather than walked. Their mounts tossed thickly maned heads and nickered, seeming to him so much like shaggy ponies that Dennis mistrusted his observation. It would be too tempting to interpret what he saw in Terran terms.

He rubbed his eyes and stared. But silhouettes were all he could make out.

One animal among the riders carried a smaller figure, coweled in a cloak of faded white—standing out in the deep gloom outside of the headlights. Something he saw in the smaller entity's carriage told him that this one was a prisoner. It carried no shiny weapons, and its arms lay motionless on the animal's neck. The hooded head slumped forward dejectedly.

As the riders passed below, the white-hooded prisoner's head lifted, then started to turn as if to look up into the undergrowth where he was hiding! Dennis ducked down, feeling his throat suddenly go dry.

One of the dark silhouettes ahead turned around in its saddle and pulled on a tether. The prisoner's mount stumbled forward, and the party passed below.

Dennis blinked and shook his head to clear it. For a moment, in the glare and confusion, he had experienced a queer illusion. It had seemed to him that the prisoner's white cloak had opened—for a brief, timeless instant—and the starlight had shown him the sad, forlorn face of a beautiful girl.

7

For a long while the image lingered in his brain—so long, in fact, that Dennis hardly noticed the end of the procession.

He felt a bit lightheaded. Yeah, that must have been it. Too much excitement had gotten him seeing things.

Dennis watched the last glimmer of the caravan pass around the far bend to the east. He still knew next to nothing about the technology and culture of the locals. All he *had* learned was that the natives shared some of humanity's less savory habits—such as the way they treated one another.

A moment later a tiny mutter of sound drifted up from the road below.

Dennis suddenly remembered the image on the camp-watch display. There had been one more tiny green dot, following the caravan from behind. In all the excitement he had forgotten about it!

He crept forward to get a better view. There were no more bright, blinding lights. *Now* he might get a good look!

He slid quietly to within feet of the road itself. At first he saw nothing. Then a tiny noise made him look to the right.

A glint of glass and plastic reflected the faint glow of the departing procession. A tiny articulated arm waved in the dim starlight. On almost silent, spinning treads, the Sahara Tech exploration robot whizzed down the alien highway eastward . . . following Dennis's instructions to the letter.

. . . finding out about the natives.

Dennis barely stifled a shout. *Idiot machine!* He rushed out onto the highway, tripping over a tree root and rolling most of the way. He made it to his feet in time to see the robot, one of its arms waving as if in farewell, pass around the bend and out of sight.

Dennis cursed softly but soundly. That robot's tapes doubtless carried all the information he needed. But he couldn't chase it or call out without bringing himself to the attention of the caravan guards!

He was still muttering softly, standing there in the middle of the dark road, when something alive dropped onto his head from an overhanging branch. Dennis gasped in alarm as the thing wrapped itself tightly over his eyes, sending him stumbling, reeling into the trees.

8

"What was the big idea, scaring me half to death?" Dennis accused hoarsely. "I might have run into something and hurt both of us!"

The object of his ire watched him from a rock a few feet away, green eyes gleaming in the light from the camp stove. The pixolet yawned complacently, apparently of the opinion Dennis was making a big deal out of nothing.

"Damn all machines and natives! Just where have you *been* the past four days, anyway? Here I rescue you from a fate worse than boredom at the hands of Bernald Brady, and in return all I ask is a friend who knows the neighborhood. What happens? That 'friend' up and leaves me all alone, until isolation eventually gets me so I'm talking to myself . . . or worse, to a stubby little flying pig who can't understand a word I'm saying . . . !"

Dennis found he could hold his hands steady at last. He poured a cup of soup for himself. Blowing on it, he muttered as his temper slowly wound down. "Stupid, practical joking E.T.s . . . damned fickle aliens . . ."

He glanced over his cup at the diminutive native animal. Its tongue was hanging out. Its eyes met his.

Dennis let out a sigh of surrender. He poured some soup into the overturned pot cover. The pixolet hopped over and lapped at it daintily, looking up at him from time to time.

When both had finished, Dennis rinsed out the utensils and crawled back into his sleeping bag. He picked up the camp-alarm and worked on its settings. Pix leaped over beside him and watched.

Dennis tried to ignore it but couldn't maintain his ire for long—not with it looking at him that way, purring, watching with apparent fascination the adjustments he made to the little machine.

Dennis shrugged and picked up the small creature. "What is it about you and machines? You sure can't *use* them. See?" He shook its little paws. "No hands!"

With the stove turned off, the forest night settled in around. In a little island in the quiet, Dennis soon found himself telling the pixolet about the constellations and all the other things he had discovered.

And he realized it *was* good to have company again, even if it was an alien creature who didn't understand a single word he said.

3

Nom de Terre

1

The next day the road began to descend into a broad river valley.

Riding on Dennis's shoulder, the pixolet peeped and grabbed a cluster of berries from an overhanging branch. It munched on a few of the purple fruits, and juice ran down its jaws. When it offered some to Dennis, he politely declined.

Dennis was feeling pretty good. His old camping skills had obviously come back. His backpack was snug now that he had found the right knots. His boots—broken in now—felt like supple extensions of his own feet as he stepped along the resilient highway. He was making good time.

But he could tell the forest would end soon. He still faced the problem of what he would do when he found civilization.

What sort of creatures were the autochthones? Would they have the technology to help him rebuild his half of the zievatron?

More important, would they decide to arrange *his* pieces neatly, by size and color, like someone had already done to the zievatron?

Maybe it might be a good idea to spy on the natives, as a first step.

"Easily suggested," Dennis mocked himself. If their facial features are a little different, I'll just use some river mud to make fake antennae and eye stalks and be in business! I might have to remove my nose and lengthen my neck a bit, of course, but only a few inches, at most.

"I wonder if I'll need scales."

As he hiked along, a number of fantasy scenarios occurred to him.

I know! I'll keep my eye out for the country estate of the eccentric squire scientist G'zvreep. I'll recognize it by the observatory dome protruding prominently from the west wing of his manor house.

Right, Dennis. *When you knock, the kindly old native savant will answer the door himself, having sent the servants to bed while he scans the skies for comets. On seeing you he'll flap his thorax in momentary revulsion at your two hideously flat eyes, your millions of tiny cranial tendrils. But when you raise your hand in the universal gesture of peace, he'll hustle you inside and say, "Enter quickly! Thank Gixgax you came here first!"*

In a meadow by the road, Dennis found the remains of a campsite. Coals were still warm in the firepit.

Dennis put down his pack. He set up the campwatch on one large stone and the pixolet on another. "All right, bright eyes," he said to the creature, "let's see if you're good for anything but company. You can keep a lookout while I do some serious detective work."

Pix cocked its head quizzically, then yawned.

"Hmmph. Well, it just goes to show how little you know. I've found something already!" Dennis pointed to the ground. "Look. Footprints!"

Pixolet sniffed, apparently unimpressed. Dennis sighed. Where was an appreciative audience when you needed one?

There were many deep impressions in the ground—apparently made by the large draft animals—and smaller hoofprints like those an unshod pony might leave. The droppings, too, indicated that this world must indeed have close analogs to horses.

After finishing with the animals, he searched for a clear set of bipedal prints and soon realized that everyone in the caravan had worn shoes.

From the sharp outlines of the corrugated tread, it was apparent these people used boots not unlike his own! *Here* certainly was evidence of technology. The tread patterns were all *identical* . . . as if some computer had come up with the perfect design that was mass-produced thereafter. He hurried about looking at the prints until a thought occurred to him.

Dennis grabbed his own left foot. Awkwardly, he tried to look at the sole of his own boot. Moving too quickly, he overbalanced and fell on his backside.

He stared at the pattern of his own boot and sighed. It was identical!

Either the computers here had come up with the same design as those on Earth had, or . . .

He looked around. The bootprints were everywhere. No doubt nearly all of them were his own.

There was a peeping that sounded suspiciously like laughter. Dennis turned and glared at the pixolet. It wore its accustomed grin.

"Don't you dare say *one* word!" Dennis warned the creature.

For once, Pix did as told.

There weren't many more clues. By the firepit he found a few crumbly sticks of dried meat. Over where the animals had been staked there were scatterings of spilled grain.

By a tall tree Dennis found a red stain in the earth. It felt sticky, like blood.

There were scuffmarks in the ground, and loose tufts of fur. Then he found one long golden strand that glinted in the morning light. He looked at it for a long moment, then carefully stuffed it into a button-down shoulder pocket.

A bit closer to the forest, he found a dead animal.

It looked like a larger cousin of the pixolet's. It had the snub nose and needle teeth, but it was the size and build of a mastiff.

The head stared at him dully from a spot three feet from the rest of the body. It had been sheared off, along with part of the shoulder, as if by a guillotine—or a high-power laser.

He stared at the carnage until the buzzing of the watch-alarm carried over from the firepit. Dennis looked up anxiously. What was coming?

He turned just as six ragged doglike things suddenly emerged from the line of trees. He did not have time to form a more accurate impression. They snarled—a low, gravelly sound—then charged.

The needler was in his hand before he had time to think. He had practiced drawing and blasting knots in tree trunks during the past few days of hiking. The exercise probably saved his life.

Balanced, legs apart, Dennis aimed just ahead of the beasts and fired.

The ground in front of the pack exploded, but the crazed things charged straight through the spray of dirt and grass single-mindedly. Dennis had no choice. He lifted his aim and fired again.

The pack tumbled into a howling mass. It divided almost instantly into the fleeing and the dead.

Dennis watched the survivors stumble away, howling in pain, their fellows bloody and still behind them. He looked down at the small weapon in his hand.

Powered by stored sunlight, the needler could peel tiny slivers off of any odd-shaped lump of metal he crammed into its ammo chamber, and fire them at high velocity. Dennis had thought it little better than a toy when he started out from the zievatron but he had begun to gain confidence in it with all the practice on the trail.

Now he stared at it in amazement.

What a killer, he thought.

2

Soon he could tell he was drawing near civilization.

The highway perceptibly widened as it dropped from the mountain pass. Some of the hillside meadows now showed signs of cultivation. A thick hedgerow now separated the highway from open fields on both sides. Through the branches he could see herds of grazing animals on the slopes.

He would run into traffic soon. A happenstance encounter on the road wasn't the best kind of first contact. He didn't want to face the sort of weapon that had severed the head of the beast back at the campsite. Dennis decided it might be best to continue his travels off the road for a while.

He searched for a break in the hedge. Pix awakened from its nap atop his backpack when Dennis drew his machete and started to chop at a thin spot in the windbreak. The little beast leaped for a high branch, then crouched and looked down at Dennis reproachfully for interrupting its siesta.

Dennis didn't find the going easy. The heavy blade bounced back from the branches, barely chipping them.

He looked at it in disgust. He had not used the machete much until now. It was covered with rust spots and the edge was dull. Dennis cursed Bernald Brady, taking what consolation he could from the fact that he had not misjudged the fellow after all.

As he sucked at scratches on the back of his right hand, he had an idea. What about the beautiful native knife he had found by the airlock? He shrugged out of his pack and retrieved the cloth-wrapped artifact from one of the bottom pouches. With a wary glance up and down the highway, he laid the cloth on the ground and unfolded it.

His eyes went wide.

A week ago he had put away a beautiful, sharp, resilient knife, an obvious product of high-tech craftsmanship.

What lay before him was still impressive, but it looked a lot more like a finely chipped piece of obsidian tied to a wooden handle by tightly wound leather strips. It was sharp and well made, but a far cry from the advanced tool he remembered first picking up.

His head felt light. *A phenomenon,* he remarked internally, touching the object lightly.

He was brought back to the present by a peeping cry from above. The pixolet chirped at him twice, shaking its head vigorously. Then it soared off into the thicket.

Dennis reached into his thigh pocket and pulled out the camp-watch. The little screen showed red lights on the road, coming this way.

He rewrapped the artifact. The mystery would keep. He hefted the pack once more and set to hacking in earnest with the machete. He *had* to get off the road!

Brambles caught at his pack and at the arm he kept up to protect his face as he bulled his way through the thicket. Finally, like a pip squeezed from a melon, he flew into the meadow and sprawled onto the grass.

Dennis rolled over, breathing heavily.

At least this *time I'll get a good look at them,* he thought as he crawled away from the break in the hedge. *At last I'll find out what the natives* look *like!*

He drew out the camp-watch again. The display showed a great many yellow lights, apparently depicting the herds of grazing animals Dennis had seen on the hillsides. To one side of the screen he saw two red dots and two yellow, coming this way down the road.

A pair of riders.

Pix's green marker was nowhere to be seen. The fickle creature must have left him again.

He was concentrating so hard on the red dots on the road that it took him a moment to notice that two small pink lights had detached themselves from a nearby herd of yellows to the south. They were moving rapidly toward the center of the screen.

Toward the center, Dennis realized . . . *that's me.*

"*Haaaa-aayy-oooaaoo!!*"

It came from behind him, a high, shrill cry that sent a shiver down his back. With the ululation came the sound of running footsteps. Someone was charging down on him from the rear!

Dennis clawed at his holster, holding little hope he could scramble about in time. At any instant he expected the sudden flash of some alien death ray to cut him down.

"Haaayyoo-oh!"

Encumbered by the pack, he rolled over onto his stomach, trying to bring his weapon up. He held the needler out in two shaky hands ready to fire at . . . the dog.

He blinked, poised to shoot . . . the small dog that growled at him, then hopped back to take cover behind a pair of small legs . . . the stubby, scuff-kneed legs of a small boy.

Dennis looked up and stared. The most ominous weapon in sight was a shepherd's crook held by a four-foot-tall towhead with a dirty face.

The first sapient extraterrestrial with whom Dennis had made contact wiped a lock of untidy brown hair out of his eyes and panted. ". . . *Ayoo-missuh* . . ." The boy breathed excitedly. *"Ooowan' seem'pop?"*

A bit numb from surprise, Dennis realized he probably looked silly laying there. Slowly, so as not to frighten the child, he picked himself up.

He decided not even to think about the incongruity of finding a human boy—apparently about eight years old—here on an alien world. There was no profit in it. He made himself concentrate on the language problem. Something about the sounds spoken by the boy had sounded strangely familiar, as if he had heard them somewhere before.

He tried to remember a few facts from the linguistics course he had taken in college in order to get out of the infamous Professor LaBelle's English 7. There were a few sounds, he had learned, that were nearly universal in meaning among human beings. Anthropologists used to use them at the beginning of contact with newly discovered tribes.

He swallowed, then ventured one of them.

"Huh?" he said.

By now the boy had caught his breath. With a sigh of exaggerated patience he repeated himself.

"You wanna see my pop, misser?"

Dennis gulped. He did manage, at last, to make his head go up and down in a nod.

3

The pup ran around them, yapping about their feet. The boy—who said his name was Tomosh—walked earnestly beside Dennis, leading him over the hilly meadow toward his home.

As they walked, Dennis saw a pair of riders pass by on the highway. Seen through breaks in the hedge, the sources of the threatening red dots that had sent him plunging into hiding minutes before turned out to be a couple of farmers cantering past on shaggy ponies.

He was just starting to adjust to all this. Of all possible first contacts, this one had to be the most benign and the most confusing. Dennis couldn't even begin to imagine how there had come to be humans here.

"Tomosh," he began.

"Yessirrr?" The boy rolled his "r's" in an accent that Dennis was only just getting used to. He looked up expectantly.

Dennis paused. Where could he even begin? There was so much to ask. "Er, will your flock be all right while you escort me to meet your folks?"

"Oh, the rickels will be fine. The dogs watch 'em. I just gotta go out an' count 'em twice a day an' give an alarrm if one's missin'."

They walked on in silence for a few more steps. Dennis didn't have much time to prepare for his first meeting with adults. Suddenly he felt very nervous about it.

Before running into the boy he had resigned himself to standing out as an alien and taking his chances. To be slain on sight by mammal-hating antmen, for instance, would have merely been unavoidable bad luck. Nothing he could have done about that.

But small details of his own behavior could affect the way local *humans* reacted to him. A simple mistake in courtesy—a careless slip—might cost him everything. And in that case the fault would be his.

Perhaps he could ask a child questions that would only cause an adult to become suspicious.

"Tomosh, are there many other farms around here?"

"Nossirr, only a few." The boy sounded proud. "We're almost the farthest! The King only wants miners an' traders to go into the mountains where the L'Toff live.

"Baron Kremer feels different, o' course. M'pop says th' Baron's got no right to send in lumbermen an' soldiers. . . ."

Tomosh rambled on about how tough and mean the local overlord was and how the King, who lived far away to the east, would put the

Baron in his place someday. The story broke down into gossip that sounded a bit sophisticated for a small boy . . . how "Lord Hern" was slowly taking over all the mines in the Baron's name and how no circuses had come to the region in more than two years because of the troubles with the King. Although it was hard to follow all the details, Dennis gathered that the local setup was a feudal aristocracy, and apparently war was not uncommon.

Unfortunately, the story didn't tell him anything about the crucial question of the world's technology. The boy's clothes, though dusty, looked well made. There were no pockets, but the belt of button-down pouches looked like it came straight out of a Kelty catalogue. Tomosh's shoes looked a lot like the tough old sneakers Dennis had worn as a child.

A rambling farmstead came into view as they crested a low hill. A house, barn, and storehouse lay about a hundred meters back from the windbreak along the road. The yard was surrounded by a high stockade. To Dennis the place looked prosperous enough. Tomosh grew excited and pulled on Dennis's hand. Dennis uneasily followed the boy down the hill.

The farmhouse was a low, rambling earth-sheltered structure with a shallow, sloping roof that gleamed in the afternoon sunlight. At first Dennis thought the reflection came from aluminum siding. But as they came closer he saw that the walls were actually laminated wooden panels, beautifully joined and varnished.

The barn was similarly constructed. Both buildings looked like pictures out of a magazine.

Dennis stopped just outside the gate. It was his last chance to ask stupid questions.

"Uh, Tomosh," he said, "I'm a stranger hereabouts. . . ."

"Oh, I could tell *that.* You talk funny!"

"Umm, yes. Well, in fact, I'm from a land far away to the . . . to the northwest." Dennis had gathered from the boy's ramblings that it was a direction about which the locals knew little.

"Naturally, I'm a bit curious about your country," he went on. "Uh, could you tell me, for instance, the name of your land here?"

Without hesitation the boy answered, "It's Coylia!"

"So your King is the King of Coylia?"

Tomosh nodded with an expression of exaggerated patience. "Right!"

"Good. You know, it's a funny thing about names, Tomosh. People in different lands call the world by different names. What do your people call it?" Dennis was determined to put "Flasteria" to rest.

"The world?" The boy looked puzzled.

"The whole world." He motioned at the earth, the sky, the hills. "All the oceans and kingdoms. What do you call it?"

"Oh. Tatir," he replied earnestly. "That's the name of the world."

"Tatir," Dennis repeated. He tried not to smile. It wasn't much of an improvement on "Flasteria."

"Tomosh!"

The shrill cry came from the farmhouse. A rather husky young woman stepped out onto the front porch and shouted again, "Tomosh! Come here!"

The boy frowned. "It's Aunt Biss. What's *she* doin' here? An' where's Mom an' Pop?" He took off toward the farmhouse, leaving Dennis standing at the gate.

Something was obviously wrong. The boy's aunt looked worried. She knelt and held his shoulders as she explained something earnestly. Tomosh was soon fighting back tears.

Dennis felt awkward. To approach before he was invited by the adult didn't seem wise. But he couldn't see just walking away, either.

Nothing looked awry about the house and yard. Real chickens pecked at the ground alongside what looked like a flock of tiny tame ostriches.

The paths about the farmyard apparently were made of the same resilient, hi-tech material as the highway. They had the same raggedy edges, almost blending into the surrounding dirt and grass.

That seemed to be the way the whole farm was put together. The windows in the house were clear and well fitted, but they were inserted at various rough approximations to level and square. Big and small windows were set side by side in no apparent pattern.

Tomosh clutched his aunt's skirt, now fully in tears. Dennis was concerned. Something must have happened to the boy's parents.

Finally he decided to approach a few steps. The woman looked up.

"Yourr name is Dennis?" She asked coolly, in the queer local dialect.

He nodded. "Yes, ma'am. Is Tomosh all right? Is there anything I can do to help?"

The offer seemed to surprise her. Her expression thawed just a little. "The boy's parents are gone. I've come to take him to my home. You are welcome to sup and stay until my man comes to gather the goods and lock up."

Dennis wanted to ask more questions, but her severe look kept him quiet. "Set here on the steps an' wait," she said. She led the boy inside.

Dennis wasn't offended by the woman's suspicion of a stranger. His accent probably didn't help any. He sat on the steps where she had indicated.

There was a rack of tools on the porch just outside the front door. At first Dennis looked them over complacently, thinking about other things. Then he looked closer and frowned. "Curiouser and curiouser," he said.

It was the strangest assortment of implements he had ever seen.

Near the door were a hoe, an ax, a rake, and a spade, all apparently shiny and new. He touched a pair of shears next to them. The edges were sharp, and they looked quite strong.

The handles had grips of smooth, dark wood, as one might expect. But the cutting edges didn't seem to be made of metal. The razor-sharp blades were *translucent* and showed faint veins and facets within.

Dennis gaped. "They're stone!" he whispered. "Some sort of *gem-stone*, I do believe! Why, they may even be single *crystals!*"

He was staggered. He couldn't imagine the technology that could provide such tools for a country farmer. The implements near the door were unbelievable!

But that wasn't the last surprise. As he scanned the toolrack, Dennis felt a growing sense of strangeness, for although the tools farthest from the door seemed *also* to be made of stone, that was all they had in common with the beautiful blades near the entrance.

Dennis blinked at the incongruity. On the far left was another ax. And *this* one might have come straight out of the late Stone Age!

The crude wooden handle had been rubbed smooth in two places, but it still had bits of bark attached to it in spots. The blade appeared to be a piece of chipped flint held on by leather thongs.

The rest of the tools fell between these extremes. Some were as crude as could be imagined. Others were obviously the products of an extremely high materials science, and computer-aided design.

He touched the flint-headed ax, lost in thought. It might have been made by the same hand that put together the mysterious knife that lay wrapped in his pack.

"Stivyung's the best practicer in these parts," a voice behind him said.

He turned. Lost in thought, he hadn't heard Aunt Biss come out onto the porch. The woman proffered a bowl and spoon, which he took automatically. Steamy aroma sparked a sudden hunger.

"Stivyung?" He repeated the name with difficulty. "The boy's father?"

"Yah. Stivyung Sigel. A fine man, sergeant of the Royal Scouts before marryin' my sister Surah. His reputation for practice was his downfall. That an' the fact that he's built just like the Baron—both height an' weight. The Baron's men came for him this mornin'."

She seemed to think she was making sense. Dennis didn't dare tell her otherwise. Much of his confusion might be due to the woman's thick accent, anyway.

"What about the boy's mother?" Dennis asked. He blew on a spoonful of stew. It was bland but compared favorably to the survival rations he had been eating for over a week.

Aunt Biss shrugged. "When they took Stivyung, Surah ran over to fetch me, then packed up an' headed for the hills. She wanted to ask the L'Toff for help." Biss snorted. "Lot o' good *that'll* do."

Dennis was getting dizzy with all the references to things he didn't understand. Who were the *L'Toff*? And what in the world was a *practicer*?

As for the story of the boy's father being arrested, Dennis could see how a farmer's pride might get him in trouble with the local strongman, but why would Stivyung Sigel be seized for being "built just like" his overlord? Was that a crime here?

"Is Tomosh all right?"

"Yah. He wants to tell you good-bye before you go."

"Go," Dennis repeated. He had sort of been hoping for some down-home hospitality, including a real bed and some trial conversation, before he tackled a larger settlement. Things didn't sound too peaceful hereabouts. He wanted to find out who made the marvelous hi-tech items and head straight for that element in society, avoiding the Baron Kremers of this world.

Aunt Biss nodded firmly. "We got no room at my place. An' my husban' Bim is locking up this stockade tomorrow. If you want work, you'll find it in Zuslik."

Dennis stared down at the bowl. Suddenly he did not want to face another night in the wilderness. Even the clucking chickens made him feel homesick.

Aunt Biss was silent for a moment, then she sighed. "Oh, wha' the hey. Tomosh thinks you're a genuine pilgrim an' not one of those layabouts we sometimes get in from th' east. I don't suppose it'll do any harm to let you sleep th' night in th' barn. So long as you behave an' promise to go peaceful in th' mornin'."

Dennis nodded quickly. "Perhaps there are some chores I can help with . . . ?"

Biss thought about it. She turned and picked up the flint-headed ax from the porch rack. "I don' expect it'll do any good, but you might as well chop some firewood."

Dennis took the crude ax dubiously.

"Well . . . I guess I could try . . ." He glanced over at the beautiful gemstone ax by the door.

"Use *this* one," Biss emphasized. "We'll want to sell it off quick, now that Stivyung's gone. There's a pile o' logs aroun' back.

"Good practice to you." She nodded and turned to go inside.

There was that word again. Dennis felt sure he was missing something important. But he judged it would be best not to ask Aunt Biss any more questions.

First things first, then. He finished the stew and licked the bowl clean. It felt like the kind of unbreakable dinnerware found in homes all over Earth. But on closer examination he realized that the bowl was made of *wood*, fashioned wafer thin and varnished to perfection.

If I ever get the zievatron fixed, and if we ever start trading with this culture, they'll be able to sell us millions of these! Their factories will be working overtime!

Then he remembered draft animals pulling sledges that slid noiselessly through the night.

What's going on here?

Casting a wistful glance at the beautiful gemstone ax near the door, he resignedly picked up the caveman special and walked around to the woodpile in back of the house.

4

The Best Way to Carnegie Hall

1

The town of Zuslik lay at the bottom of a wide valley, where low hills on both sides crowded close to a broad, sluggish river. The land was heavily wooded, with cultivated fields evenly scattered among thick patches of forest. The riverside town sat at the junction of several roads.

From a slope west of Zuslik, Dennis could see that the walled settlement was built around a hill overlooking a bend in the river. Atop this eminence, towering above the town, stood a dark, squat tower, built in a series of flat layers like a dark, brooding wedding cake.

Through his Sahara Tech monocular, Dennis could make out antlike columns of men marching in the yards surrounding the fortress. Sunlight occasionally flashed from ranks of upheld weapons. Pennants riffled from the high tower, blown by the breeze that swept up the valley.

There was no mistaking the home of the chief honcho. Dennis hoped his search wouldn't require that he go there. Not after what he had heard about the man.

The evening before last, while Dennis settled into the hayloft of the Sigels' farm, the little boy Tomosh had come out to the barn. Ostensibly it was to wish the visitor good night, but Dennis realized that the young fellow actually had come for sympathy and comfort. He didn't imagine Tomosh got much of it from his cool aunt.

Tomosh had wound up staying for a couple of hours, exchanging stories with Dennis. It had been a fair trade. Dennis had a chance to practice his accent—familiarizing himself with the muddy, strange Coylian version of English—and Tomosh, much to his delight, learned a great deal about the ways of Brer Rabbit and of flying elephants.

Dennis didn't find out much about Coylian technology—he hadn't expected to, talking with a small boy. But he listened attentively as Tomosh told "scary" stories about "Bleckers" and other fabled bogeymen, and about ancient, kindly dragons that let people ride them through the sky. Dennis filed away the tales in his memory, for one never knew what would turn out to be useful information.

More relevant, he imagined, were the tidbits Tomosh told about Baron Kremer, whose grandfather had led a tribe of hillmen out of the north to take Zuslik from the old Duke a generation ago. Kremer sounded like a good man to stay away from, according to Tomosh, especially after what the fellow had done to the boy's family.

Much as he wanted to learn more, Dennis knew Baron Kremer wasn't the best topic to dwell on. He distracted the boy from his troubles with an old camp song that soon had him laughing and clapping. By the time Tomosh fell asleep on the hay nearby, the boy had forgotten about the day's traumas.

It left Dennis feeling as if he had done a good deed. He only wished he could have done more for the little tyke.

Aunt Biss, taciturn to the end, gave Dennis a cloth-wrapped lunch of cheese and bread for his departure early the next morning. Tomosh manfully rubbed back tears when he said farewell. It had taken only a day and another morning to hike here from the farmhouse.

On the trek to town Dennis had kept a lookout for a small pinkish creature with bright green eyes. But the pixolet never showed up. It looked like the little creature really had abandoned him this time.

Dennis examined Zuslik from the bluff outside of town. Somewhere in that citadel, the boy's father was being held for mysterious crimes Dennis still didn't understand . . . because he was "built just like" his overlord and was good with tools. . . . Dennis was relieved to find out that *he,* at least, didn't resemble the warlord at all.

He decided he wouldn't learn any more about Zuslik by studying it from a distance. He got up and started putting on his pack.

Just then he caught a flicker of motion in his peripheral vision. He turned to look . . . and saw something huge, black, and *fast* come swooping straight down on him over the treetops!

Dennis flung himself to the grassy slope as the giant flying thing shot by just overhead. Its shadow was huge, and a flapping, whistling sound sent chills of expectant disaster up his back as he burrowed into the turf.

The moment of terror passed. When nothing disastrous appeared to happen, he finally raised his head, looking around frantically for the monster. But the thing was gone!

Last night Tomosh had spoken of dragons—great ferocious creatures that had once supposedly defended mankind on Tatir against deadly enemies. But Dennis had been under the impression they were of the distant past, where the fanciful creatures of children's fairy tales belonged!

He scanned the horizon and finally found the black shape. It was settling down toward the town. His throat was still dry as he pulled out the monocular and managed to focus it on the castle grounds.

Dennis blinked. It took a moment for him to realize—somewhat to his relief—that it was no "dragon" after all. His ebony monster was a *flying machine*. Small figures ran to the aircraft from a line of sheds in the castle's yard as the craft drifted to rest, light as a feather. Two small figures—presumably the pilots—dismounted and strode quickly toward the castle without looking back.

Dennis lowered the ocular. He felt a little foolish for coming to overly dramatic conclusions when there was another, simpler explanation. It wasn't really so surprising the locals had flight, was it? There had been plenty of signs of high technology.

Still, the aircraft had hardly made a sound as it passed overhead. There were no growling engine noises. It was puzzling. Perhaps antigravity merited another consideration.

There was only one way to find out more. He got up and brushed himself off, then shouldered his pack and headed down to town.

2

The market outside the city wall was like almost any small riverfront bazaar on Earth. There were shouts and calls and sudden gangs of running boys obviously up to no good. Shops and warehouses gave off pungent aromas, from rich food to the high musk of the grunting draft animals.

He entered the bazaar with what he hoped was an expression of somebody going confidently about his business. By the variety of clothing he saw, Dennis didn't feel outlandishly dressed. Boots, shirt, and trousers seemed to be conventional attire here. Some people even carried burdens on their backs, as he did.

He passed men lounging at the tables of a sidewalk cafe and gathered a few looks. But nobody seemed to stare with more than passing curiosity.

Dennis began to breathe more easily. *Maybe I can bluff my way all the way to whatever passes for a university in these parts,* he thought hopefully. He had a clear idea of the type of individuals he wanted to contact in this culture.

Even in ancient and feudal societies on Earth there had always been patches of enlightenment, and these people clearly enjoyed higher technology and culture than that. The aircraft had definitely raised Dennis's hopes of finding the kind of help he needed.

The sharp odors of drying fish and tanning hides hit him as he reached the dockyards. The piers were solid-looking structures of dowel and peg construction. They looked almost new, right down to the glossy pilings. The upper surfaces were coated with the same resilient stuff that made up the Coylian roads.

He stopped to look over one of the boats. Dennis had sailed enough to recognize a sophisticated ship design when he saw one. The hull was thin, light, and sleek. Its mast was stepped elegantly and a little rakishly over the center of gravity.

Once again, it was built of beautifully glossy laminated wood.

But if they had the technology to build boats like these, why did they use sails? Did the people of Coylia have some sort of taboo against engines? Perhaps their only machinery was in the factories where they produced these wonderful things.

Dennis wanted very much to find one of those factories and talk to the people who ran them.

Not far away, a workgang carried heavy sacks from a warehouse to the hold of a waiting boat. The sacks must have weighed forty kilos each. The stocky, barrel-chested men hummed as they shuffled along the wharf, stooped under their heavy loads.

Dennis shook his head. Could it be against their religion to use *wheelbarrows?*

After each stevedore deposited his sack in the hold, he did not return down the narrow ramp but climbed the boat's gunnels instead. In time with the groaning beat of his comrades, he chanted a brief verse, then dove into the water to make room for the next man.

It did seem like a good idea, taking a dip before swimming around the pier for another of those heavy loads. Dennis made his way around bales of waiting cargo until he was close enough to hear the chant. It seemed to be a repetitious variant of the phrase *"Ah Hee Hum!"*

The workers shuffled along to the steady beat. Dennis approached as a giant with a blue-black moustache dropped his load into the hold, then leaped lightly onto the railing. With one hand on the shrouds, he slapped his sweat-glistened chest as the men chanted.

"Ah Hee Hum!"

The giant sang:

The Mayor is wise, but we all know
      The fact is—

(Ah Wee Hoom?)

What he misses in wisdom he makes
      Up in mass!

(Ah Hee Hum!)

Only two parts of him get enough
      practice—

(Ah Wee Hoom?)

One part is his mouth and the
      Other's his . . .

The last part was drowned out by a hasty "Ah Hee Hum!" from the gang. The big fellow let himself fall into the water with a great splash. As he swam over to a ladder, his place on the gunnels was taken by a tall man with a thin fringe of hair. His voice was curiously deep.

Oh, the wife stays at home, in front of
      The mirror—

(Ah Wee Hoom?)

She must think she's a hat, or a broom,
      Or a door!

(Ah Hee Hum!)

Things practice good, but people
> Are poorer—

(Ah Wee Hoom?)

She primps, but still she looks
> Like a who—

(Ah! Hee-e-e *Hoom!)*

Dennis smiled weakly, like a person who could tell a pretty good joke was being told but who couldn't quite understand the punch line.

3

A small caravan passed slowly through the main gateway into town. There were pedestrians carrying burdens, lined up for inspection at what appeared to be a customs shed. A few men riding shaggy ponies passed through the gateway, not bothered by the guards—apparently officials riding on errands.

Teams of hulking, rhinoceroslike quadrupeds chuffed patiently outside the gate. Their harnesses led to giant sledges, apparently of the kind Dennis had glimpsed that night on the highway.

Now we'll see if it's antigravity after all! Dennis hurried forward eagerly. The mystery was about to be solved!

A few of the waiting pedestrians complained desultorily as he edged forward to the cargo sleds, but no one stopped him. His excitement rose as he approached one of the gleaming, high-sided vehicles.

As he had suspected, there weren't any wheels at all. The load was strapped to a tilted platform whose four corners ended in little skids. These fitted precisely into the two perfect grooves that ran down every road Dennis had found in Coylia.

The driver shouted at his beast and snapped the reins. The snuffling, buffalo-like creature strained against its harness, and the sled glided smoothly forward. Dennis followed, crouching for a better look.

Was it magnetic levitation? Did the tiny runners ride on a cushion of electrical force? There were devices like that on Earth, but nothing anywhere near this compact. The system seemed elegantly simple, yet incredibly sophisticated.

Dimly, he was aware that people behind him were making ribald remarks about his behavior. There was laughter, and a series of off-color suggestions in the strange local dialect. But Dennis didn't care. His mind was filled with schematics and raw mathematics as he tested and discarded explanation after explanation for the wonderful sled-and-road combination.

It was the most fun he had had in weeks!

A detached part of him realized that he had tipped over into a strange state of mind. The tension of the past two weeks had burst, and the persona best able to cope—the eager scientist—had come to the fore, to the exclusion of almost everything else. For well or ill, it was his way of dealing with too much alienness all at once.

Dennis got down on all fours and squinted close to the tiny sled in its trough. As the sled moved slowly forward, he let out a small cry of surprise. A clear *liquid* oozed from beneath the little ski as it slid along. The fluid disappeared quickly, seeping almost instantly into the bottom of the trough.

He touched the bead of wetness that followed the skid, and rubbed the drop between finger and thumb. Almost at once it spread over them in a glossy sheen. He found he couldn't press the fingertips together without their slipping aside. They barely even felt each other.

The fluid was the perfect lubricant! After a moment's delighted stupefaction, Dennis clawed through one of his thigh pouches for a plastic sampling vial. He had to hold the tube in his left hand, while he vainly tried to wipe his right to get rid of the layer of slipperiness. He pulled the stopper with his teeth.

Crawling along behind the slowly moving sled, he pushed the vial up behind the ski, catching some of the slippery, elusive fluid. Soon he had twenty-five milliliters or so, almost enough to analyze. . . .

His head bumped into the sled as it stopped suddenly. A small rain of cherrylike fruits fell over him from the overloaded wagon.

There were new voices from up ahead. Someone spoke loudly, and the crowd began backing away.

In his exalted state of mind, Dennis refused to be distracted. Drunk on the delight of discovery, he stayed crouched over, hoping the sled would start moving again so he could collect just a *bit* more of the lubricant.

A hand dropped onto his shoulder. Dennis motioned it away. "Just a minute," he urged. "I'll be with you in a sec."

The brawny hand gripped harder, turning him completely around. Dennis looked up, blinking.

A very large man stood over him, dressed unmistakably in some sort of uniform. On the fellow's face was an expression that strangely combined puzzlement with incipient rage.

Three other soldiers stood nearby, grinning. One laughed, "Tha's right, Gil'm. Let'm be! Cantcha see he's busy?" Another guard, who had been drinking from a tall ale-stein, coughed and sputtered brew as he guffawed.

"Gil'm" glowered. He clutched the bunched fabric of Dennis's bush jacket and lifted him to his feet. In his right hand the big guard held something like a two-meter quarterstaff with a shining halberd blade at one end. Dennis's gaze was drawn to the gleaming edge. It looked sharp enough to slice paper or bone with equal facility.

Gil'm called to one of the jokesters without turning or taking his eyes from Dennis. *"Fed'r,"* he rumbled. "Come an' hold my thenner. I don' wanna mess up its practice by killin' nothin' too mushy. This one I'll take care of by han'."

A grinning guard came up and took the tall weapon from Gil'm. The giant flexed fingers like sausages and tightened his grip on Dennis's jacket.

Uh-oh. Dennis at last shook himself partially free of the bemused trance. He began to recognize the harm he just might have done himself.

For one thing, he might have lost his opportunity to recite the speech he had carefully prepared for his first encounter with authorities. Hurriedly, he sought to correct the mistake.

"Your pardon, esteemed sir! I had no idea I was already at the gate of your lovely city! You see, I am a stranger from a faraway land. I've come to meet with your country's philosophers, and hopefully discuss many things of great importance with them. This marvelous lubricant of yours, for instance. Did you know that . . . *Ak!"*

The soldier's face had begun to purple strangely as Dennis spoke. No doubt that meant this was not the right approach after all. Dennis barely ducked beneath a meaty fist that passed through the spot where his nose had lately been.

The guard's face was hardly a foot from his. The fellow's breath was something to write home about.

"Aw, c'mon, Gil'm! Can't you hit a little Zusliker?" Almost the entire complement of guards had come up to watch the fun, leaving their post at the gate a dozen yards away. They were laughing, and Dennis heard one man offer a bet on how far the Gremmie's head would travel when Gil'm corrected his aim.

The civilians in the caravan backed away, looking on fearfully.

"Hold still, Gremmie," Gil'm growled. He cocked his fist back, this time aiming carefully, savoring the moment. His face took on a patient, almost beatific expression of anticipation.

This just may be serious, Dennis thought.

He looked at the guard . . . at the burly hand clutching his jacket. There wasn't time to grab his needler—as if it would help any, starting his visit by slaying members of the local constabulary.

But Dennis realized he *was* holding a small open sample bottle in his left hand.

Hardly thinking, he poured the contents over the meaty paw holding his jacket.

The giant paused and looked at him, amazed by the unprecedented offense. After a moment's thought, Gil'm decided he didn't like it much. He growled again and struck out . . . as Dennis slipped from his hand like a pat of butter. The northman's fist whistled overhead, mussing Dennis's hair with its wake.

Gil'm stared at his now empty left hand, shimmering with a thin coating of bright fluid. "Hey!" he complained. He turned barely in time to see the gremmie vanish through the gateway into town.

4

Dennis would have decidedly preferred a more leisurely first tour of a Coylian city.

Back at the gate there was a mass of confusion. The initial hilarity of the people in the caravan dissolved into shouts and screams as the guards stepped in with truncheons.

Dennis didn't hang around to watch the melee. He pounded across a beautiful, ornate bridge that arched over a canal. Pedestrians stared as he wove among gaily painted market stalls, dodging vendors and their customers. The guards' hue and cry followed only a little behind him as he fled. Luckily, most of the citizens quickly turned away in order not to get involved.

Dennis leaped past a street-corner juggler and ducked the falling pins to dive into an alley behind a pastry stall.

He heard boots pounding on the bridge not far behind him. There were yells as the guards tripped over the hapless juggler and his pins. Dennis continued dodging through the twisting streets and alleys.

The buildings of Zuslik were ziggurat high-rises, some over a dozen stories tall. All had the same wedding cake type of design. The narrow lanes were as serpentine as interdepartmental politics back at Sahara Tech.

In a deserted alley he paused to wait out a stitch in his side. All this running wasn't easy with a heavy pack on his back. At last he was about to go on when suddenly, just ahead, he heard a newly familiar voice cursing.

". . . like to burn this whole damn town to the groun'! You mean *none* of you saw that gremmie? Or those thieves who snuck in our guardhouse while we weren't lookin'? Nobody saw nothin'? Damn Zuslikers! You're *all* a buncha thieves! It's funny how a stripe or two can jog a memory!"

Dennis backed into the alley. One thing was certain, he'd have to ditch his pack. He found a dim corner, unbuckled the belt, and let it slide to the ground. He knelt and pulled out his emergency pouch, which he slung onto his Sam Browne belt. Then he looked around for a place to stash the pack.

There was rubbish in the alley, but unfortunately there were no real hiding places.

The first floor of the building next to him was little more than seven feet high. The next level was set back a meter or two, so the roof formed a parapet just overhead. Dennis stepped back and heaved the pack onto the ledge. Then he backed away again and leaped for a handhold.

Dennis swung his right leg to bring it up, but just then he felt his hold begin to slip. He had forgotten the coating of sled oil still on his right hand. His grip was too slick to hold, and he fell to the ground with a painful thump.

Much as he would have liked to have lain there groaning for a little while, there just wasn't time. Shakily, he got up for another try.

Then he heard footsteps behind him.

He turned and saw Gil'm the Guard enter the alleymouth about ten meters away, grinning happily and holding his weapon high. The halberd blade gleamed menacingly.

Dennis noted that Gil'm wasn't using his left hand at all and assumed it must still be coated with the sled oil. The stuff was insidious.

Dennis popped the flap of his holster and drew his needler. He pointed it at the guard. "All right," he said, "hold it right there. I don't want to have to hurt you, Gil'm."

The soldier kept coming, grinning happily in anticipation, apparently, of slicing Dennis in twain.

Dennis frowned. Even if no one here had ever seen a hand weapon like the needler before, his own self-assurance at least should have given the fellow pause.

Perhaps Gil'm was unimaginative.

"I don't think you know what you're facing here," he told the guard.

Gil'm came on, holding his weapon high with one hand. Dennis decided he had no choice but to play out his bluff. He felt a brief panic as his oiled thumb slipped over the safety lever twice. Then it clicked. He took aim with the needler and fired.

There was a staccato sound, and several things happened all at once.

The polished wood of the halberd's handle split into fragments as a stream of high-velocity metal slivers tore into the elevated weapon. Gil'm ducked aside as the glistening blade fell. The guard stared dully at the severed stump of his weapon.

But Dennis couldn't hold on as the recoil kicked the needler out of his slippery right hand. It bounced off his chest, then went rattling along the ground in front of him.

He and Gil'm stood in a momentary tableau, both of them suddenly disarmed. The guard's face was blank and the whites of his eyes showed. He didn't move.

Dennis started to edge forward, hoping the fellow's daze would last long enough for him to retrieve his weapon. The needler had fetched up against the fallen halberd blade, midway between him and the giant.

Dennis was reaching for it when two more soldiers in high bearskin hats appeared in the alleymouth. They shouted in surprise.

Dennis grabbed the needler and raised it. But in that telescoped moment he found that he just couldn't bring himself to kill. It was a flaw in his personality, he realized, but there was nothing he could do about it.

He turned to run but only got a dozen paces before the butt of a thrown knife struck him on the side of the head, knocking him forward into the dark shadows.

5

" 'ere, now. Easy do it. Ye'll have a bruise like a searchlight in a day or so! A real shiner it'll be!"

The voice came from somewhere nearby. Bony fingers held his arm as Dennis sat up awkwardly, his head athrob.

"Yep, a real shiner. Practice it good an' you'll be able to use it to see in th' dark with!" The voice cackled in generous self-appreciation.

Dennis could barely focus on the person. He tried to rub his eyes and almost fainted when he touched the bruise on the left side of his face.

Blearily, he saw an elderly man who grinned back at him with only half a mouth of teeth. Dennis nearly fell over sideways in a wave of dizziness, but the old fellow caught him.

"I said *easy* there, didn' I? Give it a minute an the worl' will look a lot better. Here, drink some o' this."

Dennis shook his head, then coughed and choked as his would-be nurse grabbed his hair and poured a slug of tepid liquid into his mouth. The stuff tasted vile, but Dennis grabbed the rough mug in both his own hands and gulped greedily until it was taken away.

"Tha's enough for now. You just sit an' get yer senses back. You don't gotta start workin' 'til second day, not when they bring you in lumped like this." The man arranged a rough pillow behind his head.

"My name is Dennis." His voice came out a barely audible croak. "What is this place?"

"I'm Teth, an' you're in jail, punky. Don' you recognize a jail when you see one?"

Dennis looked left and right, able at last to focus his eyes. His bed was part of a long row of rude cots, sheltered by an overhanging wooden canopy. A wattle and daub wall behind him supported the roof. Beyond the open front of the shed was a large courtyard, hemmed in by a tall wooden palisade.

On the right stood a far more impressive wall, one that gleamed seamlessly in the bright sunshine. It was the lowest and widest in a series of tiers that extended up a dozen stories or more. In the center of the shining wall was a small gatehouse. Two bored guards lounged on benches there.

Men in the courtyard, presumably his fellow prisoners, moved about at tasks Dennis couldn't identify.

"What kind of work are you talking about?" Dennis asked. He felt a little giddy, with a trace of that queer detachment from reality that had come over him before. "Do you make personalized license plates here?"

He didn't care when the old man looked at him funny.

"They work us hard, but we don' *make* nothin'. We're mostly lower-class riffraff in here—vagrants an' such. Most of us wouldn' know how to *make* anythin'.

"O' course, there's some in here for gettin' in trouble with th' guilds. An' others who served the old Duke long afore Kremer's father moved into these parts an' took over. Some o' *them* might know a little about *makin'* things, I suppose. . . ."

Dennis shook his head. Teth and he didn't seem to be talking on the same wavelength at all. Or perhaps he just wasn't hearing the fellow right. His head hurt, and he was all confused.

"We grow some of our own food," the old man went on. "I take care of new gremmies like you. But mostly we practice for the Baron. How else would we earn our keep?"

There was that word, again . . . *practice.* Dennis was getting sick of it. He got a gnawing sensation whenever he heard it, as if his subconscious were trying to tell him something it had already figured out. Something another part of him was just as frantically rejecting.

With some difficulty he sat up and swung his feet over the side of the cot.

"Here, now! You shouldn' do that for a few hours yet. You lie back down!"

Dennis shook his head. "No! I've *had* it!" He turned to the old man, who looked back with plain concern. "I'm *finished* being patient with this crazy planet of yours, do you hear? I want to know what's going on, now! Right now!"

"Easy," Teth began. Then he squawked as Dennis grabbed his shirt-front and pulled him forward. Their faces were inches apart.

"Let's get down to basics," Dennis whispered through gritted teeth. "This *shirt,* for instance. *Where* did you get it?"

Teth blinked as if he were in the grip of a lunatic. "It's bran' new. They giv' it to me to break in! Wearin' it's one of my jobs!"

Dennis clutched the shirt tighter. "This? *New?* It's hardly more than a rag! The weave is so coarse it's about to fall apart!"

The old man gulped and nodded. "So?"

Dennis snatched at a spot of color at the fellow's waist. He pulled free a square of filmy, opalescent fabric. It bore delicate patterns and had the feel of fine silk.

"Hey! Tha's mine!"

Dennis shook the beautiful cloth under Teth's nose. "They dress you in rags and let you keep something like this?"

"Yeah! They let us keep some of our personal stuff, so it won't go bad wi'out us workin' on it! They may be mean, but they're not *that* mean!"

"And this piece isn't *new,* I suppose." The kerchief looked fresh from some expensive shop.

"Palmi no!" Teth looked shocked. "It's been in my family five generations!" he protested proudly. "An' we been using it nonstop all that time! I look at it an' blow my nose in it lots of times every day!"

It was such an unusual protestation that Dennis's grip slackened. Teth slid to the floor, staring at him.

Shaking his head numbly, Dennis stood up and stumbled outside, blinking against the brightness. He walked unevenly past knots of laboring men—all dressed in prisoners' garb—until he reached a point where the outer palisade came into contact with the glistening wall of the castle.

With his left hand he touched the rough treetrunks, crudely trimmed and mud-grouted, which comprised the palisade. With his right hand he stroked the castle wall, a slick, metal-hard surface that shone translucently like a massive, light-brown, semiprecious stone . . . or like the polished trunk of a mammoth petrified tree.

He heard someone approach from behind. He glanced back and saw it was Teth, now accompanied by two more prisoners, who looked over the newcomer curiously.

"When was the war?" Dennis asked softly without turning around.

They looked at each other. A tall, stout man answered, "Uh, what war you talkin' about, Grem? There's lots of 'em, all the time. The one when th' Baron's dad kicked out the old Duke? Or this trouble Kremer's havin' with the King . . . ?"

Dennis turned and shouted, "The *Big War,* you idiots! The one that destroyed your ancestors! The one that threw you back to living off the dregs of your *forefathers* . . . their self-lubricating roads . . . their indestructible handkerchiefs!"

He brought a hand to his throbbing head as a dizzy spell struck. The others whispered to each other.

Finally a short, dark man with a very black beard shrugged and said, "Don't know what you're talkin' about, man. We've got it better'n our ancestors ever had it. An' our grandchildren'll have it better'n us. That's called *progress.* Ain't you heard of progress? You from someplace that has ancestor worship, or somethin' backward like that?"

He looked genuinely interested. Dennis let out a faint moan of despair and stumbled on, followed by a growing entourage.

He passed prisoners working in a vegetable garden. The neat rows of green seedlings seemed normal enough. But the implements the gardeners used were of the flint and tree-branch variety he had seen at Tomosh Sigel's house. He pointed to the rakes and hoes.

"Those tools are new, right?" he demanded of Teth.

The old man shrugged.

"Just as I thought! Anything *new* is crude and barely better than sticks and stones, while the rich get to hoard all the best remnants of your ancestors' ancient—"

"Uh," the small, dark man interrupted, "these tools *are* for the rich, Gremmie."

Dennis snatched a flintheaded hoe out of the hands of one of the nearby farmers and waved it under the short fellow's nose. *"These?* For the rich? In an obviously hierarchical society like yours? These tools are crude, barbaric, inefficient, clumsy—"

The fat gardener he had taken the tool from protested, "Well, I'm doin' my best! I just got *started* on it, fer heaven's sake! It'll get better! Won't it, guys?" He snuffled. The others muttered in agreement, apparently coming to the conclusion that Dennis was somewhat of a bully.

Dennis blinked at the apparent non sequitur. He hadn't said anything about the *farmer* at all. Why did he take it personally?

He looked about for another example—*anything* else to get through to these people. He turned and spotted a group of men at the far end of the courtyard. They were not dressed in crude homespun. Instead they wore finery of the most brilliant and eye-pleasing shades. Their clothing shimmered in the afternoon light.

These men were engaged in a series of mock fencing bouts using wooden dowels instead of swords. A few guards lounged about, watching them.

Dennis had no idea why these aristocrats and their guards were here in the prison yard, but he seized the opportunity. *"There!"* he said, pointing. "Those clothes those men are wearing are *old,* aren't they?"

Although it was now less friendly, the crowd nodded in agreement.

"They were made by your ancestors, then, right?"

The small, dark man shrugged. "I suppose you could say so. So what? It doesn't matter who *makes* somethin'. It's whether you keep it up that counts!"

Were these people blind to history? Had the holocaust that destroyed the marvelous old science of this world so traumatized them that they shied away from the truth? He walked purposefully over to where the dandies fenced by the wall. A bored guard looked up lazily, then returned to his nap.

Dennis had quite lost his head by now. He shouted at the prisoners who had followed him. "You don't deny that aristocrats get the best, and coincidentally the *oldest*, of everything?"

"Well, sure . . ."

"And *these* aristocrats are wearing only old things. Right?"

The crowd erupted in laughter. Even some of those in the bright clothes stopped their dour mock swordfights and smiled. Old Teth gave Dennis a gap-toothed grin. "*They's* not rich people, Denniz. They's poor prisoners like us. They's just built like some of the Baron's cronies. 'If you *can* wear a rich man's clothes, you *will* wear a rich man's clothes, whether you want to or not!' " It sounded like an aphorism.

Dennis shook his head. His subconscious was spinning and seemed to be trying to tell him something.

"Imprisoned for being 'built just like' the Baron . . . that's what Tomosh Sigel's aunt said happened to the kid's dad. . . ." Someone nearby gasped aloud, but Dennis continued talking to himself, faster and faster.

"The *rich* force the poor to wear their gaudy clothes for them, day in, day out . . . but that doesn't fray the clothes, wearing them out. Instead . . ."

Someone was talking urgently nearby, but Dennis's mind was completely full. He wandered aimlessly, paying no attention to where he was going. Prisoners made way for him, as men do for the sainted or the mad.

"No," he mumbled, "the clothing doesn't wear out—because the rich get someone *built* like them to wear their clothes all the time, to keep them in . . . ."

"Excuse me, sir. Did you mention the name of . . ."

". . . to keep them in *practice!*" Dennis's head hurt. "Practice!" he said it again and pressed his hands to his head at the craziness the word made him feel.

". . . did you mention the name of Tomosh Sigel?"

Dennis looked up and saw a tall, broad-shouldered man wearing the finery of a fabulously wealthy magnate—though Dennis now knew him for a prisoner like himself. Something about the man's face looked familiar. But Dennis's mind was too cluttered to give it more than an instant's thought.

"Bernald Brady!" Dennis shouted and struck his palm. "He said there was a subtle difference in physical law here! Something about the robots seeming to get more efficient . . ."

Dennis patted his jacket and pants. He felt lumpy objects. The guards had taken his belt and pouch but left the contents of his pockets alone.

"Of *course*. They didn't even notice them," he whispered half frantically. "They've never seen zippered pockets before! And those zippers have had *practice* getting to be better and better zippers ever since I got here!"

The crowd suddenly grew hushed as he zipped one pocket open and drew out his journal. Dennis flipped the pages.

"*Day One*," he read aloud. "*Equipment terrible. Cheapest available. I swear I'll get even with that S.O.B. Brady someday. . . .*" He looked up, smiling grimly. "And I will, too."

"Sir," the tall man persisted, "you mentioned the name of . . ."

Dennis flipped ahead, tearing at the pages. "*Day Ten . . . Equipment much better than I'd thought. . . . I guess I must have been mistaken, at first. . . .*"

But he hadn't been mistaken! The stuff had simply *improved!*

Dennis snapped the notebook shut and looked up. For the first time since arriving on this world, he *saw*.

He saw a tower that had become, after many generations, a great castle—because it had been *practiced* at it for so long!

He saw gardening tools that would day by day get better with use, until they were like the marvels he had seen on the steps of Tomosh Sigel's house.

He turned and looked at the men around him. And *saw* . . .

"Cavemen!" he moaned.

"I won't find any scientists or machinists here, because there aren't any! You don't have any technology at all, do you?" he accused one prisoner. The fellow backed away, obviously having no idea what Dennis was talking about.

He whirled and pointed at another. "*You!* You don't even know what the *wheel* is! Deny it!"

The prisoners all stared.

Dennis wavered. Consciousness flickered like a candle going out.

"I should . . . I should have stayed at the airlock and *built* my own damn zievatron. . . . Pixolet and the robot would've been more help than a bunch of savages who'll prob'ly eat me for supper . . . and *practice* my bones into spoons and forks . . . my scapulae into fine china. . . ."

His legs buckled and he fell to his knees, then went face-first into the sand.

"It's my fault," someone above him said. "I never shoulda' let him get up with a bump on his head like that."

Dennis felt strong arms grab his legs and shoulders. The world swayed about him.

Cavemen. They were probably going to put him in a cot so he could *practice* it into a feather bed just by laying in it.

Dennis laughed dizzily. "Aw, Denze, be fair . . . they're a *little* better'n cavemen. After all, they *have* learned that practice makes perfect. . . ."

Then he lost consciousness altogether.

6

It was a late-night talk show on the three-vee. The guests were four eminent philosophers.

Desmond Morris, Edwin Hubble, Willard Gibbs, and Seamus Murphy had just been interviewed. After the commercial break the show's host turned to the holo-cameras, smiling devilishly. "Well, ladies and gentlemen, we've heard a lot from these four gentlemen about their famous *Laws of Thermodynamics.* Maybe now it would be a good time to get a word from the other side. It's a great pleasure, therefore, to bring out tonight's mystery guest. Please welcome Mr. Pers Peter Mobile!"

The four philosophers stood up as one, protesting.

"That charlatan?" "Faker!" "I won't share the stage with a con artist!"

But while they fumed, the orchestra struck up a sprightly, irreverent tune. As the fanfare rose, a high-browed *chimpanzee* rolled out onto the stage, grinning a buck-toothed grin and bowing to the cheering audience.

On his head he wore a little beanie cap with a toy propeller.

The chimp caught a microphone tossed from the wings. He danced to the music, spinning the toy propeller with one finger. Then, with a scratchy but strangely compelling voice, he began to sing.

Why's it so?
Oh, why's it so?
It's an easy ride,
        I will confide,
If you know just what I know!

The refrain was catchy. Pers Peter Mobile grinned and sang a couple
of verses.

Oh, old Ed Hubble blew a cosmic bubble,
He said it did explode!
He won't confess
        to the resultant mess,
But it's gettin' awful cold!

And Willard Gibbs, His frightful Nibs,
Worked out matters' economic.
Time's arrow's the thing,
        you'll hear him sing,
And the debit's always chronic!

The chimp capered to the music, but never stopped spinning the little
propeller. The blur at the top of his head became hypnotic, like the
meshing and weaving of moiré patterns.

Pop anthropologists claim, oh, happy refrain,
That man's *defined by* tools.
Tools help us abide
        ol' entropy's tide,
But even they *obey the rules!*

And Murphy critic, pessimistic,
Cries, foreboding still,
This entropy *thing's*
        got a personal *sting,*
And what can go wrong will.

The music swelled, accompanied by the growing whine of the propeller. The dancing ape returned to the refrain.

Why's it so?
          Oh, why's it so?
It's a bloody mess
          I will confess,
But there's a secret, *don't you know!*

The blur at the top of his head no longer needed a finger to keep it going. In fact, it wasn't a *toy* propeller anymore at all! The beanie cap had become a space helmet and the whirling blades lifted him into the air, much to the dismay of the other guests.

The camera panned close to the chimp's face. Two rows of big, yellowed buck teeth grinned at the audience. The music soared to a crescendo.

Oh, there's a time and place for everything,
Or so the sages say.
If you don't like the rules
          in one stupid place,
Don't gripe, *just fly away!*

The chimp zoomed about the studio, his cap now a full ornithopter suit. He buzzed the furious philosophers, sending them diving behind their chairs in dismay. Then he swooped about in a sharp turn and streaked straight for the camera, laughing, howling, shrieking in mirth.

Just fly a-waaaa-a-a-y-y!!

"Uh!" Dennis flailed and grabbed the edge of the cot with both hands. He stared into the darkness for a long time, breathing hard. Finally he sank back against the bedding again with a sigh.

So, there was no magical, negentropic chimpanzee after all. But the *first* part of the dream was true. He was in jail on a strange world. A bunch of cavemen who hadn't the slightest idea they were cavemen had him prisoner. He was at least fifty miles from the shattered zievatron, on a world where the most basic physical laws he had been brought up to believe were queerly twisted.

It was night. Snores echoed through the prisoners' shed. Dennis lay unmoving in the dimness until he realized that someone sat on the next cot, watching him. He turned his head and met the look of a large, well-muscled man with dark, curly hair.

"You had a bad dream," the prisoner said quietly.

"I was delirious," Dennis corrected. He peered. "You look familiar. Were you one of the men I shouted at while I was raving? One of the . . . the *clothes practicers?*"

The tall man nodded. "Yes. My name is Stivyung Sigel. I heard you say that you had met my son."

Dennis nodded. "Tomosh. A very good boy. You should be proud."

Sigel helped Dennis sit up. "Is Tomosh all right?" He asked. His voice was anxious.

"You needn't worry. He was just fine last I saw."

Sigel bowed his head in gratitude. "Did you meet my wife, Surah?"

Dennis frowned. He found it hard to remember what he had been told. It all seemed so long ago and had been mentioned only in passing. He didn't want to distress Sigel.

On the other hand, the man deserved to be told whatever he knew. "Umm, Tomosh is staying with his Aunt Biss. She told me something about your wife going off to ask help . . . from somebody or something called Latoof? Likoff?"

The other man's face paled. "The L'Toff!" he whispered. "She should not have done so. The wilderness is dangerous, and things are not yet so desperate!"

Sigel stood up and started pacing at the foot of Dennis's bed. "I must get out of here. I *must!*"

Dennis had already begun thinking along the same lines. Now that he knew there were no native scientists to help him, he had to be getting back to the zievatron to try putting a new return mechanism together by himself, with or without replacement power buses. Otherwise he would never get off of this crazy world.

Maybe he could turn the Practice Effect to his advantage, though he suspected it would work quite differently for a sophisticated instrument than for an ax or a sled. The very idea was too fresh and disconcerting for the scientist in him to dwell on yet.

All he really knew was that he was getting homesick. And he owed Bernald Brady a punch in the nose.

When he tried to get up, Sigel hurried to his side and helped him. They went to one of the support pillars, where Dennis leaned and looked out at the stockade wall. Two small, bright moons illuminated the grounds.

"I think," he told the farmer in a low voice, "I might be able to help you get out of here, Stivyung."

Sigel regarded him. "One of the guards claims you are a wizard. Your actions earlier made us think it might be true. Can you truly arrange an escape from this place?"

Dennis smiled. The score so far was Tatir many, Dennis Nuel nothing. It was his turn now. What, he wondered, might not be wrought from the Practice Effect by a Ph.D. in physics, when these people hadn't even heard of the wheel?

"It'll be a piece of cake, Stivyung."

The farmer looked puzzled by the idiom but he smiled hopefully.

A touch of motion caught Dennis's eye. He turned and looked up at the layered castle to his right, its walls gleaming in the moonlight.

Three levels up, behind a parapet lined with bars, a slender figure stood alone. The breeze blew a diaphanous garment and a cascade of long blond hair.

She was too far away to discern clearly in the night, but Dennis was struck by the young woman's loveliness. He also felt sure that somehow he had seen her somewhere before.

At that moment she seemed to look toward them. She stood that way, with her face in shadows, perhaps watching them watch her, for a long time.

"Princess Linnora," Sigel identified her. "She is a prisoner as are we. In fact, she's the reason I'm here. The Baron wanted to impress her with his property. I'm to help practice his personal things to perfection." Sigel sounded bitter.

"Is she as beautiful in the daytime as she is by moonlight?" Dennis couldn't look away.

Sigel shrugged. "She's comely, I'll warrant. But I can't understand what th' Baron's thinking. She's a daughter of the L'Toff. I know them better than most, and it's hard even for me to imagine one of them ever marraiging to a normal human being."

5

Transom Dental

1

"They patrol outside the wall to keep people away," the small thief said. "After all, a lot of prisoners have family and friends on the outside, and a fair part of Zuslik's population would help in a jailbreak. Even after thirty years, Kremer's northmen ain't too popular hereabouts."

Dennis nodded. "But do the guards inspect the wall on the outside as carefully as they do inside?"

The escape committee numbered five. They were gathered around a rickety table eating the noon meal. The prisoners sat in flimsy, uncomfortable chairs. It would have been better just to stand, but practicing the chairs was another of their jobs.

Gath Glinn, the youngest member of their group, squatted in the shadows beside the nearby castle wall, huddled over Dennis's prototype escape device. The sandy-haired youth had been the first to catch on to the Earthman's idea and had been assigned to try it out. He stopped working and covered the device whenever the others indicated the guards were near.

Right now his hands moved rapidly back and forth, and the little tool he *practiced* made soft "zizzing" sounds.

The short, dark man whom Dennis vaguely remembered yelling at on his first day in jail shook his head and answered Dennis's question.

"Naw, Denniz. Sometimes they take gangs of us out to throw rocks at the wall. But mostly they make us practice it from th' inside."

Dennis was still routinely puzzled by things his fellow prisoners told him. His look must have showed it.

Stivyung Sigel looked left and right to make sure no one had approached too close. "What Arth means, Dennis, is that another of our jobs is to practice the wall itself into being a better wall."

The farmer seemed to have caught on that Dennis came from someplace far away, where things were very different from here. It seemed to puzzle him that civilization could exist in a land where things didn't get better with use, but he appeared willing to give Dennis the benefit of the doubt.

"I see." Dennis nodded. "That's why those men are allowed to chop away at the wall like that, without being stopped by the guards." He had seen groups of prisoners lackadaisically attacking the palisade, and the wall of the castle itself, with crude mallets. He had wondered why it was permitted.

"Right, Dennis. The Baron wants the wall stronger, so he has prisoners scratch at it." Stivyung shrugged at explaining something so basic. "Of course, the guards make sure they don't use *good* tools while doing it. This way, in the course of time, the outermost wall will grow more and more like the one behind us, they'll roof it over then, and the castle will grow that much larger."

Dennis looked up at the palace. He understood the wedding cake geometry now. When the Coylians built a structure it started out little better than a rude lean-to. When it was finally converted, after years of *practice*, into a solid one-story building, another crude structure was built on top. While the second story improved, the first became better at supporting weight on its roof and grew outward as lateral additions were made.

As long as someone lived in it thereafter, the building was *practiced* at holding together. Only if abandoned would it slowly revert, eventually to collapse into a tumble of sticks and mud and animal hides.

Dennis didn't imagine there would be much for archaeologists to find on this world, once a great city was abandoned.

"They also check to make sure we practice *all* the wall," Arth added. The diminutive thief claimed to be a leader among the burglars and thieves in the town of Zuslik. From the respect the other prisoners paid him, Dennis didn't doubt it.

"O' course, we always try to leave patches of wall to revert to old logs . . . so's we could *really* break through. They patrol looking for such practice gaps. It's a game o' wits." He grinned, as if certain the game could be won sooner or later.

The zizzing sound behind them suddenly ended in a sharp *snap*. Young Gath held up the severed end of the piece of wood, beaming at Dennis admiringly.

"The *flexible saw* worked!" he whispered in excitement. He looked around to make sure no guards were near, then handed the tool to Dennis.

The teeth were warm from friction. On Earth they would have shown signs of wear after cutting just that little piece of soft wood. But Gath had been thinking "Cut! Cut!" as he worked. And now, thanks to the gentle practice, the zipper was just a little sharper than before.

Dennis shook his head. It was a helluva purpose to put a zipper to. Those sealing the pockets of his overalls were all of soft plastic. He had had to rip the metal zipper from his pants—his fly was now shut with three crude buttons that he hoped would get better with use. Certainly he wasn't about to use this zipper in its old purpose again!

"Good work, Gath. We'll arrange for you to get on sick call so you can practice this saw to perfection. The night it's finished—"

Arth interrupted quickly with a comment on the weather. In a moment a pair of guards passed nearby. The prisoners developed an interest in their meal until they had gone.

When the coast was clear, Dennis offered to pass the saw around. All but Stivyung Sigel politely refused. Apparently the average person here was a bit superstitious toward those who put "essence" into a tool—the original craftsmen who "made" tools in the first place, rather than practiced them to perfection. They probably saw magic in it because it used a principle they had never seen before.

He handed the zipper back to Gath, who palmed it eagerly.

Then lunch was over. The guards started calling them back to work.

Dennis's present job was to attack suits of armor with a blunt, hollow spear—while the soldier-owners wore them! It was exacting work. If he hit the soldier hard enough to hurt, he was struck with a whip. If he struck too softly, the guards shouted and threatened to beat him.

"From now on we take turns watching over Gath to make sure he can practice undisturbed," he said as he stood up. "And we keep him supplied with wood to cut. We'll discuss the rest of the plan later."

The escape committee all nodded. As far as they were concerned, he was the wizard.

The guards called again and Dennis hurried to work. One of the punishments for tardiness was to have one's personal property taken away. Though he now wore homespun like the others, he was allowed to keep his overalls, to "practice" them on his own time. The last thing he wanted was to have them confiscated.

Three hours after lunch, a bell was rung announcing the beginning of a religious service. A red-robed prison chaplain set up an altar near the castle postern, and the cry went out for the faithful to gather.

Those who did not participate had to keep working, so most of the prisoners downed tools at once and sauntered over. In spite of a spate of irreverent chuckles, the majority participated.

A few, such as the thief, Arth, remained at work in the garden, shaking their heads and muttering disapproval.

Dennis wanted to watch the ceremony. But he saw no way to attend as just a spectator. The parishioners bowed and chanted before a row of wooden and gemstone idols.

He finally decided to stay with Stivyung Sigel. For the last hour the two of them had been assigned to chopping wood, using caveman-type axes under a guard's watchful eye.

"It doesn't look like most of our fellow prisoners take the state religion too seriously," Dennis suggested to Stivyung sotto voce.

Sigel flexed his powerful shoulders and brought his ax down in a great arc, sending splinters of wood flying in all directions. He looked incongruous chopping in Baron Kremer's brilliant clothes, but this was all part of Sigel's job. The overlord of Zuslik didn't like his clothes to bind. After this *practice* they would be supple.

"Zuslikers used to be pretty easygoing about religion under the old Duke," Sigel said. "But when Kremer's dad and grandad marched in, they right off started grantin' favors to the church and the guilds, which is funny, since the northern hillmen never were such great believers before that."

Dennis nodded. It was a familiar pattern. In Earth history, barbarians often had become the fiercest defenders of the established orthodoxy after they had conquered.

He raised his ax and took a whack at his own log. The crude stone blade bounced back, hardly making a dent.

"I take it you're not a believer, either," he asked Sigel.

The other man shrugged. "All these gods and goddesses really don't make a lot of sense. In the kingdom cities back east they're losing their following. Some folk are even starting to pay attention to the Old Belief, like the L'Toff have followed all along."

Dennis was about to ask about the "Old Belief" but the guard growled at them. " 'ere now! Pray or woork, you two. Coot th' gab!"

Dennis could barely follow the northman's guttural accent, but he got the general drift. He swung his ax. This time he got a few chips to fly, though he didn't fool himself that it was because the tool had improved perceptibly.

Even with the Practice Effect, this was slow going. He hoped young Gath was having better luck with the zipper-saw than he was having with this triple-damned hunk of flint!

2

For the following three evenings, while Gath or Sigel practiced the little saw under the blankets, Dennis snuck out of the shed and went for walks in the jailyard. He was usually tired by that time, but not so exhausted he couldn't duck past the lazy guards at the inner checkpoint.

In addition to spending his days practicing axes and armor, he had been taking lessons in the Coylians' written language. Stivyung Sigel, the best-educated of the prisoners, was his tutor.

Dennis had been forced to modify his initial opinion a little. These people did have a culture above the "caveman" level. They had music and art, commerce and literature. They simply had no "technology" beyond the late Stone Age. They didn't appear to need any.

Anything nonliving could be practiced, so everything here was made of wood or stone or hide . . . with occasional scraps of beaten native copper or meteoritic iron, both highly prized. Still, it was a wonder what could be accomplished without metal.

Their alphabet was a simple syllabary, easy to learn. Sigel was educated after a fashion, though he had been a soldier and a farmer, not a scholar. He was a patient teacher, but he could shed only a little light on the origin of humans on Tatir. That, he said, was the province of the churches . . . or of legends. Stivyung told Dennis what he knew, though he seemed embarrassed telling what were essentially fairy tales to an adult. Still, Dennis had insisted, and listened carefully, taking notes in his little book.

Finally, Dennis reluctantly concluded the stories of origin were about as contradictory as they had once been on Earth. If there was some link between the two worlds, apparently it was lost in the past.

Dennis did note that some of the oldest legends—particularly those dealing with the so-called Old Belief—did speak of a great fall, in which enemies of mankind caused him to lose his powers over the animals and over life itself.

Stivyung knew about the tale because of his long association with the mysterious tribe, the L'Toff. It wasn't much to go on. And perhaps it was just a fable, after all, like the stories Tomosh had told him about friendly dragons.

So Dennis pondered the problem alone. He scratched narrow lines of tensor calculus in his notebook in the twilight after supper. He hadn't even begun to come up with a theory to explain the Practice Effect. But the mathematics helped to settle his mind.

He needed the focus of his science. From time to time he felt brief recurrences at that strange, lightheaded disorientation he had experienced upon first arriving at Zuslik and then again on his first day in the jailyard.

No author had ever mentioned, in all the fantasy novels he had read, how difficult it really was for a normal human being to adjust to finding himself, with his life in jeopardy, in a truly strange place.

Now that he was beginning to understand some of the rules, and especially now that he had comrades, he was sure he would be all right. But he still felt occasional chills when he thought about the weird situation he was in.

On his fourth evening in the camp, after he snuck past the inner post to walk in the dim twilight past the green shoots in the garden, Dennis heard soft music as he strolled.

The music was lovely. The anomaly calculation he had been working on unraveled like shreds of fog blown by a fresh breeze.

The sound came from above the far end of the prison yard. It was a high, clear, feminine voice, accompanied by some kind of harp. The instrument seemed to weep into the night, gently and with an electric poignancy. Dennis followed the music, entranced.

He came to the point where the new wall met the old. Two parapets above, strumming a pale, lutelike instrument, was the girl he had seen so briefly that night on the road, whom Stivyung Sigel had called Linnora—Princess of the L'Toff.

Sharp spiked wooden bars kept her imprisoned on her balcony. The gleaming rods reflected the moonlight almost as brightly as did the honey yellow of her hair. Dennis listened, entranced, though he couldn't make out the words.

The lutelike instrument must have had generations of *practice* to achieve such power. Her voice filled him with wonder, though he could barely follow the accented words. The music seemed to draw him forward.

The girl stopped singing abruptly and turned. A dark figure had emerged from the dim doorway at the right end of the balcony. She stood and faced the intruder.

A tall, broad-shouldered man stepped out and bowed. If Dennis had not seen Stivyung Sigel only moments before, back at the prisoners' shed, he would have sworn it was his friend up there, advancing on the slender Princess. The big man's clothes were as fine as Linnora's, though clearly made for rougher use. Dennis heard his deep voice but could make out no words.

The L'Toff Princess shook her head slowly. The man grew angry. He stepped toward her, shaking something in his hand. She retreated at first, but then stood her ground rather than suffer the indignity of backing against the wall.

Dennis's heart beat faster. He had a wild thought to rush to her aid . . . as if she were anything to him but another of this world's enigmas. Only the knowledge that it would be perfectly useless restrained him.

The big man's words grew imperious. He threatened the girl angrily. Then he threw something to the floor and swiveled about to leave the way he had come. The curtains blew in his wake.

Linnora looked after him for a time, then stooped to pick up what he had dropped. She walked through a small doorway at the left end of her balcony, leaving her instrument to shine alone in the moonlight.

Dennis stayed in the shadows by the wall, hoping she would return.

When she finally came back, though, he felt consternation, for she went to the bars of her parapet and looked down into the prison yard in his direction. She had a bundle in her hands, and cast about as if looking for something or someone in the darkness below.

Dennis couldn't help himself. He stepped from the shadows into the pale moonlight. She looked directly at him and smiled faintly, as if she had expected him all along.

The Princess put her arm through the bars and threw the bundle. It sailed over the lower parapets, barely missing the bottom railing, and landed at his feet.

Dennis bent to pick up the torn remnant of one of his belt pouches, tied with a loop of string. Inside he found some of the things that had been taken from him. Several had been broken in clumsy efforts to find out how they worked. The crystal of his compass had been smashed, vials of medicine were spilled.

With the items was a note in flowing Coylian script. While the girl picked up her instrument and played softly, Dennis concentrated on what he had learned from Stivyung, and slowly read the message.

> *He is mystified.*

> *I could not tell him what these*
> *things are, even if I would.*
> *He has lost patience, and next*
> *will ask you himself.*
> *Tomorrow you are to be tortured*
> *to tell what you know.*
> *Especially about the terrible weapon*
> *that kills at a touch.*
> *If you are, indeed, an emissary*
> *from the realm of Lifemakers,*
> *flee now.*
> *And speak Linnora's name aloud*
> *in the open hills.*

There was a sweeping, cursive signature at the end. Dennis looked back up at her, his mind full of questions he could not ask and of sympathy and thanks he could not tell her.

The sad song ended. Linnora stood up. Lifting her hand once in farewell, she turned to go inside.

Dennis watched the breeze toss the curtains for long moments after that.

"Get up!" He shook Arth. Nearby, Stivyung Sigel was quietly awakening Gath, Mishwa Qan, and Perth, the other members of the escape committee.

"Wha, wha?" The little thief came erect swiftly, a sharpened piece of stone in his hand.

Arth claimed to have come from a long line of men who had served as bodyguards for Zuslik's old dukes—before Kremer's father had taken over the region in an act of treachery. The small man had a wiry strength that belied his size. He blinked for a moment, then nodded and got up, swiftly and silently.

The conspirators gathered by the stockade wall.

"We haven't time to prepare any further," he told them. "The moons have just set, and tonight's the night."

"But you said the *saw* wasn't good enough yet!" Gath protested "And we had other things to get ready!"

Dennis shook his head. "It's tonight or never. I can't explain, but you'll have to believe me. Arth, you'd better go steal the tools."

The little thief grinned and sped off to the shed where the gardening tools were kept, not far from the lighted window of the guard shack. It wouldn't take Arth long to swipe quietly a few items to use as weapons, should that become necessary. Dennis fervently hoped it wouldn't.

"Give me the saw."

Gath carefully handed over the onetime zipper. Dennis held it up to look at it. The teeth shone even here, and felt very sharp.

From his coveralls he took a spool of dental floss that, along with his toothbrush, had been in his pocket and not in his pack when he was captured. He tied two premeasured lengths firmly to the ends of the saw.

"All right," he whispered, "here goes."

Dennis was glad these people at least understood ropes and lassos. Stivyung Sigel took the saw from Dennis and stepped back to swing it over his head, playing out more and more line as the loop grew.

The guards routinely searched prisoners for weapons, cutting tools, and any sort of twine that might be practiced into a climbing rope. But the floss had been missed completely. For two days he had tugged at it in his spare time, *practicing* it up for this attempt.

The strand wasn't going to be used for climbing. Dennis doubted it could be done. Besides, he had a better idea.

Sigel swung one more time and let go. The loop sailed up over the sharpened end of one of the stockade logs. Dennis took the ends of line from him and tugged them straight.

He whispered, "To positions!" The thief Perth scuttled off to watch for patrols and to distract the guards, if necessary. Stivyung, Gath, and Mishwa took to the shadows, leaving Dennis to take the first shift with the saw.

He was sweating before he was even certain he had the teeth facing the right way. He wrapped rough cloth around his hands, then several loops of line, and began pulling gently back and forth—working it like a piece of floss rubbing slowly down the sides of a tooth. If he had oriented it right, the saw should be cutting away at the leather and mud bindings that held the log to its neighbors.

The cutting would begin at the weakest spot—the top, which had had the least "wall practice." As it worked its way down, the saw should get *better,* and the weight of the log itself should put stress on the remaining ties.

At least he hoped that much physics still applied in this crazy place. Dennis crouched low to the ground and applied gradually greater pressure as the saw bit into the seams. As he fell into a rhythm he had time to think—to worry about guard patrols, and to wonder about the girl on the parapet.

How had she known he would be there, below in the darkness? What had Stivyung meant when he implied that the Princess of the L'Toff was not quite human?

There were no answers in the still muggy night. Dennis wondered if he would ever have the chance to ask the right questions.

He tried to concentrate on the job at hand, thinking hard about cutting. Although some scoffed at the idea, others claimed that a focused mind tended to make practice go faster.

He sawed until his arms ached and he knew fatigue was making him inefficient. By now he had confidence in the new tensile strength of the floss and was willing to trust someone else with the cutting. He signaled Sigel to take over. The big man hurried forth to help him unwrap his hands.

Dennis grimaced in pain as circulation returned. He envied Stivyung his rough farmer's calluses. He stumbled over into the deep shadows by the wall, where Gath and Mishwa waited.

They sat together for a time in silence, watching the farmer patiently pull the line back and forth. Sigel looked like a lump in the darkness. It was amazing how well he blended in.

The minutes passed. Once they heard Arth give his warning call—an imitation of a night bird. Sigel flattened, and soon a guard patrol appeared around a corner, carrying a lantern. One cast of its beam would catch them if it were directed this way. Dennis held his breath along with the others.

But they moved on past, having counted the prisoners in the shed—including the lumpy bundles of homespun the gang had stuffed under their bedding.

Apparently routine had made the guards lazy, as Arth predicted.

When the little thief gave the all-clear, Sigel rose and went back to work, indefatigably. A faint zizzing sound could be heard where they waited, as the saw cut deeper with every stroke.

Young Gath moved a little closer to Dennis. "Is it true the Princess dropped a note to you?" the boy whispered.

Dennis nodded.

"Can I see it?"

A little reluctantly, he handed the slip of rough paper over. Gath pored over it, frowning and moving his lips. Literacy wasn't common in this feudal society. Already Dennis read as well as the youth could.

Gath gave the note back and whispered, "Someday I'd like to visit the L'Toff. There used to be more contact with them, back in the days of the old Duke, I'm told.

"You know they adopt regular humans sometimes?" the boy went on. "The L'Toff would welcome me, I know it! I want to be a *maker.*"

Gath emparted the remark as if he were trusting Dennis with a tremendous secret.

Dennis shook his head, still confused by the ways the people of Tatir had developed to deal with the Practice Effect. "A maker," he asked. "Is that someone who puts together a tool for the first time? Someone who makes starters?" A "starter" was what they called a new object or tool that had never been practiced. "I thought *making* was restricted to certain castes."

Gath nodded. He accepted Dennis's naïveté as a wizard's privilege. "Aye. There's the stonechoppers' caste, and the woodhewers' caste, and the tanners and th' builders and others." He shook his head. "The castes are closed to newcomers, and they do everything the old ways. Only farmers like Stivyung can make their own starters the way they want and get away with it, 'cause they're out in the country where nobody could catch 'em at it."

"What does it matter?" Dennis asked softly. "A starter tool soon adapts to whomever practices it, getting better with use. You could turn a fig leaf into a silk purse if you worked at it long enough."

The youth smiled. "The orig'nal *essence* that's in a starter affects its final form . . . an ax can only be made from a starter ax, not from a starter broom or a starter sled. A thing doesn't get practice becoming something unless it's at least a little bit useful from the very start."

Dennis nodded. Even here, where technology was nonexistent, people found patterns of cause and effect. "What are you in jail for, Gath?"

"For *making* sled starters without permission from the castes." The boy shrugged. "It was stupid of me to get caught. Until you came, I figured when I got out I'd try for the L'Toff. But now I'd rather work for you!"

He beamed at Dennis. "You probably know more about *making* than the L'Toff and all the castes put together! Maybe you'll need a 'prentice when you head back to your homeland. I'd work hard! I *already* know how to chop flint! And I learned how to throw pots by sneaking into th'—"

The boy was getting a bit too excited. Dennis motioned for Gath to keep it down. He shut up obediently, but his eyes still shone.

Dennis thought about what Gath had said. He probably *did* know more about "making" than everyone else on this world combined. But he knew next to nothing about the Practice Effect. In the here and now, that ignorance could be deadly.

"We'll see," he said to the lad. "When we get out of here, I may be in a hurry to get home, and maybe I could use a hand." He thought about the hills to the northwest . . . about the zievatron.

He was getting worried about all the time he had spent chasing after a mechanical civilization on this planet. Had Flaster sent anyone else through the machine? It would be just like the fellow to dither and delay and finally start searching about for another "volunteer."

On the other hand, Flaster might have given up and cut the zievatron loose, setting the Sahara Tech team to work searching once more among the anomaly worlds . . . using Dennis Nuel's search algorithm, of course.

I might have to spend the rest of my life here, he realized.

Unbidden, an image of golden hair in the moonlight came to him. It occurred to him that this world did have its attractions.

Shivering, he reminded himself that he had also received a warning of imminent torture only a couple of hours before.

Tatir had its drawbacks, too.

Stivyung Sigel hadn't called for relief yet. He worked with a fevered intensity that put Dennis a little in awe. Dennis looked up to see what kind of progress the farmer was making.

He stared in amazement. The saw had already cut almost half of the way down! How . . . ?

He looked back at Sigel and rubbed his eyes. It *had* to be the darkness, but somehow it seemed that the air around the farmer shimmered faintly. It was as if little eddies of air were churning all around him. Dennis turned to Gath to ask if he saw it too.

The young maker did indeed see it. He stared at Sigel, utterly awed, as did Mishwa, the other thief with them.

"What is it?" Dennis whispered urgently. "What's happening?"

Without taking his eyes away, Gath answered. "It's a true *felthesh* trance! They say a person's lucky to witness one once in a lifetime!"

Dennis looked back at Sigel. The man worked with demoniacal intensity, his arms pumping back and forth a blur. As they watched, the faint luminescence that surrounded him seemed to climb up the narrow thread of floss, like sparkling ionization around a high-voltage line.

Whatever mysterious thing a "felthesh trance" was, he could see that Sigel and the saw were playing havoc with the stockade bindings. A faint rain of dust fell from the growing gaps on either side of the palisade log.

Dennis found it awesome, indeed. But more immediately, he was concerned that the guards would notice this phenomenon!

Dennis decided it was time to hurry things along a bit.

He motioned to the thief, Mishwa Qan. The prisoner was a giant—larger, even, than Gilm the guard. Mishwa grinned and rose to his feet gracefully. At Dennis's beckoning he crouched at the base of the wall, braced his back against the log, and pushed. The bindings groaned slightly.

Sigel worked on without pause, without asking for relief. By now the saw had almost descended to man height but was starting to slow down. The stockade had had more wall practice at this level and was tougher.

Mishwa grunted and pushed again. The log complained softly, then tilted outward a little as its own weight began to help.

Dennis motioned for Gath to help Mishwa. Soon both were puffing together as the log groaned again.

It tipped a little farther, and then Dennis suddenly saw something that made him start. Something was moving upon the jagged rim of the palisade!

A dark figure—a little larger than a big bullfrog—bent over the growing opening and looked down at the faintly glowing zipper-saw as it cut. The nimbus of Sigel's "felthesh trance" seemed to wash over it, enveloping both the creature and the saw in a soft glow.

Green eyes glowed in the dark. Sharp little teeth flashed in amusement.

Dennis shook his head. "Pix, you blasted voyeur. *Now* you choose to show up! When'll you ever do anybody any good, hmm?"

He turned and rejoined the others, straining against the massive log. Every time it shifted, it made a racket that Dennis imagined could be heard across the valley.

Arth hurried over from his watch position. "I think they heard something," the thief whispered. "Should we shut down for a while?"

Dennis looked at the log. Stars shone through the gap. On Stivyung Sigel's face was a fierce, luminous expression that made Dennis feel a chill. The farmer's arms were a blur and the saw gave off an almost continuous quiet whir.

Dennis didn't dare disturb Sigel. He shook his head. "We can't. It's all or nothing! If the guards come you've got to distract them!"

Arth nodded curtly and hurried away.

Between heaves Dennis glanced up at the needle grin that told him the pixolet was still there, watching their struggle. *Enjoy,* he wished at the creature and joined in another push.

The log groaned, this time *really* loud. There came a yell from the compound behind them—a commotion of shadows back at the barracks. Then there were screams and shouts coming from almost everywhere.

"Hard!" he urged. They all knew they had very little time left.

Mishwa Qan bawled and battered against the barrier between himself and freedom. Gath and Dennis were thrown aside.

Flames flickered in the barracks shed. Arth's distraction had begun. Shadows moved in front of the fire. Clubs were raised high as guards and frantic prisoners struggled. High above, in the castle, an alarm gong started clanging. Out of the shadows the thieves, Arth and Perth, appeared suddenly. The small man panted. "I bought us maybe two hunnerd heartbeats, Denniz. No more."

The log moaned again, like some animal dying, as it tipped another ten degrees. "Make that *one* hunnerd beats," Arth said dryly.

Sigel hunched over and the saw sang an even higher tune. The man seemed enveloped in turbulence, and flakes of light fell from the floss cable.

Mishwa Qan stepped back about twenty feet, scuffed his feet, and let out a fierce ululation as he charged the teetering log. It toppled with a crash, and suddenly there was an opening before them. The sound carried through the night. There was no mistaking the reaction of the guards. They turned from the fire and riot and shouted to each other, pointing toward Dennis and his comrades.

Sigel stared in exhaustion at his handiwork, his hands fallen limply to his sides. The man looked spent, but his eyes were exalted.

Three guards charged out of the flickering light from the sheds, truncheons high. Suddenly a shadow on the ground rose up slightly, just high enough to trip one of them. Arth snagged the left foot of another running guard, sending that one, too, sprawling.

The third came at Dennis, uttering a fierce battle yell.

"Aw, hell," Dennis sighed. He caught the upraised club arm and punched the guard in the nose. The soldier's feet flew out from under him and he landed flat on his back, knocking the wind from him.

More guards were coming. Dennis felt a whipping breeze as Arth sped past him.

"Let's go!" Dennis shouted at Sigel and dragged the farmer toward the narrow portal to freedom.

A spear thunked into the wall near them. Stivyung shook himself, then grinned at Dennis and nodded. Together they scrambled through the opening and out into the night.

As they made their escape, Dennis caught a glimpse of something that glittered, like a necklace of diamonds in the starlight, half protruding from under the fallen log.

They did not tarry, though, and soon he and Sigel were dodging through the alleys of Zuslik, their pursuers behind them.

6

Ballon d'Essai

1

Lantern-semaphore signals flashed from the castle to all gates. Guard details were doubled, and every person trying to leave the city was thoroughly searched. High overhead, members of the overlord's aerial patrol scoured the surrounding area until dark, when they had to land.

"The Baron never put up a fuss like this before when someone got away from him. Not that he ever took it gracefully, but why the big manhunt *this* time?"

The one-eyed thief, Perth, looked out from an upper-story window in one of Zuslik's newer—and hence shabbier—highrises. He was disturbed by the flashing lights and the passing troops of marching northmen in their high, bearskin helmets.

Arth, the small bandit leader, motioned his associate away from the window. "They'll never find us here. Since when 'ave Kremer's northers ever picked out a single one of our hidey holes? Close the shutters an' sit down, Perth."

Perth complied, but he cast a sidelong look at the other fugitives, who sat talking at a table near the kitchen while Arth's wife prepared dinner. "You and I know who they're lookin' for," he told Arth. "The Baron don't like losin' one of his best practicers. An' even worse, he don't like losin' a wizard."

Arth couldn't help but agree. "I'll bet Baron Kremer regrets lettin'

Denniz sit in the jailyard for so long. He probably figured he had all the time in the world to get around to torturin' him.''

Arth rubbed the plush arms of his recliner. Once a day, one of the free members of the band had sat in it to keep it in practice for him. Arth was pleased because it showed they had believed he would get out eventually. "Anyway," he told Perth, "we owe those three our freedom, so let's not begrudge 'em the Baron's wrath."

Perth nodded but wasn't mollified. Mishwa Qan and most of the other thieves were out now, scouring the city for the items Dennis Nuel had asked for. Perth didn't like having a foreigner boss Zuslik thieves around—wizard or no.

Gath looked from Dennis's drawings to the Earthman. The boy could barely restrain his excitement. "So the bag won't have any flying essence until the hot air is put inside it? Will it really fly then? Like a bird, or a kite, or one of th' dragons of legend?"

"We'll find out as soon as the Lady Aren returns with the first bag, Gath. We'll experiment with a model and see how much practice improves it overnight."

Gath smiled at mention of the old seamstress. Clearly the youth did not think much of Lady Aren and her strange delusion. The old woman lived down the hall, making a paltry living as a seamstress. Yet she maintained high manners and insisted on being addressed as she had been as a young courtier in the days of the old Duke.

Right now their entire plan depended on the skill of one crazy old lady.

Stivyung Sigel sat beside Gath, puffing slowly on a pipe, content to listen and voice an occasional question. He seemed fully recovered from the effects of his felthesh trance. In fact, he had held off on his initial idea—trying to climb the city walls—only on Dennis's assurance that there was a better way to get out of town and look for his wife.

Arth and Perth joined the three of them at the table. Dennis and Gath cleared the drawings away as Arth's wife, Maggin, brought out a roast fowl and mugs of ale.

Arth ripped off a drumstick and proceeded to make his beard greasy with it, apparently feeding himself as an accidental side effect. The others took their turns stabbing the bird after the host, as courtesy demanded. Maggin brought a steaming bowl of boiled vegetables and joined them.

Arth spoke with his mouth full. "We had a messenger from th' boys while you were so intent on makin' those drawings, Dennis."

Dennis looked up hopefully. "Did they find my backpack?"

Arth shook his head, mumbling around his food. "Ye weren't too awfully specific, Dennzz. I mean, there're a lotta buildings near th' west gate, and some of 'em use their parapets as balconies an' gardens, in which case your pack's been picked up by now."

"No leads at all? No rumors?"

Arth took a drink, letting red, foamy ale run around the mug and into his beard. He obviously relished home cooking after his time in jail. He wiped his mouth on his cuff. Dennis noted that Arth's shirts all seemed to have gradually developed built-in sponges on their left sleeves.

"Well, I'll tell you, Dennzz, there *are* some strange rumors going about. They say someone's seen a Krenegee beast sneakin' around town. Others say they've seen the ghost of the old Duke come to take revenge on Baron Kremer.

"There's even a story about a strange critter what doesn't eat at all, but spies on people from their windows and moves faster than lightning . . . somethin' nobody's ever seen before, with five eyes." Arth spread his open hand on the top of his head, fingers up, and rotated it, making a whistling sound. Perth coughed in his ale and guffawed. Maggin and Gath laughed out loud.

"But my backpack . . . ?"

Arth spread his hands to indicate he had heard nothing.

Dennis nodded glumly. He had hoped the thieves would recover the pack intact. Or, barring that, they might hear about pieces of his "alien" property in the underworld grapevine. Perhaps one or two items might turn up on sale in the bazaar.

More likely, the pack was in Baron Kremer's hands already. Dennis wondered if even now Kremer was shaking his campstove or his shaving kit under the pretty nose of the L'Toff Princess, Linnora, demanding to know what they were for.

For all their reputation for mystery, the L'Toff would be as perplexed by Dennis's goods as anyone else on Tatir. Linnora wouldn't be able to help Kremer. Dennis hoped he hadn't somehow helped make her incarceration any worse than it already was by angering her captor.

There came a faint knock on the door. The men tensed until they heard it repeat five times, then two, in the proper sequence.

Perth went to unlatch the bolt, and an old woman in an elegant black gown entered. She set down a large sack as the men rose and bowed to her politely.

"My lords," the old lady said and curtsied. "The *global tapestry* you asked for is finished. As you requested, I embroidered only the faintest outlines of clouds and birds on the sides. You may practice the scene to perfection on your own. If this small globe is to your satisfaction, I will commence on the larger version as soon as you bring me the materials."

Arth picked up the sewn arrangement of frail velvet sheets and pretended to inspect it briefly. Then he handed it to Dennis, who took it eagerly. Arth bowed to Lady Aren.

"Your Ladyship is too gracious," he said, his speech suddenly almost aristocratic. "We'll not sully your hands with paper money or amber. But our gratitude will not be denied. May we contribute to the upkeep of your manse, as we have in th' past?"

The old woman grimaced in feigned distaste. "One imagines it would not be too unseemly if it were handled thus."

Tomorrow a basket of food would appear outside her door, as if by magic. The pretense would be maintained.

Dennis did not observe the transaction. He was marveling at the "global tapestry."

Coylians did possess a few respectable technologies. There were certain things that had to be usable from the day they were "made" and could not be *practiced* without ruining them. Paper was an example. A piece of paper might have to sit and wait in a drawer for weeks or months until it was needed for a note or letter. Then it had to have all of its "paperness" instantly ready for use. Once written upon, then, it might be stored for years before being needed for reference. It should not degrade, as happened here to abandoned things whose qualities existed purely because of practice.

No wonder they used paper money here and no one complained. The stuff had intrinsic value almost as great as amber or metal.

With papermaking came felting. Dennis had asked the thieves to "acquire" a dozen square yards of the finest felt they could find. If the experiment worked, they would want to follow that up by stealing virtually the entire supply of this small metropolis.

Dennis was mildly surprised at how little guilt he felt over being an accessory to a major heist. It was all part of his general reaction to this world, he realized with just a touch of bitterness. Earthlings had had to struggle and experiment for thousands of years to reach a level of comfort these people achieved almost without thinking. He could easily rationalize taking what he needed from them.

Anyway, the chief paper merchant of Zuslik was a close crony of the Baron. His monopoly and his flaunted wealth made certain few in the lower town would feel sorry for him.

The "global tapestry" was a sewn sphere of paper-light cloth with one open end. Its sides were vaguely embroidered with clouds and birds. The stitching was really rather uneven, though Lady Aren obviously thought herself an artiste.

Eventually, if practiced long enough by appreciative eyes, the figures would seem to come alive. Besides science, Dennis realized, art, too, had been stunted by this beneficent Practice Effect.

Dennis and Sigel and Gath waited while Lady Aren gossiped with Arth and Maggin. Sigel gave Gath a sharp look when the boy started drumming his fingers on the table. The wait seemed interminable. And Arth appeared in no hurry to end it. The little thief actually seemed to be enjoying himself!

Dennis forced himself to relax. He'd probably enjoy a little gossip, too, if he'd just returned home after a long imprisonment. He found himself longing to know who had been doing what to whom back at old Sahara Tech.

Idly, he wondered if Bernald Brady had had any luck winning the heart of fair Gabriella. He raised his cup and drank a toast to Brady's luck in the venture.

Finally the old lady departed. "All right," Dennis said, "let's finish it."

He spread the limp globe out on the table. Gath and Sigel took several soft tallow candles and began rubbing them carefully against the felt paper, laying down a thin coating of wax. Meanwhile, Dennis carefully tied a small gondola of string and bark to the open end. By the time he had affixed a candle to the tiny basket the others announced they were finished. Arth and Perth and Maggin watched, puzzlement on their faces.

Dennis and Gath carried the contraption to a corner, where a rough wooden frame had been prepared.

"It's called a *balloon*," Dennis said as he laid the fabric over the frame.

"You told us that much," Perth said a little snidely. "And you said it would fly. A *made* thing would fly . . . and indoors where there's no wind . . ." He obviously didn't believe it. In the here and now there was one way to fly—by building, and slowly practicing, a great tethered kite.

Long ago, some Coylian genius who hated getting wet had invented an umbrella—now a common item owned by nearly everybody. Later, after a freak windstorm had caused a large umbrella to rise up with the wind, carrying its owner on a brief, harrowing ride, someone had a second conceptual leap. It was the birth of kites on Tatir. Furious practice led thereafter to the development of tethered wings, carrying men high above the surface to look at the ground below.

Those kites had helped Baron Kremer's father, a minor nobleman from the northern hill country, to defeat the old Duke and force the King of Coylia to grant him domain over the upper valley of the Fingal.

Only in the past few years had the step to true gliders been taken—this time by Kremer himself. Though other armed forces now had kites, at the moment he, and only he, possessed a true air force. It was a major tactical advantage in his current conflict with royal authority.

Dennis wondered why no one else had ever developed gliders. Perhaps it had something to do with the imagery that took place when a person practiced an object. One had to have an idea of what one wanted in mind. Perhaps no one could conceive of an untethered kite as anything but fatal to the rider, and so they always were until Kremer made his breakthrough.

Dennis arranged the candle directly below the opening in the bottom of the trial balloon. He smiled with assurance. "You'll see, Perth. Just make sure those buckets of water are handy in case we have an accident."

He acted confident, but he was less than entirely certain. In a science-fiction story he had read as a boy, another Earthling had, just like himself, been transported to another world where the physical laws were also different. In the story, *magic* had worked, but the hero's gunpowder and matches had all failed!

Dennis suspected that the Tatir Practice Effect merely supplemented the physics he knew, rather than supplanted it. He certainly hoped so.

Clear smoke rose from the candle, entering the balloon through the hole at the bottom.

Arth offered Dennis and Stivyung his best loungers and pulled out a few string-and-stick chairs that "needed a lot of work anyway," he insisted. He gave Dennis and Stivyung two very nice pipes and happily puffed away on a hollowed twig and corncob contraption—working it slowly toward perfection, or at least staving off a decline to uselessness.

Dennis shook his head. The Practice Effect took a lot of getting used to.

"Will someone explain to me just what Baron Kremer is trying to pull?" Dennis asked as they waited for the bag to fill. "I take it he's defying the central authority . . . the King?"

Stivyung Sigel puffed moodily at his pipe before answering.

"I was in the Royal Scouts, Dennis, until I married and retired. The Baron has been hard on us royal settlers out on the western frontier. He doesn't care to have me and my kind around, whose loyalty he can't count on.

"The Baron's supported by the maker guilds. The guilds don't like homesteaders setting up too far from the towns. We *make* our own starters—chip our own flint, tan our own hides and ropes, weave our own cloth. Lately we've even found out how to start makin' our own paper, if the truth be told."

Arth and Perth looked up, their interest piqued. Gath blinked in surprise. "But the paper guild's the most secret of the lot! How did you learn . . . ?" He snapped his fingers. "Of course! The L'Toff!"

Sigel merely puffed on his pipe. He said nothing until he noticed that all eyes were on him and he was clearly expected to go on.

"The Baron knows now," he said, shrugging. "And so do the guilds. Common folk might as well find out, too. What's happening out here is the sharp edge of something big that's shaping up back in the estates an' cities to the east, too. People are getting tired of the guilds, and churchmen, and petty barons pushing them around. The King's popularity has gone way up ever since he cut the property requirement to vote for selectmen and since he's been calling an Assembly every spring instead of one year in ten."

Dennis nodded. "Let me guess. Kremer's a leader in the cause for barons' rights." It was a story he had heard before.

Sigel nodded. "And it looks like they've got the muscle. The King's scouts and guards are the best troops, of course, but the feudal levies outnumber them six or seven to one.

"And now Kremer's got these free-flying kites to carry scouts wherever he wants. They scare the daylights out of the opposition, and the churches are spreading word that they're the ancient dragons returned to Tatir again . . . proof that Kremer's favored by the gods.

"I've got to give Kremer credit there. No one ever thought of gliders before. Not even the L'Toff."

One more mention of the L'Toff brought Dennis's thoughts back to Princess Linnora, Baron Kremer's prisoner back at the castle. She had begun to show up in his dreams. He owed her his freedom, and he didn't like to think of her still trapped in the tyrant's power.

If only there was a way I could help her, too, he thought.

"*Balloon* is almost full." Gath used the word as if it were a proper name.

The bag was starting to stretch from the pressure of hot air within. It didn't form a very even sphere. But here it didn't pay to lavish excess attention on most "made" goods, anyway, so long as they started out useful enough to be practiced.

The candle was less than half gone. The balloon bobbed within its frame, straining at the tiny gondola's shrouds. The basket bounced on the floor, then lifted away entirely.

There was a hushed silence, then Maggin laughed out loud and Arth clapped Dennis on the back. Gath crouched beneath the balloon, as if to memorize it from every angle. Stivyung Sigel sat still, but his pipe poured forth aromatic smoke, and his black eyes seemed to shine.

"But this thing won't lift a man!" Perth complained.

Arth turned on his subordinate. "How do you know what it'll eventually be able to do? It's not even been *practiced* yet! Weren't you the one sneering at 'new-made' things?"

Perth backed down nervously, licking his lips as he stared superstitiously at the slowly rising balloon.

"Actually," Dennis said, "Perth's right. After practice this one will probably lift better than any similar balloon on . . . in my homeland. But in order to lift several men we'll still have to make a much bigger balloon in that empty warehouse you told me about, Arth. We'll practice it there, then Gath and Stivyung and I will use it to escape at night, when the Baron's flying corps is in its sheds."

Arth had a mercenary gleam in his eye. "You an' Gath an' Stivyung won't forget about the message to the L'Toff, will you?"

"Of course not." All three of them had good reasons for heading straight for the mysterious tribe in the mountains once they got out of town. Dennis intended to tell them about their captive Princess and offer suggestions how she might be rescued.

Arth expected to rake off a nice reward from the L'Toff for his part in all this, as well as have the pleasure of giving the Baron *tsuris* in the process.

The balloon bobbed against the ceiling. "All right," Dennis said, "you all were going to teach me how to concentrate to get the most out of practice. Why don't we start?"

They took their seats. Stivyung Sigel was the acknowledged best practicer, so he explained.

"First off, Dennis, you don't *have* to concentrate. Just using a tool will make it better. But if you keep your attention on the thing itself, and what you're using it to accomplish, the practice goes faster. You give the tool tougher and tougher jobs to do, over weeks, months, and think about what it could be when it's perfect."

"What about that trance we saw you under in the prison yard? You practiced the saw to perfection in a matter of minutes!"

Stivyung considered. "I have seen the felthesh before, when I dwelled, for a time, among the L'Toff. Even among them, it is rare. It comes after years of training, or under even more rare circumstances. I never imagined I would ever enter that state.

"Perhaps it was some magic of the moment and the desperation of our need."

Stivyung seemed pensive for a long moment. He shook himself at last and looked at Dennis. "In any event, we cannot count on the ax falling twice in exactly the same spot. We must rely on normal ways as we practice your 'balloons.' Why don't you tell us again just what this example is doing now and how it could gradually come to do it better. Don't get too far ahead of what it *is,* or it won't work. Just try to describe the next step."

It sounded like a children's game to Dennis. But he knew that here "wish and make it so" had a very serious side to it. He squinted as he looked at the balloon . . . trying to see an ideal. Then he started to describe what none of them had ever before imagined.

2

Two days later, the search for the escapees had finally died down. The guards at the city gates were still diligent, but street patrols went back to normal. Dennis at last got to take a tour of the town of Zuslik.

On his first attempt, when he had arrived almost two weeks ago, Dennis had been full of vague ideas about how to get along in a strange city.

(One made contact with the local association of one's profession, he imagined, hoping a local colleague would insist you stay at his home—and maybe offer his charming daughter as a tour guide, as well. Wasn't that the way he had envisioned it just a short while back?)

His plans had gone awry before he passed through the city gates. Still, he had probably acquired a more intimate acquaintance with the local power structures than he would have as a tourist . . . and without the typical banes of the gawking traveler—beggars, bunions, and muggers.

He and Arth took lunch in an open-air cafe overlooking a busy market street. Dennis washed down his last bite of rickel steak with a heady swallow of the dirt-brown local brew. After a long day and night practicing the balloon, he had built up a hearty appetite.

"More," he belched, bringing the beer stein down with a thump.

His companion stared at him for a moment, then snapped his fingers to the waiter. Dennis was a bit larger than the average male Coylian, but his appetite was nevertheless causing a bit of a sensation.

"Take it easy," Arth suggested. "After I've paid for all this I won't be able to afford to take you to a physic for yer upset stomach!"

Dennis grinned and plucked a rough toothpick from a cup by the rail. He watched a heavy cargo sled slide past the restaurant, almost silent on one of the self-lubricating roadways, pulled by a patient, lumbering larbeast.

"Have your boys managed to collect any more slippery oil?" he asked the thief.

Arth shrugged. "Not too much. We use street urchins to do the collectin', but the drivers have taken to throwin' rocks at 'em. And the kids waste a lot of the stuff playin' 'greased pig.' We've only got a quarter of a jug or so by now."

Only a quarter jug! That was almost a liter of the finest lubricant Dennis had ever encountered! Arth had certainly not acted this casually when Dennis first demonstrated the stuff to him. He had gone almost crazy with excitement.

It would make a useful commercial product, of course. It would also greatly facilitate burglary . . . until shop owners began practicing their doors to resist the stuff. Last night's paper heist had depended completely on a surprise use of sled oil.

Dennis wondered why these people had never discovered the very substance that made their roads work. Were they that uncurious? Or did it come from operating under a totally different set of assumptions about the way the universe worked?

Of course, history showed that most of Earth's cultures had been caste-structured, and slow to improve on the way things had been done for centuries. Here, where innovation was less necessary, people had not developed a tradition for it until very recently. The war between Baron Kremer and the King seemed to be part of that change.

This morning he and Arth had rented a warehouse. The growing fear of war had caused a decline in river commerce, and the landlord was desperate to find any tenant at all. Someone had to occupy the place and keep it fit until times improved. Already the walls were showing a creaky roughness, starting to resemble wooden logs again.

Arth was quite a bargainer. The landlord would actually *pay* a small sum for them to move in for a while!

Last night had come the great felt heist. Arth's thieves had arrived at the warehouse furtively carrying bolts of the fine cloth. Lady Aren and several assistant seamstresses, all from families that had been brought down in class by Kremer's father, were soon at work. And young Gath was at this moment constructing a gondola for the big balloon. The lad was ecstatic over the chance to *make* something new—something that would be of use almost before its first *practice*.

Arth paid the luncheon bill, muttering over the total. "Now what?" he asked.

Dennis motioned with his hands. "What else? Show me everything!"

Arth sighed resignedly.

Their first stop was the Bazaar of Merchants and Practicers.

Unlike other open-air markets, with their collections of practice-on-your-own goods, this plaza featured high-quality merchandise. The ziggurat buildings were gleaming and tasteful. Their first floors, open to the street, were supported by arching, fluted pillars. Well-dressed men and women hawked wares at long tables before the openings.

Dennis examined keen-edged chisels and razors, ropes of marvelous strength and lightness, bows and arrows that had obviously been practiced against targets thousands of times and would have sold on Earth for handsome prices.

There was no sign whatever of screws or nails, and hardly any metal. Nowhere was there anything resembling a wheel.

At one end were cheaper items—crude axes, body armor consisting of tanned strips of leather sewed together. Below each table was the sigil of the appropriate maker guild—a sign that the "starter" was sanctioned by law.

Dennis looked up at a banging sound. Two men walked lackadaisically around the third-story parapet, striking the walls with clubs.

Arth explained. "They're gettin' the clubs better at bashin', and gettin' the walls better at keepin' out bashers." He winked at Dennis. "Bashers like us."

Burglary here usually involved breaking through the walls of a house while the tenant was away. Sometimes people forgot that living in a house practiced it well to stand sturdily and keep the rain out, but nothing more.

The owners of this building clearly had not forgotten.

The plaza was crowded with aristocrats from the upper town and from estates outside Zuslik's walls. The gentry were accompanied by their servants.

Master and lackey generally dressed identically, and usually they were about the same size and build. They could be told apart only by the nobles' imperious manner, their hair styles, and the bits of metal jewelry they wore.

On Earth the rich flaunted their status by acquiring large amounts of property that was rarely used. Here such property would quickly decay to its original, crude state. To maintain appearances, then, the affluent needed servants who not only performed housework, gardening, and other tasks, but who kept their employers' property practiced for them, as well.

Dennis perceived some of the social implications.

When they were so busy always wearing their master's clothes, the servants had no time to *practice* their own. They might look good all the time, but the fine threads on their backs weren't theirs. If they left their employer they would have nothing at all of their own!

It would be a symbol of status among the rich, of course, never to be seen wearing or using anything that truly *needed* practicing.

Besides food and land, metal and paper, the chief commodity of value here was the human man-hour. Even when exhausted from a hard day's labor in the fields, a serf's time was not his own. In relaxing he practiced his master's chair; in eating, he practiced his mistress's spare dinnerware. He couldn't save to buy his freedom, because anything saved away had to be maintained, or face decay!

No wonder there was trouble brewing in the east! The combination of the guilds, the churches, and the aristocracy made sure that change would come hard, if at all.

Fixxel's Practicorium, at the north end of the plaza, was a tall building that reminded Dennis of home.

For one thing, its walls were in large part brilliantly transparent, as if of the clearest glass, slightly tinted to moderate the afternoon sunlight.

Arth explained that the panes had started out as sewn paper sheets, practiced hard during dry seasons, until they were weatherproof and clear. After many years of this they were probably better than any windows on Earth.

Facing the boulevard were displays of men's and women's clothes, tools, pottery, and rugs. "Nothing New! All Old and Used!" a sign stated proudly.

The window displays were constantly changing. Workers removed items and replaced them as Dennis watched.

The furnishings on exhibition were stunning. Realistic mannequins were draped in what looked like exquisite silks and brocades. Some of the gowns would surely have gone for thousands at Neiman-Marcus.

"Come on," Arth said, nudging Dennis. "Don't give old Fixxel a free push."

Dennis blinked. He had been entranced by the beautiful things. Then, all at once, he realized what Arth meant. He laughed out loud in admiration of the scam. By just looking at the merchandise, and appreciating its beauty, he had helped just a little to enhance that beauty! No wonder the mannequins looked so lifelike. They were *practiced* by generations of passersby!

What a racket!

Still, Dennis couldn't help but wish his camera wasn't lost with his backpack. The clothing designs alone would be worth a fortune back on Earth.

Under Dennis's urging, they went around back to peek into the great practice arena at the rear of the building. It was a scene of furious activity.

Teams of men and women poured water into and out of long lines of pitchers, cups, and goblets. Others kept busy digging holes with shovels, and then refilling them, or slicing great logs into kindling, practicing shiny tools in the process.

There was a large open area in which men muffled in layers of clothes sat on half-finished chairs and threw weapons at targets. The crudest knives were being tossed against near-finished suits of glossy leather armor.

No wonder technology never developed here! It didn't pay to specialize. Wherever a person could practice three or four items at once, it paid. The niceties of concentration seemed less important than keeping as many things busy as possible all the time.

This was the equivalent of an Earthly factory, but something about it struck Dennis as terribly futile. All this hard work would be for nothing if the constant maintenance stopped for just a few weeks or months. Left alone long enough, each of these products would decay to its original state.

Still, Dennis thought, there were no mountains of garbage here, either—no great landfills heaped with worn-out, unwanted things. Almost anything these people created was utimately recycled to nature.

On neither world, it seemed, was there any such thing as a free lunch.

Later, in another part of town, Dennis and Arth watched a religious procession pass through one of the main squares. A trio of yellow-robed priests and their followers carried a pillowed platform on which a gleaming sword was carried. At the four corners of the palanquin were set freshly severed human heads.

"Priests of Mlikkin," Arth identified them. "Bloody panderers. They appeal to th' more unsavory cit'zens of Zuslik with their murderin' ways." He spat.

Dennis made himself watch, though his gorge rose at the grisly sight. From what he had picked up during the past week, he could tell that the priests were engaged in a campaign to inure the people of the town to the idea of death and war.

Sure enough, when the procession stopped at a platform set up at one end of the square, the chief priest held up the sword—obviously a product of generations of daily practice by acolytes of Mlikkin—and harangued the rowdy crowd that had gathered. Dennis could not make out much, but clearly the fellow thought little of the "eastern rabble." When he began speaking ill of King Hymiel, some parishioners looked at each other nervously, but nobody cried out in disagreement.

A number of Zuslikers, though, frowning in distaste, hurried off, leaving the square to the celebrants.

With one exception. Dennis noticed that an old woman knelt in a far corner of the plaza, before a niche in which was set a dusty statue. With age-wracked hands, she cleared away layers of debris and replaced flowers in the twisting, helical pedestal.

Something about the shape of the shrine made Dennis's neck tingle. He started forward, with Arth trailing along nervously, complaining that this was not a healthy place for them to be.

"What is it?" Dennis asked his companion about the shrine.

"It's a place of th' Old Belief. Some say it was here b'fore even Zuslik was founded. The churches tried to have it pulled down, but it's been practiced so long it's impossible to scratch. So they dump offal on it an' have gangs of toughs push around people who try to pray there."

No wonder the old woman glanced up and around nervously as she went through her devotions. "But why should they care—"

Dennis stopped, still twenty yards away. He recognized the figure at the top of the pedestal. It was a *dragon*. He had seen its likeness on the haft of the native knife he had found by the zievatron.

In the dragon's grinning mouth was a malevolent, demoniacal figure —a "blecker," as Arth identified it. Covered with layers of filth and graffiti, the dragon nevertheless gave a frozen wink to passersby. Its open eye shone with gemstone brilliance.

But it was the pedestal beneath the mythical beast that seized Dennis's attention. The fluted column was a delicate double helical coil, held together by delicately knotted rails, like the rungs of a twisted ladder.

It was a chain of DNA, or Dennis was the pixolet's blood uncle!

Dennis felt a return of that nervous feeling of unreality that had plagued him since his arrival on this world. He approached the shrine slowly, wondering how these people ever could have learned about genes lacking the tools or mental disciplines required.

"Hssst!" Arth nudged Dennis. "Soldiers!" He nodded toward the main street, where a troop was strolling in their direction.

Dennis glanced longingly back at the statue, but then nodded and hastily followed Arth into an alley. They watched from the shadows as a patrol passed by. The squad marched along haughtily, their "thenners" raised port high. The big sergeant, Gilm, paced alongside, heaping verbal abuse on civilians not quick enough to get out of the way.

From the way the townsfolk scattered, Dennis presumed Kremer's northern clansmen still didn't think of themselves as Zuslikans, though the town had been the Baron's capital for a generation.

When Dennis next looked back at the little niche-shrine, the old woman had departed, no doubt scared away. Gone also was his best chance to find out more about the Old Belief.

The troop of soldiers was followed by nearly a score of young civilians, downcast and tethered to one another at the wrist.

"Press gang!" Arth whispered harshly. "Kremer's buildin' up th' militia. War can't be far off now!"

It reminded Dennis that he was still a hunted man. He looked up and saw, high in the sky, a set of broad black wings sailing in an updraft. A pair of small human figures sat in a light wicker framework beneath the glider, steering it lazily toward a thermal south of town. The underside was painted to resemble leathery wings, to take advantage of the traditional dragon reverence that filled most Coylian fairy tales.

Fortunately, these people had never developed telescopes. Those scouts would not be likely to pick them out in Zuslik's crowded streets. He and Arth only had to worry about foot patrols.

When they made their break in the balloon, however, it would be a different story. Those gliders might present a problem.

Discretion seemed well advised. He let Arth lead him away from the busy square, resolving though to return to study the statue in more detail later.

The Hall of the Guild of Chairmakers was overrun with children.

The chairmakers' guild was the poorest of the maker castes. Unlike that of the stonechoppers, the hinge and door builders, and the papermakers, it had no secrets to protect. Anyone could make a chair or table "starter" with twine and sticks. Only the law kept the guild in its monopoly.

Youngsters ran all over the place. The floor was a litter of string and shredded bark. Arth explained that open guilds like the chairmakers' hired mostly children and old people—unsuited for the high-volume practicing that took place at salons like Fixxel's.

Under the supervision of a few master chairmakers, boys and girls assembled furniture starters to go into the homes of the needy. After a year or so of using these tables and chairs, the poor would sell the practiced models to somewhat better-off folk and buy another set of crude starters with part of the proceeds. The furniture would slowly work its way along the socioeconomic ladder as it grew older and better —upward mobility for things, if not people.

A red-robed priest moved among the children, accompanied by two master chairmakers, blessing the finished starters. Dennis couldn't remember which deity the red gown represented, but something about the color seemed almost to remind him of something.

"Another patrol, Dennzz." Arth pointed out a troop of guards passing by, one street over. "Maybe we better be gettin' back."

Dennis nodded reluctantly. "All right," he told Arth, "let's go." It would be at least a week before the escape attempt, and there would be other chances to explore the town.

They ducked down a side alley and emerged on the Avenue of Sweetmeats. Arth bought pastries, and Dennis tried to make sense out of the chaotic but apparently efficient sledrail traffic pattern as they walked.

Still, he couldn't shake the image of the red-robed priest from his mind. Somehow it made him feel simultaneously angry and frustrated.

Arth grabbed Dennis's arm as they were approaching the little thief's neighborhood. He looked up and down the street suspiciously. "Let's take a shortcut," he said, and led Dennis between a pair of stalls into another alley.

"What's the matter?"

Arth shook his head. "Maybe I'm just nervous. But if you sniff a trap five times, and you're wrong four of 'em, you're still ahead if you avoid th' smell."

Dennis decided to take Arth's word as the expert. He saw a stack of crates against the wall of one of the wedding cake buildings. "Come on," he said, "I've got a tool that's super at detecting traps. We can use it up on the roof."

They climbed to the first parapet, then up a garden trellis to another level. Dennis reached under the robe Arth had lent him and pulled the little camp-watch alarm out of one of his overall pockets.

Arth stared at the flashing lights, entranced. He appeared totally confident in the Earthman's wizardry, sure that Dennis would be able to tell, from this magic, whether it was safe to go out onto the streets.

Dennis twiddled with the tiny dials. But the screen remained a chaos of unreadable garbage. The alarm, over a week out of practice, kept trying to go off regardless of what he did.

Dennis sighed and reached into another pocket. The slim, collapsible monocular had been in the packet Linnora had thrown him. Fortunately, it had only been scratched in Kremer's futile attempts to open it.

Dennis used it to scan the streets below.

There were crowds up and down the main boulevard—farmers come to town to market their produce and purchase starters, aristocrats with their clonelike entourages, an occasional guard or churchman. Dennis looked for suspicious clumps of activity.

He focused on a group of men at the far end of the street. They idled about in front of a pub, apparently lounging.

But the spyglass told a different story. The men were armed, and they glanced intently at passersby. They had the high cheekbones of Kremer's northmen.

Dennis adjusted the focus. A tall, armed man with the look of an aristocrat emerged from a building behind the toughs. He was followed by a short, stooped fellow with a patch over one eye. They were conversing in an agitated manner. The one-eyed man kept pointing in the direction of the waterfront. The aristocrat just as insistently seemed to indicate that they would wait right where they were.

"Uh, Arth"—Dennis's mouth felt dry—"I think you'd better look at this."

"At what, that little box? Are you lookin' *through* it, or at somethin' inside it?"

"Through it. It's like a sort of magic tube that makes things far away look bigger. It may take you a minute to get used to it, but when you do, I want you to use it to look at that tavern at the end of the street."

Arth squatted forward and took the monocular. Dennis had to show him how to hold it. Arth grew excited.

"Hey! This is great! I can see like th' proverbial eagle of Crydee! . . . I can count th' steins on th' table over at . . . *Great Palmi!* That's *Perth!* An' he's talkin' to Lord Hern himself!"

Dennis nodded. He felt a hollowness within his chest, as if fragile hope had suddenly turned into something heavy and hard.

"That scum!" Arth cursed. "He's turnin' us in! His dad even served with mine under th' old Duke! I'll have his intestines an' practice 'em into hawsers! I'll . . ."

Dennis slumped back against the wall behind them. He was fresh out of ideas. There didn't seem to be any way to warn his friends back at Arth's apartment, or in the waterfront warehouse, where construction of the escape balloon had just begun.

He felt so helpless that, once again, the strange detachment from reality seemed to fall over him. He couldn't help it.

Arth made a grand art out of cursing. He had quite a vocabulary of invective. For a while it kept him busy while the Earthman simply felt miserable.

Then Dennis blinked. A brief, sharp reflection had caught his eye from one of the neighboring rooftops not too far away.

He sat up and looked. Something small was moving about among the vents and rooftop debris.

"They've got somebody!" Arth declared, still staring through the monocular at the scene at the cafe. "They're draggin' him down from my place. . . ." Arth whooped. "But they've only got one! The others must have got away! Perth don't look happy *at all!* He's tuggin' at Lord Hern's arm, pointin' to th' waterfront.

"Hah! By th' time they get there all our people will be gone! Serves 'em right!"

Dennis barely heard Arth. He got up slowly, staring at the shape on the rooftop several blocks away; it glistened and scuttled from hiding place to hiding place.

Arth exclaimed. "It's *Mishwa* they've caught! And . . . and he's broken free and managed to jump Perth! Go get him, Mishwa! They're tryin' to get him off before he—Hey! Dennis, give that back!"

Dennis had snatched away the monocular. Ignoring Arth's protests, he tried not to shake as he focused it on the roof a hundred meters away. Something quick and blurry passed in front of his line of sight.

It took him a few moments to find the exact spot. Then for seconds all he could see was the roof vent the thing had ducked behind.

At last, something rose from behind it—an *eye* at the end of a slender stalk that swiveled left and right, scanning.

"Well, I'm the son of a blue-nosed gopher. . . ."

"Dennzz! Give me back th' box! I gotta know if Mish got that rat Perth!"

Arth tugged at his trouser leg. Dennis shook free, focusing the monocular.

What finally moved out from behind the roof vent had changed subtly since the last time Dennis had seen it, on a highway late one dark night. It had turned a paler shade, blending well with the color of the buildings. Its sampling arms and cameras scanned the crowd below as it moved.

On its back it carried a passenger.

"Pix!" Dennis cursed. The little animal voyeur had found the perfect accomplice for its favorite activity, sidewalk superintending. It was riding Dennis's Sahara Tech exploration 'bot like its own personal mount!

The multiple coincidences and irony were overwhelming. All Dennis knew was that the robot was the key to everything . . . to rescuing his friends and the Princess, to getting out of Zuslik, to repairing the zievatron . . . to *everything!*

What couldn't a man who knew what he was doing accomplish, simply by using the Practice Effect on a sophisticated little machine like that? It could help him build more machines, even a new return mechanism!

He needed that 'bot!

"Pix!" Dennis shouted. "Robot! Come to me and report! At once! Do you hear me? Right away!"

Arth grabbed furiously at his arm. In the street below people were looking up curiously.

The strange pair on the far roof seemed to pause briefly and turn his way.

"Prior orders are overridden!" he screamed again. "Come to me *right now!*"

He would have shouted more, but then Dennis was knocked down as Arth took him behind the knees in a powerful tackle. The little thief was wiry and strong. By the time Dennis managed to pull free to look again, the robot and pixolet had disappeared from sight.

Arth was cursing at him soundly. Dennis shook his head as he sat up, rubbing his temple. His attack of tunnel vision had evaporated, almost as suddenly as it had come on. But it might already be too late.

Oh, boy, he realized. *What I just did.*

"All right," he told Arth. "Let me go! Let's get out of here. We can go now."

But moments later, when soldiers climbed onto the roof, Dennis realized that he was wrong again.

7

Pundit Nero

1

On the morning after the evening of his second imprisonment, Dennis awoke with a crick in his neck, straw in his ear, and the sound of voices in the corridor outside his cell.

He tried to sit up, and winced as movement prodded his bruises. He sank back into the straw and sighed.

"Argh," he said concisely.

It was surprisingly easy to recognize his surroundings. Although he had never been in a dungeon before, he had visited countless examples in stories and movies. He looked this one over, impressed with the verisimilitude.

Apparently it had been well *practiced* as a dungeon. It was dank, cold, and apparently lice-infested. Dennis scratched.

It even *sounded* like a dungeon, from the slow, monotonous, drip-dripping of wall seepage, to the hollow clacking of passing boots in the corridor and the gravelly voices of the guards.

". . . don't know why they had to bring in a strange-looking foreigner to help us down here. Even if he does come wit' hoity-toity references," he heard one voice say.

"Yeah," another agreed. "We was doin' just fine . . . a little torture, a few convenient accidents, light practice. But this place sure has been lousy since Yngvi arrived. . . ."

The voices faded as the footsteps receded down the corridor.

Dennis sat up and shivered. He was stark naked—they weren't about to make for a second time the mistake of leaving a wizard with his own property. He felt around for the one filthy blanket his captors had given him.

He found it wrapped around his cellmate. Dennis nudged the fellow with his foot. "Arth. Arth! You've got two blankets now! Give me back mine!"

The little thief's eyelids opened, and he stared at Dennis blankly for a moment before focusing. He smacked his lips.

"Why should I? It's 'cause of you I'm here. I shoulda said good-bye an' let you go your own way right after we got out of th' stockade."

Dennis winced. Arth was right, of course. He had been in a confused state when he screamed at the pixolet and the robot. It wasn't the sort of thing a storybook adventurer would do.

But Dennis was a man. He was susceptible to the psychological pressures of his unusual and highly dangerous situation. He might *think* he'd adjusted to being stranded in a strange world with strange rules, sought by enemies for reasons he barely understood—then a disaster shook his equilibrium, making him disoriented, estranged, lightheaded.

But he couldn't explain this to Arth. Not while he was freezing. Anyway, if they were to have any chance, they would have to cooperate. That meant making Arth respect his rights.

"I'm sorry about this mess, Arth. You have my wizard's vow that I'll make it up to you someday. Now, give my blanket back, or I'll turn you into a frog and take *both* of them for myself."

He said it so evenly, so calmly that Arth's eyes widened in reaction. No doubt his opinion of Dennis had plummeted since the episode on the rooftop. Still, he remembered tricks the foreigner had pulled in the past.

Arth snorted in disgust and tossed Dennis the blanket. "Wake me when breakfast comes, Dennzz. Then see if you can turn *it* into somethin' edible!" He rolled over the other way under his blanket.

Dennis wrapped himself as well as he could and tried to *practice* the blanket while he waited for Baron Kremer to decide his fate.

Time passed slowly. The tedium was punctuated by the occasional pacings of the jailers up and down the halls. The guards muttered constantly under their breath. Eventually Dennis was able to make out that they were repeating over and over a dolorous evaluation of the condition of their clients.

"Sure is dank an' gloomy in here," Guard One commented as he passed.

"Yep. Dank. Gloomy," the other responded.

"Sure wouldn't want ta be a prisoner. It's awful down here."

"Sure is. Awful."

"Will you stop repeatin' what I say? Do I have to do all th' work? It's really irritatin'!"

"Uh-huh. Irritating. Sure is . . ."

Anyway, it solved one mystery. The way they kept the dungeon in practice was by having cycles of jailers constantly comment on how terrible it was down here. Presumably the prisoners were too distracted to put up much resistance. Perhaps Kremer even hired local masochists to come down and enjoy themselves.

It was an unsavory corner of the Practice Effect Dennis wished he'd never learned about.

They finally came for him a couple of days later, after the evening swill. Dennis stood up as the wooden bolt was raised and the door swung wide. Arth watched moodily from the corner.

An officer in a severely elegant uniform casually entered the cell. Behind him stood two tall soldiers, whose conical bearskin headgear brushed the hallway ceiling.

The tall aristocrat looked familiar. Dennis finally remembered seeing him on the street on the day they were captured, arguing with the betrayer, Perth.

"I am Lord Hern," the officer announced. "Which one of you is the wizard?"

Neither of them replied.

Lord Hern glanced at Arth, then made a decision. With a bored motion he indicated for Dennis to follow him.

"Good luck, Arth," Dennis said. "I'll be seeing you." The little thief merely rolled his eyes and sighed.

The sun was setting behind the western mountains as they emerged on one of the lower parapets. Dennis shaded his eyes, so long had he been in the dimness belowground.

Two more guards fell in behind. Dennis was led down service corridors, then upstairs to an elegant hallway. None of the servants turned to look at the shabby fellow clutching a blanket around him who passed by.

Another pair of guards flanked a door at the end of the hall. They opened it at a nod from Lord Hern.

Dennis followed his escort into a well-appointed room without windows. There was a king-sized bed, with a richly elegant brocade covering. A pretty young servant was laying out an elegant dark brown outfit with puffy sleeves. Through a door on the opposite side came steam and the sound of water being poured.

"You will dine with the Baron tonight," Lord Hern announced. "You will behave well. The Baron has been known to lose track of inconsiderate guests."

Dennis shrugged. "So I've heard. Thanks. Will you be there?"

Lord Hern looked down his nose. "I shall not have the pleasure. I shall be on a diplomatic errand. Perhaps another time."

"I'll look forward to it." Dennis nodded pleasantly.

The aristocrat barely returned the nod. He left without another word.

Coylians, apparently, were an unenlightened and unsophisticated people. The guards merely looked curiously at the odd arm and finger exercise Dennis performed in the direction of the departing lord's back.

He didn't need to be told a bath was being drawn. Dennis dropkicked the blanket over into a corner and made his way toward the sound of pouring water.

2

Cavemen, Dennis reminded himself again and again as he walked to the banquet room.

Remember, boy, they're only cavemen.

It was hard to keep it in mind. The grand hallway was lined with brilliant mirrors alternating with ornate tapestries. His boots and those of his escort clacked on a mosaic floor that reflected glistening highlights from sparkling chandeliers.

Guards with sun-bright leather armor and gleaming halberds stood at even intervals, at rigid attention.

Dennis wondered. Was this an ostentatious display, keeping these men here when even their leisure time was more valuably spent practicing things?

Then it occurred to him that they *were* practicing something—this very hall. They were *looking* at the mirrors and hangings and each others' uniforms, making them more beautiful by appreciating them.

These guards, he realized, were undoubtedly selected less for their prowess than for their good taste!

His escort glanced at him as he whistled appreciatively.

As they approached two high, massive doors, Dennis tried to relax.

If the local honcho expects a wizard, my best chance is to *act* like a wizard. Maybe this Baron Kremer isn't unreasonable. Perhaps I can strike a deal with the fellow—freedom for myself and my friends, and aid in fixing the zievatron, in exchange for teaching one of the maker guilds the principle of the wheel?

Dennis wondered if the nobleman would trade Princess Linnora for the "essence" of lighter-than-air flight.

The great doors opened soundlessly as Dennis was ushered into a broad dining room with a vaulted, open-beamed ceiling. The center of the chamber was dominated by an ornate table carved from some impossibly beautiful dark wood. Subdued light came from three rich candelabras. The crystal on the embroidered tablecloth sparkled in the candlelight.

Although four places were set, only servants were visible at the moment. One brought forth a tray with an assortment of beverages and offered Dennis his choice.

He needed *something* to calm his nerves. It was hard to keep in mind that a savage—a caveman—owned all this. Everything in the room was meant to make the guest know his place in a stratified society. In a room such as this on Earth, Dennis would be about to meet royalty.

He pointed to a bottle, and the servant poured the liquor into a crystal goblet the color of fire.

Dennis took the glass and wandered about the room. If he were a thief and had a working zievatron within reach, he could retire on Earth on just what he could carry in his hands.

Providing, of course, the things retained their current state when they left the ambience of the Practice Effect. Dennis smiled, imagining irate customers whose wonderful purchases slowly decayed before their eyes into the crude products of a kindergarten workshop!

The lawsuits could go on for years.

The sense of alienation was back again. It felt inexorable. And this time he wasn't sure it wouldn't be a help. He had to appear confident this evening, or risk losing whatever chance remained of ever getting home again.

In a contemplative daze he passed through elegant French doors onto the balcony. He looked upon the starry night, with two small moons casting their light on the drifting cumulus clouds, and brought the goblet to his lips.

The pensive spell was broken instantly as he gagged. He coughed and spat the stuff out onto the brilliant parquet floor. He wiped his lips on his lacy sleeve and stared in disbelief at the cup in his hand.

Once again he had been trapped by his own assumptions. In this kind of lavish environment he had expected fine vintages, not elephant piss!

From the shadows to his right there came musical, feminine laughter. He turned quickly and saw that someone else stood on the balcony with him; her hand briefly tried to cover a grin of amusement.

Dennis felt blood rush to his cheeks.

"I know how you feel," the young woman hurried to say in sympathy. "Isn't it awful? You can't *practice* wine, and you can't cook it. So these cretins put what they have in fancy bottles and are happy, unable to tell the difference."

From his brief glimpses and the stories he had heard about the L'Toff, Dennis had built in his mind an almost elfin image of Princess Linnora —as someone fragile and almost ethereal. Up close she was, indeed, beautiful, but much more human than his imagination had drawn her. She had dimples when she smiled, and her teeth, while white and brilliant, were slightly uneven. Though she was clearly a young woman, sorrow had already planted faint lines at the corners of her eyes.

Dennis felt his voice catch in his throat. He essayed a clumsy bow as he tried to think of something to say.

"In my country, Lady, we would save such vintages as this one for periods of penance."

"Such penance." She seemed impressed with the implied asceticism.

"Right now," Dennis went on, "I'd trade this rare goblet and all the Baron's wealth for a good Cabernet from my homeland—so I could raise it to your beauty, and the help you gave me once."

She acknowledged with a curtsy and a smile. "A convoluted compliment, but I think I like it. I admit, Sir Wizard, that I expected never to see you again. Was my help so poor?"

Dennis joined her at the rail. "No, Lady. Your help made our escape from the jailyard below possible. Didn't you hear the commotion you indirectly caused that night?"

Linnora's lips pursed and she turned away slightly, obviously trying not to laugh undemurely out loud at the memory.

"The look on my lord host's face that night repaid any debt you owed. I only wish his net had remained empty this time."

Dennis had it in his mind to say something stylishly gallant such as,

"I could not stay away but had to return to you, my Lady." But the openness in her gray eyes made it seem verbose and inappropriate. He looked down.

"Well, uh," he said instead. "I guess even a wizard can get a little clumsy once in a while."

Her warm smile told him he had given the right answer. "Then we shall have to hope for another opportunity, shall we not?" she asked.

Dennis felt unaccountably warm. "We can hope," he agreed.

They stood quietly for a while, looking at the reflections of the moonlight from the River Fingal.

"When Baron Kremer showed me your possessions for the first time," she said at last, "I was convinced that someone strange had come into the world. They were obviously tools of great power, though I could feel almost no *Pr'fett* in them."

Dennis shrugged. "In my land they were common implements, your Highness."

She looked at him closely. Dennis was surprised to notice that *she* seemed nervous. Her voice was subdued, almost hushed. "Are you then from the place of miracles? The land of our ancestors?"

Dennis blinked. *Land of our ancestors?*

"Your tools had so little *Pr'fett,*" Linnora went on. "Yet their essences were *strong,* like nothing else in the world. Only once before have I encountered the like—in the wilderness shortly before I was captured."

Dennis stared at her. Could so many threads come together all at once? He took a step closer to Linnora. But before he could speak, another voice cut in.

"I, too, would be interested in learning about the wizard's homeland. That, and many other things, as well."

They both turned. A large shadow blocked part of the light from the banquet hall. For a brief instant Dennis had a sudden joyful impression he was seeing Stivyung Sigel.

But the man stepped forward.

"I am Baron Kremer," he said.

The warlord had a powerful cleft jaw to complement his broad shoulders. His silvery-blond hair was cut just below the ears. His eyes remained in shadows as he motioned toward the glittering table within.

"Shall we dine? Then perhaps we'll have a chance to discuss such matters as different types of *essence* . . . and other worlds."

3

Deacon Hoss'k spread his arms in an expansive gesture, barely missing a glittering candelabrum in the process.

"So you see, Wizard, nonliving things were compensated for the advantages the gods gave to the living. A tree may grow and prosper and spread its seeds, but it is also doomed to die, while a river is not. A man may think and act and move about, but he is fated to grow old and decrepit with time. The tools he uses, on the other hand—the nonliving slaves that serve him all his life—only get better with use."

The deacon's exposition was a strange mixture of theology, teleology, and fairy tale. Dennis tried not to look too amused. The roast fowl on his plate was a definite improvement on his dungeon diet, and he wasn't about to risk going back to prison fare by grinning at the ramblings of his host's resident sage.

At the head of the table, Baron Kremer listened quietly to Hoss'k's pedantic presentation, occasionally serving Dennis with a long, appraising gaze.

"Thusly, within all inanimate objects—including even that which once lived, such as hide or wood—the gods imbued the *potential* to become something greater than itself . . . something *useful.* This is the way the gods chose to make plenty inevitable for their people. . . ."

The portly scholar was dressed in an elegant white evening coat. As he gestured, the sleeves fluttered, displaying a glimpse of a bright red garment underneath.

"When a maker later converts the *potential* of an object into *essence,*" Hoss'k continued, "the thing may then be *practiced.* In this way the gods preordained not only our life-style but our blessed social order as well."

Across from Dennis Princess Linnora picked at her meal. She looked bored, and perhaps a bit angry over what Hoss'k had to say.

"There are those," she said, "who believe that *living* things have potential, too. They, also, may rise above what they are and become greater than they have been."

Hoss'k favored Linnora with a patronizing smile. "A quaint notion left over from ancient superstitions taken seriously only by a few obscure tribes such as your own, my Lady, and by some of the rabble in the east. It manifests a primitive wish that people, families, and even *species* can be improved. But look around you! Do the rabbits, or rickels, or horses get better with each passing year? Does mankind?

"No, clearly man himself cannot be improved. It is only the inanimate that may, with man's intervention, be practiced to perfection." Hoss'k smiled and took a sip of wine.

Dennis couldn't escape a vague feeling that had nagged him for an hour, that he had encountered the man before and that there was some cause for enmity between them.

"Okay," he said, "you've explained *why* inanimate tools improve with use . . . because the gods decreed that it be so. But *how* does a piece of flint, for instance, become an ax simply by being used?"

"Ah! A good question!" Hoss'k paused to belch good-naturedly. Across the table from Dennis, Linnora rolled her eyes, but Hoss'k did not notice.

"You see, Wizard, scholars have long known that eventual fate of this ax you mention is partly determined by the *essence of making* imbued into it by an anointed master of the stonechoppers' guild. The essence that is put into an object at its beginning is just as important as the *Pr'fett,* which the owner invests through practice.

"By this I mean that practice is important, but it is useless without the proper essence at the beginning. Try as he might, a peasant cannot practice a sled into a hoe, or a kite into a cup. An implement must *start out* at least a little bit useful in its designated task to be made better through practice. Only master makers have this skill.

"This is something not well enough appreciated by the masses, particularly lately, with all of this intemperate grumbling against the guilds. The rabble-rousers chant about 'value added' and the 'importance of practice labor.' But it's all ignorant foolishness!"

Dennis had already realized that Hoss'k was the type of intellectual who'd dismiss an urgent and unstoppable change in his society, blithely ignoring the forces that pulled all about him. His kind always fiddled while Rome burned, all the while explaining away the ashes with their own brand of logic.

Hoss'k sipped his wine and beamed at Dennis. "Of course, I don't have to explain to a man such as yourself why it is so necessary to control the lower orders."

"I haven't any idea what you're talking about," Dennis answered coolly.

"Now, now, Wizard, you need not dissemble. From inspecting the items you have so kindly, er, lent us, I can tell so very much about you!" With an indulgent smile the man bit into a pulpy dessert fruit.

Dennis decided to say nothing. He had eaten slowly and spoken little this evening, aware that the Baron was watching his reactions closely. He had barely touched his wine.

Dennis and Linnora had shared glances as they dared. Once, when the Baron was speaking to the butler and while the scholar addressed the ceiling expansively, the Princess puffed her cheeks and mouthed a nattering mimicry of Hoss'k. Dennis had had to struggle not to laugh out loud.

When Kremer had looked at them curiously, Dennis tried to keep a straight face. Linnora assumed a mask of attentive innocence.

Dennis realized that he was well on his way toward falling in love.

"I am curious, Deacon," Kremer said. "What can you divine about our guest's homeland from only his tools and his demeanor?"

The Baron lounged back on his plush, thronelike chair. He seemed filled with a restless energy, carefully, calculatedly restrained. It showed from time to time as he crushed nuts in his bare hands.

Hoss'k wiped his mouth on his napkin-sleeve. He bowed his head. "As you wish, my Lord. First, would you tell me which of Dennis Nuel's tools are of most interest to you?"

Kremer smiled indulgently. "The far-killing hand weapon, the far-seeing glass box, and the box that shows shining insects moving as dots."

Hoss'k nodded. "And what do all of these things have in common?"

"You tell us."

"Very well, my Lord. Clearly these implements contain essences wholly unknown here in Coylia. Our lady of the L'Toff"—Hoss'k inclined his head to Linnora—"has confirmed this fact for us.

"Although he has endeavored to hide the details of his origins, our wizard's plain ignorance of some of the most basic facts about our way of life indicates that he comes from a distant land, easily beyond the Great Desert beyond the mountains—a land where the study of essence has developed along radically different lines than it has here.

"Perhaps *essence* itself is different there, such that the tools they practice are constrained to develop in totally divergent ways." Hoss'k smiled, as if he knew he were making a daring speculation.

Dennis sat up in his chair. *Perhaps this fellow is no dolt after all,* he thought.

"The box of lights, in particular, tells me much," Hoss'k went on, confidently. "The tiny trained insects it contains behind its clear cover are unknown in these parts. They are smaller than the tiniest firefly. What are they called, Wizard?"

Dennis sat back in his chair again, almost sighing aloud in disappointment. *Cavemen,* he reminded himself.

"They are called *pixel array elements,*" he answered. "They are made up of things called liquid crystals, which—"

"Living crystal elementals!" Hoss'k interrupted Dennis. "Imagine that! Well, I feared at first that the little creatures were dying under my care. After a time they grew dim, and I could find no airholes nor any way to supply them with food. Finally I learned—almost by accident, I will confess—that they recovered quite nicely when fed *sunlight!*"

Dennis couldn't help reacting with a raised eyebrow. Hoss'k took note and grinned in triumph.

"Ah, yes, Wizard. We are not bumpkins or fools here. This discovery was particularly pleasing to my Lord Baron. Until that time his new weapon, the small "needle-caster" you so graciously provided, had stopped functioning. *Now,* of course, that tool is also fed its fill of sunlight every day as it is practiced."

The portly scholar beamed as Baron Kremer acknowledged this coup with a faint smile and nod. Kremer obviously had plans for the needler. Dennis frowned but remained silent.

"Like the bugs in the wonder box," Hoss'k continued. "Something inside the weapon must at intervals eat from the sun. Indeed, when the weapon is used one can hear the faint scamperings of captive animals inside it.

"I did find a little food door on that machine. And now we provide the creatures inside with the metal they apparently require besides sunlight.

"These demons of yours have expensive tastes, Wizard. My Lord has used up the price of several serfs just keeping the weapon in practice!"

Dennis kept his face impassive. The fellow was clever, but his deductions were diverging more and more from reality. Dennis tried not to think about how Kremer might be "practicing" his needler.

"And just what does all this tell you about my homeland?" he asked.

Hoss'k grinned. "Well, first off we have seen that part of your magic is in taking the *essence* of living things and imbuing them into tools before practice even begins. This suggests to me a society with less regard for the dignity of life than we have here in Coylia."

Dennis couldn't help smirking sardonically. Of all the fatuous conclusions to reach! He glanced at Linnora to share his feelings in a secret glance but was shaken by the look she gave him. She obviously didn't think much of Hoss'k, but his latest deduction obviously disturbed her. She fingered her napkin nervously.

Couldn't she tell that the scholar was only flailing around blindly?

Hoss'k went on. "Some time ago I took some of the items Dennis Nuel brought with him from his homeland—those that my Lord Baron did not require for other purposes—and put them in a dark closet, where they received neither light nor practice. I wished to observe them as they reverted to their original forms and find out what principles of essence were at the heart of each.

"To my shock I found that, after a few days, the tools stopped devolving altogether! Left in a dark room, his knife remains sharp as it was a week ago. Some of this may be due to the fact that it is made of a prince's ransom in iron, but the fastenings on his clothing and backpack also remained frozen in intricate shapes that could have been made by no craftsman alive."

Dennis glanced at Kremer. The Baron listened with hands clasped in front of him. Heavy brows cast his eyes into shadows.

Linnora's gaze darted from Hoss'k to Dennis to Kremer with an expression of apparent anxiety. Dennis wondered what was going on. Was it something the fool had just said? He decided to stop this foolishness before it got any more ridiculous. "I don't think you. . . ."

But the scholar wouldn't be interrupted. "The wizard's things are positively amazing. Only once before have I encountered their like," he said. "In our recent expedition into the western mountains north of the lands of the L'Toff, I and my escorts found a tiny house in the wilderness, all made of metal. . . ."

Dennis stared at Hoss'k and felt his hands become fists. *"You!"* He knew, now, that he had seen the deacon one time before, on the tiny screen of the Sahara Tech exploration 'bot. It was *this* fool, dressed in his red formal robes, who had overseen the dismantling of the zievatron!

"Ah," the scholar nodded. "I see from your reaction that that little house was yours, Wizard. And that does not surprise me. For I found a little box in the side of the house, which opened under prying. And there I found a *storehouse* of incredible little tools! I took home a few to examine at my leisure and, while I have not been able to make them do anything discernible, they, like the items in your backpack, have not changed a whit since I acquired them!"

Hoss'k reached into his voluminous robes and pulled out a handful of small objects.

"A few of these came from a pair of rather large, ferocious demons we found guarding the little house. But they were no match for the thenners of my Lord's brave guardsmen."

Bits and pieces of shiny electronics spilled from his hand onto the table. Dennis stared at a claw arm from a "ferocious" little Sahara Tech exploration robot, and a broken elevatronics circuit board whose components alone were worth hundreds of thousands of dollars!

"Of course, we could not stay long enough to pursue a full investigation, you'll understand. For that was when we encountered the Princess. It took our men two whole days to—ahem—track her from the little metal house to the rock cleft where she had become lost. . . ."

"I wasn't lost! I was hiding from your thrice-cursed northmen!" Linnora bit out.

"Hmm. Well. She claimed that she had come to the mountain glade because she sensed that something unusual had recently occurred in the area. I felt it wise to invite her to accompany our expedition back to Zuslik . . . for her own safety, of course."

Dennis could barely contain himself. "So *you're* the cretin who tore apart the return device," he growled.

Hoss'k laughed. "Oh, Wizard, I completed the job of dissection, but our L'Toff Princess had already begun investigating the strange cabin when we arrived."

He glanced at her to see if this was true, but Linnora only looked away, fanning herself. At that moment Dennis didn't feel any favoritism. He gave Linnora some of the hot glare he had offered Hoss'k. *Both* of them had meddled where they had no business!

"Anyway, Wizard," Hoss'k went on, "no harm was done, I'm sure. When my Lord Baron decides it is time for you to return to your homeland with your property, I'm sure we can return the metal I took and lend you all the help you'll need in order to practice your little house back to perfection."

Dennis swore softly in Arabic, the only way he could properly express his opinion of the idea.

Hoss'k seemed to sense some of the message, if not the meaning. His smile narrowed. "And if my Lord decides otherwise, why, then I will lead another expedition to the little house and reclaim all of that wonderful metal for my Lord's treasury."

Dennis sat back in stunned silence. If the airlock itself were ever actually moved, let alone dismantled, he would spend the rest of his life here!

Kremer had remained quiet during this exchange. Now he cut in.

"I believe we have strayed from the topic, my good Deacon. You were explaining to us what was so unusual about the tools once owned by our alien wizard. You said that they appear to remain unchanged, no matter how long they are left unpracticed."

"Yes, my Lord." Hoss'k bowed. "And there is only one way known to *freeze* a tool into its practiced form so it will remain in that condition forever, unable to revert to its starter state. In our land this technique is controlled only by the L'Toff."

Linnora sat rigidly, not looking at Hoss'k or even at Dennis.

"The technique, as we all know, involves a member of the L'Toff race willingly investing a portion of his or her own life-force into the tool in question, spending a part of his or her life-span to make the *Pr'fett* permanent."

Kremer spoke pensively. "A great gift, is it not, Wizard? The priests claim that the L'Toff were chosen by the gods . . . blessed with the talent to be able to make beautiful things beautiful forever.

"But all gifts have a price, do they not, scholar?"

Hoss'k nodded sagely. "Yes, my Lord. The talent has been a mixed blessing to the L'Toff. With their other gifts, it elevated them above other peoples. It also led to many unpleasant episodes of, well, what might be called attempted exploitation by others."

Dennis blinked. This was all coming too fast, but even without reflection he could imagine how the L'Toff had suffered for their talent.

The Princess looked only at her own hands.

"Of course, the rest of the story is common knowledge," Hoss'k said, chuckling. "Fleeing the greed of mankind, the L'Toff came to the western mountains, where an ancestor of our King Hymiel ceded them their present territory and made the old dukes of Zuslik their protectors."

And Baron Kremer's father deposed the last of the old dukes, Dennis realized.

"We were speaking of the wizard's property," Kremer reminded softly but severely.

Hoss'k bowed. "Of course. Now, what *can* we suppose when we find that the wizard's property does not decay, does not devolve into crude *starters?* We are forced to conclude that Dennis Nuel is a member of the aristocracy of his homeland, a homeland in which both metal and life itself are cheap. Furthermore, it seems clear that the equivalent of the L'Toff in his country have been enslaved and put to use freezing *Pr'fett* within practiced objects so that they remain refined even when left unused for long periods. This exploitation has gone so far as to freezing even Nuel's clothing. Here in Coylia no one has ever considered squandering the L'Toff talent on *clothes—*"

"Now just a darned minute," Dennis cut in. "I think there are a few things that need to be—"

Hoss'k grinned and hurried on, cutting Dennis off. "—We must conclude, at last, that their expertise at different kinds of essence—including the enslavement of little animals as integral parts of tools—plus this power over the L'Toff of their own land explains the wizardry of Dennis Nuel's country.

"He may be an exile or an adventurer. I cannot say which. In either case our guest clearly comes from a most powerful and ruthless warrior race. This being so, he should be treated as a member of the highest caste while he remains here in Coylia."

Dennis stared at the man, dumbfounded. He wanted to laugh, but it was too preposterous even for that!

He started to speak twice and stopped each time. It occurred to him to wonder if he should interfere at all. His initial impulse to protest might not be the right strategy at all. If Hoss'k's sophistry led to the granting of high status and respect here, should he even interfere?

While he considered, Princess Linnora abruptly stood up, her face very pale. "My Lord Baron. Gentlemen." She nodded left and right but did not look at Dennis. "I am fatigued. Will you excuse me?"

Her chair was withdrawn by a servant. She did not meet Dennis's gaze, though he stood and tried to catch her eye. She bore stoically the Baron's lips upon her hand, then turned and left, accompanied by two guards.

Dennis's ears burned. He could well imagine what Linnora thought of him. But all considered, it was probably best that he had remained silent right now, until he had a chance to think about what was to be done. The time for explanations would come later.

He turned to see Kremer smiling at him. The Baron took his seat and sipped from a goblet whose lacquer had, over the years, developed into a magnificent, arsene blue.

"Please sit down, Wizard. Do you smoke? I have pipes that have been used every day for three hundred years. As we relax, I am certain we will find matters of mutual benefit to discuss."

Dennis said nothing.

Kremer eyed him calculatingly. "And perhaps we can work out something that will benefit the lady as well."

Dennis frowned. Were his feelings that obvious?

He shrugged and sat down. In his position, he had little choice but to deal.

4

"It's a good thing the palace has lots of well-practiced indoor plumbing," Arth said as he worked to join two ill-fitting pieces of tubing, binding them with wet mud and twine. "I'd hate to have to make our own pipes out of paper or clay and have to practice 'em up ourselves."

Dennis used a chisel to trim a tight wooden cover to fit over a large earthen vat. Nearby, several kegs of the Baron's "best" wine awaited another test run. The maze of tubes overhead was a plumber's nightmare. Even the sloppiest Appalachian moonshiner would have shuddered at the sight. But Dennis figured it would be good enough for a "starter" distillery.

All they had to do was get a few drops of brandy to come out the other end of the condenser. A little final product was all they needed for it to be useful and therefore practicable.

Arth whistled as he worked. He seemed to have forgiven Dennis since being released from the dungeon and assigned work as "wizard's assistant." Now wearing comfortably old work clothes and being fed well, the short thief was enthralled by this extended making task, unlike anything he had ever done before.

"Do you think Kremer's goin' to be satisfied with this *still*, Dennizz?"

Dennis shrugged. "In a couple of days we should be producing a concoction that'll knock the Baron's fancy, two-hundred-year-old socks off. It ought to make him happy."

"Well, I still hate his guts, but I'll admit he pays well." Arth jingled a small leather purse a quarter filled with slivers of precious copper.

Arth seemed satisfied for now, but Dennis had his private doubts. Making a distillery for Kremer was a stopgap measure at best. He was sure the warlord would only want more from his new wizard. Soon he would lose interest in promises of new luxuries and trade goods and start demanding weapons for his upcoming campaign against the L'Toff and the King.

Dennis and Arth had been at this task almost a week. Here and now, few spent much more than a day *making* anything. Kremer was already showing signs of impatience.

What would he do when the distillery was operational? Show the Baron how to forge iron? Teach his artisans the principle of the wheel? Dennis had hoped to keep one or two of those "essences" in reserve, just in case Kremer decided to renege on his promise. The warlord had vowed eventually to heap wealth on Dennis and provide him with all the resources he'd need to repair his "metal house" and go home. But he might change his mind.

Dennis was still ambivalent. Kremer was clearly a ruthless S.O.B. But he was competent, and not particularly venal. From Dennis's readings of Earth's history, a lot of men who were revered in legends weren't exactly pleasant people in real life. Although Kremer certainly was a tyrant, Dennis wondered if he was particularly terrible as founders of dynasties went.

Perhaps the best thing to do would be to become the fellow's Merlin. Dennis could probably make Kremer's victories overwhelming—and therefore relatively bloodless—and in so doing become a power at his side.

Certainly that would win him a freer hand, perhaps even to repair the zievatron and return home again.

It did sound like the right plan.

Then why did it feel so unpalatable?

He could think of at least one person who wouldn't agree with his decision. The few times he had seen Princess Linnora since the banquet they had been at least two parapets apart, she escorted by her guards and he by his. She had nodded to him coolly and swept away with a swirl of skirts even as he smiled and tried to catch her eye.

Dennis could see now how Hoss'k's logic at the banquet would sound compelling to someone raised in this world. The misunderstanding irked him all the more because it was so unfair.

But there was nothing he could do. Kremer was keeping her in Dennis's sight but out of earshot. And he couldn't insult the Baron in her presence—spoiling all of his plans—just to regain favor in her eyes, could he? That would be shortsighted.

It was perplexing.

He and Arth built their still in a broad court not far from the enclosed jailyard they had escaped from only weeks before. Except for their small corner, the broad field was taken up by drilling grounds for the Baron's troops. Near the outer wall of sharpened logs, sergeants marched militia from the town and neighboring hamlets—practicing both the ragged weapons and their equally motley bearers.

Nearer the castle, regulars in bright uniforms used their battle-axes and halberds to slice at chunks of meat hanging from tall gibbets. The gleaming blades sheared through meat and bone alike. The chops were collected in tubs and carted off by drudges to the palace kitchens.

Even the pair of guards assigned to watch Dennis and Arth kept busy. They took turns striking each other lightly with dull blades, working on their armor.

Overhead, the Baron's aerial patrol went through their maneuvers. Dennis watched them dive and swoop around each other, as facile as the sprightliest gliders of Earth, staying aloft for hours at a time in the day thermals near the castle. They practiced throwing clusters of small, deadly darts at ground targets in midflight.

No one else on Coylia had anything like these gliders. The innovation was said to have come one day when the observation kite the Baron himself had been riding was cut loose in an assassination attempt. Practiced to perfection as a kite, the untethered airfoil instantly went into a spinning fall.

But instead of plummeting to his death, Kremer had been caught in a powerful winter updraft. Showing unusual imagination, the Baron had recognized almost instantly that something new was involved. He concentrated desperately on *practicing* the unwieldly glider, rather than resigning himself to certain death, and the amazing happened. To the awe of all those watching, he and the kite had shimmered for a few moments in the sparkling nimbus of a felthesh trance. The fabric contraption changed before everyone's eyes into something which flew!

In the end, Kremer merely broke his leg, but he had discovered a new principle in the process.

Seventeen killed and maimed "volunteers" later, he had his corps of one-, two-, and even four-man gliders. They were getting better day by day. And although Kremer never again was able to produce another felthesh, his reputation was made throughout Coylia.

Dennis watched the gliders thoughtfully. The hangar shed was guarded, and the launching tower as well. But their greatest protection was the fact that Castle Zuslik contained the planet's only supply of trained pilots. Even if some other lord managed to steal a glider, he wouldn't be able to *practice* it in time to prevent it from decaying back to a pile of sticks and string and hides.

But unbeknownst to Baron Kremer, there was one more potential pilot on Tatir.

No. Dennis shook his head. You've chosen a plan. Stick with it.

Arth approached, holding up a piece of condenser. "Say, Dennzz, where does this thing you called a . . . a *gizmo* . . . fit? Does it go into the *thingumbob?* Or the *doohickey?*" Arth pronounced each name as he had memorized it.

Dennis returned to the task of fostering an industrial revolution.

5

"Master, you must get dressed for the party now."

Dennis looked up from a sheaf of notes covered with the arcane notations of anomaly mathematics.

"Oh, is it time already, Dvarah?"

The servant girl smiled and gestured over to the ancient bed by the wall. Dennis saw that she had laid out a formal dinner suit. It had fancy sleeves and a wide, puffy collar.

The girl curtsied. "Yes, my Lord. And tonight you will dress in a manner befitting your station. These garments are over two hundred years old. And the practicer we found for you has been wearing them nonstop for over a week. They have just been laundered and are ready for you now."

Dennis looked at the suit and frowned. It wasn't just that the clothes were frilly and decadent for his tastes. After all, he was the foreigner here and should adapt to local fashions.

But he didn't like to think that some poor citizen of Zuslik had been shanghaied into durance style—just to *practice* these clothes for him.

Dvarah had been assigned to Dennis after the dinner meeting with the Baron. The pretty, petite brunette brought him his meals and tended his sumptuous new quarters.

She coughed demurely. "Master, you really mustn't keep my Lord Baron waiting."

Dennis cast a brief, wistful glance back at the papers on his desk. It had been fun, almost relaxing, to play with the symbols and numbers, trying to figure out how the Practice Effect came to be. While lost in the equations, Dennis could almost forget where he was, and pretend he was, once again, a comfortable terrestrial scientist with nothing at all to fear.

Kremer had actually been quite generous, by his own lights. He had, for instance, given Dennis all the paper he wanted for his studies. But he had stopped at letting Dennis have any of his Earthly equipment.

There was no use complaining. Dennis had to win the warlord's trust. Without the wrist comp, for instance, all these calculations were inevitably futile. Eventually, he was sure, Kremer would let him have his gear.

He got up to dress. Kremer was bringing together all the burghers and guildmasters tonight, to show off his new wizard. Dennis would have to put on a good show.

Dvarah came over and began unbuttoning his shirt.

The first few times it had happened, Dennis had stammered and pushed her away. But that only seemed to hurt the girl's feelings—not to mention her professional pride. *When in Rome* he realized at last, and learned to relax while having things done for him.

Actually, it was rather pleasant once he got used to it. Dvarah smelled nice. And over the past few days she had apparently become quite devoted to him. It seemed her duties included considerably more than he had taken advantage of as yet. His politeness toward her, and his reluctance to assert those privileges without considerable further thought, seemed to surprise and please her.

Dvarah was straightening his cravat as a knock came on the door.

"Come in!" Dennis called.

Arth stuck his head in. "Ready, Dennizz? Come on! We gotta get the brandy set up for the party!"

"Okay, Arth. Just a sec."

Dvarah stepped back and smiled approvingly at her master's elegance. Dennis gave her a wink and followed Arth out into the hall.

Along with two of the ever-present guards, there waited four burly men with a heavy cask on two rails. As the guards turned to lead the way, the bearers heaved and lifted the cask on their shoulders, following behind.

Dennis had considered inventing something to make their task easier. Then, on thinking about it, he decided to hold off for a while. The wheel was too much of an ace to play just yet.

"I got a message from th' missus . . ." Arth whispered to Dennis as they walked down the elegant hallway.

Dennis walked steadily ahead, without missing a step. He asked, softly, "Are the others all right?"

Arth nodded. "Mostly. Guards caught two o' my men . . . and Maggin found out what happened to Perth." He spat the name as if it were something vile.

"Did Mishwa . . ." Dennis let the question hang.

"Yeah. He took care of the rat, all right! Just before they conked him. Perth never got a chance to give away th' exact location o' the warehouse, so Stivyung an' Gath were able to—"

Arth shut up as the grand doors to the ballroom swung wide before them. But Dennis got the general idea.

He was relieved his friends were all right. Perhaps in weeks, or months, he would have enough influence over Kremer to intercede for other prisoners. For now, though, he would rather not test it. Gath and Stivyung deserved a chance to make their own escape.

Dennis could only describe the party as a sort of quasi potlatch, with a dash of Louis XIV's Sun King court thrown in.

The local elite were out in force, in a sea of elegant finery, but there was less dancing and socializing than there would be at a party on Earth. Instead, there appeared to be a whole lot of ceremonious exchanging of gifts. The rituals bemused Dennis. Here, it seemed, there was a complicated way in which status was maintained by giving things away. The more practiced the donated items were, the better.

Dennis was reminded of similar rites he had read of in preatomic New Guinea and in the Pacific Northwest. The gift-giving had little generosity to it but rather an aggressive *bragging* overtone heavily dependent upon status.

He saw the recipient of a particularly frilly, silky, useless-looking garment briefly blanche and stare in horror at what she had been given, before hurriedly putting on a casual expression and thanking the giver through her teeth.

Yes, it was very much like an ancient Earthly potlatch. But Dennis soon saw that the Practice Effect had twisted the ritual in strange ways.

It cost many man-hours to maintain a tool or an object at its peak of perfection, for instance. So unlike similar social arrangements on Earth, the gifts could be stockpiled in advance only at great cost to the giver. Their number was limited by the overall ability of a magnate's servants and bondsmen to *use* things . . . and just before one of these parties the serfs must be run ragged practicing their masters' best gifts.

Dennis moved about the grand hall, casually watching the rich people bow and make convoluted compliments to each other. They traded their gifts with elegant gestures of surprise and feigned spontaneity.

Arth had explained it to him. The receiver of gifts was caught in a bind. Covetousness was counterbalanced against caution. A rich man might desire a beautiful, ancient thing but fear the investment of man-hours it would take to maintain it. A gift received had to be displayed later, and any deterioration would bring terrible shame.

It was like watching an elegant pavane. Several more times Dennis saw unmistakable chagrin on the face of a recipient who had made a false move, and received too much.

At the station being manned by Arth, the brandy cask had just been opened. Servants were circulating small goblets of amber-colored fluid.

A chain of gasps and coughing exclamations rippled across the crowd, just behind the waiters.

Dennis looked for Linnora. Maybe here, at the party, he would have a chance to explain to her that he was not from a land of monsters. He had to convince her that by playing a waiting game he could become so necessary to Kremer that one L'Toff prisoner would be meaningless to him in comparison. Dennis was certain he could win Linnora's release within a few months.

But there was no sign of the Princess in the crowd. Perhaps later, he hoped.

The minor nobles and guildmasters—most of them sons and grandsons of men who had helped Kremer's father seize power—moved about with their wives, followed by personal servants who modeled the gifts their masters had been given. It was like watching a crowd filled with sets of almost identical twins, only the sibling apparently bearing more riches always walked behind the less heavily laden, and the one wearing all the flashy junk *never* partook of food or drink.

Dennis had managed to beg off being assigned a "tail," as the accompanying servants were called. It was bad enough knowing that someone, somewhere, was spending hours practicing Dennis's formal outfits for him. He didn't want to have to force another fellow to take on such a disgusting role, no matter how well accepted it was here.

Anyway, it helped establish Dennis as an anomaly. By now everyone knew he was a foreign wizard. The more conventions he broke, Dennis figured, the better the precedent and the less likely they'd try to hold him to other tribal stupidities.

Not stupidities, he reminded himself—*adaptations!* The patterns of behavior all fit when one thought of combining feudalism with the Practice Effect. One might not like them, but the rituals did make a certain amount of brutal sense.

"Wizard!"

Dennis turned and saw that Kremer himself was motioning him over.

Nearby stood Deacon Hoss'k in his bright red robes, and a crowd of local dignitaries. Dennis approached as he was bid and gave Kremer a calculatedly respectful nod.

"So this is the magician who has shown us how to practice wine into . . . *brandy.*" A richly dressed magnate held up his goblet in admiration. "Tell me, Wizard, since you seem to have found a way to practice consumable items, will you now teach us to turn cornmeal into rickel steak?"

The fellow laughed loudly, accompanied by several of those around him. He had obviously already had a fair sampling of Dennis's first product.

Baron Kremer smiled. "Wizard, let me introduce you to Kappun Thsee, magnate of the stonechoppers' guild, and Zuslik's selectman for the Assembly of our Lord, King Hymiel."

Dennis bowed just a little. "Honored."

Thsee nodded slightly. He tossed back the brandy in his glass and motioned to a servant for more.

"You did not answer my question, Wizard."

Dennis didn't know what to say. These people had a fixed way of looking at things, and any explanation he gave would involve new assumptions the Coylian aristocrats were ill prepared to hear.

Anyway, at that moment he saw Princess Linnora enter the room, accompanied by a servant.

The crowd near the entrance parted for her. When she nodded and spoke to someone, the response was almost always an exaggerated, nervous smile. In her wake people frankly stared. She stood out brilliantly in the sea of flushed, anxious faces, cool and reserved as her mountain people were reputed to be.

"I am afraid that is not the way of it, my dear Kappun Thsee."

Dennis turned quickly and saw that it was the scholar Hoss'k who had spoken, filling the long pause in the conversation. Dennis had had a brief illusion that it had been Professor Marcel Flaster, somehow transported directly from Earth, beginning one of his infamous, ponderous lectures.

"You see," Hoss'k expanded. "The wizard has not *improved* wine into brandy. He has used wine much as your stonechoppers use flint nodules. He *makes* brandy by infusing it with new essence."

Kappun Thsee's eyes shone with ill-concealed greed. "The guild that gains the license to this art—"

Baron Kremer laughed out loud. "And why should this wonderful new secret be given to any of the present guilds? What, my friend, does chopping stone have to do with creating liquor with the flavor of fire?"

Kappun Thsee flushed.

Dennis had been trying to keep track of Linnora's progress through the crowd. He quickly turned back as Kremer put his arm over his shoulder.

"No, magnate Thsee," Kremer said, grinning. "The new essences brought to us by our wizard *might* be divided up among the present guilds. Then again, perhaps each should have its own, new guild. And who better to be guildmaster than he who brought these secrets to us?"

One of the women gasped. The other aristocrats stared.

In the silent moment Dennis suddenly saw with perfect clarity what was going on.

Kremer was manipulating them beautifully! Holding out the possibility of access to a whole set of new "essences," he was accompanying the carrot with an implied stick. He already had the monopolistic guilds on his side. Now they'd positively be baying to do his will.

At the same time, Dennis realized that Kremer had just offered him more wealth and power than he had ever imagined.

He saw that even the ebullient Hoss'k was subdued, as if he were seeing Dennis in a new light—less as his own personal discovery and more, perhaps, as a dangerous rival.

That suited Dennis fine. The man had been the direct cause of stranding him on this crazy world. He had already promised himself to teach Hoss'k a lesson.

Dennis noticed that Linnora had come closer but was avoiding approaching the area where the baron stood. He turned to Kremer. "Your Grace, some may think that my brandy is nothing but a more potent form of wine. May I perform a demonstration to prove that it is, indeed, something truly different?"

Kremer nodded, betraying a faint smile.

Dennis called for a brandy-filled goblet and a small table to lay it on. Then he reached into the folds of one of his fancy sleeves and pulled out a bundle of small sticks, each painted at one end with a blob of crusty paste.

It had taken him days to hunt down and purify the right materials to perform this demonstration. It would be just the sort of thing to solidify his reputation.

"Baron Kremer spoke of the flavor of fire. From the way some of our local notables are weaving about the hall, it certainly seems that the blood in their veins has grown more than a little warm."

The crowd laughed. Indeed, several magnates had already become tipsy, falling prey to other players of the gift-giving game. Their servants were stumbling under quantities of fine, ancient things that would ruin their masters in expensive practice time.

Dennis noticed that Linnora watched from a nearby pillar. She had smiled at the reference to the foolish guildsmasters.

Encouraged, Dennis went on.

"In this evening of marvelous gift-giving, I, a poor wizard, have little to offer. But to Baron Kremer I now offer the essence of . . . fire!"

He struck two of the little sticks together. At once the two ends erupted into flame.

The crowd moaned and pulled back in awe. They were rather crude matches, smoking and stinking of sulfur and nitrates, but that only made the display more impressive.

Dennis had seen the firemakers they used here. They were efficient but used that ancient principle of a rotating friction stick. Nothing in Coylia could do what he had just done.

"And now," he added dramatically, waving the matches for effect, "the *flavor* of *fire!*"

He brought one of the matches down to the goblet.

A flickering blue flame popped audibly into place to meet it. The onlookers sighed. There was a long, stunned silence.

"The essence of fire . . . captured in a *drink?*" Dennis turned and saw that Hoss'k was goggle-eyed.

"A marvelous feat," Kremer agreed, quite calmly. "It is akin, per- haps, to the fashion in which the wizard's people enslave those tiny creatures within his little boxes. They have found a way to trap fire as well, it would seem. Wonderful."

"But . . . but . . ." Hoss'k spluttered. "Fire is one of the *life* es- sences! Even the followers of the Old Belief agree with that. It is re- served for the gods who *make* and *practice* men! We may release the essence of fire from that which once lived . . . but we cannot trap it!"

Dennis couldn't help it. He laughed. Hoss'k was nervously licking his lips, and seeing the deacon squirm gave Dennis a moment's satisfaction. Here, at last, was some repayment for what the fellow had done to him.

"Did I not say it?" Kremer's laughter boomed. "Dennis Nuel knows how to trap *anything* within a tool! What wonders might we expect if he is but given our full support?"

The crowd applauded dutifully, but Dennis could tell they were cowed. Their faces were touched with superstition and uncertainty.

Dennis glanced to his left, still grinning over giving Hoss'k the shock of his life. Then he saw Linnora, her face a mask of concern and fear.

The Princess favored Dennis with a withering glance, then swept about in a flourish to leave the hall, followed by her maid.

Now he recalled what Hoss'k had said about "the Old Belief." Ap- parently his little demonstration had reawakened her fear of those who abused life essences. Dennis cursed softly. Was there *anything* he could do here that wouldn't be misinterpreted by her?

It had been the Baron who declaimed on what Dennis had done, he realized, at last. Kremer had put his actions in a light that boxed him in a corner, insuring that Linnora would misunderstand.

He was outclassed by the man. He could not oppose that kind of manipulative skill. How could there be any choice but to go along?

He only hoped that someday Linnora, too, would understand.

6

A bit foggyheaded from the party, Arth and Dennis were late reporting to the still the next morning. When they arrived, they found that the crew had had a celebration of their own and left the still a shambles in the process.

The prisoners groveled, terrified of the wizard's wrath.

Dennis just sighed, "Aw hell," and set the men to work fixing the damage. Keeping busy helped him not think about his overall situation.

He had made progress in his plan to win influence over the warlord, Kremer. He still thought it the most logical plan—best for himself, for his friends, for Linnora, and even for the people of this land.

Yet the episode last night left him with a sour feeling. He worked hard, and tried to drive the memory away.

A little after noon, a bugle cried out from the front gate. The call was answered by trumpets on the castle tower. Troops in the yard hurried to fall into formation along a corridor from gate to castle.

Dennis looked at Arth, who shrugged. The little thief-*cum*-moonshiner had no idea what was happening.

Down a ramp from the keep came Baron Kremer and his entourage, their bright, centuries-old robes almost painful to look at in the sunshine. The tall plumed helm of Kremer's cousin, Lord Hern, stood out in the crowd of courtiers.

They halted at a dais overlooking the massed companies and watched as the outer gate swung back.

In rode a small procession on horseback.

"It's th' embassy from th' L'Toff!" Arth breathed.

They had been told such a party was coming. The L'Toff were searching for their missing Princess and no doubt suspected she was being kept here.

The rumors must have spread far and wide since the jailbreak, and especially since Zuslik's aristocracy were let in on it, Kremer was publicly feigning innocence until it suited his purposes to do otherwise. But apparently he was no longer worried about suspicions.

For all of his apparent good favor with the warlord, Dennis had not been invited to attend the meeting of the welcoming committee. It was another sign of Kremer's masterful insight into people. He clearly knew the foreign wizard was not trustworthy on the subject of the L'Toff Princess.

Dennis looked up at the third-level parapet, where he had often seen Linnora walk. She wasn't in sight, of course. Her guards would keep her well secluded during the brief visit by her kinfolk.

He walked over to the low fence enclosing his work area and put a foot up on one of the rough wooden rails. He and Arth watched the embassy pass the arrayed soldiers to approach Baron Kremer's platform.

There were five riders, all wearing soft cloaks in muted colors. They looked normal enough to Dennis's eyes, though all five wore beards, unfashionable among Coylians. They seemed a trifle more slender than the people of Zuslik, or Kremer's northmen. The five rode looking straight ahead, ignoring the xenophobic stares of the troops, until they came within a dozen yards of the dais where Kremer waited.

Two L'Toff held reins for the others as they dismounted and saluted the Baron.

Dennis could see Kremer's face better than he could the emissaries'. He couldn't hear what was said, but Kremer's answer was obvious. The warlord smiled with unctuous sympathy. He raised his hands and shook his head.

"Next he'll say he's had scouts out scourin' the countryside far an' wide for their Princess," Arth said.

Sure enough, Kremer waved an arm at his troops and at a squad of mounted horsemen. Then he pointed to the gliders circling patiently in the updraft over the castle.

"The two L'Toff on the right aren't buyin' it," Arth commented. "They'd like to take th' castle apart, startin' with th' Baron hisself."

The gray-bearded leader of the embassy tried to stifle one of his companions, a brown-haired youth in dark-brown body armor, who shrugged off restraint and shouted hotly at the Baron. Kremer's guards muttered angrily and shifted weight, poised for a nodded command from their Lord.

The young L'Toff looked contemptuously at the tense guards and spat on the ground.

Arth chewed on a grass stem speculatively. "I've heard it used to be the L'Toff were pacifists. But they've had to become fighters the past two hunnerd years or so, in spite of the protection o' th' King and the old Duke. Some of 'em are said to be about as good as th' King's own scouts."

Arth pointed to the tall, angry young L'Toff. "That one may make it hard for the ambassador to get outta here without a fight."

Arth sounded like he was handicapping horses. From what Dennis had heard, one of the major spectator sports here in Coylia seemed to be watching men hack each other to bits and betting on the outcome.

The Baron did not rise to the young man's challenge. Instead he grinned and whispered to one of his aides, who sped away.

Kremer waved forward trays of refreshment, which he diplomatically sampled first. He had seats brought for his guests as the troops stepped back to create a broad aisle from the dais to the courtyard wall.

The L'Toff looked suspicious, but they could hardly refuse. They sat nervously near their host. As they turned his way, Dennis thought he saw, in the face of the angry young man, a family resemblance to Linnora.

He wondered if her fey sensitivity had informed the Princess that relatives were only a few hundred meters away. Dennis had finally become convinced Linnora really had such a gift. Over a month ago the power had led her to the zievatron, where she was captured. It had enabled her to know him in the dark prison yard weeks later.

Unfortunately, it wasn't enough to keep her from falling under the spell of Hoss'k's fallacious logic, or to let her see through Kremer's manipulative explanations.

In any event, her talent was apparently intermittent and quite rare even among the L'Toff. Kremer didn't seem afraid of it.

Arth clutched Dennis's shoulder and gasped. Dennis followed his pointing finger.

A cluster of guards were dragging a prisoner from one of the castle's lower gates. Dust rose from the struggle, for the captive was very big and very angry.

Dennis suddenly realized it was Mishwa Qan, the giant whose strength had been key to their breakout from jail. Mishwa bellowed and heaved against his bonds. When he saw they were leading him to a scarred, upright post, the battle became furious.

But the guards had been chosen carefully to be almost his equal in size. Dennis saw his old nemesis, Sergeant Gil'm, pulling a rope tied to Mishwa's neck.

Kremer motioned the scholar Hoss'k forward from his entourage.

Hoss'k bowed to the dignitaries and brought forth items to show them, one at a time. Dennis stirred when he saw that the first was his camp-watch alarm.

As the L'Toff stared at the lights on the screen, Dennis wondered what changes practice had wrought in the tiny machine since the last time he had seen it.

No doubt Hoss'k was pointing out how difficult it would now be for an enemy to approach the castle undetected.

Then he demonstrated Dennis's monocular, showing the L'Toff how to use it, pointing out various objects. When the ambassador put the scope down he was visibly shaken.

Dennis felt a slow burning rise within him—a combination of shame and deep anger. In spite of the strategy he had chosen, for very good reasons, his natural sympathies were with the L'Toff.

Dennis didn't like it one bit when Hoss'k turned and pointed directly at him. Kremer smiled and bowed slightly to his wizard. The Baron's well-rehearsed personal guard shouted Dennis's name in unison.

He scowled. If only there were some way of communicating with the L'Toff privately!

By now Mishwa Qan had been dragged to the post and tied into place. Dennis had already figured out that they planned to execute the man. He had witnessed many executions during the past week, and there was nothing at all he could do. Arth knew that as well and stood almost rock-still.

The guard, Gil'm, marched up to the overlord and bowed. Kremer drew something small from his robe and handed it to the trooper, who bowed again and turned to march back down the dais toward the prisoner.

Realization struck Dennis. "No!" he cried aloud.

Gil'm marched halfway to the target post. Mishwa Qan glared back at him, hands flexing uselessly under his bonds. The big thief shouted a challenge at Gil'm which everyone in the yard could hear, offering to take the trooper on blindfolded, with any choice of weapons.

Gil'm simply grinned. He lifted a small black shape.

Dennis felt a purple outrage. *"No!"* he screamed.

He vaulted the fence and ran toward the execution aisle, dodging one set of guards, then plowed through two more who ran to cut him off. He flattened one with a round house. Those on the dais turned to look at the commotion as one of Dennis's own guards tackled him from behind. At that moment Gil'm aimed Dennis's needler and pulled the trigger.

In the confusion only a few people were actually looking at the prisoner when the burst of tiny metal needles struck at hypersonic velocity. But everyone heard the explosion. Dennis heard Arth's astonished gasp.

Fighting partway free of a pile of guardsmen, Dennis struggled up far enough to see a bloody stump where the target post had been sheared in half. Beyond that lay a gaping hole in the wooden wall.

The needler had, indeed, been getting practice. Gil'm grinned and held the weapon up to the sun.

A wave of revulsion and shame overwhelmed Dennis. He snarled and flailed at those around him, biting at one hand that grabbed near his face. Then a heavy object struck him from behind and turned off the lights.

7

Linnora stared at the little creatures that arranged themselves in such orderly rows on the face of the little box. At the far right they shifted and reformed with great rapidity, hopping into new positions almost faster than she could follow with her eyes. The group next to the left shifted their formations more slowly, and so on. At the far left, the tiny bugs were patient, and seemed to take about half a day to make their next move.

The little box wasn't much more than four times the size of the first digit of her thumb. On each side it had two straps, one of which ended in little metal pieces whose purpose she had yet to divine.

Hesitantly, Linnora tried pressing a few of the many little nubs that protruded from the half of the box where no bugs danced. The bugs hopped into new patterns every time she touched one of the nubs.

A part of her wanted to laugh at the antics the little creatures went through—there was an urge to play and make them dance some more.

No. She put the little box down and withdrew her hand. She would not experiment with living things. Not without knowing what she was doing and having a clear idea of her purpose. That was one of the oldest credos of the Old Belief, handed down from parent to child from the earliest days of the L'Toff.

Only a deep conviction that they needed to be within the box to survive kept Linnora from breaking it to set the little slaves free.

That and a lingering uncertainty that they really *were* slaves.

The ordered patterns had a *feeling* to them . . . not joy exactly, but *pride,* perhaps. She sensed that very much had gone into the *making* of the little box and its tiny occupants. There was more complexity here than she had ever encountered before one month ago.

If only I could know for certain, she sighed silently.

Deacon Hoss'k had made such a consistent and logical case! The wizard's people must have used ruthless means to accomplish such wonders . . . especially to freeze the state of practice in each of these amazing tools. The lives of many of the equivalent of the L'Toff in Dennis Nuel's homeland must have been sacrificed so these things would remain in unchanged perfection.

Or must they? Linnora shook her head, confused.

Could the whole logic of making and practicing be different somewhere else?

Once upon a time it had not been the same here on Tatir, according to the Old Belief. In ancient days, before the fall, it was *life* that had been perfectible, and tools had no powers at all.

That was what the stories said.

Resting her elbows on the dressing table, she let her face fall into her hands. Hope had been fragile since that day when Hoss'k's men boiled out of the forest near the wizard's mysterious little house. Now, with Kremer pressing his demands harder than ever, with the L'Toff searchers come and gone without contact, she felt more desperate than ever.

If only there were a way to believe in the wizard! If only he were the kind of man she had originally felt him to be, instead of serving Kremer and living high—in his plush new rooms with his pretty serving wench —proving himself a complacent syncophant to Kremer's rising star like all the others!

She wiped her eyes, determined not to weep again. On the table before her the little bugs continued their mysterious dance, whirling on the right, shifting slowly on the left. Marking time.

8

Dennis woke up feeling as if his body had been used to *practice* baseball bats. The first few times he tried to move, he only managed to rock from side to side a bit. He hurt all over.

At last he succeeded in rolling to one side and got his eyes blearily open.

Well, he wasn't in the luxurious quarters he had been assigned before. Still, he wasn't in the dungeon either. The room had the rough-hewn, half-finished look of the newer, higher parts of the castle.

Guards stood by the door—two of Kremer's northland clansmen. When they saw that he had awakened, one of them stepped out into the hall and spoke a few words.

Dennis sat up in the cot, groaning aloud just a little at the twinges. His throat was sore and dry, so he reached over to the rickety bedstand to pour himself a cup of water from an earthenware jar. His cut lip stung as he drank.

He put down the cup and settled back against the rough pillow, watching the clansmen watch him. He said nothing to the guards and expected no words from them.

His status had declined, apparently.

There were heavy bootsteps in the hallway. Then the door was flung back. Baron Kremer stepped over the threshold.

Dennis had to blink at the brilliance of the man's clothing in the sunlight that streamed behind him. Kremer regarded Dennis silently, his dark eyes in shadow below heavy brows.

"Wizard," he said at last, "what am I going to do with you?"

Dennis sipped again from the cup. He licked his stinging lips gingerly.

"Uh, that's a real toughie, your Lordship. Let's see, though. I think I might have an idea.

"How about this? You're going to help me and my friends, in utter sincerity and to the best of your ability, to return to our homes in good health, both mental and physical?"

Kremer's slow smile was not particularly appreciative.

"That *is* a thought, Wizard. On the other hand, it occurs to me that the palace torturer has been complaining that his spare tools are getting out of practice. Only the main set has had any work the past month or so. Remedying that situation seems equally appealing."

"You face a quandary," Dennis sympathized.

"It *is* a difficult choice." The Baron shook his head.

"I am certain you'll work something out, though."

"Are you, really? Ah! Such confidence from a wizard is inspiring. Still, the two options do seem mutually contradictory. I was wondering if you might be able to suggest a compromise solution. Just a hint, mind you."

Dennis nodded. "A *compromise*. Hmm." He scratched his stubble. "How about something midway in between, like me doing your bidding quickly and cheerfully, giving you whatever you desire, in return for which you will keep me in a moderate level of comfort, and string me along with minor rewards and vague promises of eventual freedom and power?"

Kremer smiled. "An amazing solution! No wonder they call you a wizard."

Dennis shrugged modestly. "Oh, it was nothing, really."

The Baron cracked his knuckles. "Then it is settled. You have two more days to complete the *making* of your beverage 'distillery' and to teach my servants to practice it. Then you shall begin work on something of more immediate practical value, such as more of the beautiful long-range killing weapons. If, as you claim, the animals needed to drive such devices are lacking in my realm, I shall require that you come up with something else of military value.

"Is our *compromise* clear, then?"

Dennis nodded. He was thinking, and he had had enough of bantered wisecracks for now. They hadn't really helped all that much, anyway.

"One more thing, Wizard. Should you ever again embarrass me in front of outsiders, or attempt to thwart me in any way, you will find my torturers have planned something special for you. There will be no repeat of yesterday's unfortunate demonstration. Am I understood?"

Dennis said nothing. He looked at the tall blond man in the resplendent costume, and nodded, barely.

The Baron acknowledged with a possessive smile. "You will be happy here, Dennis Nuel," he promised. "Eventually—perhaps soon, if you behave well—we will improve your quarters again. Then you and I can talk as gentlemen once more. I would be interested in learning how your people persuade *their* recalcitrant L'Toff to become pliant. Perhaps Princess Linnora can be a test case."

He grinned, then turned and left. The door closed, leaving Dennis alone with a single guard. For a long time there was silence; only the distant shouts of drilling troops carried up from far below.

The Earthman sat on his cot. He could almost imagine it perceptibly changing, minute by minute, into a better and better bed as he lay in it.

Logically, his options were still the same, only put off a little. In a year or two of feeding Kremer wonders he felt sure he could gain the man's trust and gratitude, especially if he invented gunpowder for him, ensuring his conquest of all Coylia.

Dennis shook his head, making up his mind. He hadn't thought about it much before, but there were few worse criminals on any world than the engineer who blithely and knowingly hands over to a tyrant the tools of oppression. Come plague or ruin, he wasn't going to give Kremer gunpowder, or the wheel, or the secret of metal smelting, or anything else he could use to make war.

What options did that leave, then?

Only escape. Somehow he had to get out of here again.

9

Hot iron pincers closed upon his thumbs. A steaming stench rose where the flesh shriveled back, rolling away on black, curling ash.

Dennis moaned. He felt a wet splash against his face and he opened his eyes, breathing hard.

Arth looked down at him worriedly. "You were dreamin', Dennizz. It must've been a bad one. Are you all right now?"

Dennis nodded. He had been taking a nap near their work area after supper. It was twilight already, out in the shadow of the castle.

"Yeah," he muttered, "I'm okay." He got up and dried his face on a towel. He still felt shaken from the dream.

"I just got back from the jailyard," Arth told him. "I said I wanted to go and personally pick the guys to run the new still."

Dennis nodded. "Did you find out anything?"

Arth shook his head. "Nobody's seen Stivyung or Gath or Maggin or any more of my boys, so they don't seem to've been caught."

Dennis was glad. Perhaps Stivyung would eventually be reunited with his wife and son. The news helped lift his spirits a little.

"So what's the plan now?" Arth asked, too low to be overheard by the guards. "Do we try to make another *balloon?* Or do you have somethin' else in mind, like that *saw* that can break through walls?"

After the execution of his friend, Arth was no longer tempted by life within the castle walls. All he wanted was to get away from here, to see his wife again, and to hurt Baron Kremer as badly as possible. The thief looked to the Earthman with complete confidence.

Dennis wished he could share the feeling.

As twilight fell, a squad of soldiers climbed a pedestal in the court-yard where Dennis's needler was kept during the day. When not being practiced or stored for the night, it was exposed to sunlight, always surrounded by at least six guards.

Dennis had run through a few calculations. Clearly the needler was approaching the theoretical limit of capability for that type of weapon. No matter how efficient it became, it could only throw slivers of metal with the amount of energy it could absorb through a five-square-centimeter solar collector.

That gave Dennis one more reason to get out of here. Kremer had talked of using the needler to blast down the walls of cities. Dennis didn't want to be around when the Baron found out the deadly little weapon could be practiced only so far.

He watched the guards cautiously remove the needler from its little solarium. No. The device was guarded much too closely. He clearly wasn't going to be able to reclaim his property and blast his way to freedom. There would have to be another way.

He had considered building a wheeled cart and practicing it into an armored car. Theoretically, it should be possible. But it could take months or years, at the rate things normally improved here. It just wasn't feasible under the circumstances.

As dusk settled, the watch kites were pulled in. The Baron's glider corps had already swooped down from their training flights for the night.

Dennis thought again about those glider sheds. They were lightly guarded. It took long training to learn to fly one of the gossamer-winged things, and Baron Kremer apparently assumed he controlled the only corps of qualified pilots in the world.

He was right. Dennis had never flown even a fixed-wing glider, not to mention one of these kite things. But he had taken a few private flying lessons in single-engined prop planes. He had always intended to go back and get his license.

The two kinds of flying couldn't be that different, could they?

Anyway, he had seen lots of movies and talked to hang-glider pilots about how it was done. And he had taken courses in the physics of aerodynamics. The principles seemed simple enough.

"Have you managed to pick a way in and out of your room yet?" he asked Arth.

"Of course." The small thief sniffed. "They bolt th' door, but you can't keep a fellow like me in a room that hasn't been practiced as a jail."

"Especially with the help of a little slippery oil."

Arth shrugged. They had been careful to collect the stuff when nobody was looking, so they only had a little. Still, just a little bit of the perfect lubricant could go a long way.

"I can get about the cruder parts of th' castle pretty well after dark. The hard part's the outer walls, where they've got dogs, an' sniffer beasts, an' lights and guards by the dozens. I could pilfer half the stuff in Kremer's banquet room if I knew I could get off the castle-mount with it."

"Do you think you could snatch one of those?" Dennis nodded toward the shed where they had watched the pilots carefully fold their machines earlier.

Arth looked at Dennis nervously. "Uh, I dunno. Those gliders are kinda bulky. . . ." He bit his lower lip. "Your question's just . . . uh, hypothetical." He carefully spoke the word Dennis had taught him. "Isn' it? It doesn' have nothin' to do with your idea on how to escape from here, does it?"

"It does, Arth."

Arth shuddered. "I was afraid you'd say that. Dennizz, do you know how many men Kremer lost before they learned to handle those things? They *still* lose nearly half their new pilots. Can you actually fly one?"

Dennis needed Arth's help. To get it he would have to inspire faith. "What do you think?" he asked confidently.

Arth smiled slightly, tentatively. "Yeah, sure. I guess only an idiot would try to take off in one of those things, in th' dark, without knowin' what he's doin'. I'm sorry, Dennizz."

Dennis managed not to wince visibly at his friend's way of putting it. He clasped Arth's shoulder. "Right. Now, do you think you'll be able to hide the glider until we need it? Kremer's people don't seem to understand inventory control, but they may miss it anyway."

"No problem." Arth grinned. "My room's stuffed with heaps of cloth and lumber for our 'experiments.' The servants've got orders to give us any junk we want, whatever's not sharp or made of metal. I can hide it in there easy."

"Will you want me to help in the heist?"

Arth shivered. "Uh, no, Dennizz. Some things are best left to experts. You walk like a bull rickel tha's lookin' for a female under a house. No offense, but I'll do it m'self. Don't you worry about a thing."

"All right, then." Dennis looked at the settling twilight. "Maybe you'd better retire a bit early this evening, Arth. You look pretty tired."

"Huh? But it's only . . . oh." Arth nodded. "You want me to do it tonight." He shrugged. "Ah, well, why not? That means we make th' break tomorrow night?"

"Or the night after." Dennis was under a time limit. Kremer would not be stalled much longer.

"Okay." Arth had picked up the expression from Dennis. The little thief yawned exaggeratedly for the benefit of the guards. He spoke out loud. "Well, I think I'll work on improvin' my cot for a while!" He nudged Dennis with his elbow and winked. "See you in the mornin', boss!" Then he added under his breath, "I hope."

"Good luck," Dennis said softly as Arth walked away, followed by his guard. Dennis felt bad asking him to risk his neck like this. But the fellow knew his job and would do it cheerfully. Dennis counted himself lucky to have him as his friend.

Nearby, a small stream of pungent liquor had begun to drip from the end of the condenser. If that kept up, the crew's main job would be simply to watch and practice the distillery as a unit. The hard part was teaching them to change the wine mix properly.

Dennis found his thoughts drifting several parapets higher. Now that he was committed to trying an escape soon, he would have to settle his feelings about Princess Linnora.

If he was really serious about doing something for her, somehow during the next twenty-four hours he would have to get in touch with her, somehow regain her trust, and find a way to get her away from her guards for a rendezvous with the glider at the castle peak.

It sounded next to impossible.

He only hoped that she would give him a chance to explain if the time ever came.

The distillery crew huddled around the condenser, watching the slow drip-dripping of brandy into a flask.

Dennis caught some brandy on his fingers and shuddered as he sniffed, wishing nostalgically for the bottle of thirty-year-old Johnny Walker Swing that presumably still sat in his closet back at Sahara Tech.

He popped a few drops into his mouth and then sucked air. The stuff *did* have a bite to it, he had to admit.

The evening shift of practicers arrived to relieve the day crew. It was time to change the pot anyway, so he ran the Coylian prisoners through the routine several times to make sure they had it down right.

By the time they had finished, the stars were coming out. He made sure all was in order, then picked up his cloak from the railing. "I want to stretch my legs," he told his guards.

The northmen bowed slightly and followed behind. Although his privileges had been sharply reduced, he was still at least officially a quasiguest . . . and a wizard. He had freedom of the yard so long as he was accompanied.

He strolled the long way, past the glider sheds and then the main gate. As he neared the section of the castle where the L'Toff Princess had her rooms, his doubts returned. Every parapet was rimmed with sharp stakes, practiced every day by teams of soldiers armed with slabs of meat. To land a glider upon one and take off again would be as impossible as climbing those sheer walls appeared to be.

Should he take an already risky plan and reduce its chance to negligible by trying to free Linnora as well? Would that be fair to Arth?

Dennis rounded a corner and felt his pulse rise. In the light from the flickering wall cressets, he saw a slim girl dressed in white holding onto the bars three levels up. The L'Toff Princess stared into the starry night, the breeze tugging at her filmy gown. As Dennis approached, his guards keeping a steady five paces behind, he saw the girl turn. Someone else had come out onto her balcony.

Dennis bent in the shadows to tie the laces of his boots, and he looked up as casually as he could. He saw Baron Kremer come forth and confront Linnora. She looked terribly small before him.

The warlord spoke to her and she shook her head in reply. She tried to turn away, but he grabbed her arm and spoke again, more sharply. Dennis still couldn't make out what was being said, but he could catch the tone.

Linnora struggled, but Kremer only laughed and pulled her close, holding her against his broad chest in spite of her resistance.

One of the guards behind Dennis made a rough joke. Obviously they thought their Lord was giving the haughty tribeswoman only what she had coming.

Dennis felt under his waistband. Four carefully selected smooth stones made a lump there. He hadn't had any opportunity to *practice* his crude weapon. It would only be as good as he had *made* it. All told, it was not much better a makeshift sling than the cummerbund he had used for the same purpose at that last Sahara Tech party.

Still, he could probably get one or two stones off before the guards brought him down. And Kremer was a big target.

If I were one of Shakespeare's characters I'd consider it worthwhile to die for a lady's virginity, he thought. *Or at least her honor.*

Dennis's shoulders sagged. Most of Shakespeare's characters had been poetic idiots. Even if he succeeded in striking down Kremer, it would only buy Linnora a respite. At the cost of his own life.

It wasn't worth it. Not when he might be able to get her out of here tomorrow if he were patient. He was willing to *risk* his life for her, but he would not throw it away uselessly.

There was the sound of ripping cloth.

He turned away so he wouldn't have to witness it. At least by forcing the guards to follow him, he could spare the girl an audience to her humiliation. He walked away quickly, shoulders hunched. The guards chuckled as they followed.

He got ten paces, then a hint of motion in the sky caught his eye.

Dennis stopped. He looked to the south.

Something in the southern sky was blocking a small patch of stars. It moved in the night, faster than a cloud and more regular in outline, growing larger as it came closer. He squinted, but with his night vision ruined by the tower torches, he couldn't make it out.

Then a smile came unexpectedly. Could it be . . . ?

At the southern edge of the encampment there was a sudden outcry, then a clamor of anxious shouts. Men came running out of the barracks, struggling into armor as an alarm bell began to clang.

Out of the night gloom, into the light of the tower torches, a giant round shape suddenly loomed. It had two great eyes that shimmered and glared angrily. At the bottom of the huge, looming face was a great maw. A fire burned within.

"Ha-ha!" Dennis jumped and struck at the air with his fist. "Kremer *didn't* catch the others! They *practiced* it, and it flies! It really flies!"

A giant globe of fabric and hot air hissed and bobbed over the outer wall, slowly gaining altitude. In a wickerwork gondola below the globe, the dim shapes of his friends were vague shadows against the flames.

Still, something seemed to be wrong with the balloon. It wasn't rising as fast as Dennis would have hoped. And worse luck, it was headed right for Kremer's castle! It looked like it would barely clear the palace peak!

"Come on, guys," he muttered while his guards pointed fearfully, their eyes outlined white in fear. "Up! Rise up and get *out* of here!" Dennis stared hard at the balloon, practicing it at climbing.

And it did seem to rise faster now, gaining slowly. Tiny faces peered from the gondola down into the courtyard below. A few soldiers threw spears and stones but none quite reached the majestic, silent craft.

Dennis turned to see how Kremer was taking this. It would be great for something to stick in the tyrant's imperturbable craw.

The Baron had let go of Linnora, who huddled against the wall, rubbing her bruised arms and weeping silently.

But unlike his men, Kremer did not appear frightened at all. Instead, a smile spread across his lips as he reached into his tunic.

"Oh," Dennis said, realizing. "Oh, no you don't, you son-of-a-bitch."

He hurriedly unraveled his waistband as his guards cowered underneath the glowering shadow of the balloon. There was a thumping sound as two bags of sand exploded into spray nearby, sending men fleeing.

Dennis's carefully selected stones popped into his hand. He ran toward the first parapet, stretching out his sash and praying he would be in time.

Kremer was savoring the moment, bless him, letting the crude aerostat approach as he fondled the Earthmade needler. Dennis measured out a length of waistband, dropped a stone into the fold, and began swinging the makeshift sling over his head.

Except for that evening at S.I.T., he hadn't used a sling much since his Boy Scout days. If only he had been able to practice!

Kremer raised the needler and languidly aimed it at the great balloon just as Dennis cast loose.

The stone struck a parapet spike just in front of the Baron and ricocheted noisily into the night. Kremer jumped back in surprise. He looked about for a second, then saw Dennis in the lighted courtyard below, struggling to ready another stone.

Kremer grinned and aimed downward, at the Earthman. Dennis knew, in that telescoped moment, that there wasn't time to get off another stone. He had barely begun his second swing when Kremer fired.

A hail of deadly slivers tore up the ground a few meters to Dennis's right. Dennis blinked in surprise as he found himself alive. The reason was readily apparent. A small storm of blond hair and fingernails had struck the Baron, spoiling his aim a second time.

A little amazed but not yet counting his luck, Dennis swung the sling, looking for a clear shot. But now Linnora was in the way. The Princess was all over her captor, struggling to take the handgun from him.

Dennis's arm was beginning to tire. If only she'd move aside now!

The balloon was directly overhead and moving fast. All the aeronauts needed was maybe another half minute to get away. . . .

Kremer got a grip on Linnora's arm and flung her down. There were scratch marks on his face, and at last he looked perturbed. Kremer cast Dennis a look that seemed to say his turn would come, and he lifted the needler to bear on the balloon.

Dennis's guards must have caught on at last. He finished swinging even as he heard them running toward him. He felt a *rightness* as he let go of the second stone just in time.

The stone struck Kremer's left temple at the same moment as the balloon reached the zenith, and several hundred pounds of guard tackled Dennis from behind.

As the ground came up to meet him, Dennis thought, *I've got to stop meeting people like this.*

8

"Eurekaarrgh"

1

It was getting monotonous, this waking up not knowing where you were, feeling like something dragged in from a refuse heap.

He could tell without even opening his eyes that he was back in the dungeon again. Sharp bits of straw stabbed his naked back, thwarted only where bandages covered his worst cuts and bruises.

Still, someone in authority apparently had decided to keep him alive for the present. That was something.

Strangely, in spite of the greater severity of his welts—and they seemed really to have worked him over this time—Dennis felt better than he had on the other occasions when he had been beaten up here on Tatir. This time, at least, he had gotten his own licks in. The brief memory of Baron Kremer tipping over like a fallen tree seemed to lessen the pain.

He shivered and sat up slowly, wincing, and gingerly examined himself until he was fairly certain nothing had been permanently damaged.

Yet, he reminded himself.

From somewhere down the dank hallway he heard a faint "thunking" sound . . . like someone chopping something with a sharp object. Perhaps the headsman was practicing his ax.

Time passed, measurable only by his sparse meals, by his thoughts, and by punctuated screams from some poor devil down the hall.

Dennis passed some of the time wondering at his bandages, which seemed never to need changing. They breathed easily, remained clean, and were comfortable to wear. Of course, he realized, they were probably well practiced. No doubt the baron gave his people free emergency care during peacetime so the medicinal supplies would be up to par when war came along. Here in the castle the dispensary would have dressings hundreds of years old.

It was a peculiar thought.

Bandages were among the things he would bring home to Earth if he ever got the chance—not gemstone tools, or works of art that would presumably only decay once they were released from the field of the Practice Effect, but things whose properties could be analyzed and then duplicated by the *making* wizards of Earth.

In the dark hours he made lists of things to take back. To help pass the time, he rehearsed the report he would give to the dubious folks back home.

He concluded that even if he ever did escape this place, and somehow managed to fix the zievatron and get home, he had better bring back some pretty convincing novelties. Otherwise nobody would ever believe him.

They fed him a thin gruel at infrequent intervals. Dennis lost all track of time. For a day or so the screams from down the hall ceased. Then some unfortunate new victim seemed to have been recruited to practice certain specialized tools.

Dennis tried to do anomaly calculations in his head. He brought up long-untended memories of home. He listened hard for anything to relieve the monotony.

Once he heard the jailers talking excitedly out in the corridor.

". . . first here, then high in the tower, then out in the yard, and now down here again! And nobody knows what it is!"

"It's a *monster* is what 'tis!" the other retorted. "It's the spawn of that great demon who struck down the Baron four nights ago. I tell you it's unlucky to keep wizards and L'Toff under a roof! I can't wait 'til the Baron's recovered and makes a judgment. . . ."

The voices passed down the hallway.

Dennis got up to grab the bars in his door's tiny window. "Guard!" he called. "Guard! Did you say Kremer lives?"

The jailers had answered none of his questions before, but this pair sounded different. Perhaps they had just been rotated down to the dungeon.

They looked at each other in the flickering light from a wall cresset. One of the jailers shrugged and gave Dennis a snaggle-toothed grin. "Yeah, Wizard. No thanks to that demon you conjured up to drop rocks on his Lordship. Baron Kremer should be up an' aroun' in a few days. 'Til then Lord Hern's in charge."

Dennis nodded. So. He had figured that these cavemen never even invented the sling. It was a miracle they had bows and arrows. Probably no one but Kremer himself knew exactly what Dennis had done.

Everyone else quite correctly blamed him for the Baron's condition, but for the wrong reason, thinking he had managed it by metaphysical means. They wouldn't do anything further to him until Kremer was ready to choose an appropriate fate himself.

Dennis didn't doubt it would include a protracted visit to the technicians down the hall.

He scratched his stubble and asked the guards if he could have a razor in order to shave.

They grinned at each other as if they had read his mind. "Naw, Wizard," the snaggle-toothed one said, grinning. "Even Lord Hern don't forgive incomp'tents who let a prisoner take the easy way out."

The other jailer smiled. "Tell ya' what, though. We'll letcha have some *brandy*"—he said the word with hushed reverence—"if you'll promise to keep us safe from those devil-spawned critters you've let loose around here. I got a friend on the *still* detail, an' he sneaks me some." He held up a flask that sloshed.

Dennis shrugged as the man poured a cupful and passed it between the bars. He hadn't the slightest idea what the fellow was talking about. Devil-spawned? Critters? It sounded like a load of superstitious nonsense.

He took a swallow of the wonderfully vile liquor. After the fire had settled warmly into his stomach, he asked the guards about Arth.

They told him the little thief had been placed in charge of the distillery. Dennis suspected Arth had actually bribed the guard to pass the entire flask on to him.

Another swallow of the horrible stuff made him cough. But he swore he'd make it up to Arth someday.

The jailers knew nothing of Linnora. Mention of the L'Toff Princess made them nervous. They made small warding motions with their hands and claimed pressing duties elsewhere.

Dennis sighed and returned to the straw pallet. At least the spot where he lay was getting slowly more comfortable. It had to.

He tried practicing a small stone into a chisel, to pry apart the stones of his cell. But he knew he was really only practicing the dungeon itself. The pebble wasn't anywhere near as good at chiseling as the wall was at being a wall. No doubt it was an old story on this world. Unless he came up with something unusual, a prisoner was stalemated.

2

He awakened suddenly from a dream about monsters.

There was a feathery touch of vague horror to the images that clung to Dennis's mind as he blinked in the darkness . . . scrabbling shapes and sharp, ominous claws. For a long time after waking, he felt filled with a heavy lethargy.

In the dark silence he thought he heard something. Then, for a time, he dismissed the faint scratching sound as a lingering remnant of his nightmare.

Then it changed and became a soft hissing.

Dennis shook his head to free it of mental cobwebs. He turned in the gloom and then blinked. A fiery spark had appeared at one corner of the door to his cell, a bright speck in the almost total blackness.

The spark climbed slowly, leaving a glowing line behind it, until it reached a height of about two feet. Then the hot glow jogged right. Faint light from the hallway shone through the charred trail the flame left behind.

Dennis backed away, suddenly remembering what the jailers had said about "devil-spawned critters" loose in the castle. They had blamed him, but Dennis knew he had nothing to do with demons. Something was cutting its way into the cell, and it was not of his liking!

The burned trail turned another right angle, descending at an even pace toward the floor. Dennis clutched his sharpened stone as the wooden segment finally fell away, leaving an opening in the door just above the floor.

Dennis tried to call out, to summon the guards—*anybody*—but he couldn't find his voice.

For a moment the new opening was dark and empty. Then two gleaming red eyes appeared in the smoking opening—eyes larger than ought to belong to any living thing. They shone at him in the dimness for several heartbeats.

Then the thing that owned them moved slowly forward into the cell.

In his half-starved condition, with the catalepsy of sleep still in his muscles, Dennis felt far from ready for a fight. Against his will he closed his eyes, holding his breath as the softly chittering monster approached.

Then it stopped. He could sense it poised only a few feet away, muttering slowly to itself.

Dennis waited. Then his lungs started to burn. He couldn't hold his breath any longer. He opened one eye to look, ready for anything . . .

. . . and exhaled in a long sigh. "Oh, lord."

There, waiting patiently on the cool stones, was his long-missing Sahara Tech exploration 'bot. It sat complacently, its sensors whirring quietly, ready—at last—to follow his instructions, to report.

Even in the dim light he could tell that the thing had changed. It rode lower, sleeker, with a sly pattern of coloration on its back. It had been . . . *practiced* . . . become better at the job he had assigned it. His most recent instructions, shouted briefly several weeks ago, had been to come and report to him. No Earthly robot could have managed it. But here it was, hardly "Earthly" anymore.

The thing must have followed his trail ever since that escapade on the rooftops of Zuslik, patiently working past obstacles until it overcame them, one by one.

But how? A tool had to have a user to benefit from the Practice Effect, didn't it? Could he really be thought to have been *using* the 'bot when it was out of sight and mind?

This played havoc with the theory he had formed, that the Practice Effect was at least partly a psi power exercised by humans on this world.

Then he remembered. The last time he had seen the robot it *had* been accompanied by a living thing—someone who loved to watch tools being used, the more complicated the better.

"Come on in, Pix," he whispered. "All is forgiven."

Two bright green eyes appeared in the little gap in the door. They blinked, then were joined by a Cheshire grin of needle-sharp teeth.

The little animal launched itself into a short glide and landed on Dennis's lap. It purred and snuggled as if it had left him only hours ago.

Dennis sat there, stroking the little creature's fur and listening to the quiet hum of the robot. Unexpectedly, tears welled. Hope seemed to fill him suddenly. After so long alone in the dark, to have companions and allies again . . . for a few minutes it was too good to be endured.

In the corridor outside, he found one of the jailers sprawled unconscious next to a bench. Dennis stripped the man of his clothes and left him inside his own cell, bound and gagged. He propped the rectangular piece of doorway into place. It was crude, but it was all he could do.

There was a bowl of stew and a slab of bread by the guard's bench. Dennis wolfed them down while he hurried into the jailer's clothes; they were too tight around the shoulders for him and too wide around the girth. When he finished, the pixolet took its old place on his shoulder, grinning at everything.

The robot had originally been equipped with a small stunner to acquire specimens of animal life. Apparently it had improved the device through practice and now was capable of knocking out anyone who stood between it and its job. Undoubtedly that ability would come in handy during the hour ahead.

Dennis knelt and spoke clearly and carefully to the machine.

"New instructions. Take note." The 'bot hummed and clicked in response.

"You are to accompany me now, and zap unconscious anyone I point at like this."

He demonstrated, cocking his thumb and miming a pistol firing. It was a pretty complicated concept, but he was wagering the machine had grown sophisticated enough to comprehend.

"Indicate if you understand and are capable of carrying out this function."

The green assent light on the machine's turret winked. So far so good.

"Secondary orders. Should we become separated, you are to preserve your existence and make every effort to discover my whereabouts again and report."

Again the light flashed.

"Finally," he whispered, "should you find that I am dead, or in any event after three months, you will go back to the zievatron and await anyone from Earth. Should such a person arrive, report what you've observed."

The robot assented. Then across its tiny display screen came a request to begin its encyclopedic report on the denizens of Tatir. The 'bot seemed quite anxious to discharge its duty.

"Not yet," Dennis said. "First we have to get out of here. I've got friends to rescue. Or at least one friend—and someone else I'd very much like to have as my friend. . . ."

He realized he was babbling. Hope was a mixed blessing. He found he was capable of being afraid once more.

"Okay, then. Everybody ready?" His two little companions didn't look like awfully formidable allies in an assault on a fortress. The pixolet would likely desert upon the first sign of danger, anyway.

He straightened his guard's uniform and pulled the cap down low, then set off with his strange crew.

He didn't even have to help the robot with the stairs. The thing was, indeed, a marvel.

I must get it home to Earth when all this is over and find out what's happened to it! he thought.

Princess Linnora had little choice but to use some of the beautiful things in her room.

She sat before the ancient vanity table and looked at her reflection in the centuries-old mirror. She didn't want to help practice her captor's property, but there was so little else to do, trapped alone in the elegant room. She found that brushing her hair helped to pass the time.

At first she had tried to give Kremer nothing, not even the benefit of her good taste. She refused to pay attention to her environment, lest her appreciation of subtleness and beauty help make Kremer's palace a little nicer for him.

The room had formerly been occupied by one of Kremer's mistresses. The peasant girl's tastes had made a heavy impression on the furnishings. After the first month of her captivity, Linnora had had enough of the bright, garish colors and flashy decorations. She took down the worst and began concentrating on her own image of the room.

It had been a subtle sort of setback, using some small fraction of her powers to make her imprisonment a little more tolerable. Kremer obviously intended to break her down a little at a time. And Linnora wasn't at all certain she could prevent it. His will was strong, and he had her life in his hands.

She picked up the lovely antique brush and stroked her hair, watching her reflection in the mirror, trying to imagine a way to stay out of Kremer's bed once he recovered, or to prevent being used as a hostage against her own people.

She concentrated on seeing Truth in the mirror. It was a form of fighting back. The next person to look into the mirror would see more than just flattering images of themselves.

She looked at a young woman who had made mistakes. From that day when she had gone off riding on her own, far from her brother Proll, in search of the strangeness she had felt come into the world—from that day when she was captured by the Baron's men at the small metal house in the forest—she had committed errors.

She recalled how Dennis Nuel had looked at her, those days after the banquet and before the sky monster appeared. She had been convinced by Deacon Hoss'k's logic that the wizard could only be an evil man. But might other logic than the obvious apply to someone from so very far away?

What if there were other ways to create the alien essences than the trapping into them of life forces?

Could an evil man have been so gallant, fighting her enemy when her need was greatest?

On the night of the sky monster, the wizard had done battle with Kremer. Linnora was still confused over what had happened. Had Dennis Nuel conjured up the great glowing air-beast on seeing Kremer attack her? She wanted to believe it was so, but then why had he been forced to throw stones to bring Kremer down at last? And why did the monster fly away then, leaving its master to be overcome?

She put down the hairbrush, shaking her head at her reflection in the mirror. She would probably never learn the answers. Her guards had said the wizard was as good as dead in the Baron's dungeon.

She picked up her klasmodion and plucked its strings idly, letting the soft notes come one at a time and in no particular order. She didn't feel much like singing.

There was a tension in the evening quiet of the palace, as if something strong was about to happen. She felt a sense of danger in the night, and it was intensifying! She stopped playing, her senses suddenly alert.

From outside her door came a strange, high-pitched sound. Then something fell with a thump in the hallway. Linnora stood. She laid down the instrument and picked up her hairbrush, the only thing handy that was heavy enough to serve as a weapon.

There came a faint knock at her door. Linnora edged back into the shadows. There was something familiar in the presence in the hallway, like that faint feeling she had had a week ago that had seemed to say that Proll had briefly been nearby.

There was also something out there so alien that just the hint of it made her shiver.

"Who is it?" She tried to keep her voice steady and regal. It came out sounding merely young. "Who is there?"

A voice in the hallway whispered hoarsely, "It's Dennis Nuel, Princess! I've come to offer you a chance to get away from here, if you're interested. But we've got to hurry!"

Linnora ran to the door and opened it.

The aroma of unbathed male was almost overwhelming. Filthy, bruised, and unkempt, Dennis Nuel smiled, holding the bunched waist of an oversized guard's uniform.

It was more than enough to surprise a girl. But Linnora gasped when she saw the thing in the hallway behind him.

The hairbrush fell clattering to the floor as she fainted.

Well, Dennis thought as he rushed forward to keep her from falling, *a guy could get a less flattering reception. I wish I could be sure it was gratitude that's overcome her, and not BO.*

He knew he must be a treat for the senses. His bruises were a still brilliant shade of purple, and he hadn't bathed in two weeks.

Behind him the Sahara Tech 'bot poked at the fallen guards. While it awaited further orders it proceeded with its second priority and took tiny blood samples from the unconscious soldiers for comparison purposes.

Fainting princesses were fine—in storybooks. But slender or not, Linnora felt heavy to Dennis in his weakened state. He carried the girl into the room and laid her on the bed.

"Princess! Linnora! Wake up! Do you recognize me?"

Linnora blinked, recovering quickly. She got up on one elbow. "Yes, of course I recognize you, Wizard . . . and I'm happy to see you alive. Now would you please release my hand? You're squeezing much too hard."

Dennis hurriedly let go. He helped her sit up.

"Is escape truly possible?" Linnora asked. She assiduously avoided looking at Dennis's companion in the hallway. If it was one of *his* demons, it surely wasn't about to consume her, she assumed.

"I'm not sure," Dennis answered. "I'm on my way to the tower to find out. I stopped here to offer you a chance to come along. I don't suppose either of us has anything to lose."

Linnora managed an ironic smile. "No, we do not. One moment, then. I will be right back."

She stood and hurried quickly to a closet.

Dennis dragged the supine guards into the room. It had been a harrowing climb from the dungeons to the storerooms, to the kitchens, and beyond, constantly ducking from shadow to shadow. He and his companions had made it to the second story before being spotted. A pair of guards saw him entering a stairwell. They called and hurried after in chase.

As Dennis had expected, the pixolet deserted the moment it came to any action.

But the robot was stalwart. It waited with Dennis just inside the stairwell until the two soldiers sped through between them.

Dennis heard the second guard slump to the floor before he was half finished throttling the first into unconsciousness. He left them both bound and gagged behind the staircase, and then they hurried on.

Five minutes later he had a chance to witness the robot in action.

From the stairs he pointed pistol-like at the two guards standing watch outside Linnora's room. The little machine had sped out into the hall, faster and more quietly than Dennis would have believed possible. The guards barely had time to turn before it scuttled up to them and touched each on the leg. They groaned in brief surprise and collapsed to the floor.

Dennis was just a little in awe of what the Earth machine was becoming.

While Linnora gathered a few things, he tied up the guards. Of course, someone was sure to notice they were missing. But he couldn't just leave them in the hall.

"I'm ready," Linnora announced. "I found a cloak that might fit you." She handed him a thick, hooded garment of lustrous black material. He noted with approval that she had changed from her accustomed white into dark clothing.

"Also, this is yours, I believe. I hope I did it no harm looking at it. Its purpose is a mystery to me."

"My wrist-comp!" Dennis cried out as he took it.

The Princess watched in amazement as he put it on his arm. She had never seen a crimp clasp before.

"So that is what those little straps were for!" she said.

"I'll show you the rest of what the comp can do if we ever get out of here," Dennis promised. "Now we'd better be going. If Arth isn't still in his room in the tower, this is going to be an awfully short trip."

3

When Arth heard thumping noises outside his room, he opened the door with a cudgel in his fist, ready for anything. But he grinned broadly when he saw the young woman and the wizard standing there, an unconscious guard slumped at their feet.

Arth just about reopened Dennis's wounds, slapping him on the back. The normally quiet and taciturn thief could barely restrain himself.

"Dennizz! Come in! You too, Princess! Y'know, I *figured* you'd show up at some point. That's why I stayed here even when Lord Hern promoted me to distillery manager. Come on in an' have some brandy!"

Arth kicked the guard's limp body aside to make room for Linnora to pass. Then the little thief stopped as he spied the robot whirring quietly behind them. He gulped. The glassy eyes stared back patiently.

"Uh, is that a fren' of yours, Dennizz?" Arth spoke without taking his eyes away.

"Yes, it is, Arth." Dennis ushered Linnora inside and pulled Arth along when the man lingered to stare.

Linnora was glad to get inside, away from the glint of bright lenses. Although she had watched the robot in action in the dark hallways, helping Dennis overcome two more pairs of guards on their way here, she still glanced at the machine nervously.

She had begun wondering what kind of man kept such strange familiars. Never before had she encountered anything that reeked so of both Pr'fett *and* essence as this "robot." It felt like a thing . . . yet it moved and acted as if it were alive!

Dennis ordered the robot to keep watch outside and closed the door.

The room was a clutter of bits of wood and leather and cord—piles of lumber and rough cloth, and flimsy contraptions that would have done a kindergartner on Earth proud.

"Hey, Dennizz," Arth said, pouring three cups of brandy from a brown bottle, "I've been tryin' my hand at *makin'*, like you do! Can I show you some of my projects? I think I've figured out a real good way to trap mice, for instance."

"Umm, I don't think we have the time, Arth. The alarm should be out any time now."

Linnora coughed. Her cheeks flushed and she stared at the cup in her hand. She sniffed at the liquor, then attempted another sip.

The thief nodded. "I suppose you'll want to see the glider, then."

Dennis had been afraid to ask. "You did it! I knew you could!"

"Aw, t'wasn't no big thing." Arth reddened. "Th' slippery oil made it a snap. It's over here under this pile of rubbish. They let out quite a fuss when they found it missing. But with the Baron out of action they never got a good search together."

Dennis helped him pull the debris off. Soon a neatly folded roll of silky fabric and slender wooden struts came into view. "It's a good thing you made it up here tonight," Arth mused critically. "Another couple of weeks an' the thing would have lapsed back into being a kite. I guess you won't have any trouble flyin' it now, though."

From your mouth to my ear, Dennis thought as he helped Arth carry the heavy, two-man glider out the doorway and up to the palace roof.

Dennis had to reassemble the thing almost by himself in the moonlight. The others tried to help, but Linnora was frightened by the great, flapping wings, and Arth kept making irrelevant suggestions and needlessly urging him to hurry.

The rising wind pulled at the fabric, frequently tugging it almost out of Dennis's hands. He managed to get the glider's wings extended and was searching for the locking mechanism when the alarm finally sounded below. It began in one corner of the castle, down near the bottom story, and spread until the night was filled with a chaos of bells, shouts, and running feet.

They must have found one of the sets of guards he and the robot had knocked out.

He found the latch at last. The cloth wings, which had been flapping in the stiff breeze, suddenly snapped taut with a loud report.

From two parapets below Dennis heard worried queries. Of course Arth's guard failed to answer. Soon there were footsteps not far below.

"No time for experimentation," he muttered. "Arth! Slip into the rear saddle to anchor it down!"

The big glider bucked and hopped until Arth had settled in. Even then it would not stay still. Dennis motioned for the robot to come. He knelt, still holding the edge of one flapping wing.

"Instructions!" he told the little automaton. "Go below and delay those who are approaching until we are gone. After that, attempt to survive and follow however you can. We'll try to head west by southwest!"

The 'bot's green acceptance light flashed. It swiveled and sped away, swiftly negotiating the plank ramp they had used to climb onto the roof.

Dennis heard booted footsteps on the stairwells below this level. They didn't have much time.

Arth was in his place in the strap saddle, as Dennis had showed him. Arth looked completely confident. He had seen the "balloon" soaring through the night and knew now that Dennis could manage flying things. The distinction between a balloon and a glider was inconsequential to him.

"This is a two-man glider," Dennis said, "but you two don't weigh much more than one big man. Linnora can ride with Arth on the rear seat. All we have to do is make it out of town, anyway."

But Linnora clutched her cloak around her, staring at the great flapping wings. She looked at Dennis, all her doubts brought back at once.

I don't blame her, Dennis thought. *She's a savvy lady, but she's not prepared for this.*

All three of them could die in this attempt. Some might say that what Kremer had in store for her would be worse than death. But while one lived there was always a chance.

She held her klasmodion to her breast as the gusty wind tugged at the great kite, almost dragging Dennis and Arth along the roof. The glider was like a powerful bird, straining at a tether—eager to be airborne.

Suddenly there were thuds and dismayed shouts from the landing below. The robot was making its stand at the head of the stairs.

Dennis looked at the L'Toff Princess, and her eyes met his. He could tell she wanted to trust him. But this was all too sudden, too alien for her.

He couldn't drag her along by force. But neither could he bring himself to leave her behind.

Linnora caught sight of it first, when the small figure appeared clambering over the ledge. She gasped and stared to the left. Dennis swiveled quickly and saw a tiny face—a pair of small green eyes and two rows of grinning, sharp teeth.

"A Krenegee!" Linnora said with a sigh.

The pixolet grinned. It scrambled onto the roof, then launched itself into the breeze. With outspread wing membranes it sailed lazily to Dennis and landed on his shoulder. Tiny claws bit into his cloak and jabbed his skin underneath.

Dennis had to struggle with his skidding feet, grappling with the bucking glider, cursing the wind and the stupid, irritating creature purring by his ear.

But Arth stared with superstitious awe, and when Linnora spoke, Dennis could barely hear her over the wind.

"The Krenegee chooses whom it will—and those whom it chooses make *the world . . ."* she said.

It sounded like a litany. Perhaps the pixolet's species was some sort of totem for her people. Maybe Pix might do some good for somebody after all!

He held out his hand to Linnora, and this time she stepped forward and took it readily, as if in a daze. He guided her into the rear saddle, in front of Arth, and told the thief to hold on to her as he would his life.

There came a series of screams and loud crashes from below as another group assaulted the head of the stairs.

He felt a little guilty leaving the robot to face all that alone. It was only a machine, of course. But here on Tatir, that *only* wasn't as easy an excuse as on Earth.

The soldiers were getting organized. Dennis heard officers shouting and what had to be entire platoons trooping quickly up the stairs. It wouldn't be long now.

The wind rose again. Dennis had to fight down a wave of uncertainty as he looked out upon the rough, dimly perceived terrain. The spires of Zuslik town lurked against the hulking mountains beyond. The twisting, moonlit river glistened. Jagged outlines told of ship masts by the docks.

He looked back at his passengers. The pixolet purred and Linnora's eyes now shone with a confidence he could not understand, though it felt good.

Somewhere below, a captain with a shrill voice was haranguing his men for a charge. It was definitely time to go.

"All right," he told Arth and Linnora, "now I want you all to think *up* very hard, lean the way I lean, and jump with me when I say the magic word—'Geronimo!' "

4

The very instant they were airborne, Dennis was filled with a not unreasonable wish he could go back and try to think of something else.

"Dennizz! Watch out for that spire!"

A high tower appeared out of the darkness, directly in their path. Dennis swung his weight leftward in the hanging saddle. "Lean hard!" he shouted, hoping Arth and Linnora would try to mimic his actions.

The glider tipped slowly. The top story of one of Zuslik's higher buildings passed a scant two meters to their right. Through a brightly lit window Dennis glimpsed a scene of merriment. Some sort of celebration was in progress. There was a brief sound of high laughter. None of the partiers noticed a dark, swift shape whistle past their window.

Dennis fought to realign the glider. The bank had dropped them into a layer of turbulence. The craft bucked and fluttered as it followed the hillside down to the city proper.

Behind them the castle was in an uproar. Searchlamps cast sharp beams from every peak and parapet. Dennis didn't dare look back, but he did hope the robot had managed to scuttle away at the end.

Zuslik's wedding cake towers passed swiftly below them. The outer wall of the town lay less than a mile ahead, and beyond it the river. They were still losing altitude. It would be close.

Behind him Dennis could hear Arth's teeth chattering. But Linnora's grip on his waist was firm. Good girl. She wasn't even trembling!

The glider surged as they passed through a pocket of warm air rising from a chimney. By the time Dennis regained control the town's outer wall was coming toward them fast.

"Come on!" he urged the glider. "Come on, baby! Lift!"

He was talking to his craft, as almost every other pilot had. But in this case the entreaties might actually do some good. Any additional practice the glider got couldn't hurt.

The pixolet gripped his shoulder with its front claws and spread its wing membranes wide so its hind legs trailed behind. Was the darned thing actually trying to *help* for a change? It grinned, watching Dennis's every move as the neophyte glider pilot threaded the higher towers toward the wall.

Hey! I'm not so bad at this! Dennis thought, grinning as the glider swooped around the steeple of a Coylian temple. *A fellow could get to enjoy this.*

A minute later he changed his mind. *We're not going to make it.*

Zuslik was a maze of twisting streets and pointed structures. In the darkness there was no way he could pilot the glider to a safe landing down there. He had brought them all to this predicament. Now it looked as if only the pixolet, with its built-in parachute, would escape catastrophe.

Suddenly the streets opened up, and the city wall loomed. It was at least a couple hundred yards ahead and now only a few meters below, waiting to flick them out of the air.

He glanced at Arth and Linnora. The little thief grinned back. In his adrenaline rush he looked like he was having the time of his life, totally confident in Dennis's magical abilities.

Linnora's eyes were closed, a peaceful expression on her face as she whispered quietly. Though her face was hardly a foot from his own, Dennis could not make out the words over the rushing wind.

Her chant seemed to resonate with the purring of the tiny animal on Dennis's shoulder. For an instant she opened her eyes. She smiled at Dennis happily.

The pixolet purred louder.

Dennis piloted the glider past the last obstacle, and the stretch before the wall was ahead.

"Come on!" he urged the flying machine.

The ground swept past. Linnora's chant and Pixolet's purring seemed to meld with Dennis's concentration. Reality seemed to shimmer around him. The struts and cables shuddered with a faint, musical thrill, almost as if the glider were *changing* under his very fingers. It felt familiar, somehow.

Dennis blinked. The wall was only twenty yards away now. Soldiers walked along the parapet carrying torches, their attention on the ground below.

Maybe . . . Dennis began to hope.

The glider seemed to hum excitedly. From the L'Toff *Princess* there streamed a feeling of power. And a great amplified echo seemed to come from the creature on his shoulder!

The glider felt electric under his hands, and the faintest shimmering light seemed to run along its cables. The taut fabric rippled with only the faintest luffing as the wall passed a bare man's height below them. One guard stared up, slack-jawed. Then the wall was behind them, swallowed by the night.

Suddenly they were over the river. Faint starlight reflected from its surface.

The brief *felthesh* trance was fading. It had gotten them over the wall alive. But Dennis realized that no miracle of practice could get them across the water. Limited to a glider's essence, their craft could only fall in the cool air, no matter how efficient it became.

To the left were the cluttered masts of the docks. He doubted they could clear them and get to the farmland beyond.

"Can everybody swim?" he asked. "I sure hope so, 'cause we're going in."

The wharves were dark. Only a rare light gleamed through a window here and there. "Cut loose your straps!" he told Arth. "Drop when I tell you to!"

The thief obeyed at once, his knife slashing the leather harness. Linnora wrapped her klasmodion in her cloak and nodded that she was ready.

Dennis tried to angle their descent parallel to the docks. The water swept past only two meters below, a blur under their feet.

"Now! Let go!"

Linnora gave Dennis a quick smile, then she and Arth jumped. The glider jounced and Dennis fought with it. It had been practiced to carry more weight, and the center of mass had shifted.

Centroid, Dennis reminded himself as he pushed backward. Where's your centroid now? He heard two splashes behind him, then he was busy trying to negotiate his own landing.

It was too late to jump. He had to ride it out. He fumbled with his own strap and got it loose just as his feet began dragging through the water.

As he raised his legs he realized the pixolet was gone. Somehow it didn't surprise him at all.

Suddenly his knees were plowing furrows in the river. The glider settled around him as the water pulled him into a wet embrace.

5

"Dennizz!"

Arth rowed as quietly as he could. He had muffled the oars of the skiff they had stolen. Even so, he hated having to row out into the open river. Search parties had already sallied forth from the castle—horsemen and infantry patrols would soon be scouring the countryside.

"Can you see him?"

Linnora peered into the darkness. "Not yet. But he must be out this way! Keep rowing!"

Her clothes were plastered to her body, and the valley winds blew along the water. But her only thoughts were on the river and her rescuer.

"Wizard!" she called. "Are you out there? Wizard! Answer me!"

There was only the soft squeaking of the oars and, in the distance, the shouts of the Baron's troops.

Arth rowed.

Linnora's voice cracked. "Dennis Nuel! You cannot die! Guide us to you!"

They paused to listen, barely breathing. Then out of the darkness came a faint sound. "That way!" She grabbed Arth's shoulder and pointed. He grunted and pulled at the oars.

"Dennis!" she cried. She heard faint coughing somewhere ahead. Then a rough voice called back.

"The terrestrial has sblashed dowd . . . fortunately, my ship floats. Are you guys the local Goast Guard?"

Linnora sighed. She didn't understand more than a word or two of what he had said, but that was all right. Wizards were supposed to be inscrutable.

"I'b gonna *have* to find a way to phode hobe," the voice in the darkness muttered. Then a loud sneeze echoed over the water.

Dennis clutched the floating frame. A great bubble of air kept the glider afloat, though it was leaking out quickly. Onshore the search parties were getting closer. Against the distant flicker of lanterns he finally made out the moving shadow of the rowboat.

When Arth pulled up alongside all he could see of the little thief was his grin. But he couldn't mistake Linnora's outline as she bent to reach for his hand. In spite of his situation, Dennis had to appreciate what the water had done to her gown.

He shivered as he clambered into the boat. She wrapped some sail-cloth around him. But as Arth moved back to the oars, Dennis stopped him.

"Let's try to salvage the glider," he said, trying to overcome his stopped-up sinuses. "It'd be best if they weren't completely sure how we got away. I'd rather they suspected it was magic."

Linnora smiled. Her hand was on his arm.

"You have an amazing way with words, Dennis Nuel. Who in the world would think that what we have just been through was anything *but* magic?"

9

Discus Jestus

1

The farm had begun to deteriorate.

From the open gate Dennis looked down the walk to Stivyung Sigel's house. The home that had looked so comfortably lived-in a couple of months back now had the appearance of a place long abandoned to the elements.

"I think the coast is clear," he told the others. He helped Linnora lean against the fence post so she could take her arm off of his shoulder. The girl smiled bravely, but Dennis could tell she was almost done in.

He motioned for Arth to keep watch, then hurried across the yard to look into the house through one of the yellowing windowpanes.

Dust had settled over everything. The fine old furniture within had begun to take on a rough-edged look. The decay was sad, but it meant the farm was deserted. The soldiers combing the countryside for them hadn't set up an outpost here.

He returned to the gate and helped Linnora while Arth carried the disassembled glider. Together they slumped exhausted on the steps of the house. For a while the only sound other than their breathing was the hum of the insects.

The last time Dennis had sat on this porch, he had been bemused by a row of tools that seemed partly out of Buck Rogers and partly out of the late Stone Age. Now Dennis saw that more than half of the implements were missing from the rack by the door . . . the better half, he noted. The wonderful tools that Stivyung Sigel had practiced to perfection were probably with young Tomosh at his aunt's and uncle's, along with the Sigels' better household possessions.

The remaining tools on the rack had been left because they couldn't be kept employed. Most had begun to look like props from a low-budget Hollywood caveman feature.

Arth lay back on the porch, hands clasped across his chest, snoring.

Linnora painfully removed her shoes. In spite of the intense practice of the past two days, they still weren't appropriate for rough country. She had picked up several terrible blisters, and for the last day she had been limping on a twisted ankle. She had to be in great pain, but she never mentioned it to either of her companions.

Dennis heavily got up to his feet. He shuffled around the corner of the house to the well, and dropped the bucket in. There was a delayed splash. He pulled the bucket out, untied the cinch, and carried it, sloshing and leaking, back to the porch.

Arth roused himself long enough to take a deep drink, then sagged back again. Linnora drank sparingly, but dampened her kerchief and dabbed at the dust streaks on her face.

As gently as he could, Dennis bathed her feet to wipe away the dried blood. She winced but did not let out a sound. When he finished and sat down next to her on the dusty porch, Linnora rested her head against his shoulder and closed her eyes.

They had been dodging patrols for almost three days, eating small birds Dennis brought down with a makeshift sling, and fish scooped from small streams by Linnora's quick hands. Twice they had almost been spotted—by men on horseback one time, and again by a swift, nearly silent glider. The Baron, or his regent, certainly had the countryside in an uproar looking for them.

Linnora nestled comfortably below his chin. Dennis breathed in the sweet aroma of her hair, knotted as it was from three days in the wilderness. For a short time they were at peace.

"We can't stay here, Dennizz." Arth spoke without moving or opening his eyes.

On the evening of the escape, he had wanted to hang around the outskirts of Zuslik until it was safe to sneak back into town. Arth wasn't comfortable out in the open. But the fuss that was being raised and the thoroughness of the search had persuaded him at last to go along with Dennis and Linnora—to try for the land of the L'Toff.

"I know we can't, Arth. I'm sure the Baron's men have been here already. And they'll be back.

"But Linnora's feet are bleeding, and her ankle's swollen. We had to go somewhere for her to rest up, and this was the only place I could think of. It's deserted and it's in the direction we wanted to go."

"Dennis, I can go on. Really." Linnora sat up, but her slender body began to sway almost at once. "I think I ca—" Her eyes rolled upward and Dennis caught her.

"Give a yell if the army comes," he told Arth as he gathered her into his arms. He stood up unsteadily and managed to nudge the door open with his foot. It creaked loudly.

Dust was everywhere inside the house. Dennis could almost feel the love and taste Stivyung Sigel and his wife had practiced into this home, and now it was well on its way to reverting to a hovel of sticks and thatch and paper.

He wondered what had become of the tall farmer, and Gath, the bright young lad who had wanted to be a wizard's apprentice. Did they survive their adventure in the balloon? Was Sigel even now searching for his wife in the forests of the L'Toff?

Dennis carried Linnora down a narrow hallway to the Sigels' bedroom and laid her gently on the bed. Then he half collapsed into a chair nearby.

"Jus' gimme a minute," he mumbled. Exhaustion was like a heavy blanket weighing him down. Once he tried to get up but failed.

"Aw, hell." He looked at the young woman now sleeping peacefully nearby. "This isn't the way it's supposed to work the first time the hero gets the beautiful Princess into bed. . . ."

In his half sleep, Dennis's mind wandered. He found himself thinking about Pix and the robot . . . imagining how a passerby would have seen them some weeks back, the little pink creature with the bright green eyes, and its companion, the alien machine, together invading the human-filled streets of Zuslik, scuttling among the roofs and culverts, spying on the denizens of the town.

No wonder there had been rampant rumors of "devil-spawned critters" and ghosts.

Linnora had told him that the "Krenegee beast" shared with humans the ability to imbue a tool with *Pr'fett,* yet they weren't tool users themselves, nor apparently even truly sentient.

Sometimes a wild Krenegee established a long-term rapport with a human being. When this happened the human's practice became tremendously powerful. A month's improvement might be accomplished in a few hours' time. Even the L'Toff, whose mastery of the art of practice was unsurpassed, could not match the accomplishments of a man accompanied by a Krenegee, especially if the combination resulted in an occasional true practice trance.

But the Krenegee were notoriously fickle. A human counted himself lucky if he saw one once in his lifetime. A rare person who made lasting acquaintance with one was called a *maker of the world.*

Dennis imagined the pixolet roaming the city roofs on the back of an automaton, pushing it ever toward perfection at its programmed function—a function Dennis had originally given it. The results had been amazing.

Fickle Pix might be, but Dennis had wronged it in calling it a useless creature.

He couldn't help feeling guilty over the robot, though he knew he shouldn't. He saw it in his imagination, bravely holding off the guards on the night of their escape.

Dennis slumbered fitfully, dreaming of green and glowing red eyes, until a hand came down to shake his shoulder.

"Dennizz!" The hand shook him. "Dennizz! Wake up!"

"Whazzat? . . ." Dennis sat up quickly. "What is it? Soldiers?"

Arth was a silhouette in the dim room. He shook his head. "I don't think so. I heard voices out on the road, but no animals. I scooted before they opened the gate."

Dennis got up heavily and went over to look through a gap in the curtains. The dusty, yellowed window looked out on the farmyard. At the right edge of his field of vision he saw a flicker of movement. There were footsteps on the wooden porch.

The only way out was through the living room; they would have to face whoever it was. And the three of them weren't fit to take on a pack of drugged Cub Scouts.

He motioned Arth over behind the door and picked up a small chair. The footfalls were in the hall now.

The latch slid and the bedroom door squeaked slowly open. Dennis raised the chair high.

He swayed and almost overcompensated when the door swung wide to reveal a stocky, middle-aged woman. She saw Dennis and gasped as she hopped back at least four feet, almost knocking over a small boy behind her.

"Wait!" Dennis called.

The woman grabbed the boy's arm, dragging him frantically for the front door. But the small figure resisted.

"Dennz! Ma, it's only Dennz!"

Dennis put down the chair and motioned for Arth to stay put. He hurried down the hall after them.

The woman paused uncertainly at the open front door. Her grip was white on the arm of the young boy Dennis had met early in his stay on this world. Dennis stopped at the hallway entrance, his empty hands raised.

"Hello, Tomosh," he said quietly.

" 'lo, Dennzz!" Tomosh said happily, though his mother yanked him back when he tried to come forward. Suspicion and fear still filled her eyes.

Dennis tried to remember the woman's name. Stivyung had mentioned it several times. Somehow, he had to convince her he was a friend!

He sensed movement behind him.

Damn Arth! I told him to stay back! One more strange man in the house will be enough to spook this woman!

Mrs. Sigel's eyes opened wide. But instead of fleeing, she sighed. "Princess!"

Dennis turned and couldn't help blinking a little himself. Even with disheveled hair, sleepy-eyed and standing on bloody, bare feet, Linnora managed to look regal. She smiled graciously.

"You are right good woman, though I don't believe we have ever met. I must thank you for the hospitality of your beautiful home. My gratitude, and that of the L'Toff, are yours for all your days."

Mrs. Sigel blushed, and curtsied awkwardly. Her face was transformed, no longer hard at all. "My home is yours, your Highness," she said shyly. "An' your friends, of course. I only wish it were more presentable."

"To us, it is as fine as the greatest palace," Linnora assured her. "And far nicer than a castle where we have recently been."

Dennis took Linnora's arm to help her to a chair. She caught his eye and winked.

Mrs. Sigel made a great fuss when she saw the condition of the girl's feet. She hurried to a corner of the room and pried up a floorboard to reveal a hidden larder. She brought out clean, decades-old linen and a jar of salve. She insisted on immediately attending to Linnora's blisters, pushing Dennis to one side gently but irresistibly.

The boy Tomosh came over and hit Dennis affectionately on the leg, then began a torrent of eager, uncoordinated questions. It took ten minutes for Dennis to get around to telling Mrs. Sigel that he had last seen her husband two hundred feet in the air, riding a great balloon.

Eventually he had to explain what in the world a "balloon" was.

2

"We could try to arrange a hiding place for you here," Surah Sigel told Dennis much later, after the others had gone to bed. "It'd be dangerous for sure. The Baron's mobilized the militia, an' his men will be back here again soon. But we could give it a try."

Surah looked as if she had little faith in her own suggestion. Dennis already knew what the problem was.

"Sniffers," he said simply.

She nodded reluctantly. "Yah. Kremer'll have them out in force, huntin' for you. Sniffers can find a man anywhere by his scent, given 'nuff time."

Dennis had seen a kennel of the big-nosed animals while he resided in the castle. They looked like distant relatives of dogs, but Dennis could think of no real analogs on Earth. They were slower than bloodhounds but had three times the sensitivity. Arth had told him there were ways to stymie sniffers in town, but out in the country they were unstoppable.

Dennis shook his head. "We have to be going as quickly as possible. You're as generous and brave as Stivyung described you, Surah. But I can't be responsible for what would happen to you and Tomosh if Linnora and I were found here.

"We'll leave the day after tomorrow." Privately, Dennis dreaded waiting even that long.

"But the Princess's feet won't have healed by then! Her ankle is still swollen!"

Mrs. Sigel had offered earlier to take Linnora to her sister's and to try somehow to disguise her. But Linnora would hear none of it. It wasn't just her unwillingness to put innocent people in danger. She was also determined to deny Kremer even the possibility of ever using her as a hostage. And her people had to be warned of Kremer's new weapons. She would climb the western mountains even if she had to crawl.

"I'd not even stay the extra day," Dennis said. "But I have to try to *make* something . . . something that will enable us to take Linnora along even if her feet haven't healed."

Mrs. Sigel sighed in acceptance. A wizard was a wizard, after all. She had listened to Arth's stories about Dennis's miracles with wonderment. "All right, then. At first light I'll go fetch those tools you need from Biss's house. Tomosh'll watch the road and warn you if soldiers come. I'd draw you a map to show you the way to the L'Toff, but you've got the best guide in the world, so I don't suppose you'll need it."

Linnora and Tomosh had retired after a Spartan but nourishing meal from the Sigels' secret hoard. Arth snored softly in a chair, practicing it in return for his hostess's hospitality. Although he wasn't much of a smoker, Dennis puffed diligently at one of Stivyung Sigel's pipes for much the same reason.

Surah told Dennis about her own adventure, from which she had only just returned—her journey into the mountains of the L'Toff. Her eyes seemed to light up as she spoke of her travels.

Stivyung had often spoken of his career in the Royal Scouts. Brought up in a society that still rigidly controlled the options open to women, Surah had thrilled to her husband's stories of adventure in the wild border reaches, of encounters with strange peoples including, of course, the mysterious L'Toff.

From his descriptions she knew that they were not fairies or devils but people on whom the gods had bestowed some mixed blessings. Since their exodus during the reign of Good King Foss't, they had lived pretty much to themselves in their mountain retreat. After the fall of the old Duke, their last strong protector in the west, the only Coylians who had regular contact with them were a few traders and the Scouts.

When the Baron's men took Stivyung away, Surah suddenly found herself behaving as she never had imagined before. She ran to her sister's and told her to pick up Tomosh. Then she threw together a pack and headed west with no definite plan in mind, thinking only to find some of Stivyung's former comrades and beseech their help.

She did not recall much about her journey into the mountains, except being frightened most of the time. Though she had grown up on the edge of the wilderness, she had never spent nights alone under the trees before. It was an experience she would never forget.

The first sign she was in L'Toff country came when she encountered a small patrol of stern, fierce men, whose spears had the burnished look of deadly practice. They were agitated and questioned her closely. But eventually they let her proceed. Only later, when she passed through the outer hamlets and finally came to the main village of the L'Toff, did she learn that Princess Linnora had disappeared.

That explained the anxiety of the border guards, certainly. Surah began to realize that her own problems were small eddies of a larger storm brewing.

Linnora's father, Prince Linsee, ruled a virtually independent realm, answerable only to the King of Coylia himself. This irritated the great lords and the temples. But like the isolation of their mountain home, it was for the tribe's protection.

In return, the crown monopolized the trade in rare treasures whose *Pr'fett* had been "frozen" into a permanent state of practice. Each item generally cost some L'Toff a measure of his vital force—a week, month, or a year out of his or her life. The frozen goods were very rare—and coveted greedily.

Relations between the L'Toff and the great nobles had grown worse since the demise of the old Duke, and especially as Baron Kremer's cabal of gentry and guilds prepared to confront the King.

Obviously the aristocrats would be well served if they had a lever on the L'Toff, the King's strongest allies in the west. If they had a hostage to ensure Prince Linsee's neutrality, they could turn their attention fully to investing the cities of the east, with their royalist, antiguild rabble.

Fate had delivered Kremer his hostage against the L'Toff the very same day that soldiers had come to take Surah's husband away.

When Surah arrived in the mountains, the L'Toff were searching far and wide for their beloved Princess. Linnora had slipped away from her maids and escort nearly two weeks before, claiming in a cryptic note that she had sensed "something different" come into the world.

While everyone respected Linnora's fey powers, Prince Linsee had feared the results of his daughter's impetuousness. He suspected she had fallen into the Baron's hands.

So, too, thought Demsen, the tall, homely leader of a detachment of Royal Scouts that had arrived just before Surah. Demsen was sure that Kremer was holding Linnora in secret, until a hostage was needed to keep the L'Toff passive at his rear.

Surah found out all of this because she was right there in the thick of it. Since she knew something of the situation in Zuslik, Surah was invited to sit at table with Linsee and Demsen and the captains and elders, all of whom attentively listened as she nervously answered their questions.

At the assembly, young Prince Proll had demanded permission to storm Zuslik and rescue Linnora by force of arms. Proll's courage and charisma influenced many. The younger L'Toff could think of nothing but their beautiful Princess languishing in prison.

But Linsee knew that Kremer's forces were more than a match for his own in open battle, especially since the perfection of the Baron's terrifying glider corps. It would take years of dangerous experimentation to duplicate that accomplishment. Long before then, the war would begin.

Linsee had sent a delegation, led by the Chief of the Council of Elders, and Prince Proll, to visit Kremer and inquire. It would probably accomplish nothing, but it was all he could do. Reluctantly, he ordered the defenses strengthened such as they were.

Surah listened to all of this and came to a numb realization that she would find no help here for her own, personal crisis. If the L'Toff and the Royal Scouts could do nothing to save Linnora, what could they do about a simple farmer—even a retired scout sergeant—whom Baron Kremer had seized on a whim?

Prince Linsee gave her a donkey and some provisions and wished her well. Except for the border guards, no one even noticed when she left.

She returned to find the countryside in an uproar. Preparations for war were well under way, and the area was being scoured for important fugitives.

Life had to go on, whatever the magnitude of great affairs around her. She retrieved her son from her sister's house and headed home to keep up the farm as best she could, against the hope that Stivyung would someday return to her.

And at home she found the fugitives hiding in her own bedroom.

Surah Sigel sighed and refilled Dennis's cup with hot thah.

"I've not had a big voice in th' happnin's of the time," she said in conclusion. "I'm just a farmwife, for all of Stivyung's teachin' me to read an' all.

"Still, it does seem to me that I'll have witnessed an' had a small part in the events." She looked up at Dennis with an idea. She spoke a little timidly, as if speaking an idea she was afraid he would laugh at. "Y'know, maybe someday I'll write a *book* about what I saw an' tell about all the people I met before th' war began.

"Now, wouldn't that be somethin'!"

Dennis nodded in agreement. "It would at that."

She sighed and turned to stir the coals.

3

It had been years since Dennis had done any useful carpentry, and the tools he used now were unfamiliar. Nevertheless, he started work early the next morning.

He trimmed two long, stout poles from a pair of half-practiced hoes he had found on the porch, then he cut out several flat planks from one of the hay cribs. When Mrs. Sigel returned from her sister's farm with better tools, Dennis drilled four holes in the sides of a light-framed watering trough, and slid the poles through the holes.

Perched on a stack of hay, her feet swathed in white bandages, Linnora worked on a leather harness. She deftly used an awl to punch holes in straps of hide, in places where Dennis had made marks, then fastened them together with thongs. She hummed softly and smiled at Dennis whenever he looked up from his work. Dennis grinned back. It was hard to feel tired when encouraged like that.

Arth puffed into the barn, carrying a small chair Surah Sigel had donated to the project. He put the chair down and examined the contraption Dennis was building.

"I get it!" The little thief snapped his fingers. "We put the chair in the tub an' the Princess rides inside. Then we grab those poles an' lift! I heard of those things. They call 'em 'litters.' When the Emperor from across the big sea came to visit our King's father years back, I hear he was carried aroun' in somethin' like that. A couple of our big nobles tried to copy the idea an' almost had riots on their hands before they gave up."

Dennis just smiled and kept working. Using a beautiful saw with a serrated gemstone edge, he cut four identical round disks from a flat slab of wood. They were about a meter diameter and an inch thick.

Arth thought for a minute, then frowned. "But we'd need four men to carry this thing! There's just you an' me an' the L'Toff donkey Surah's given us! Who's gonna support the fourth side?" He scratched his head. "I guess I still don't get it."

Dennis used a sharp-bitted drill carefully to cut a small circular hole out of the center of each disk.

"Come on, Arth," he said when he had finished. "Help me with this, will you?"

Under Dennis's direction, the bandit leader lifted one of the poles penetrating the sides of the trough. Dennis slid one of his disks over the end, then removed it to trim the center hole a little wider. When he tried again, it wedged into place a few inches down the shaft. He pounded it farther with a cloth-muffled hammer.

Arth lowered the tub. It lay canted at an odd angle, propped up at one corner by the upended disk. Linnora put down her work and edged forward on the hay to watch.

"What is it, Dennis?" she asked.

"It's called a *wheel,*" he replied. "With four of these in place and with the help of Surah's donkey, we should be able to carry you out of here tomorrow night almost as fast as if you could walk. Of course, it'll force us to use the roads at first, but there's no helping that. The road's the only way over the pass, anyway."

Dennis directed Arth to lift one corner at a time. He pounded a wheel onto each.

"This whole device is called a *cart*. Back in my homeland, this crude thing wouldn't last more than a few hours, at best. I imagine at first it'll scrape along little better than if we were dragging the trough on its belly. There's no bearing between the axles and the holes in the body, for one thing. That'll play hell with the rolling friction coefficient. Of course, with practice we can expect a lubrication effect to come into play eventually. . . ."

Arth and Linnora glanced at each other. The wizard was getting opaque again. They had grown used to it by now.

"I could've made a better starter," Dennis said as he drove the last wheel firmly into place. "But there's no time. Right now they're ranging all over the countryside looking for us, but once the sniffers find our trail, they'll concentrate. We'd better be well into the mountains by that time.

"We're going to have to count on the Practice Effect to fix this wagon up. Tonight Arth and I will take turns pulling it around the farmyard. By tomorrow maybe . . ."

Dennis stepped back and looked at the cart. He saw bewilderment on Arth's face. But Linnora wore an expression of deep concentration. Her eyes were narrowed and she moved her hand as if trying to visualize something she had never seen before.

Suddenly she clapped her hands and laughed out loud.

"Push it! Oh, Dennis, push it and make it move!"

Dennis grinned. Linnora did not have the mind of a caveman. Her ability to envision the way things worked was just short of amazing, considering her background.

He lifted his foot and gave the back of the cart a shove. Groaning loudly, it rattled and rolled down the gravel path and out the barn doorway.

Someone shrieked, and there was a loud thump outside. Dennis hurried out and found Surah Sigel seated on the ground, staring wide-eyed at the contraption. It had rolled to a stop a few feet away. Beside her a cloth bag of provisions lay open, its contents half scattered.

"I thought it was *alive* when it came out at me like that!" She blinked at the cart.

"It's just a machine," Dennis reassured her as he helped her up. "It's what we're going to use to carry the Princess. . . ."

"I can see that!" Surah brushed his hands away and straightened her clothes stiffly. She started gathering the provisions—dried meats, fruit, and sacks of cornmeal—and shooed Dennis away when he tried to help.

"Tomosh just came back with word from my cousins down the road," she said. "They've been quartering four of the Baron's troopers for a week. And now the soldiers are saying they're going to move out the day after tomorrow. They won't say where, but my cousin thinks it's westward."

Dennis cursed softly. He and the others had to be through the pass before the troops entered the mountains. If they waited until tomorrow night they would still be on the road when the main force reached the gap!

"Tonight, then," he said. "We've got to go tonight."

Tomosh came running out of the house. He stopped and stared at the little wagon.

Arth supported Linnora as she hobbled over to take her seat in the cart. She laughed as Arth and the boy pushed it slowly about the farmyard.

Dennis shook his head. *The little red wagon I had as a child would be more useful,* he thought, *than that creaky thing will be on its first day.*

They started out soon after nightfall, while the moons were still down. The donkey snorted uncomfortably as it pulled the rickety cart. When it stopped at the gate and threatened to balk, Linnora strummed her klasmodion and sang to the restive animal.

The donkey's ears moved; its breathing slowly settled as the girl's melody calmed it. Finally, it responded to Arth's gentle tugs and pulled at its awkward burden. Dennis helped push until they were out onto the road proper. There they stopped to bid the Sigels farewell.

Linnora whispered to Tomosh while Dennis shook hands with Mrs. Sigel.

"Good luck to y'all," Surah said. "Tell Stivyung we're fine if you see him." Surah looked at the motley party dubiously. Dennis had to admit that they didn't look like much of a force to take on Kremer's patrols.

"We'll do that," Dennis said, nodding.

"You'll be back ag'in, Dennizz!" Tomosh promised as he whacked the Earthman on the thigh affectionately. "You 'n my pop an' the Royal Scouts'll come back an' fix old Kremer once and for all!"

Dennis tousled the boy's hair. "Maybe so, Tomosh."

Arth clucked to the donkey. The crude cart squeaked up the dark, sloping road. Dennis had to push for an uphill stretch. When he looked back, Surah and her son were gone.

Except for the narrow, mirror-focused beam of their small oil lantern, the night was black all around them. The wind brushed through the trees lining the highway. Even on the smooth, superresilient highway, the cart thumped and bumped and shook. Linnora bore it bravely. She plucked her klasmodion softly, with a dreamy, distant expression on her face.

She was already hard at work, using her L'Toff talents to help the cart practice.

On Earth the rickety contraption could be expected to fall apart anytime from a few minutes to a few hours after construction. Here, though, it was a race between wear and practice. If only it lasted long enough, the thing would get better. Maybe.

Dennis pushed the noisy cart, wishing the pixolet was around to help.

4

Murris Demsen, commander of the Green Lion company of the Royal Scouts, poured another cup of winter wine for Prince Linsee, then looked to see if anyone else wanted a refill.

The boy from Zuslik, young Gath, nodded and grinned. The winter wine of the L'Toff was about the best thing he had ever tasted. He was already well on his way toward getting tipsy.

Stivyung Sigel held his hand over his goblet. He knew the potency of the stuff from his days in the Scouts.

"The latest word is that Kremer's patrols have been applying pressure all along the border," Demsen said. The gangly scout commander put down the beautiful, ancient decanter and pulled a sheaf of notes from a folder. "There are also reports that the baronies of Tarlee and Trabool are mobilizing, and setting up outposts in L'Toff territory. Even Baron Feif-dei appears to be getting ready for war."

"That is indeed bad news," Prince Linsee said. "I had counted him a friend."

Stivyung Sigel stood slowly. He bowed to Prince Linsee, to Demsen, and to Linsee's son, the brown-haired Prince Proll.

"Sirs, I must ask once again for permission to return to my home. You say my wife is no longer here. Therefore I must go to her and my son. And once I see that they are safe, there are friends I must try to help, who at this moment languish in the tyrant's dungeons."

Prince Linsee looked to Demsen, then back at Sigel. He sighed. "Stivyung, have you heard nothing? The border is closed! Any day now we expect to be under attack! You can't make it over the pass while it's choked with troops!"

Demsen agreed. "Sit down, Stivyung. Your place is here. I need you, Prince Linsee needs you, your King needs you. We can't let you throw your life away."

At the end of the table Prince Proll slammed his own goblet down. "And why stop him?" the young man demanded. "Why should you stand in his way?"

"My son . . ." Linsee began.

"He, at least, is willing to take chances—to dare all to rescue those he cares for! Meanwhile, we let Linnora suffer in the clutches of that amoral spawn of tree lizards, Kremer! Tell me, what good will waiting do when the forces of all the baronies west of the Fingal march on us? Oh, for the gods' sakes, let Sigel go! And let me *strike* while they can still be taken one at a time!"

Linsee and Demsen shared a look of exasperation. They had been through this too many times of late.

"We shall strike, my son," Linsee said at last. "But first we must prepare. Stivyung and Gath have brought us this 'balloon' device of the alien wizard's—"

"Which is nothing compared with the weapons the alien has given Kremer! What good is it, anyway? It was ripped to uselessness when Sigel landed!"

"It was damaged, yes, Prince," Demsen said. "But it is almost repaired. Duplicates are being made and practiced. Why, this may be the very thing we have been looking for—a way to counter Kremer's gliders! I will grant that I do not yet see how it will be used, but what we most need is time. My scouts and your companies must buy Prince Linsee time!

"Meanwhile, young Gath and Sigel, my old comrade-in-arms, must do their part in supervising the making of more balloons—"

"Making! What can you accomplish by *making?*" The young prince turned and spat on the fire. He sank back into his chair.

"My son, do not blaspheme. Making is as honorable as practicing, for according to the Old Belief, did we not once have the power to make life itself? Before the blecker threw us down to savagery?"

Proll stared at the fire, and finally nodded. "I will try to control my temper, Father."

Still, they all knew Proll had a point. It took *time* to make things. And even among the L'Toff it took more time still to practice them. Time was something Kremer wasn't about to give them.

In all their minds, also, was the dread of how Kremer intended to use his hostage. Would he display Linnora at the battlefield? The effect on the morale of the troops could be devastating if Kremer timed his move right. And Kremer was a past master of timing.

Conversation lapsed. Finally Demsen unrolled the grand map, and he and the Prince examined still more ways to distribute their meager forces against the hordes they expected soon.

Young Gath paid little attention to the talk of strategy. He was not a soldier. But he was an . . . an *engineer*. Dennis Nuel had taught him that word, and he liked the flavor of it.

Gath felt certain that the key to saving the L'Toff—and eventually rescuing Dennis and Arth and the Princess—lay in perfecting the *balloons*. So far Gath had been kept busy just supervising the repair of the original and the construction and practice of new models. But that didn't keep him from turning his mind to new design problems.

Such as how to use them in battle! How could one make the balloon go where one wanted it to go and then keep it there? It had been almost impossible to maneuver the first balloon in their escape from Zuslik. Only a small miracle of wind had taken it into the mountains where he and Stivyung wanted to go. From their landing site it had taken days to seek out the fastness of the L'Toff.

Somehow there must be a way, he thought.

Paper was much too valuable for casual doodling. So Gath dipped his finger in the wine and traced out sketches on the beautifully ancient, varnished tabletop.

5

Baron Kremer sat in bed, a pile of reports spread wide on the silky, ancient coverlet. He worked doggedly, reading messages from the other great lords of the west, who were due to arrive soon for a meeting he had called.

Those messages were satisfying to read, for not one of the western barons and counts had demurred.

But the rest of this garbage! There were reams of lists of accounts to be paid for war materiel. There were bills from hundreds of freeborn practicers, requisitioned for the duration, and complaints from the guilds over his demand of even greater subsidies for his campaign against the liberal King.

The pile was daunting. Paperwork was the one thing in this world that Kremer feared.

If anyone noticed that the Baron's lips moved as he read, nobody said anything. The three scribes who assisted him also carefully averted their eyes from the purple welt that discolored their overlord's left temple.

Kremer slammed down a long scroll.

"Words, words, words! Is this what it means to carve out an empire? To conquer, only to wade neck deep into a storm of *paper?*"

The scribes looked down, knowing their Lord's questions were rhetorical.

"This!" Kremer shook a roll out. It spread like a long, thin flag to float out over the floor. The fine sheet was in itself worth nearly a peasant's yearly income. "The guilds cavil over a pittance! A *pittance* that will win them security and me a crown! Do they want Hymiel and his rabble to have their way in the east?"

Kremer growled and shoved the stack aside. Reports flew out across the floor. The scribes scuttled to recover them.

Taking a moment's satisfaction, Kremer watched them stack the sheets and rolls. But it was a poor distraction from the nagging little irritations that seemed to abound on the very eve of his triumph!

The guilds were useful, he reminded himself—besides serving as rich allies. For instance, the monopoly of the paper guild kept their product rare and expensive. If the stuff were cheap, the number of reports would probably double, or even triple!

Kremer chafed. He had been told to stay in bed by the palace physician—an old gentleman who had treated him as a child, and one of the few men alive whom he respected. He had to be healthy in a week's time, when the main campaign against the King was to begin. Without good cause, he couldn't justify breaking the doctor's advice. The advance against the L'Toff was a sideshow that his commanders were competent to handle without his presence.

Everything seemed to be going according to plan. Still, he half hoped for an emergency just to have an excuse to get out of here!

Kremer's fist pounded on his thigh. The tension brought back the twinge in his temple. He winced and brought up a hand to touch the spot, gingerly.

Ah, there will be an accounting, he thought. *There will be much to pay for this. A certain individual owes much.*

From under his pillow he drew out Dennis Nuel's metal knife, now practiced to a razor edge. He contemplated the shiny steel while his scribes waited silently for him to return from wherever he had gone.

What pulled the Baron back from his feral reverie was an explosion that blew the curtains about like cracking whips. The delicate windows bowed and rattled in their frames as the detonation pealed like thunder.

Kremer threw aside the coverlet, sending the papers flying again. He strode quickly between the blowing curtains onto the balcony and looked out onto the courtyard. He saw men running toward an area just under the wall out of view. Shouts carried from the site of the commotion.

Kremer grabbed his two-hundred-year-old robe. The senior physician was not present, but his assistant protested that the Baron was unready, yet, to venture outside.

Being picked up by the shirtfront and thrown halfway across the room changed the fellow's mind. He quickly pronounced his Lordship ambulatory and scuttled away.

Kremer hurried downstairs, his bedrobe flapping about his ankles. Four members of his personal guard, all intensely loyal clansmen from the northern highlands, clicked into step behind him. He strode quickly downstairs and out into the courtyard. There he found the scholar Hoss'k poking through a pile of charred wood splinters and pottery shards.

Kremer caught up short, staring at the wreckage of the distillery Dennis Nuel had built. Steam rose from twisted, blackened tubing. The deacon stood in the midst, coughing and waving smoke away. The scholar's resplendent red robes were singed and soot-coated.

"What is the meaning of this!" Kremer demanded. At once the soldiers who had been gawking at the wreckage turned and snapped to attention. The slaves who had been in charge of the distillery dropped to their bellies in abasement.

Except for three who took no notice of him. One of the latter was clearly dead. The other two cringed not from him, but from their own badly seared hands and arms. Pantrywomen were working to bandage the wounded.

Hoss'k bowed low. "My Lord, I have made a discovery!"

From his appearance, Hoss'k must have been here when the disaster occurred. Knowing Hoss'k, that implied the man had *caused* all this somehow, by meddling with Dennis Nuel's beverage manufacturing device.

"You have made a catastrophe!" Kremer shouted as he looked about at the ruins. "The one thing I was able to squeeze out of that wizard—before he betrayed my hospitality and made off with a valuable hostage—was this distillery! I had counted on its products to bring me great wealth in trade! And now you, you and your meddling—"

Hoss'k held up his hand placatingly. "My Lord . . . you *did* instruct me to study the essence of the alien wizard's devices. And as I was stymied by most of his other possessions, I decided to see if I could discover how this one works."

Kremer regarded him, his expression ominous. Onlookers glanced at each other, making silent wagers over the scholar's expected life-span.

"You'd better have discovered the essence behind the still," Kremer threatened, *"before* you destroyed it. Much depends on your ability to rebuild it. You might find it hard to practice your fancy clothes without a head on your shoulders."

Hoss'k protested, "I am a member of the clergy!"

At one look from Kremer, Hoss'k ducked down and nodded vigorously. "Oh, be not concerned, my Lord. It will be easy to rebuild the device, my Lord. Indeed, the principle was devilishly clever and simple. You see, this pot here—er, what is left of the pot—contained wine that was made to boil slowly, but the vapors from the boiling were restrained—"

"Spare me the details." Kremer waved the man to be silent. His headache was getting worse. "Consult with the crew. I want to know how long it will take to get it running again!"

Hoss'k bowed and hurriedly turned to talk to the surviving members of the distillery gang.

The Baron stepped over an injured soldier. The palace midwife who had been tending the moaning man's wounds scuttled to get out of his way.

Even as he walked through the ruins, Kremer's mind was turning back to his main preoccupation—how to distribute his forces to recapture the wizard and Princess Linnora, and how simultaneously to begin his campaign against the L'Toff.

The alliance was shaping up well. A squadron of his gliders had gone on tour, impressing the gentry for a hundred miles to the east, north, and south, and cowing the restive peasantry by playing up to the traditional superstition regarding dragons.

All the great lords would be here shortly for a meeting. Kremer planned an impressive demonstration for them.

Still, the barons would not be enough. He would need mercenaries, too, and it would take more than demonstrations to acquire those!

Money, that was the key! And not this paper trash that kept its value by an artificially maintained scarcity, but real, *metal* money! With enough money Kremer could buy the services of free companies and bribe every great noble in the realm! No demonstrations or rumors of magical weapons could match the effect of cool, hard cash!

And now this idiot deacon had destroyed the number one money-maker Kremer had been counting on!

"Uh, my Lord?"

Kremer turned. "Yes, scholar?"

Hoss'k bowed once more as he caught up with the Baron. Hoss'k's black hair was coated with soot.

"My Lord, I did not intend, in experimenting with the still, to destroy it. . . . I—"

"How long will it take?" Kremer growled.

"Only a few days to begin getting small quantities—"

"I don't care about the *making!* How long will it take until the new still is *practiced* to the level of performance the old one had reached this morning?"

Hoss'k looked very pale under his sooty coating. "Ten—twenty—" His voice squeaked.

"Days?" Kremer winced as the twinge returned. He clutched his head, unable to speak. But he glared at Hoss'k, and it seemed that only his unspeakable headache was extending the deacon's life.

Just then a runner hurried through the palace gateway. The boy spotted the Baron, ran over, and saluted snappily.

"My Lord, the Lord Hern sends his compliments and says to tell you that the sniffers have found the fugitives' scent!"

Kremer's hands clasped each other. "Where are they?"

"In the southwest pass, my Lord. Runners have been sent to all the camps in the foothills with the alert!"

"Excellent! We shall send cavalry, too. Go and order the commander of First Spears to gather his troopers. I will be there shortly."

The boy saluted again and sped off.

Kremer turned back to Hoss'k, who was clearly making his peace with his gods.

"Scholar?" he said quietly.

"Y-y-yes, my Lord?"

"I need money, scholar."

Hoss'k gulped and nodded. "Yes, my Lord."

Kremer smiled narrowly. "Can you suggest a place where I can get a lot of money in a very short time?"

Hoss'k blinked, then nodded again. "The metal house in the forest?"

Kremer grinned in spite of the ache in his head. "Correct."

Hoss'k had suggested, earlier, that the metal house might have some intrinsic value far beyond its huge content in metal. The foreign wizard had been very clear in insisting that it be left alone if he was to do any word for Kremer.

But Dennis Nuel had betrayed him, and Hoss'k no longer had much to say around here.

"You leave with a fast troop of cavalry at once," he told the portly churchman. "I want all that metal back here in five days."

One more time, Hoss'k merely swallowed and nodded.

6

A day and a half after setting off from the Sigels' farm, Dennis had almost begun to hope they might make it through the cordon undetected.

All through that first night on the road, the small party of fugitives had passed the flickering light of encampments in the hills—detachments of Baron Kremer's gathering western army. Arth and Dennis helped the little donkey pull, while Linnora did her part by concentrating, practicing the cart to be silent.

Once they stole nervously past a roadblock. The militiamen on duty were snoring, but in Dennis's imagination the cart was barely quieter than a banshee until they passed beyond the next fringe of forest.

Come morning they were high in the pass. They had left behind the main units of the army poised to invade the lands of the L'Toff. There were probably only a few squads of pickets between them and the open country.

But to proceed during daylight would be madness. Dennis pulled his little group off into the thickets beside the mountain highway, and they rested through the day, alternately sleeping, talking quietly, and sampling from the picnic basket Mrs. Sigel had prepared for them.

Dennis amused Linnora by showing her some tricks on his wrist-comp. He explained that there were no living creatures inside, and demonstrated some of the wonders of numbers. Linnora caught on very quickly.

They must have been more tired than Dennis thought, for when he finally awakened, it was dark again. Two of Tatir's small moons were already high, making the forestscape eerily and dangerously bright.

He roused Arth and Linnora, who sat up quickly and stared in surprise at the darkness. They arose and loaded the little wagon once again. Dennis insisted that Linnora continue to ride in the cart. Although her feet were better, the Princess clearly wasn't ready yet to walk very far.

The shadowy hillsides hulked around them as they set out. They pushed on silently.

Dennis recalled the last time he had been through this pass, three months ago. Back then he hadn't any idea what lay ahead. He had imagined the river valley filled with amazing alien creatures and still more amazing technology.

The truth had turned out to be even more bizarre than anything he had imagined. Even now, from time to time he felt a faint recurrence of that sense of unreality, as if it were hard really to believe that this amazing world could exist.

He thought about the probability calculations he had set up back in Zuslik. With his wrist-comp he just might be able to work out the odds of such a strange place as Tatir—and its even stranger Practice Effect—coming into being.

But then, Dennis thought as they trudged under a dark canopy of trees, wasn't *Earth* a strange place when you came right down to it? Cause and effect seemed so straightforward there, yet entropy always seemed to be conspiring to get you!

Dennis hardly knew three or four engineers back home who didn't secretly, in their hearts, devoutly believe in gremlins, in glitches, and in Murphy's law.

Dennis couldn't decide which world was the more perverse. Perhaps both Earth and Tatir were improbable in the grand picture. It hardly mattered. What was important right now was survival. He intended to use the Practice Effect to the hilt, if that's what it would take.

He helped push the little cart. Already it seemed much easier. The wheels didn't seem to squeak much anymore. Linnora was no longer jostled and tossed like a sack of potatoes as they rolled along.

The Princess looked up at him in the moonlight. Dennis returned her smile. Everything would be all right, if only he could get Linnora safely to her people in the hills. No matter how great Kremer's strength, the L'Toff could surely hold out long enough for Dennis to whip up some Earth magic to save the day.

If only they could make it in time.

Dawn came earlier than he expected.

Ahead, in the growing light, was the crest of the pass. Dennis switched the donkey to hurry it along. He felt sure there would be an outpost up here.

But when the road peaked without any sign of trouble, he began to hope. The pass flattened out in a mist of early-morning haze. Dennis was about to call a rest when there came a sudden shout from their left.

Arth cursed and pointed. Up on the hill to that side was a small red campfire they had missed, in spite of their watchfulness. In the dawning light they could see bustling movement and the brown uniforms of Kremer's territorial militia. A detachment was already beating their way toward them through the underbrush.

The road ran slightly downhill ahead, around the flank of the mountain. Dennis slapped the tired donkey's flank.

"Get going, Arth! I'll hold them off!"

Arth stumbled after the cart, mostly carried along by inertia. "All by *yerself*? Dennizz, are you crazy?"

"Get Linnora out of here! I can handle them!"

Linnora looked back at Dennis anxiously. But she was silent as the muttering Arth led the donkey at a trot around the bend in the road.

Dennis found a good spot and planted himself in the center of the highway. Fortunately, the territorials weren't the best troops Kremer had—mostly drafted farmers led by a smattering of professionals. Most of them would undoubtedly rather be at home.

Nevertheless, this would have to be a pretty good bluff.

When the patrol tumbled out of the brush onto the road, Dennis saw only swords, spears, and thenners. Fortunately, there were no archers. A good bowman was rare in these parts. A practiced bow required a lot of attention, and few had that kind of time or energy to spend on weapons.

His plan just might work.

He waited in the center of the road, fingering a handful of smooth stones and a strip of silky cloth.

The gathering soldiers seemed nonplussed by his behavior. Instead of charging, they came forward at a walk, urged by a growling sergeant. Apparently they had heard who the chief fugitive was, and they weren't exactly boiling over with excitement at the idea of attacking an alien wizard.

When they were within a hundred feet, Dennis dropped a stone into his sling. He whirled it three times and flung.

"Abracadabra! Oooga booga!" he shouted.

In the dense packing of militiamen, he couldn't miss. Someone howled and dropped a clattering weapon to the ground.

"Oh, demons of the air!" he invoked the sky. "Teach these fools who dare to try to thwart a wizard!" He whirled and flung another stone.

Another soldier clutched at his stomach and sat down, groaning.

A few of the militiamen began melting away from the rear, suddenly developing an intense interest in the breakfast they had left behind.

The others stopped uncertainly, their eyes wide with superstitious dread.

A sergeant in a gray cloak began shouting at the men, and commenced kicking a few rumps. After a moment, the line began to approach again raggedly.

Dennis couldn't let this continue. Sure, he could make them pause again with another stone. But if they became habituated to his attack they would soon see that only a few men were getting hurt—and only getting the wind knocked out of them, at that. They would see that in a massed charge they could easily overwhelm him.

Dennis put down his sling and pulled from his belt a long leather thong. At one end was tied a hollow piece of hardwood he had whittled back at the Sigels'.

"Flee!" he called out in his best deep movie voice. "Do not make me call forth my demons!" He advanced slowly and began whirling the thong over his head.

The hollow tube bit into the air, and began to let out a rumbling, groaning sound. He hadn't had much time to practice the bull roarer. It would have to do as he had *made* it. In a moment he had it moaning loudly, though, an eerie, hackles-raising noise.

It was a chancy business, certainly. Dennis wasn't even sure Coylians were unfamiliar with the device. Just because he had never witnessed one in use and Arth had never heard of it didn't mean none of these men had.

But the soldiers began to swallow nervously and back away as he advanced. Several more dropped out from the rear of the troop and hurried away.

The sergeant cursed and shouted again. His voice had the accent of Kremer's northmen. But the rising growl of the bull roarer seemed to fill the forest with reverberations. It sounded as though there were animals out there, in the half light beneath the branches. The echoes were like strange creatures' voices, answering the summons of their master.

Dennis concentrated on making the noisemaker *better,* though he knew he lacked the talent to cause things to change so quickly. Only a talented L'Toff could occasionally purposely manage a rare felthesh trance—or a fortunate man who won the help of a fickle Krenegee beast. Still, the groaning noise rose until the hairs on the back of his own neck stood on end.

The militiamen were backing up now, staring about themselves fearfully in spite of the northman's curses. Finally the sergeant seized a spear from one of his frightened soldiers. With a yell he cast it toward Dennis.

Dennis watched the spear sail toward him. But he kept a smile on his face and advanced evenly. To turn and run, or even step aside, would put heart into these men. He had to seem not to care, and to trust that the sergeant was too nervous himself to be much of a marksman!

The spear slammed into the ground inches from Dennis's left foot. It vibrated musically as he walked past it.

His legs felt like water. He laughed—though, to be honest, it felt more hysterical than humorous to him.

At the sound of his laughter, the soldiers moaned in terror almost as one. They threw down their weapons and fled.

The sergeant offered a brief grimace of defiance. But when Dennis shouted "Boo!" he spun about and followed his men, rushing pell-mell down the road to Zuslik.

Dennis found himself standing there in the misty morning light, whirling his little noisemaker, amid a scattered pile of shiny, abandoned weapons.

Finally he was able to make himself bring his arm down and stop the infernal racket.

When he hurried down the road, calling out their names, Arth and Linnora pulled out of a dark hole in the trees. Arth looked Dennis up and down, then smiled sheepishly, as if ashamed ever to have doubted him. Linnora's eyes shone, as if to say that she at least had never worried.

She plucked at her klasmodion as they resumed their march. Only by accident did Dennis, a short time later, glimpse her nudge Arth and hold out her hand. Arth shrugged and handed over a small wad of ragged paper bills.

7

Soon they were passing the flint quarries Dennis had observed during his first week here. Now he understood why he had seen nobody back then. The preparations for war had already cleared the mountains. And here on Tatir, when people evacuated an area they took all their practiceable possessions and left nothing behind.

They made good time. The cart was clearly improving with use. As the morning passed, however, Dennis still worried. Surely the fleeing militiamen would have reported in by now. Kremer would have better troops sent after them.

They arrived at a fork in the road. Ahead of them the highway continued along the flank of the mountains, westward toward the big flint mines of the Graymounts.

Linnora got up and hobbled over to the less-used fork, the one heading south. "This is the trade route. It is the way I first came when I felt the presence of the little metal house come into the world."

She frowned and scuffed the side trail, as if unhappy over its level of practice. Trade had been particularly poor during the past few years. If the neglect lasted much longer the beautiful surface would start to fade away to a dirt track.

Dennis turned and looked to the northwest. Out there, a couple of days' foot march north of the main highway, lay his "little metal house."

If he could be at all sure he could pull it off—slap together a new zievatron and *practice* it up sufficiently in time—he would be willing to take the gamble. He would offer to take Linnora and Arth away from this violent madness, to a world where everything was difficult, but sensible.

But there was no time, and anyway they had other obligations. With a heavy sigh he took the donkey's bridle and led it onto the southward trail. "All right. We have another big climb ahead of us and another pass to get through. Let's make tracks."

The highland vale dropped behind them satisfactorily. Under Linnora's gentle urging, with Arth's and Dennis's help, the little cart had begun to turn itself into something really quite useful. The axles spun in narrow grooves in the body of the wagon, apparently lubricating themselves much as the runners of the Coylian sleds did in the native roads. The leather straps Dennis had contrived for Linnora to pull seemed to grow better and better at steering the front wheels around tight switchbacks behind the donkey, as Dennis and Arth pushed.

They were only a mile or so from the verge of the higher southern pass when Arth touched Dennis's shoulder.

"Look," the small man said, pointing behind them.

Below, and about two miles back, a column of dark shapes moved quickly on the trail under the trees. Dennis squinted, wishing for his monocular.

"They are runners," Linnora told them, rising in her seat to bring her sharp eyes to a level with theirs. "They wear the gray of Kremer's northmen."

"Can they catch up with us?"

Linnora shook her head, indicating uncertainty. "Dennis, these are the troops with which Kremer's father defeated the old Duke. They run tirelessly, and they are professionals."

Though Linnora clearly admired Dennis for his exploits, among other things, she also clearly knew he had his limits. These were not peasants, to be frightened with stones and a little noise.

She stepped out of the cart. "I think I had better walk now."

"You can't! Your feet will start swelling again!"

Linnora smiled. "Climbing uphill, you all cannot pull me as quickly as I can hobble. It is time I started doing my own part." She took Dennis's arm.

Arth clucked at the donkey, who pulled gamely at the lightened cart.

Dennis glanced back at the line of dark figures behind and below. They seemed larger already. The soldiers jogged on, and sunglints flashed from their weapons.

The fugitives turned and continued their climb toward the heights of the southern pass.

Both pursuers and pursued slowed as they approached the crest.

Now that Linnora was walking after a fashion, Dennis considered cutting loose the cart, or at least abandoning the little glider that lay bundled in the back. But although it would lighten their burden, for some reason he relented. A lot of practice had been invested in those things. They still might be useful.

The limit to their speed was Linnora's pace, anyway. She knew this. Her face grew hard as she forced herself onward. Dennis dared not interfere or force her to rest. They needed every moment.

His own legs hurt, and his lungs complained in the thinner air. The ordeal dragged on for what felt like hours.

It took them by surprise when, suddenly, a new vista opened before them to the south—a new watershed. Worn out, finally they slumped to the ground at the crest of the high pass.

Linnora looked out over the chain of mountains, like stalwart giants glowering in an arc to the south. This side of the peaks lay in shadows as the afternoon sun sank slowly to their right.

"There," she said, pointing to a series of glacier-girdled peaks. "That is my home."

To Dennis, the mountainous realm of the L'Toff looked like they might as well be as far away as the gentle hillsides of Mediterranea, back on Earth. How could they ever make it that far, pursued as they were?

Dennis stood in contemplation for a moment, catching his breath as Arth and Linnora sipped from one of the canteens Surah Sigel had provided.

Dennis looked at the twisting road that fell away before them to the south, along the flanks of the mountain. He turned and looked at the little cart that had served them so well so far. He whistled a faint tune as he felt an idea begin to emerge.

Could it work? It would be a desperate gamble, for sure. Probably it would get them all killed in a short time.

He glanced at his compatriots. They appeared almost done in. They certainly couldn't outmarch the troopers who were only a little way behind them.

"Arth," he said, "go keep a lookout."

The little thief groaned. But he got up and limped back up the road a piece.

Dennis poked under the nearby trees until he found a pair of stout sticks. He cut some rope from a coil Surah had given them and set to work attaching the sticks to the cart, along the railing just above and ahead of the rear wheels. He had hardly finished when there was a cry.

"Dennizz!"

Arth waved frantically from the northern edge of the pass. "Dennizz! They're almost here!"

Dennis cursed. He had hoped for just a little more time. The Baron's northerners were certainly fine troops. They must be pushing their human limits to maintain such a pace.

He helped Linnora into the cart even as Arth tumbled back to them. Arth began tugging at the exhausted donkey's tether, shouting imprecations as the animal became stubborn.

"Leave it alone," Dennis told him. He went over and cut the tethers, setting the creature free. Arth stared in surprise.

"Get in, Arth, there in back," Dennis told him. "From here on, we *all* ride."

8

The commander of the Blue Griffin company of the Zuslik garrison puffed alongside his troops. An ache tore at his side, where his laboring lungs complained in agony. The commander clamped down hard. He was determined not to be left behind by his men, most of whom were young volunteers from noble families, few over the age of twenty.

At age thirty-two, he knew he was getting too old for this. Perhaps, he thought as he wiped away the sweat clouding his eyes, perhaps he should arrange a transfer to the cavalry.

He spared a moment to glance at his men. Their faces were strained and sweaty, too. At least a dozen of his two score had fallen out already and were lying, gasping, by the side of the road all the way down the mountain.

The commander allowed himself a faint smile even as he fought for every new breath of thin air.

Maybe he would put off that transfer for a little while yet.

The minutes of agony seemed to crawl by. Then, at last, the pass crested under them. His feet felt feather-light as the slope flattened. He almost collided with the man ahead of him, who slowed down and pointed.

"There . . . ! Just . . . ahead . . . !"

The commander felt jubilant. Baron Kremer would be generous to the one who reclaimed the foreign wizard and the L'Toff Princess. His reputation would be made!

At the summit a clump of his soldiers, hands on their knees, were breathing raggedly and staring downhill. The commander, too, stopped there and blinked in surprise when he came into view of the southern slope.

Only a few yards away a little donkey grazed contentedly, leather straps hanging loosely from its harness.

Down the road, only a hundred yards or so, three people sat closely together inside a little *box.* He could tell at once that they were the fugitives he was after. They appeared to be just *sitting* there, helplessly waiting to be captured!

Then the commander noticed that the box was moving! No animal was pulling it, yet it moved!

How . . . ?

He realized suddenly it had to be the wizard's work. "After them!" He tried to shout but managed only a croak. "Up! Get up and after them!"

About half of his men got raggedly to their feet and staggered after him down the road.

But the little box was only speeding up. The commander saw the smallest fugitive—the little thief he had heard was instrumental in the escape from the castle—glance backward and flash them a sudden, malicious grin.

The box swung swiftly around a bend and out of sight.

9

"Watch out for that turn!"

"I *am* watching out for the damned turn! You just pay attention to the brakes!"

"Breaks? The cart's *broken?* Where!"

"No! *Brakes!* Those two sticks . . . When we're coming near a turn . . . twist those sticks so they rub against the rear wheels!"

"Dennis, I seem to remember a very tight turn just ahead—"

"What did you say, Linnora? Where? Oh, no! Hold on!"

"Dennizz!"

"Dennis!"

"Lean hard! No! The other way! Princess, I can't see! Get your hands off of my eyes!"

With a shuddering hum that vibrated their very bones, the cart squealed around the hairpin, then shuddered and swept on down the sloping highway. Rough scrub bushes and scraggly trees whizzed by them.

"Hooeee! Izzit over yet? Can I leggo these broken stick things? I don't feel so good. . . ."

"How about you, Linnora? Are you all right?"

"I think so, Dennis. But did you see how close we came to that precipice?"

"Uh, fortunately no. Look, will you check on Arth, please? I think he fainted."

The road ran straight for a little while. Dennis managed to get the cart running stably.

"Umm . . . Arth is coming around now, Dennis, though I think he looks a little green."

"Well, slap him awake if you have to! We're starting to speed up again, and I want him riding those brakes. You'd better help him by *practicing* them as well as you can!"

"I'll try, Dennis."

Dennis fought the bucking cart around the mountainside. Just in time, he felt Arth back on the brakes. The little thief was cursing foully, indicating a return to health.

"Thanks, your Highness," Dennis sighed.

"You're welcome, Dennis. But I ought to tell you . . . I think there is another switchback just ahead."

"Wonderful! Is it as bad as that last one?"

"Umm, worse, I think."

"Oh, lord, you're right! *Hold on!*"

When the downgrade finally ended they nevertheless coasted several hundred yards, and even climbed a little way up the opposite slope. By now the wagon's bearings were practiced to almost frictionlessness—a small blessing during that downhill careen.

They finally rolled to a stop in the middle of a narrow mountain vale —a summer pasturage. An abandoned shepherd's shack stood not far from the roadside. Momentum carried the little cart to within a few meters of its door.

Arth set the brakes securely, to lock the cart in place. Then he leaped out and fell to the ground, laughing.

Linnora followed, a little less nimble but just as delirious. She, too, collapsed to the lush grass, holding her sides as her bell-like laughter rolled. Tears streamed from her eyes.

Dennis sat at the front of the cart, quivering, his hands still wrapped in the biting thongs with which he had steered for ten or twenty of the most terrifying miles of his life. He cast a withering sidelong glance at Arth and Linnora. Though they were his friends and comrades, it was just as well he didn't have the energy or balance to get up, walk over to where they lay, and *strangle* them right there!

Like children, they whooped it up, making zooming motions with their hands. They had been like that ever since those first terrifying moments on the downslope. Once they realized that the "wizard" had done it again, it never even occurred to them to be frightened.

Their joyful shrieks had almost made him lose control a half-dozen times, nearly sending them over razor-edged cliffs!

Slowly, carefully, Dennis unwrapped the steering thongs. Returning circulation brought on a wave of intense pain. The "cart sickness" that had almost overwhelmed him during the wild ride came back. He stood up unsteadily, and stepped carefully out of the crazy little contraption, holding onto its side.

"Oh, Dennis." Linnora limped over to grab his arm. She had barely stopped laughing. "Oh, my Lord Wizard, you made such fools of them. And we flew faster than the very wind! You are wonderful!"

Dennis looked into her gray eyes, seeing in them the love and admiration he had often longed to find there—and came suddenly to realize that there were priorities that came before even a dream come true.

"Uh." He gulped and swayed. "Hold that thought."

He pulled away from her then, and stumbled quickly over behind a clump of bushes to become very sick.

10

Sic Biscuitus Disintegratum

1

It was an evening demonstration, performed by moonlight and the flickering luminence of a hundred bright torches. The noble observers watched with growing nervousness as preparations were made. Rank upon rank of troops filed into place in the parade yard. Then the rumbling drums fell silent.

There was a long pause, then the sudden quiet was split by a loud, terrifying sound. The crashing explosion was followed by another silence as the guests stared in stunned amazement at what had happened. Then a thousand men let out a single, bloodthirsty roar of approval.

Sergeant Gil'm turned and marched smartly back toward the dais. Out on the parade ground, at the end of the execution aisle, there was a new hole in the outer wall. A bloody stump stood where only moments before a defiant L'Toff prisoner had shouted epithets at Baron Kremer and his noble guests.

Kremer accepted the needler from his sergeant. He turned back to his peers, the great lords of the west, who had gathered to discuss the final alliance against the King's authority.

The counts and barons were pale. A couple looked like they just might be ill. *Yes,* Kremer thought, *the demonstration has been effective.*

"Well, my lords? You have seen my aerial corps in action. I have shown you my far-warning box. And now you know what my most precious new weapon can accomplish. Are there any now among you who doubt my plan?"

The Duke of Bas-Tyra frowned and shook his head. "We cannot but be impressed, my Lord Kremer . . . although it would be good actually to *meet* this foreign wizard who created these wonders for you, and of which so much is rumored."

He looked at Kremer expectantly. But the Lord of Zuslik merely waited, saying nothing, watching under darkly hooded brows.

"Ah, well," the Duke continued, "we are certainly in agreement that our Lord King Hymiel must needs be taught a lesson in the rights of his vassals. Still, some of the methods you propose . . ."

"You still seem not to perceive the true situation," Kremer said with a sigh. "You will have to be shown."

He turned to his cousin, Lord Hern. "Have them bring out the special prisoners," he commanded.

Lord Hern passed on the order.

The great lords muttered among themselves. Clearly they were deeply disturbed. This was getting to be more than they had bargained for. A few eyed Baron Kremer nervously, as if they had begun to suspect what he had in mind.

Lord Hern's messenger arrived at the postern, and soon a chain of bound men were led out into the courtyard, their guards yanking on their tethers.

There was a gasp from the assembled notables.

"Those are Royal Scouts!"

"Indeed. So it is war, like it or not!"

"And look! A Kingsman!"

Amid the chain of Scouts was a man wearing the blue and gold of a royal commissioner—a Kingsman—who had the power of royal writ.

"Kremer!" the man shouted. "You dare to treat the very *body* of the King in this way? I came out here as an emissary of peace! When my royal Lord hears of this he will have your—"

"He will have my fist!" Kremer roared, interrupting the commissioner's defiance. His troops, as one, shouted a cheer.

Kremer turned back to the assembled noblemen. He gestured to the prisoners.

"Hang them," he said.

The stunned Duke of Bas-Tyra said, "Us? You want us to hang royal messengers? *Personally?*"

Kremer nodded. "Right now."

The nobles looked at each other. Kremer saw a few eyes drift to glance at the gliders circling overhead in the torchlight, at the thousand disciplined troops—a fraction of his might—and at the needler in his hand. He saw the light dawn on them.

One by one, they bowed.

"As you wish . . . your Majesty."

One by one, they moved to obey. Kremer watched them descend, each to take a doomed man in tow.

That left only the mercenary captains on the dais with him. He turned and regarded them—six hardened veterans of dozens of scrappy little wars. These ones had no lands or property to think of. Able to have their forces simply melt away under threat, they had far less to fear from gliders and magical weapons. If in doubt, they would simply move on.

Kremer needed them if he was to put under siege the cities of the east and their "democratic-royalist" rabble.

And to keep them over a long campaign, he would need money.

"Gentlemen," he said, "would any of you care for some more *brandy?*"

2

"Dennis?"

"Hmmph? Wha—what is it, Linnora?" Dennis lifted his head. He had to rub his eyes to see. It was still dark outside. Across the floor of the little shepherd's cabin, Arth snored softly.

Linnora had slept curled next to Dennis, under the same blanket. Now she sat up, gray eyes blinking in the pale moonlight.

"Dennis, I just felt it again."

"Felt what?"

"That sense that someone or something has come into the world. Like the time I *knew* your little metal house had arrived, many months ago . . . and when I felt you, as well, arrive on Tatir."

Dennis shook his head to clear it. "You mean someone's using the zievatron?"

Linnora didn't understand. She merely stared into the night.

He wondered. Could Linnora really tell when the zievatron was operating? If she could, then did that mean someone else had just stepped through the reality transfer machine, following him onto this world?

Dennis sighed. He pitied the poor sucker, whoever it was. There was nothing he could do to help the fellow right now, that was for sure. The guy was in for one series of rude shocks.

"Well, no sense worrying about it," he told the Princess. "Come back and get some sleep. It'll be a busy day tomorrow."

3

As the dawn light spread across the upland meadow, the little alien house shone with the colors of a King's ransom in metal. The scholar Hoss'k whispered for his guards to keep still.

Hoss'k eyed the little house speculatively. The gods only knew how he was going to take the damnable thing apart. There had been a reason he had refrained from harvesting the whole thing months back. And it hadn't only been the need to get the captured Princess back to Kremer as quickly as possible.

Anyway, the whole question might be moot. Just like the last time, Hoss'k had arrived only to find somebody here ahead of him! A solitary figure paced impatiently about the clearing, muttering softly and carrying boxes out of the little metal house.

In the dim light, Hoss'k could half imagine that it was the foreign wizard himself! After all, the metal house was one of the obvious places to look for the fellow.

Perhaps Nuel could be made to disassemble the house *for* him! In any event, capturing and returning the wizard to Kremer would do a lot to relieve the warlord's wrath.

Hoss'k was disappointed when the growing light revealed the intruder to be a light-haired man. It wasn't Dennis Nuel at all, although the fellow did seem rather tall, like the wizard.

And as he and his guards listened from the cover of a nearby copse of trees, it seemed the fellow did speak with the same outrageous accent. Hoss'k strained to pick up the words as the foreigner mumbled to himself.

". . . bloody mess! . . . return mechanism torn apart . . . stuff strewn around on the ground . . . crazy note about local *intelligent beings!*" The foreigner snorted as he picked through a pile of items pulled from crates on the ground.

". . . getting even with me, that's what he's doing. Just because I went to N-Mart for his gear instead of that expensive wilderness store he picked . . . probably decided to go play explorer, and really did a number on the damned zievatron just to make certain nobody else could fix it . . . must've known Flaster'd pick me next. . . ."

Hoss'k had heard enough. One wizard would do in place of another. Maybe this one would be more tractable!

He motioned for his guards to spread out to surround the unsuspecting alien.

4

"Watcha doin', Dennizz?"

Dennis looked up from his work. In the predawn half light he felt tired and irritable. Arth was supposed to be with Linnora, helping prepare breakfast for their busy day ahead. "What does it look like I'm doing, Arth?"

"Wellll . . ." Arth rubbed his chin in what he had adopted as his "engineer's" stance. He clearly thought Dennis's question was Socratic, not sarcastic.

"Uh, it looks to me like you're attachin' the glider to th' cart, makin' its wings into sails, like on a boat."

Dennis shrugged.

Arth snapped his fingers. "Sure! Why not? There's lots o' wind up in these heights. Might help us along some o' those uphill stretches ahead!" He turned and called back to the shack, where cooking smells were beginning to waft.

"Hey, Princess!" Arth shouted, "come lookit what th' wizard's come up with!"

Dennis sighed and worked steadily. They would have to get out of here soon. They had gained a good head start yesterday afternoon. But Kremer's troops couldn't be far behind them. He only wished he were really as sure as Linnora and Arth were that he could get them out of their next jam. He would hate to see the disappointed looks on their faces when he finally let them down.

5

"Father, the attacks have begun!"

Prince Linsee looked up from the great map table as his son, Proll, strode into the conference room.

"Where have they struck?"

"All of the passes to the east are under assault by Kremer's toady allies. The attacks were synchronized by messengers riding his accursed gliders. We expect another major force to hit us along the northern trade route within a day at most."

Linsee looked to Demsen. The leader of the Royal Scouts detachment shook his head. "If all the western lords have joined Kremer, I cannot get a message out to the King, especially not when those gliders are aloft. The plains of Darb are too broad to cross in a single night, even on a fast horse."

"Perhaps with a *balloon?*" Linsee suggested.

Demsen shrugged. "And risk the few we have? Sigel and Gath are doing their best, but unless one of your people can lure a coven of Krenegee to help, I doubt the flotilla will be ready in time."

Prince Linsee looked downcast. There seemed to be little hope.

"Don't worry, old friend." Demsen clasped Prince Linsee's shoulder. "We shall give them a fight. And something may come up."

6

"I thought those sails were supposed to help us!" Arth grunted as he pulled on the little cart. From behind, Dennis pushed.

"So maybe it doesn't work! Not every good idea pans out. Sue me!"

They pushed the cart up a steep incline and finally reached a long, even stretch where they could rest. Dennis wiped perspiration from his brow and motioned Linnora to climb back aboard.

"I can walk some more, Dennis. Truly I can." Linnora looked angry at being forced to ride and having to watch as the two men did all the work.

Dennis was impressed with her stoicism and courage. Surely her feet and ankles still caused her great pain. Yet it was she who seemed the most anxious to press on rather than find a place in the hills to hide and wait out the coming battles.

"Sure you can probably walk some more," Dennis said firmly. "But pretty soon you may have to *run*. I want you to be able to do it when the time comes."

Linnora looked as though she were about to become stubborn. Finally she sighed.

"Oh, all right! I shall practice the cart some more and work on your sails for you."

She reached up, grabbed Dennis by the hair, and kissed him soundly. When she finished, she nodded "Hmmph!" as if by doing so she had established some important point. Then she climbed into the cart and took her accustomed seat, looking straight ahead.

Dennis blinked in confusion for a moment but decided not to question anything that felt so nice.

"Uh, Dennis?"

Dennis looked up. Arth was gesturing down the mountainside behind them.

Dennis was frankly getting a little sick of this habit of Arth's of pointing out bad news. He turned around and looked where the little man indicated.

There, in the bottom of the little mountain pasturage, was a large column of swiftly moving shapes.

Galloping past the shack where they had spent the night swept a troop of cavalry at least two hundred strong. A detachment stopped to search the shepherd's hut. The rest hurried on, their gray pennants flying as they swept up the trail after the fugitives.

It wouldn't take them more than twenty minutes to get here.

Dennis shook his head. Looking at the rolling upland country ahead of them, he saw no place to hide for several miles, at least. The trail was constrained to the side of the slope, with rugged banks or drop-offs on either side.

Okay, he thought, *what's going to get us out of this one?*

Arth and Linnora were looking at him expectantly. Dennis felt very tired.

I'm fresh out of ideas.

He was about to turn and tell them so when he caught sight of a small flurry of movement to the northeast, in the rough brush that covered the slopes in the direction that led, eventually, to the town of Zuslik. He peered at the strange phenomenon. The disturbance was moving toward them at high velocity.

"What the—?" Linnora and Arth turned and looked the way he indicated.

There was no way they could run from it if it turned out to be something dangerous. Whatever was shaking up the dry bushes, sending dust flying into the air, was moving their way at terrific speed.

Arth and Linnora looked as perplexed as he. "You know," Dennis thought aloud, "I think maybe it just might—"

The disturbance stopped suddenly, twenty yards away. There was a brief pause, as if the thing below the bushes, whatever it was, were taking its bearings. Then the trail of havoc turned and sped directly toward them!

Arth backed away, lifting one of the swords Dennis had taken from the militiamen he had driven off yesterday. Dennis moved to put himself between whatever it was and Linnora, though he had begun to suspect . . .

A shrub by the road parted in a shower of flinders. The cloud of debris settled slowly, to finally reveal a mound of dust—a pile that advanced on them in a whir of spinning treads.

With a faint whine the Sahara Tech exploration robot's turret opened. A pair of green eyes winked from the cupola within. Two rows of needle-sharp teeth grinned out from under the metal hood.

"Well," Dennis said, "it sure took you two long enough to catch up with us." Nevertheless, he smiled.

The robot beeped. The pixolet just grinned back at him through the cloud of floating dust. Then it shook its head vigorously and sneezed.

7

On the third fork of River Ruddik, the battle was not going particularly well for either side.

To Baron R'ketts and Count Feif-dei, the advance up the narrow canyon was a slow and dangerous undertaking, wasteful of both time and men. They watched from horseback atop a small hillock in the middle of the steep gorge as their forces trooped past in two columns.

The larger file headed westward, ever higher into the mountains, past heaps of rubble from the most recent of the many costly skirmishes in this hit-and-run war.

The very hill the barons stood on had been formed only this morning, when an avalanche of boulders had rained down upon this spot, trapping twenty soldiers beneath instant headstones.

The toll might have been far worse but for the prowess of the new King's glider corps. Kremer's crews had dived in, recklessly brave in the tricky air currents, and strafed the men of the L'Toff with hail-storms of deadly darts. They soon cleared the mountainside of defend-ers, allowing the lords' armies to move on.

Baron R'ketts watched the advancing column with an air of grim satisfaction. Even Baron . . . make that *King* Kremer . . . couldn't complain much over the pace they were making. At least not reason-ably.

In spite of these early reverses Baron R'ketts still expected an easy victory and looked forward to the harvest of this campaign. He had heard wondrous stories of the wealth of the L'Toff. It was said that L'Toff men could practice tools and weapons to perfection in minutes, and the items would stay in that condition forever after! It was also said that L'Toff women had the gift of being able to practice *men* . . . restoring in their users the virility that had once been theirs.

Baron R'ketts's spine hurt from all this time on horseback. But he kept telling himself it was worth it. Kremer had promised him wealth and pleasure beyond his fairest dreams.

He licked his lips in anticipation. He could *dream* of an awful lot!

Count Feif-dei watched the passing invasion with a more dour eye. Whereas his brother Lord gazed upon the stream of armed men climb-ing into the hills, Feif-dei could only watch the thinner trickle going the other way—farmers, yeomen, practicers, and even journeymen makers from the villages in his county—holding bandages to wounds, wincing on makeshift crutches, or leaning upon one another as they picked their way downslope to the aid stations.

Feif-dei knew that the best, most practiced bandages were saved for the nobility. Many, if not most, of these men would die—if not from blood loss, then from the wasting sickness that devoured the blood from within.

The troops seemed to have little of the bubbling enthusiasm with which they had begun this campaign. Mostly they were tired and hun-gry and getting just a bit frightened.

Still, there were a few here and there who spoke excitedly about the wealth they would win when they captured the enemy stronghold. Of his own blue-clad troops, he recognized some of the braggarts. They talked big, but unless they were watched closely they had an uncanny talent for being elsewhere when it came to any real fighting.

Count Feif-dei cursed softly, careful so his neighbor would not hear.

War was hell, and Baron R'ketts was a fool to savor it. He, Feif-dei, had once visited the lands of the L'Toff and been hosted courteously by Prince Linsee. He had tried several times to explain to R'ketts that the L'Toff were not tremendously wealthy. This campaign had one purpose only, to protect Kremer's rear for the real war to the east.

But R'ketts would listen to none of Feif-dei's accounts of what lay ahead, preferring to believe his own fantasies.

Count Feif-dei sighed. Ah, well. At least this struggle would keep R'ketts off of *his* back for a time. His folk and his lands would probably be as safe under the new King as under the old.

Just let it be a clean victory, he prayed, with as few skilled farmers and guildsmen lost as possible.

From up ahead there came a trumpet sound—a shrill warning. The lords heard a loud clatter of falling rock.

"Oh, no. Not again!" Baron R'ketts moaned and covered his eyes. He sat immobile on his horse, shaking his head.

Feif-dei quickly turned to his aides. "Hurry back to the semaphore post. Inform them of the new ambush and have them call for air support."

A messenger sped off. Baron R'ketts was still commiserating with himself, making no effort to investigate the situation. Count Feif-dei shook his head in disgust and spurred his horse toward the sounds of fighting.

8

"We strike and fall back, strike and fall back . . ." the courier explained hoarsely. "We have them stopped on all the other fronts, but in the Ruddik Valley the tide of lowlanders is endless! They just keep coming!"

Prince Proll thanked the exhausted messenger and ordered him taken away to find rest. He turned to his father.

"May I have leave, my Lord, to take forth with our reserves and crush the force in the Ruddik?"

Prince Linsee looked tired. He sat beneath a camouflaged canopy, under the trees near the eastern front. Outside they could hear the sounds of messengers coming and going at a run or a gallop. In the outer pavilion the battle staff argued over the tactical disposition of the L'Toff forces with their sparse royal allies.

"No, my son." The gray-haired Prince shook his head. "Your forces must remain in the north, with Demsen's scouts. That is where the main attack will come—where Kremer's full might will fall."

He did not add that the northern road was probably where the rebellious Lord would reveal his hostage—Princess Linnora—at a moment well chosen to strike at the defenders' morale.

When that moment came, they would need their best leaders to rally the men for the struggle of their lives. Old men, competent tacticians, could handle the delay along the eastern tributaries, especially when the balloon corps was ready to make its sally. But it would take sharp young fighters, such as Proll and Demsen, to give their soldiers heart, to adapt, to recover, and to continue harrying Kremer's northmen.

For once, Proll seemed to understand. The young man did not complain. He merely nodded and resumed pacing near the doorway, awaiting news.

At last Linsee spoke again. "Send for Stivyung," he told an aide. "I must know at last if his project is going to bear fruit in time."

9

"Who the hell *are* you guys? Let go of me! What do you think you're doing? Where are you taking me?"

The guards held the tall foreigner tightly and dragged him over to where the scholar Hoss'k waited in his red robes, sitting below the trees on a hundred-year-old portable chair.

The sandy-haired alien looked Hoss'k up and down. He straightened his shoulders. "Are you the grand high potentate around here? You'd better tell me what's going on! Never mind what you did with Nuel . . . I want to know what you did to our zievatron!"

"Be silent," Hoss'k said.

The foreigner blinked. He reared back. *"Listen,* fatso, I'm Dr. B. Brady, of the Sahara Institute of Technology. I am a representative of Dr. Marcel Flaster, who happens to be—"

There was a loud thump as the alien hit the ground, knocked flat by the burly backhand of one of the guards. "The scholar said to be silent!"

The fellow rolled over slowly and looked up, blearily. He did not open his mouth again.

Hoss'k smiled in satisfaction. This one would indeed turn out to be more tractable than Dennis Nuel had been. His bluster meant he had few internal reserves and would bend quickly once shown the way of things. He already showed the signs.

Apparently the guard had used too much force, though. The foreigner was slow to become lucid again.

No matter, Hoss'k thought. *By the time we are on our way back again, the high passes will be filled with my Lord's troops. I'd rather make a procession past them, with my new prize, than journey down that silent, eerily empty road one more time.*

10

"Are they gone yet?"

Linnora turned and went "Sshhh!" at Arth, who ducked quickly back under the bushes and was quiet.

Dennis watched anxiously as the Princess peered through the underbrush at the side of the road. The dust of the last of the cavalrymen settled slowly.

She had insisted on being the lookout. Dennis wasn't too happy about it, but he had to admit that she was right. The job didn't put much strain on her feet, and she was less exhausted than the two men. Besides, Dennis had witnessed few things more remarkable than the girl's eyesight.

He lay back on the dry sticks and needles beside the little cart. They had pushed the wagon into this thicket fifteen minutes before. It had been just in time, as the lead elements of Kremer's cavalry pounded around the rim of the mountain only moments later.

He and Arth had fallen to the ground exhausted, hardly noticing the apparently endless procession of horsemen who galloped past. It was only in the past few moments that the roar in Dennis's ears—and the laboring of his lungs—had quieted enough for him to hear anything at all.

Dennis felt a sharp tug on his sleeve. He turned his head and saw the robot standing only inches away. It had nudged him with one manipulator arm. Its red "attention" light flashed.

Dennis rose onto one elbow and looked at the small line of text that appeared on the machine's little screen.

"Oh, hell. Not now!" he told it.

The thing still wanted to fulfill the very first function he had given it —to report what it had found out about the inhabitants of this world. No doubt it had discovered a lot, but now certainly wasn't the time for a debriefing!

He patted the little robot on its turret. "Later, I promise, I'll listen to everything you have to tell me."

The machine's lights winked in response.

"Okay," Linnora said. She used the Earth term she had picked up from Arth. "The last of the horsemen are gone. From what we saw on high, they cannot be followed closer than an hour by any other forces, even more cavalry."

"All right," Dennis said, groaning as he sat up. "We chance the road again."

It was the only way deeper into the mountains. And deeper to the south they had to go if they were to arrive in time to do the beleaguered L'Toff any good.

Dennis stood up and held out his arm. The pixolet swooped down from its vantage point on a branch overhead, from which it had watched the cavalcade of horsemen. Grinning, it seemed to think the episode a wonderful joke.

Of course, they never would have made it this far without Pix and the 'bot.

This forest thicket in which they had hidden had been more than three miles away when they first caught sight of their pursuit. He and Arth could never have hauled the cart this far in time.

But the robot proved to be powerful when he ordered it to lend a hand—or claw. It was at least as good a tractor as the donkey had been. They covered those three miles quickly.

During the race for shelter, Dennis was certain that he had felt that queer resonance effect again between the humans and the Krenegee, directed at the tools they were using. It had been a mild version of the *felthesh* trance. He was sure the cart and robot had changed again even over that short stretch.

At his command, the 'bot took its place under the wagon again. Two of its three arms clamped onto the undercarriage to hold on.

Already the arms were beginning to look suited to the task.

Linnora and he pushed the cart through a gap in the bushes, while Arth ran back up the road to keep watch. Once they were onto the highway, Linnora climbed aboard and reset the glider sails. Dennis almost stopped her, but then he shrugged and let her finish. Who could tell? The flapping things might frighten some party of troops they came upon.

Arth came hurrying back. "Th' whole army's headed this way, Dennizz! At th' rate they're comin' we got no more'n an hour's head start."

"Okay. Let's get going."

Linnora belted herself into the cart, its sleek, almost streamlined sides glistening in the sunshine. Arth climbed aboard and took the brakes, whose friction bars and bindings had begun to look almost like machine-designed units.

Dennis remained on his feet to help push. He would hop in when they came to a downhill slope.

Linnora had already begun to enter her practice meditation. Maybe he was becoming more sensitive, or maybe it was the presence of the pixolet, but Dennis could already feel its traces begin to fill the space around him.

The pixolet, seeing a better place to position itself than his shoulder, abandoned him and launched itself to the top of the twin masts. The sails drooped under its weight, but the creature seemed happy enough. Its purring intensified the feeling that strange powers were already at work, helping mould the cart into something better.

Fine, Dennis thought, *but I'd still rather have an armored personnel carrier,* made *from scratch by the Chatham Works in England.*

With a sigh he nodded to his motley crew, and signaled the robot to commence pulling at top speed.

Dennis pushed on the upslopes, and ran alongside on the downhill sections while Arth applied the brakes and Linnora steered. The robot whirred and the sails flapped.

Above them all, the little Krenegee beast purred, amplifying the queer resonance that seemed to glow around them like an aura. The afternoon felt crystalline, like a faceted gem, and the *use* of the cart became like a complicated dance to music just beyond the edge of hearing.

Clearly they were getting better at working together to make the practice trance work.

It gave Dennis a strange sense of exhilaration. Through the pixolet, he could almost feel Linnora's thoughts as she concentrated. It seemed to tie them together, somehow closer than they otherwise might have been. Arth, too, became part of the matrix, although the Krenegee did not focus upon the little thief quite as much.

Dennis caught occasional glimpses of Pix perched upon its drooping sails. The creature grinned, enjoying the flow of *purpose* that flooded through it into the machine their lives depended on.

And it *was* changing. Dennis pushed the cart until he found he had to run simply to hang on! At the top of a steep rise he ordered the robot to stop, and he climbed aboard up front to take the reins from Linnora. The straps, he found, had grown softer and easier to hold.

He was about to start off again when Arth nudged his shoulder and pointed. Dust rose from the trail behind them. Only a mile or so off, they could see another troop of horsemen, followed by a seemingly endless column of foot soldiers, winding along the mountainside.

Trapped! They couldn't afford to go much faster, or they'd catch up with the units ahead of them. But to slow down would be disastrous!

"I'm going to take down these blasted sails," Dennis said. "Look at how they're drooping. They'll just attract attention, and there never was much wind, anyway."

Linnora stopped him. "Don't, Dennis. I am certain they have helped us remain stable and have slowed us safely over a few of those steep downhill stretches, although I admit I don't understand why. I am sure the cart is practiced for them by now. Removing them would only hurt."

Dennis could only trust her fey second sense. He kissed her quickly, then turned forward and told the robot to proceed.

They sped off down the mountain road.

Less than a mile farther on, they rounded a corner to sweep by a squad of resting cavalrymen. There were at least ten surprised faces, caught in a blur as the cart fluttered past like some great running bird. Men dove to both sides to get out of the way, tumbling in the dusty slope. Shouts followed the fugitives and soon there were charging troopers after them.

Dennis concentrated on his steering. The cart was already screaming along faster than ever. *This* time, however, he felt he was in control. In the grip of the practicing trance, he felt lightheaded and powerful.

Let 'em follow! They can eat our dust!

He heard Arth laugh from the back of the car, taunting their pursuers. Linnora was singing softly, an old warriors' song, with a strong beat and tone of defiance. It wove itself into the trance they shared. Dennis shouted in exhilaration.

The road turned then, and they came into sight of a battle.

Just ahead, in a flat clearing between the hills, the first fighting was taking place.

It looked like the invaders had caught a party of L'Toff by surprise. About fifty of Kremer's cavalrymen rode around a harried band of warriors dressed in faded green. The mountain men defended themselves in a disciplined manner with their pikes. No horseman dared approach too closely. But neither could the spearmen withdraw. And from their nervous glances to the north, it was clear they knew the rest of the invading army was not far away.

The defenders looked up in consternation as Dennis drove the car over the lip of the hill. A few cavalrymen, expecting nothing but help from that quarter, shouted in triumph.

The shouts turned to dismay as a great flapping juggernaut zoomed down on them. Dennis had no choice but to head into the thick of them. The ground on the right was too rocky, and on the left, only a dozen meters away, was a steep drop-off.

The cavalry horses were well trained, but not for anything like this whirring, flapping contraption! They screamed and bolted, carrying their hapless riders in every direction.

Dennis could sense Arth, standing up in the rear of the bouncing cart, striking out right and left with a staff and yelling with all his might. One knight who charged alongside seemed about to slash at the broad sails with his battle-ax, but just in time Arth's swinging pole knocked him completely off his horse.

A glimpse behind told Dennis that more of Kremer's soldiers were coming. And about a quarter mile ahead, a large contingent of green-clad fighters was approaching from the south, to the rescue of the beleaguered pikemen. A fair-sized battle was brewing.

He urged the robot to speed up. Their only chance was to get beyond the fighting, quickly!

Swerving hard to the left, Dennis struggled to avoid a collision, sending another pair of horses rearing in panic in their dusty wake.

If their sudden appearance had thrown off the invaders' tempo and enabled a few defenders to escape, that was all to the good. But Dennis's top priority was to get the cart to the other side of this little vale intact. Once beyond, they would be safely behind friendly lines. They could ride unopposed all the way to Linnora's home!

He felt something move between his legs. He glanced down and saw the pixolet grin back at him from deep within the cart, out of harm's way. The little Krenegee clearly knew how to take care of its own skin.

On looking up again, Dennis cursed quickly and slewed hard to the left. The wagon swept past a cluster of frightened pikemen, missing the stunned soldiers by the breadth of one of the sails.

"Dennizz!" Arth flailed. Dropping the quarterstaff, he plopped down into the cart. "Dennizz, where are you *goin'*?"

"Where do you *think* I'm—*Oh, no!* Robot! Full reverse!"

The little machine tried to comply. Its treads screamed. Clouds of dust rose from below them.

The steep slope before them had been hidden by a thin hedge of shrubs beside the road. They plowed straight through the narrow barrier in a shower of branches. Then they were over, rushing pell-mell down a forty-degree embankment!

"Aaaaagh!" he heard Arth say.

"Hoooyyy!" Linnora contributed.

Dennis struggled to steer as the cart bounced and flew downslope. "Slow down!" he urged loudly. He *practiced* slowing the descent as hard as he could and could feel the others doing the same.

"Slow down!"

Ahead, less than a hundred meters away, was the edge of a precipice. And there didn't seem to be any way to stop in time.

11

Et Two Toots

1

"Now, remember what I told you all!" Gath shouted at the other aeronauts. From the undercarriages of ten bobbing balloons came cries of assent.

Gath turned and gave thumbs up to Stivyung Sigel, riding the lead balloon of the south contingent. The big farmer nodded. He brought his hands to his mouth.

"Cast off!" There were two trumpet calls.

Axes split the tethers. Sandbags dropped. Hands spread fresh coals onto the smoldering fires beneath the open bags. One by one, the bright balloons rose past the tall trees and into the sky.

They had waited long for a favorable wind. At last one had come that blew the right way but that would not force them past the battle too soon.

Underneath rode a convoy of support troops ready to catch anchoring ropes when the time came to tether the lighter-than-air flotilla.

Gath was filled with excitement. To be aloft and in action was wonderful after all the waiting. It was a vindication of all the work he and Stivyung had put in with the L'Toff makers and practicers.

They drifted eastward with the wind. It felt like hours, but actually they were soon over the Ruddik heights, where the enemy had made their deepest penetration so far. Stivyung's contingent floated over the south spur, rimming that side of the canyon. There his aeronauts dropped anchors to waiting men. The L'Toff soldiers below scampered over the rocks to seize the anchors and tie them down.

When Gath's forces were over the north spur, they repeated the procedure.

The aeronauts had not had a chance to practice the technique. Fortunately, only one balloon from the south contingent drifted free, floating unanchored off to the east, rising rapidly.

That was a smaller loss than Gath had expected. They had planned to send one eastward anyway, with a report to the King of Coylia. Even Kremer's gliders could not stop the message if the balloon gained enough altitude in time.

If the L'Toff on the ground cheered when the balloons hove into view, the enemy below stared up in dismay. Rumors had already spread of the great, round monster that had roared into Zuslik one night, months ago. And now here were *ten* of the behemoths, glaring down with fierce, painted faces. The attackers fell back nervously from the high redoubts and muttered nervously while their captains conferred over this new development.

Here, where the L'Toff had chosen to make their chief stand, the terrain was extremely rough. A series of deadly prearranged rockfalls would make any direct ground assault costly.

But all these defenses required that Kremer's gliders be kept away so the L'Toff fighters on the heights could work unmolested.

That was the purpose for which the balloon detachment had been sent. The test was not long delayed.

"There!" One of the young bowmen in Gath's gondola pointed.

Against the sunlit clouds, high in the noontime sky, at least two dozen black shapes were outlined. The gliders looked like hawks in the distance, and they stopped, suddenly, like great birds of prey.

"Get ready!" the captain of a neighboring gondola cried.

The enemy looked small and distant for what seemed the longest time. Then, in an instant, they were down upon them! All around Gath, his bowmen were shouting.

"There! Shoot!"

"They're coming in too fast!"

"Quit complainin', kid! Just stop em!"

The babble of voices was almost as unnerving as the wicked black wings that rushed amongst them.

"Yahoo! I got one!"

"Great! But don't get cocky!"

"Watch out for those darts!"

There were screams of pain and cries of triumph, all in a matter of seconds. Then, almost as swiftly as they had come, the gliders were speeding away along the ridgetops toward carefully charted updrafts. They left behind three of their squadron, wrecked and scattered on the rubble below.

One more glider, unable to recover from a tear in its dragon wing, crashed directly into a cliff face as Gath watched. The defenders, both above and below, cheered.

"All right!" Gath yelled hoarsely as soon as he caught his breath. "They'll be back, and it won't be as easy to drive them off next time!

"Until they return, though, we concentrate on the enemy on the ground! Mark your targets, and make those arrows count!"

It would be difficult to get more ammunition. Resupply would be slow and chancy by bucket. And now the enemy's ground commander would certainly throw everything he had at the points where the covering balloons were anchored. Already Gath could see the invaders marshaling their forces for an assault on the other slope of the crumbled canyon, where Stivyung Sigel's four balloons were moored.

The attacks came, thereafter, at hourly intervals. The archers took a terrible toll of invaders on the ground. But each arrow lost was precious —in the making, in lost practice, and in the difficulty of hauling up supplies under fire.

And the defenders died in ones and twos as the battle went on. The L'Toff fighters on the surface fought to hold their ground and to defend the anchor points. The forces of the barons fought just as desperately to take those ridges.

The long afternoon passed like a slow agony, punctuated by moments of sheer terror. Within a few hours, the tactical picture began to emerge.

Here on the northern spur, the defense was going well, for now. Gath's archers took a heavy toll of attackers trying to climb the slopes and beat back three separate glider sorties.

But on the southern spur things had begun to go badly. Before the sun passed beyond the highest peaks, two of Sigel's southern balloons were lost, one when its bag was pierced. It settled slowly to the ground. The other one drifted off over the eastern plains when its anchor point was taken. It was too slow at ascending and finally fell under a rain of darts as Kremer's gliders converged from all around, like wolves upon a wounded lamb.

Gath wondered if Stivyung could hold out until nightfall. The two remaining southern balloons couldn't give each other much support.

Gath watched helplessly as enemy reinforcements arrived late in the afternoon . . . including a dozen fresh gliders. Kremer seemed to have an endless supply of them! Either that or his generals were stripping the other fronts of air support to handle this sticky spot in the center.

As the afternoon wore on, Gath watched as the entire flock of gliders swooped down on the two balloons on the lonely slope. And there was nothing he could do to help!

2

"Slow down! Slow down!"

Dennis realized that both Arth and Linnora had taken up his chant. The practice resonance was fully upon them.

Silvery fire seemed to dance around the body of the cart, and their acceleration down the tumbled slope did, in fact, seem to be slackening. But that didn't keep them from moving inexorably toward the cliff. It loomed ahead ten meters, five meters, two meters away.

At the very last minute the robot's whirling treads took hold and brought them to a stop in a boiling cloud of dust, teetering at the edge of the precipice.

Arth grabbed the narrow trunk of a shattered sapling that had partly broken the cart's momentum. The little thief held on for dear life.

Dennis wiped floating grit from his eyes and purposely avoided looking down. He tried to clear his throat of dust so he could politely ask the robot to redouble its efforts to back them away from the cliff edge. But the cart chose that moment to settle forward a few more inches. It dropped with a thump, leaving the robot's treads hanging out over open space.

"Okay," Dennis sang, a little bit upset by this time. "Linnora? Arth? You folks all right? I've got an idea. Let's all sidle backward, nice and easy." He felt Linnora begin to loosen her strap. She obviously had the same notion. It was time to get the hell out of here.

Something whizzed past Dennis's head. At first he thought it was some huge insect, but as he turned he glimpsed a second arrow passing through the space his ear had just occupied a second before.

"Hey!" Arth howled. An arrow quivered in the sapling's trunk inches from his fingers.

Up the talus slope Dennis saw at least a dozen of Baron Kremer's gray-clad archers working their way cautiously downward, getting into position to administer the coup de grâce. Capture, apparently, was no longer an option at this point.

They didn't really have to bother, Dennis realized. Arth was visibly weakening and soon would have to let go of either the tree or the glider. He and Linnora could never slide back quickly enough to make a difference.

Is this it? Dennis looked around for some way out—while arrows zinged past them or stuck, humming, to the sides of the cart.

Linnora was fumbling for her knife. Dennis wondered what she was trying to do. Then it hit him.

The *glider!* If we can only detach it from the cart in time, we might be able to escape on it!

But first the wings would have to be let down. They were being held up—vertically, like sails on a boat—by a stout length of rope. Linnora was going for it with her knife.

It took almost half a second for it to occur to him to remember the amount of tension that was in that cable. He cried out in dismay, "No! Linnora, don't!"

It was too late. She sliced the rope. The wings snapped down violently, knocking two deadly arrows out of the air.

Perhaps it was a rational decision, but Arth was never able to explain why he let go of the tree and not the cart. But when the little wagon bucked suddenly, like a mad stallion, Arth tumbled into the back of the cart behind the great wings. Linnora and Dennis were whipped around to face forward as their strange vehicle teetered dangerously, rocking unstably on the edge.

The pixolet had hopped onto Dennis's lap from the floor. The little creature had the expression of one who by this time had had quite enough. This trip was no longer fun.

About to abandon us again? Dennis thought at the thing, unable to do anything else.

The Krenegee shrugged, as if it understood. It flexed its wing membranes in preparation to depart. Then, for the first time, it took a good look over the rim of the cart into the canyon below.

"‼" it peeped out loud and shivered. Its little glider membranes were never meant for true flight. They wouldn't keep it from being smashed to jelly after a fall like that! Dennis almost laughed as the smug little thing at last showed consternation.

All of this took about one second of telescoped time as the cart rocked, and then slid over the edge. A flight of arrows missed them by inches as their trusty machine toppled over the precipice. The pixolet wailed. Arth cried out. Dennis held on as the canyon opened up below them.

At that moment it was Linnora who saved them.

She started to sing.

The first, high note was of such startling clarity, that it seized their attention away from the hypnotizing view of the onrushing canyon floor. As a practice team, they had worked together for a long time. Her call served as a focus. Out of habit—quicker than volition—the *felthesh trance* snapped into being all around them.

Dennis felt Linnora's mind touch brush against his own. Then he felt Arth, and even the Krenegee beast—taking this all seriously for the first time since he had known the smug little thing. Space around them seemed to flash and burn with energy. The power was there, and the desperate will to change reality.

Unfortunately, there was no focus. One had to be *using* something for the Practice Effect to operate!

Dennis's conscious mind was in no condition to provide an answer. It was a good thing, then, when his unconscious stepped in and took over.

In that instant, with the ground rushing up at them, Dennis seemed to feel time contract all around him. In a haze of chaotic energy that felt strangely like the field around a zievatron, he blinked once, twice, then closed his eyes.

When he opened them again, he found himself sitting next to a dark-haired young man with a thick, waxed moustache. The fellow wore a white leather coat that flapped in the stiff breeze, and a pair of old-fashioned flight goggles over his eyes.

They sat together in a strange contraption of white canvas and wooden struts, laced together by piano wire. Although air rushed past them, the hazy-edged reality that surrounded them seemed entirely gray and motionless.

"You know, we had the most bully awful time getting the proper approach to warping the wings," the fellow explained over the rush and roar. He had to shout to be heard. "Langley never really understood, you see. He rushed ahead without testing his designs in a proper artificial wind tunnel, as Wilbur and I did. . . ."

Dennis blinked in surprise. And in the time it took to close his eyes and open them, his surroundings changed.

". . . so I had to test the X-10 personally, get it? The engine took up over half the damned thing's length! Busted the first few props we tried to smithereens! They called it a flying bomb! Couldn't ask anyone else to take it up, see?"

The man with the handlebars and goggles was gone, replaced by a fellow with a thin moustache, a sardonic expression, and a floppy fedora hat. He shook his head and laughed.

"Hard work is what it took. Sure, I had inherited money and got to stand on the shoulders of giants. I admit it! But I sweated blood straight into each of my designs."

The space around them was still that hazy, half real shimmering, like the boundaries of a dream. But the flimsy array of wood and canvas had been replaced by a thrumming cocoon of riveted metal and glass, vibrating with the power of a thousand horses.

"And don't think I don't already feel the shoes of later inventors sometimes," the pilot of the monoplane grinned, "right here." He patted his own shoulder and laughed.

The fellow looked familiar, though he couldn't place him—like someone he had read about in a history book somewhere. Dennis blinked again, and when he reopened his eyes the dreamlike scene had shifted again. The dark-haired man and the cramped cockpit were gone.

It was only a brief glimpse, this time. The engine roar had muted somewhat. There was the scent of chrysanthemums, and for the moment his eyes were open he saw a woman wearing a straw hat and a bright, pink scarf. She smiled at him from her controls, and winked. Through the cockpit window he saw water, all the way to the horizon. Then the transition happened again.

Now he was seated at the copilot's station in a huge twin-engined airplane—a bomber, from the looks of it. There was the smell of gasoline and rubber. In his hands a wheel vibrated with a powerful rhythm. A balding man in a khaki uniform smiled at him from the other set of controls.

"Progress," the gangly fellow grinned. "Boy, you sure are doing it the easy way, fella. It took us old-timers years and plenty of sweat to get this far, I'll tell you!"

For the first time in this crazy dream, Dennis thought he understood what someone was talking about. He recognized this man's face. "Uh, I know. I guess you really could have used the Practice Effect back in your day, Colonel."

The officer shook his head. "Naw. It was a whole lot more fun doing it for ourselves, even if it *was* slower. I only ask that the universe be fair, not that it grant me any special favors."

"I understand."

The Colonel nodded. "Well, each of us does what we have to do. Say, do you want to hang around here for a little while? We just took off from the *Hornet,* and we're on our way to have a little fun."

"Uh, I think I'd better be getting back to my friends, sir. But thanks, anyway. It was a pleasure to meet you and the others."

"Think nothing of it. It's only a shame you couldn't stick around to meet some of the jet jockeys and astronauts. Talk about pilots!" The Colonel whistled. "Ah, well. Just remember, my boy. *Nothing* substitutes for hard work!"

Dennis nodded. He closed his eyes once more as the wind roared and the dream unraveled around him like fog melting in the dawn.

Seconds that had seemed telescoped into years evaporated, and as the crystalline shimmer at last parted, Dennis found himself flying!

He wasn't exactly sure how much time had passed, but a powerful lot of changes had been made in the cart-and-glider combination—as evidenced by the fact that they were still alive.

Even as he looked around, a pale, shimmering light was leaving the struts and fabric of the wings—now anchored firmly to the wagon-fuselage, sweeping rakishly outward and back like those of a swift. The cart itself seemed to have lengthened and grown a nubby tail. Its narrow nose aimed proudly upward, into the rising thermal in which they slowly climbed.

It must have been one of the most powerful *felthesh* trances in Tatir history. The pixolet slumped exhausted on his lap, breathing hard and staring about in disbelief. Dennis was still tentative enough in his control of the glider not to be willing to turn around, but he'd be willing to wager Arth and Linnora were in similar shape.

His dream still lingered at the fringes of Dennis's mind. He could almost smell, again, the gasoline and oil, and feel humming metal.

If the dream had gone on, no doubt he would have met more of the heroes of aviation, called up by his unconscious to provide a focus for the intense practice trance. But it had lasted long enough, and it left him with a vague feeling of pride. Such men and women were the heritage of Earth. By pluck and ingenuity they had carved miracles out of reality—the hard way.

Dennis leaned out over the side to look. The updraft was petering out. It wouldn't take them back to the level of the mountain road they had fallen from. He would have to find another place to land within gliding range.

There was a plateau nearby, a spur jutting eastward out from the mountains. Cautiously, Dennis leaned left and sent their craft into a gentle bank. He had seen a flat spot on the mesa. It would have to do. Beyond that was only a tumbled plain of boulders as far as the eye could see.

Still, they couldn't stay up here forever.

Dennis wished there was some way to get the robot up in the cockpit with them. He didn't want it damaged in the landing. But it would just have to take its chances. He called down for the machine to prepare as best it could.

The precaution was probably unnecessary, he realized. The rugged little thing could well be the only one of them to survive their encounter with the ground.

He used up some height gliding far out over the plain. It took a while to reach a position along what he hoped was a gently appropriate glide path, then bank around and begin his approach. It had to be just right, because they weren't going to get another chance.

While he got ready, he spared a moment to glance back at the others. Arth was soaked in sweat but gave the thumbs-up sign. Linnora simply looked exalted, as if she could ask no more than to have experienced what they had just gone through. She leaned forward slightly and pressed her cheek against his. Dennis smiled hopefully and turned back to make ready for the landing.

"All right, everybody. We're going in!"

The "flat spot" that rushed up at them was actually a sandy bank with at least a ten-degree slope from left to right, only a dozen meters from the plateau's northern rim. A crosswind came from twenty degrees left of the nose. Dennis steadied the balance so the wings compensated as well as possible. He felt Linnora's hands grip tightly around his chest. At the last moment he brought up his knees and braced himself.

The fabric wings luffed slightly as the glider swooped in like an albatross and touched down gently on the soft sand. One wingtip briefly touched ground, slewing them around slightly as they jounced along the embankment. Gravel flew up behind them as Arth put all his weight into the brakes and the robot's treads spun furiously.

Dust was everywhere! Blinded, Dennis steered entirely by instinct.

At last they rolled to a stop. When the sand had settled and tears had washed some of the dry powder from his eyes, Dennis looked out to see that the glider had halted close to the edge of the mesa. Another jumbled drop of about fifty meters lay only six feet away.

One by one—first Arth, then Linnora, and finally Dennis—they loosened their straps and stepped out. Barely able to keep to their feet, they stumbled to a thin patch of grass under the sparse trees.

Then Arth and Linnora fell to the ground, dizzily, and laughed. This time Dennis collapsed with them and joined in.

Several minutes later, the pixolet raised its head from the well of the craft. It still twitched and shook, from fright and from the power of the trance it had been forced to take part in. For a long while it simply stared at the crazy humans.

Finally, as the sun settled behind the western peaks, it sniffed disgustedly and dropped back down beside the gently humming robot to fall instantly to sleep.

3

In spite of their leisurely pace, Bernald Brady was saddlesore well before the stout character in the red robes called a halt for the night.

It was the first time Brady had ever ridden a horse. If ever he got a chance to decline further invitations, he was certain it would also be his last. He dismounted clumsily. A guard came over and loosened his bound hands, motioning him to hobble over and sit beneath a tall tree by the campsite.

Soon there was a fire, and the smell of trail cooking wafted through the air.

One of the soldiers scooped a thick dollop of stew and came over to hand Brady a beautiful, feather-light ceramic bowl. The Earthman ate as he marveled at the bowl. He had never seen anything like it before. It helped him justify the theory he had come up with.

Although his "captors" played a good game at this business of acting like primitives, they couldn't hide their true nature. Things like this beautiful, high-tech bowl gave their game away.

These people clearly came from an advanced culture. One look at the road, and the wonderful self-lubricating sleds, told him that. There was only one explanation for what was going on here.

Obviously Nuel had spent the last three months living among the locals. And all that time he had been plotting, knowing that if he only waited long enough Flaster would surely send him, Brady, over to try one more time to fix the zievatron. In all that time Nuel had no doubt ingratiated himself with these people, perhaps promising them rich trading rights with Earth! In return, all they would have to do would be to help him pull one great big practical joke!

It sounded like Nuel's way of setting up priorities!

No doubt members of an advanced civilization would have plenty of leisure time on their hands. Brady had witnessed "midaevalists" on Earth, who liked to ride horses and play with old-fashioned weapons. Nuel must have hired a troupe of history-nuts like those to help him pull a fast one on the next guy to come through the zievatron!

These fellows played pretty rough. They had really put a scare into him for a while, especially when the fat boy kept questioning him about every piece of his gear.

Brady sniffed. That had been carrying it too far! Imagine, people who could make swords out of gemstones being perplexed over his rifle and his porta-microwave!

Oh, these people knew Nuel, all right. Whenever he mentioned the fellow's name the big "priest" got a funny look on his face. The "soldiers" clearly knew exactly who he meant, though they never admitted a word.

Yeah, Brady nodded, by now convinced. They were all in it together. Nuel was having his revenge on him for switching those chips on the replacement circuit boards.

Well enough was enough! It was going to stop here! The game had gotten altogether too rough. His hands were chafing and he had been battered and bruised . . . Brady decided it was time to stand up for his rights. With his jaw set he put down the now-empty bowl and started to get up.

At that moment one of the "soldiers" screamed.

Brady blinked as he saw one of the men stagger about the campsite with an arrow protruding through his throat. Suddenly, everyone else was diving for cover!

This was carrying realism just a bit too far! Brady watched the stricken soldier gurgle and die, choking on his own blood. He swallowed and had the uneasy feeling that maybe his theory might need some amending.

He heard someone shout, "Guerillas! Sneakin' aroun' behind our lines!"

One of the "officers" barked an order. A detachment of men hurried off eastward into the trees beside the road. There was a long wait, followed by a series of loud noises—clangings and loud screams. Then, a little while later, a messenger came running back into camp.

The courier hurried over to the fat man in red, who was taking no chances, huddled beside a tree nearby.

Brady crawled to the edge of his own tree where he could listen.

". . . ambush coverin' a turn in th' road. I guess one of 'em musta got impatient, waitin' for us, and sprang th' trap early. That was a lucky break for us. But we're still stuck here until we can get word to our army."

The fat man in red, the one called "Hoss'k," licked his lips nervously.

"We used our last pigeon to inform my lord Kremer that we had captured another alien wizard! How shall we get a message through, then?"

The officer shrugged. "I'll send a dozen men in different directions after dark. All we need is for just one to get past 'em. . . ."

Brady crawled back around his tree and sat there a long moment, blinking. His comfortable theories dissolved around him, and he was left with a confusing, dangerous reality.

I didn't want to come here in the first place! he complained silently to the universe.

He sighed. I should never have let Gabbie talk me into volunteering!

4

"My Lord, we have received a message from Deacon Hoss'k. He is on his way to North Pass now. He claims to have found—"

Baron Kremer turned and snarled, "Not now! Send word to the fool to stay where he is and not to get in the way of the northern force!"

The messenger bowed quickly and ducked out of the tent. Kremer turned back to his officers. "Proceed. Tell me what is being done to clear Ruddik Valley of the floating monsters."

Kremer had only just arrived, as the new day dawned, by three-man glider. His head throbbed and he felt just a little sick. His subordinates sensed that he had a short fuse, and they hurried to comply.

"My Lord, we were stopped yesterday by the coming of night. But Count Feif-dei's forces are now closing in upon the two monsters remaining on the southern rim of the canyon. We are going to provide heavy air support, assisted by the reinforcements you ordered sent from the other fronts.

"As soon as the last two southern monsters are eliminated, we'll be able to assault the ridge beyond. It will be costly, but the L'Toff positions will then be untenable. They will have to fall back, and the remaining four monsters on the northern slope will then be surrounded. There will be nothing they can do."

"And how many gliders will have been lost by then?" the Baron asked.

"Oh, not many, my Lord. Perhaps fifteen or twenty."

Kremer slumped into a chair. "Not many . . ." He sighed. "My brave, lucky pilots . . . so many. A quarter, almost a third lost, and none at all left to support the northern force."

"But your Majesty, the monsters will all be gone. And by now the L'Toff and the Scouts are fully engaged on all fronts. A breakthrough anywhere, and we shall have them! That is especially true here. If we cut through to the west today, it will split the enemy in half!"

Kremer looked up. He saw enthusiasm on the faces of his officers, and he began to feel it himself once again.

"Yes!" he said. "Have the reinforcements brought up. Let us go to the head of the Ruddik and watch this historic victory!"

5

When morning came, Dennis and Linnora lay side by side, wrapped in one of Surah Sigel's blankets on the sandy bank, watching the sun rise over the bank of eastern clouds.

Dennis's muscles felt like limp rags that had been all used up. Only here on Tatir a rag that was so thoroughly used wouldn't be in as bad shape as he was. It would only be getting better at cleaning up.

Nearby he heard Arth doing his best to throw together a breakfast from the scraps left over from Surah's larder.

Linnora sighed, resting her head on Dennis's chest. He was content just to drift, semiconscious in the soft, sweet aroma of her hair. He knew they would have to start thinking about a way off of this plateau soon. But right now he was reluctant to break the peaceful feeling.

Arth coughed nearby. Dennis heard the fellow shuffle near the edge of the precipice, mutter unhappily for a moment, then walk back to the trees.

"Uh, Dennizz?"

Dennis did not lift the arm from over his face. "What is it, Arth?"

"Dennizz, I think you'd better have a look at somethin'."

Dennis uncovered his eyes. He saw that Arth was pointing to the west.

"Will you *stop* doing that?" Dennis asked as he and Linnora sat up. He couldn't quite quash a feeling of irritation toward Arth's penchant for pointing out bad news.

Arth was gesturing toward the ridge they had fallen from as dusk fell yesterday, with arrows slicing through the air around them. According to Dennis's wrist-comp, it had been less than ten summer hours since they had plunged over that cliff, straight into the heart of the Practice Effect.

Dennis could hear faint sounds of fighting from that direction. A dust plume of battle rose from the ridgeline above them. The cloud seemed to be moving slowly, inexorably southward.

The L'Toff were clearly being pushed back.

But that wasn't what concerned Arth. He pointed to a place just behind and below the dust of battle. Dennis looked carefully at the ridge face, illuminated by the rising sun. Then he saw them.

A small detachment of men had dropped away from the fighting on the heights. They were working their way downslope along the slash in the cliff that a spring waterfall had gradually made. They were descending carefully, belaying each other with ropes over the steeper parts.

So Kremer's troops weren't letting go yet. They knew how badly their Lord wanted the fugitives and had sent a contingent to chase them, even to this lonely plateau.

Dennis estimated they would be here in a little more than two hours, perhaps three.

Linnora touched his shoulder. Dennis turned around, and winced when he saw that *she* was pointing now, as well!

You too? He looked at her accusingly before following her gesture.

Off in the south, where she indicated, something bright moved against the sky. Several somethings. He envied Linnora her prodigious eyesight.

"What . . . ?"

Then he knew. The bigger object was a *balloon*, drifting in the morning light. Its great gas bag was aflame, and several dark, malign objects darted and swooped about it, closing in for the kill.

So. In spite of a brief, peaceful respite, the battle still raged around them on many fronts. It would be best to get off this mesa before Kremer's rangers made it down here. It might also be desirable to see what their little band of adventurers could do to help the good guys.

And Dennis thought he just might have a way.

He drew out the sharp, hundred-year-old knife Surah Sigel had given him, and turned to Linnora and Arth.

"I want both of you to find me a big piece of sturdy wood, about *so* thick by *so* long." He indicated with his hands.

When Arth started to ask questions, Dennis merely shrugged. "I want to do some carving," was all he would say.

Linnora and Arth looked at each other. *More magic,* they thought, nodding. They turned without another word, and hurried into the brush to look for what the wizard wanted.

When they returned they found the Earthman deep in conversation . . . partly with himself and partly with his metal demon. He had pulled the glider to within a few feet of the edge of the cliff and installed the robot underneath it once again. A pile of gear lay on the sand beside the craft.

"We found a stick," Arth announced.

"And it looks like what you asked for," Linnora finished for him.

Dennis nodded. He took the five-foot branch and immediately started whittling it, chopping away loose bark and shaving slivers away in long, curved arcs. He mumbled to himself distractedly. Neither Linnora nor Arth dared interrupt him.

The pixolet arose out of its slumber within the cart/glider and clambered up onto the windshield to watch.

Linnora frowned in concentration. "I think he wants to take off again," she whispered to Arth. She could tell, for instance, that he had already started emptying the craft to lighten it. "Come and help me," she told the thief, and started tugging at the chair and bench to tear them out of the glider.

Only once in a while did they look up to see the progress Kremer's rangers had made in moving steadily downslope. They were getting closer all the time.

Arth and Linnora had just about completed their task when Dennis finished his.

Linnora had thought herself long past surprise at anything the wizard would ever do. But then Dennis stopped carving, admired his handiwork for a second, then reached under the glider to give the stick to the robot!

"Here," he told it. "Take it firmly in the middle with your center manipulator arm. Yeah. Now spin it clockwise. No, I want a rotary motion along the axis of that arm. That's right!

"Don't strain yourself at first, but spin it as fast as you can. Your *purpose,*" he emphasized, "is to cause a *breeze* to blow back toward us, and generate forward lift."

He turned back to the others and smiled. When they only stared back at him, he tried to explain. But all they really were able to get down was the name of the new tool . . . a *propeller,* he called it.

The stick turned faster and faster. Soon it was only a blur, and they began to feel a stiff wind.

Dennis asked Arth to stay on the ground, holding onto the rear of the craft to keep it from moving. Linnora climbed aboard and took her accustomed position.

Dennis picked up the Krenegee, who whimpered slightly in exhaustion. "Come on, Pix. You've still got a job to do." He climbed in front of Linnora and nodded for her to begin the practice trance.

"Propeller." Linnora mouthed the new word to memorize it. She picked up her klasmodion and strummed.

On Tatir, sometimes even people benefited from practice. The four of them slipped into another felthesh trance as if they had been born to it. It was nowhere near as intense as the powerful storm of change they had wrought so desperately the day before. But soon there was a familiar shimmering to the air near the front of the glider, and they knew alterations were taking place.

Now it was a gamble against time.

6

The last of the balloons on the south spur floated away just after sunrise as the defenders of its anchor rope fell before the dawn onslaught. These aeronauts, at least, had learned from prior disasters. Immediately they dumped overboard all of their sandbags, weapons, clothes, anything that could be cast loose. The balloon shot up into the sky, past the waiting, vulturelike gliders. The lighter-than-air craft caught a fast air current to the east and relative safety.

Gath watched it happen and hoped that balloon was the one with his friend Stivyung aboard.

Well, at least they had managed to hold off the inevitable for an entire day. During the night the smoldering glow of the balloon maws had been a reminder to the troops below that Kremer wasn't having everything his own way.

"The gliders will now be free to attack our forces on that ridge," a L'Toff bowman in the gondola with him said. "They'll sweep the southern spur, enabling invader troops to follow and enfilade our forces in the valley."

Gath had to agree. "We need reinforcements!"

"Alas, our reserves have all been pulled back to stay the thrust from the northern front."

Gath cursed. If only he had been able to come up with a way to drive balloons against the wind. Then they might have been of some use in the northern fight as well. Then they would not have been sitting ducks for those damned gliders!

"Here they come again!" one man shouted.

Gath looked up. Another stoop of the damned dragon-winged devils was on the way. Where had they all come from? Kremer must have brought in every one he owned to finish them off.

He picked up his bow and made ready.

7

Arth struggled to maintain his grip on the tail of the cart-glider. His heels skidded in the powdery sand. The blowing air was filled with floating grit.

"I can't hold it back!"

"Just hold on a little longer!" Dennis urged over the backwash. The wind from the whirling stick was now a roar, blowing their hair about wildly. The cart kept bucking and heaving as the rushing air made the wings strain and hum.

Linnora leaned into the brakes, her long, blond hair whipping around her.

Arth shouted again, "I can feel it slippin'!"

Dennis yelled back, "I've got the robot running its treads in reverse.

In just a minute you can hop aboard, Linnora can release the brakes, and I'll tell the robot to take off!"

"You'll tell the what to *what?*" Arth was straining as hard as he could.

"I *said,*" Dennis shouted, "I said I'll tell the *robot* to *let go!* Then you can—"

He never finished his sentence. There was a sudden shift in the whine below them as the treads stopped whirling in reverse and immediately slammed into forward gear.

"No! I didn't mean now!" Dennis was whipped back against Linnora as the craft bolted forward like a racehorse released at the gate.

Caught in a spray of sand, Arth let go just in time. He sprawled face first to the ground, inches from the cliff edge. "Hey!" He coughed and spat and sat up, complaining. "Hey! Wait for me!"

But the "cart" had already leaped out of earshot. It was out over the boulder canyon, doing cartwheels in the air.

Arth watched, enthralled, as the flying machine zoomed high, stalled, fell into a steep career, then recovered into a series of powered loop-the-loops.

The maneuvers certainly were amazing, Arth thought. The wizard must be showing off for his sweetheart. And who could blame him? Arth's heart soared with the wild, capering dance of the airplane.

Still, for one brief moment he thought he heard a loud, foul-tempered curse as the machine flew past the plateau.

He watched, amazed, until a noise reminded Arth about Kremer's soldiers. A hurried look around a small bluff told him the party of rangers had finally arrived. Arth decided then that he had better go about finding himself a hiding place.

Linnora was laughing again. And once again, it was hardly a help.

Dennis's pulse pounded and he gasped for breath. The Princess clung so tightly to him that it was hard to breathe!

He tugged at one of the strings he had attached to the robot so he could control the crude airplane by hand and not have to shout all of his commands. He pulled gently, so as not to overcompensate, having learned that lesson the hard way. Several times he had almost stalled the little craft, or sent it into uncontrollable spins.

Finally, the damned thing steadied down. The robot spun the propeller at an even rate, and Dennis got the contraption flying smoothly away from the vicinity of cliffs, rock walls, and downdrafts. He set the plane into a slow climb, then sagged back against Linnora's soft, strong embrace, hoping he wasn't about to be sick.

Linnora laughed richly, and hugged him out of sheer exhilaration.

"Oh, my Wizard," she sighed. "That was marvelous! What a great lord you must be in your homeland. And what a land of wonders it must be!"

Dennis felt his breath returning. In spite of that period of panic and almost disaster, things had turned out pretty much as he had planned this time. It looked like he was getting the hang of the Practice Effect!

He couldn't help feeling happy, sitting back as she rubbed the muscles of his neck and played happy nuzzle games with his ear. He controlled the plane with gentle nudges, letting it gain practice with use.

The pixolet peered over the side, bright-eyed with amazement as they cruised leisurely across the sky.

Although he was content to rest there in her arms for the moment, Dennis realized he would have to set Linnora straight about one thing quite soon. She had altogether too much confidence in him. No doubt about it. She frequently had the habit of assuming he *knew* what he was up to when all he was doing was improvising to survive!

The forests and plains of Coylia stretched out below them, a sea of ambers, greens, and blues. Soft white clouds arrayed in drifting columns as far as the eye could see.

Dennis ran his hand along the laminar smooth side of the craft they flew . . . handiwork he had created, helped by his comrades, in only two days' time! He marveled at the wonderful adaptations that had converted a rickety little hand-carved cart into a sleek flying machine.

True, the thing would not normally have been possible, even here. It had taken a combination of his own inventiveness and the rare practice resonance—derived from the melding of man, L'Toff, and Krenegee. But still . . .

Pix hopped up onto his lap. Apparently it had decided to forgive him. The creature settled in for a long purr. Dennis stroked its soft fur. He looked up at Linnora, remembering her last remarks, and smiled.

"No, love. My world is no more wonderful than this one, where nature's so kind. It's usually been a hard life there. And if it's become anything but brutal and futile in the past few generations, it's thanks to the sweat and hard work of millions. Given the chance, any man or woman of Earth would choose to live here instead."

He looked out over the plains and realized that he had made a surprising decision. He would remain here on Tatir.

Oh, he might return to Earth temporarily. He owed the land of his birth any help he could give it from what he had learned here. But Coylia would be his home. Here was where Linnora was, for one thing. And his friends . . .

"Arth!" He sat up suddenly. The plane rocked.

"Oh, my, yes!" Linnora cried. "We must go back!"

Dennis nodded as he gently turned the plane around.

And then there was the war, too. That madness had to be dealt with before he thought any more about settling down in this land and living happily forever after.

From his hiding place under a fallen tree, Arth heard the cries of the soldiers. For a long time they stood out on the plateau while he listened to their amazed exclamations. They were clearly more than a little surprised by what they had seen. He heard superstitious mutterings and the Old Tongue word "dragon" repeated over and over.

The minutes passed. Then there came more excited shouting. Arth heard a terrifying roar, followed by sounds of panicked flight. The sequence was repeated several times. Each time the roar seemed louder and the frightened yells sounded farther away.

Finally, he crawled out of his hole and cautiously emerged to look around.

He saw Kremer's rangers running for their ropes, trying desperately to escape the plateau as if the devil himself were after them.

Even he flinched at first as the large, roaring form swooped down toward him from the clouds. Then he saw two small shapes wave at him from the cockpit of the plane.

Arth could understand the soldiers' flight. His own heartbeat sped as he watched the thing, and he knew what it was!

Arth understood that it would be dangerous to try another landing on the sloping, sandy embankment. The chance wasn't worth taking while there was still a lost war to be won. He was only grateful Dennis and Linnora had taken the time to drive the rangers away before moving on to more important matters.

Arth waved farewell to his friends, and watched as the flying machine accelerated away to the south. He shaded his eyes and followed it as it headed toward the line of battle, far down the line of mountains.

Finally, when it had become a mere dot on the horizon, he went over to the pile of supplies Linnora had emptied onto the gravel bank. There he also found several backpacks, dropped in panic by the departing soldiers.

He sighed as he picked through the detritus. There was enough here to live off of for quite some time.

I'll give them a couple days to win th' war and come to get me, he thought. *If they don't come back by then, maybe I'll try to build one of them flyin' things myself!*

He hummed softly as he fixed himself a meal and imagined soaring in the sky, no slave to the winds.

8

The battle was going badly. About noon, Gath ordered every spare implement cast overboard in preparation for a desperate bid at escape.

It did little good. The next flight of gliders to attack sent a hail of darts tearing through the canopy. Fewer arrows than ever rose to meet the black shapes. The great gas bag began to sag as heated air escaped.

Another of the bowmen was killed in the onslaught. The body had to be cast overboard without ceremony. There was no time to do otherwise.

Below, the men guarding the tethers were hard pressed. All knew that it was only a matter of time until the forces holding the south rim fell back under pressure from the air, leaving their flank unguarded.

Kremer had obviously seen the opportunity his salient up the Ruddik offered. He had drawn reinforcements away from the northern front, where Demsen's Royal Scouts had been putting up stiff resistance. Gath had seen several contingents of mercenaries arrive, along with companies of Kremer's gray-clad northmen, only minutes before the most recent glider sortie. The final assault on the salient would not be long delayed. And once they broke through here, the heartland of the L'Toff would lie open.

Their balloon was leaking steadily now. Gath couldn't even estimate how long it would stay aloft, practice notwithstanding.

Then, as if all that weren't enough, one of his men grabbed his shoulder and pointed, asking, "What's *that?*"

Gath squinted. At first he thought it was another damned glider. In the bright afternoon light something new seemed to have entered the sky battle . . . a large winged thing, with a span greater than the biggest of Kremer's aerodynes.

This thing *growled,* and it flew as no glider he had ever seen. There was something powerful about the way it prowled across the sky.

Gath's men muttered fearfully. If Kremer had added another element to the fray . . .

But no! As they watched, the growling thing rose high, then dove into the updraft at the canyon mouth to attack the slowly rising column of gliders there!

Gath stared in amazement. The intruder swooped about the lumbering wings, disturbing the smooth air they depended upon. The turbulence of its passage sent them out of control. One after another, the black shapes shook, tumbled, and fell!

Most of the glidermen ultimately regained control of their bucking craft, but not in time to reach another updraft. The skilled pilots desperately sought flat areas and had to settle for crash landings on the rough slopes.

Angry airmen stumped or hobbled out of their wrecked flying machines to stare up at the buzzing thing that had brought them down like a hand swatting down flies.

A few of Kremer's gliders managed to stay in the updraft. They escaped on the first pass of the growling monster, struggled for altitude, and then dove on the intruder.

But the hawk-winged shape easily maneuvered out of reach of the deadly darts. Then it turned nimbly and pursued its pursuers, hounding them out over the arid plain. Each time the inevitable result was another glider wrecked or stranded on the tumbled prairie.

In a matter of minutes, the sky was clear! The L'Toff stared, unable to believe what had happened. Then a cheer rose from the defenders' lines. The attackers—even the gray-clad professionals—drew back in superstition and awe as the droning *thing* came around to fly high over the canyon.

As if that weren't enough, at that moment there came a peal of horns that echoed resoundingly down the rocky vale. Emerging from the heights overlooking the canyon, a detachment of armored men appeared. As a breeze stiffened, they unfurled the royal pennant of Coylia. A great dragon, its broad, sweeping wings outlined in bright green piping, flapped in the wind and grinned down at the combatants.

Gath knew that a bare dozen Royal Scouts had been hiding on the slopes above, to make a big show at some appropriate time. The tacticians had been counting on the Scouts' reputation to slow the enemy at some crucial moment.

The effect was magnified far beyond what Demsen and Prince Linsee had hoped for. The association between the unknown flying thing and the dragons of legend was unmistakable. In the armies below there were, doubtless, sudden foxhole conversions to the Old Belief.

That was when the great growling monster above chose to swoop upon the army of plainsmen.

No arrows rose to meet it, for although it dropped nothing lethal, its bass moaning struck terror in the invaders' hearts. They dropped weapons and fled their positions without looking back.

Gath breathed easily for the first time in days. He had very little doubt who the pilot of that noisy, dragon-like glider had to be.

9

"Your Majesty! All is lost!" The gray-cloaked rider swerved in front of his liege lord.

Kremer reined up his horse. *"What?* What are you talking about? I was told we had them in our grasp!"

Then he looked up and saw the rout in progress. Like a flash flood, the green, red, and gray uniforms cascaded unstoppably down the canyon, only a little way behind the mounted messenger.

The warlord and his aides were caught in the flood of panicked troops. It quickly became apparent that shouting and beating at the men with their swords would not rally them. It was all Kremer and his officers could do to spur their nervous animals over to high ground at the side of the canyon, out of the tide of fleeing soldiery.

Clearly something had gone desperately wrong. Kremer looked up, searching for his chief weapon, but not one of his gliders was in the sky!

Then he turned at a faint noise and saw an unfamiliar shape flying low down the canyon, chasing his men! From long experience, he knew that no glider could fly that way, ignoring the tricky little niceties of air rise and rate of fall. It screamed like a great, angry bird of prey, and around it shimmered the faint ambience of *felthesh*.

The troops that fled before it had clearly had enough of surprises this campaign. First those nasty, bobbing, floating "balloon" monsters—and now this!

The warlord muttered angrily. As the thing approached, Kremer touched the butt of the needler he wore on his hip. If only it would come close enough. If he could shoot it down, it might restore heart to his men!

But the monster did not cooperate. Its task apparently accomplished, it rose and turned about northward. Kremer had no doubt it was headed toward the battle in the northern passes.

In his mind's eye he saw it all—the foreign wizard had done this, and there was no way to stop it.

He couldn't fight this new thing—not *now*, at least. His battle plan had relied too heavily on his gliders, and they were no match for the monster.

Of course, once news of this disaster reached the east, the great lords would flock to King Hymiel. Within days there would be armies heading west, competing for a price on his head.

Kremer turned to his aides. "Hurry to the semaphore station. Order a complete retreat, both here and in the north. Have my hillmen gather in the Valley of the Tall Trees, in our ancestral highlands of Flemmig. The ancient redoubts there are strong. There we shall not have anything to fear from either armies or the wizard's flying monsters."

"Your Majesty?" The officers stared at him in disbelief. One moment ago they were serving the clear and certain future ruler of all the lands from the mountains to the sea. Now he was telling them that they were to live as their grandfathers had, in the northern wilds!

Kremer understood that few men could see the lay of things as quickly and clearly as he. He couldn't blame them for being stunned. But neither would he countenance slowness to obey.

"Move!" he shouted. He touched the holstered needler at his side and saw them quail.

"I want word to go out at once. When that is done we shall message our garrison in Zuslik. They will strip the town of wealth and food. . . . We will need it during the months and years ahead."

10

It was late, even for a Tatir summer day, when the miracle "dragon" returned to the heartland of the L'Toff. The welcoming party on the ground had to follow in zigs and zags until both they and the pilot of the flying machine found a clearing large enough. By then, it seemed, half of the population—those not still harrying the retreating armies—had gathered to greet their saviors.

The craft swooped in low, a glistening shape that shone in the golden twilight. It touched down lightly and finally rolled to a stop not far from a stand of tall oak trees.

The crowd virtually exploded in joy when they saw the slim form of their Princess stand from the body of the flying craft. They gathered around, cheering, and some even tried to lift her up and carry her off on their shoulders.

But she would have none of it. She motioned them all back and turned to help another person stand. A tall man for an outlander, he was dark-haired and bearded, and he looked very tired.

But the biggest surprise came when they saw the thing that sat upon the man's shoulder—a little creature with two green eyes shining and an impish grin. The Krenegee purred as the people stepped back and fell into a hushed, reverent silence.

Then the L'Toff sighed, almost as one, as the foreign wizard took their Princess into his arms and kissed her for a very long time.

12

Semper Ubi Sub Ubi

1

When Dennis finally awakened he felt a bit strange, as if a lot of time had passed, as if he had dreamed a great deal. He sat up, rubbing his eyes.

Through a filmy curtain, sunlight streamed into the bright-canopied pavilion. He flung aside the silky bedspread and got up from the soft pallet on which he had slept. He found he was naked.

There were excited shouts coming from outside the gaudy tent, and the sound of galloping messengers coming and going. Dennis searched for something to wear and found a pair of soft buckskin breeches and a satiny green blouse laid out over a white-fringed chair. Black leather boots lay nearby . . . his size. Dennis didn't bother with the underwear. He put the clothes on quickly and hurried outside.

Only a dozen meters away, Prince Linsee spoke animatedly with several of his officers. The lord of the L'Toff listened to a report from an out-of-breath messenger, then chuckled and clasped the courier on the shoulder in gratitude.

Dennis relaxed a little when he heard the Prince's laughter. Dennis's exhausted sleep had been disturbed by recurring guilty thoughts that he ought to be up and about, helping the L'Toff secure the victory he had brought them. Several times he had half awakened, intending to get busy devising new weapons, or to use his new aircraft to harry the enemy. But his exhausted body had refused to cooperate.

That wasn't to say his sleep had been disturbed all the time. At intervals he had dreamed of Linnora, and that had been nice.

"Dennizz!"

One of the L'Toff officers grinned as he saw Dennis. Dennis had to stare for a moment. He had been introduced to so many faces in the blurry twilight. . . . Had it been last night, or the night before?

"Dennizz! It's me. Gath!"

Dennis blinked. Why, so it was! The lad seemed to have grown in the past two months or so. Or perhaps it was the uniform.

"Gath! Has there been any word from Stivyung?"

The youth grinned. "We got a message only an hour ago. He's okay. His balloon landed in a barony loyal to the crown, an' he's headed back with a column o' troops to help chase Kremer!"

"Then Kremer—"

Dennis stopped in the middle of his question, because the Prince had turned and was walking over. Linsee was a tall, slender man, with a gray goatee. He smiled and took Dennis's hand.

"Wizard Nuel. It is good to have you up at last. I trust you had a good rest?"

"Well, yes, your Highness. But I'm rather anxious to know about—"

"Yes," Linsee said, laughing. "My daughter, and your betrothed, by my warrant. Linnora is communing in a nearby grove. She will be sent for." At the Prince's nod a young page hurried off with the message.

Dennis was glad. He wanted very badly to see Linnora again. On the night of their landing he had felt as nervous as any young suitor when the Prince arrived and she introduced him. He was greatly relieved when Linsee delightedly consented to their betrothal.

Still, it was the progress of the war that concerned him at the moment. From the air, on that tumultuous evening of battle, he had seen the tyrant's gray-clad troops retreating on all fronts. Their multihued allies—the mercenaries and liege men of other barons—had melted away after the first pass of his flying machine, leaving the northmen to hurry their retreat, glancing up nervously over their shoulders.

But the retreating gray soldiers were not broken. In spite of their fear, they had pulled back in good order. They were excellent troops, who delayed the pursuing L'Toff fiercely so their fellows could escape.

When approaching darkness had forced him and Linnora finally to seek a landing in the L'Toff homeland, Dennis had worried that, come tomorrow, the enemy might reorganize and return.

"What about Kremer?" he asked.

"Not to worry," Linsee grinned. "Kremer's allies are all gone over to the King by now. And an army of volunteer militia is on its way from the populous east. Kremer has stripped Zuslik of everything movable and is even now on his way to his ancestral highlands.

"Sadly, I doubt even the armies of all the kingdom, aided by a flock of your buzzing and bobbing varieties of flying monsters, could pry him out of those craggy clefts."

Dennis felt relieved. He had no doubt Kremer would cause more trouble someday. A man as brilliant and ruthless as he would find ways to pursue his ambitions, and regard this as only a temporary setback.

Still, for now the crisis was over.

Dennis was glad to have helped Linnora's people. But most of all he was happy that no tyrant would force him to invent devices for which this world was simply unprepared.

He would have to watch that, in the future. Already he had unleashed on Tatir the wheel and lighter-than-air craft. And Gath had probably figured out the principle of the propeller by now, just by looking over the cart/airplane.

Dennis would have to see what the Practice Effect made of these innovations, once they were mass-produced, before unleashing any more wizardries on these innocents.

A page hurried up to Prince Linsee. Linsee bent to hear the message.

"My daughter asks that you meet her in the meadow where you landed the night before last." He told Dennis. "She is there, by your miracle machine.

"No one has disturbed your craft since you arrived," the prince assured him. "I let it be known that anyone who touched the great growling dragon-thing would be gobbled up alive!"

Dennis noticed from Linsee's wry smile that he shared Linnora's sharp wit. No doubt while he had slept the Princess had filled her father in on everything that had happened since her capture.

"Uh, that's good, your Highness. Could you assign someone to show me the way?"

Linsee called forth a young girl page, who stepped forward and took Dennis's hand.

2

Linnora awaited Dennis in the open meadow by the gleaming aircraft. She sat cross-legged in L'Toff leather and hose before the nose of the plane, while three of her gowned ladies whispered together at the edge of the glade.

From overheard snippets as he approached among the trees, Dennis could tell that the maids didn't approve overmuch of their Princess dressing like a soldier, not to mention sitting on the turf in front of an alien machine.

The ladies gasped and turned quickly when Dennis said good morning. (Good *afternoon,* he corrected himself as he saw the lay of the sun.) The maids bowed and backed away. Their attitude was respectful, but it also nervously conveyed that they thought he was just a little likely to grow fangs or walk on air. Clearly the run-of-the-mill L'Toff weren't all that much more sophisticated than the average Coylian.

That could change, though, Dennis reminded himself as he walked toward the plane.

Dennis frowned in puzzlement. Linnora was all scrunched over, her head poked under the front of the onetime cart. Although he admired the girl's limberness, to twist about in such a contortion, he wondered what in the world she was doing.

"Linnora," he called, "what are you—"

There was a sudden thud. "Ow! . . ." Her cry was muffled by the airplane's undercarriage. Dennis blushed as there followed a quick chain of expletives Linnora could have learned from only one source. The words certainly weren't in the Coylian dialect of the English language!

The Princess withdrew from under the craft and sat up rubbing her head. But her muttered invective stopped the instant she saw who it was. "Dennis!" she cried out. And then she was in his arms.

Finally, a bit breathless, he got a chance to ask her what she had been up to down there.

"Oh, that! Well, I hope it was all right. I mean, I hope I wasn't fooling around dangerously with things I don't understand well enough. But you were asleep for *so* long, and some busybody went and told Father I'd dressed for war, so he's had me watched ever since to make sure I didn't go ride off after Kremer's ears or something. I was starting to get *bored,* so bored that I decided I wanted to see—"

She was clearly excited about something. But it was all coming just a bit too fast for Dennis. "Uh, Linnora, your ladies seemed a bit shocked seeing you burrowing under there like that."

"Oh!" Linnora looked down at her muddy knees. She started trying to dust herself off, then stopped and shrugged. "Oh, well. They'll just have to get used to it, won't they? In addition to being your wife, I expect to be taught wizarding, you know. And that seems to be a dusty business, from what I've experienced so far."

The twinkle in her eye told him that there were certain things she would expect from her lord husband. Clearly, he wouldn't have to look far from home for an apprentice.

"Anyway," she went on, "I came down here and found everything just as we left it when we landed. Your Krenegee was here, too. But he seems to have gone off, now. Perhaps he's hunting. I've been under there a long time, and maybe I've lost track of time."

Dennis despaired of his beloved ever getting to the point. "But what were you *doing* under there?" he insisted.

Linnora stopped for a moment, her torrent of words cut off as she traced her train of thought.

"The robot!" she declared suddenly. "I was bored, so I decided to talk to that wonderful creature-and-tool you brought from your world!"

"You were *talking* to . . ." It was Dennis's turn to blink. "Show me," he asked at last.

The L'Toff ladies were shocked even more when they saw the wizard and their Princess crawl down together into the grass and dirt. The women made ready to turn modestly away if their worst fears proved true.

They gave out relieved sighs. Linnora hadn't been *so* debased down in the lowlands. But then what were they *doing* squirming under there like that?

The ladies realized, with regret that things would never be the same as they once were.

3

They had not really needed to crawl under the plane to examine the robot. Dennis realized later that he could have ordered the little automaton to drop the propeller, and its grip on the undercarriage, and come out. But by now it looked so much a *part* of the craft that it never even occurred to him at the time. The series of powerful practice trances, amplified by the magic of the Krenegee beast, had transformed the machine until it looked inseparable from the gleaming wooden flyer.

When Linnora said she had been "talking" to the robot, she meant that she had done the actual speaking. The 'bot had replied using its little display screen.

Dennis frowned as he looked at the rows of flowing Coylian script on the pearly rectangle. He couldn't read the alien tongue as quickly as it sped past. Besides, he wondered, how had the robot learned to . . .

Of course, he realized quickly. Since almost his first moment on Tatir, the machine had been gathering information on the inhabitants, at his command. Naturally, that included learning the writing they used here.

"Split screen," he commanded. "Coylian script on the left, Earth English translation on the right."

The text parted into two versions of the same report. He and Linnora had to crawl in a little farther to read, then, but that only brought them closer together, and he couldn't think of that as a disadvantage.

Immediately he noticed something interesting. Though Coylian letters were part of a syllabary, and English/Roman letters were a true alphabet, the two systems clearly shared a common style. The "th" sound in Coylian, for instance, looked like a mutated "t" and "h" melded together.

Dennis recalled some of the calculations he had played with during his imprisonment. With a growing sense of excitement, he began to suspect that one of the theories he had come up with back then just might be true.

He read the text for a while. It was a summary of early Coylian history, found on some ancient scrolls the 'bot had pilfered temporarily from a temple in Zuslik. The scrolls had referred specifically to the Old Belief, once followed widely on Tatir, but now adhered to only by the L'Toff and a few others. It seemed to consist mostly of apparent myth and legend, but interspersed through the gaudy stories, Dennis thought he saw a pattern.

Dennis asked the robot to skim back to earlier entries, then ahead again. Linnora watched, fascinated, and from time to time suggested passages she had read earlier. Occasionally she stopped to explain a meaning he had not come across before.

They spent a long time together under the cart, reading the correlated history of a world.

Dennis was starting to get a crick in his neck when he finally felt he had enough data. The conclusion seemed incontrovertible.

"This isn't *only* another planet!" he declared. "It's also the future!"

Linnora rolled over and looked at him.

"Yes, for you it is, my wizard from the past. Does this change things? Would you still marry with one who might be your distant descendant?"

Dennis moved closer and kissed her. "I had no strong ties to my time," he told her. "And you can't be my descendant. I never had any kids."

Linnora sighed. "Well, that, too, can be remedied."

Dennis was about to kiss her again, and the ladies at the edge of the grove might have been shocked even more. But there came a sudden shout from somewhere directly overhead.

"Dennizz! Princess!"

This time there were two thumps and two series of muttered oaths. Both Linnora and Dennis emerged rubbing their heads. But they grinned when they saw who awaited them.

"Arth!"

It was, indeed, the diminutive thief. A crowd of L'Toff had gathered, and they watched in hushed admiration from the edge of the glade, for a Krenegee sat on Arth's shoulder, purring.

Dennis clasped his friend. "So Proll's men were able to find you! I was afraid our description of that plateau wouldn't be good enough and we'd have to go after you in the plane. We were worried about you!"

Arth scratched the purring pixolet under the chin. "Oh, I was okay," he said nonchalantly. "I spent th' time bangin' sticks together to *make* another flyin' cart. Woulda tried it out, too, but th' L'Toff an' Demsen's scouts came for me."

Dennis shuddered at the thought. He would have to have a good talk with the fellow—and with Linnora and Gath and anyone else who suffered under the illusion that Earth technology could just be *banged together*. Practice Effect or no, some things had to work right the first time!

"Well, just as long as you're all right."

"Sure, I'm fine. Sent a message to Maggin with Demsen's troops. Asked th' little lady to come out here from Zuslik to join me here for a vacation—with your Highness's permission, o' course." He bowed to Linnora. Linnora only laughed and hugged the little thief.

"Oh, by th' way," Arth went on, "I don't know if you both have heard, but I guess you'd be interested. It seems Demsen's boys caught up with a company of Kremer's men out near North Pass. And guess who was with 'em? None other than our old friend Hoss'k!"

"Hoss'k!"

"Yeah. Th' deacon got away, worse luck. But th' Scouts did capture a strange fellow who was *with* Hoss'k. A prisoner, it seems. They got him back at Linsee's tent now.

"Funny thing, though. You know he talks a lot like you, Dennizz? All funny an' open in th' back of the throat, with that strange accent o' yours.

"An' some of th' captured hillmen said he was another wizard!"

Dennis and Linnora looked at each other. "I think we had better look into this," the Princess said.

4

"Well, Brady. So Flaster chose you to come after me. He sure took his time about it."

The sandy-haired fellow sitting gloomily in the camp chair turned quickly about and stared.

"Nuel! It's you! Oh, lord, it's good to see a fellow Earthman!"

Bernald Brady looked harried and exhausted. He had a bruise on his forehead, and his typical snide expression had been replaced by apparently genuine delight and relief at the sight of Dennis.

Linnora and Arth followed Dennis into the tent. Brady's eyes widened on seeing the creature riding Arth's shoulder, and he backed away.

The pixolet apparently remembered Brady, too. It hissed unappreciatively and bared its teeth. Finally Arth had to take it outside.

When they were gone, Brady turned imploringly to Dennis. "Nuel, please! Can you tell me what is going on here? This place is crazy! First I find the zievatron in pieces, and your weird note. Then all my equipment shows signs of acting funny. Finally, I get conked on the head by some big slob who acts like Minister Calumny himself and has a bunch of thugs strip me of all my gear. . . ."

"They took your weapons? I was afraid of that." Dennis grimaced. Kremer already had his needler, and there was no telling what other arms the ever-cautious Brady had brought along. No doubt Brady had not stinted quality in outfitting *himself*. With all that stuff, Kremer could still turn out to be a big pain down the road.

"They stole everything!" Brady groaned. "From my campstove right down to my wedding ring!"

"You're married, now?" Dennis's eyebrows rose. "To whom? Anybody I know?"

Brady suddenly looked anxious. Clearly he did not want to offend Dennis. "Uh, well, when you didn't come back—"

Dennis stared. "You mean you and *Gabbie?*"

"Uh, yes. I mean, you were gone so long. And we discovered we had so much in common—well, you know." He looked up sheepishly.

Linnora, too, was looking concerned.

Dennis laughed. "Never mind, Bernie. We never had anything going, anyway. I'm sure you're better suited to her than I ever would have been. Congratulations. Sincerely."

Brady shook Dennis's hand uncertainly. He looked from Dennis to Linnora and back and seemed to understand the situation.

But that only appeared to make him more miserable. The fellow wasn't merely afraid and homesick. He was in love.

"Well, we'll see to getting you back to her as quickly as possible," he told his erstwhile rival compassionately. "I've got to visit Earth temporarily anyway. I'd like to trade a few local works of art for some items I can buy from N-Mart."

Dennis had plans. For the sake of both worlds he would make sure Linsee kept a tight guard on the zievatron, restricting the flow between the worlds carefully. They certainly didn't want to create any paradoxes in time!

But in a limited way trade could probably profit both realities.

Brady shook his head. "Even if we could put a new return mechanism together from those parts you buried, we'd never get it finished in time! Flaster gave me only a few days, and those are about used up!

"And when the airlock mechanism was wrecked, it destroyed the calibration settings. I don't even know Earth's reality coordinates!"

"Well, I remember them," Dennis assured him.

"Oh, yeah?" A touch of Brady's familiar sarcasm returned. "Well, have you figured out the coordinates for *this* crazy place yet? We never were too sure of them back in Lab One. We just sort of stumbled onto the settings. And now those, too, are ruined!"

"Don't worry. I can calculate them as well. You see, I think I know not only where we are, but *when* as well."

Brady stared. And Dennis started to explain.

"Think about the most important discoveries of the twentieth and twenty-first centuries," Dennis suggested. "Clearly the most dramatic were bioengineering and zievatronics.

"Physics was a dead end by the year 2000. Oh, there were lots of abstract problems, but nothing that seemed to offer a way to bring other worlds within mankind's grasp. The solar system was a pretty barren place, and the stars remained awfully far away.

"But with recombinant DNA, there appeared the possibility of creating almost any type of viable life-form, for whatever purpose. Work only beginning at Sahara Tech and at other institutions when we were there seemed to be leading to a world filled with wonders—giant chickens, cows that gave yogurt, even unicorns, dragons, and griffins!

"Then there was the zievatron, which promised to reopen the road to the stars relativity seemed to have closed off forever.

"Now imagine both of these trends," Dennis asked, "taken into the future.

"When, in a hundred years or so, the ziev effect was finally perfected, bands of migrants would travel to other worlds, to colonize or find space for their own diverse ways of life.

"And by that time they wouldn't take with them many tools, only the very minimum that could fit through the zievatron. After all, when you can tailor-make organisms for any function, why burden yourself with clumsy hunks of metal?

"Self-repairing, semi-intelligent robots made of living matter would drive you to work, toil in the fields, and clean your house. Walking brains would record your messages and recite any information verbatim at command. Fiercely loyal great flying 'dragons' with laser eyes would protect your new colonies against any danger. All these specialized organisms would be 'fueled' by food generated at special facilities.

"In the future, colonists would not go in starships, nor would they carry cold metal with them. Why should they, when they could simply step through a gate to their new worlds and design creatures for any function?"

Brady scratched his head. "That's a lot of speculation, Nuel. You can't tell what's going to happen in the future."

"Oh, but I can," Dennis said with a smile. "Because this is it! This is the future, Brady."

Brady stared.

"Imagine a group of colonists who belong to a fringe group with antimachine sentiments," Dennis said. "Let's say this group finds a beautiful world, accessible through the zievatron. They save up to pay transmission charges and then leave the complicated society of Earth for their paradise, shutting the door behind them.

"At first all goes well. Then, all of a sudden, the complicated bioengineered creatures they depend upon start dying!

"Their scientists finally find a cause. It is a plague, created by another race that plies the ziev space, one with whom man has by this time had skirmishes for several centuries. The enemy are called the *Blecker,* and they have chosen this isolated outpost of humanity to test their new weapon.

"The Blecker had released a disease on Tatir, which is what the world was named. The plague could not kill any life-form capable of independent existence—able to find its own way in the wild—but it destroyed the synthetic food supply. Without that food the delicate symbiotes upon which the colonists' civilization depended were doomed.

"The scientists of Tatir discovered the attack too late to stop it. The dying was well under way, beginning with the huge but delicate dragons upon whom the planet's defense relied.

"Desperate, they reopened the zievatron link to Earth, to beg for help."

Brady sat on the edge of his seat, listening intently. "What happened then?" he asked.

Dennis shrugged. "Earth was anxious not to get contaminated. They sent through a powerful device that would scramble the zievways to Tatir for a thousand years, until a cure could be found. When the machine had done its work, neither Earth *nor* the invaders could get through to this world.

"But"—Dennis raised one finger—"before doing that, they sent through a gift!"

From outside they heard Arth's voice call. "I think th' critter's settled down now. I'll bring him in. You all sit still!"

The curtain parted and Arth entered again. The pixolet rode his shoulder. When it saw Brady it glared but was quiet. It spread its wing membranes and glided over to Linnora's lap. She stroked the beast and soon it was purring again.

Linorra whispered, "We of the L'Toff never forgot the gift from Earth, did we, my little Krenegee?"

"No, you didn't," Dennis agreed. In the centuries of savagery that followed the inevitable fall of Tatir civilization, almost everything was lost. The few machines rusted away and were forgotten. Since most of the transports had been hovercraft, even the principle of the wheel was forgotten.

"Most of the specialized animals died off, leaving only the sturdiest Earth stock and local fauna. The language started to change as virtually all learning and lore were lost.

"The people were soon reduced almost to the level of beasts. It took a long time for the legends of written speech to inspire some genius to reinvent writing.

"Back on Earth they had known all this would happen. And yet they could not help without risking a spread of the infection to the home world.

"So they opened the portal just a crack, before sealing it for a millennium. They sent through the very latest product of their great research —the culmination of two converging fields, biology and reality physics.

"What they sent through was an animal immune to the disease, for it could fend for itself, but one who carried with it a *talent*. That talent would pervade this world and give its people a chance.

"With time, the people of Tatir absorbed some of the talent for themselves. Those who lived closest to the creatures absorbed the most of it and became the L'Toff."

Dennis finished, "The gift the Earth sent was a miracle, from our twenty-first-century perspective. It saved the people of this planet. And to think I once thought it useless."

Brady followed Dennis's look.

"That thing?" He pointed incredulously at the pixolet. The creature preened, and grinned back with a row of needle-sharp teeth.

"Yes, that," Dennis said with a nod.

"Of course, I'm only going by pieced-together accounts from legends more than a thousand years old. But I'm pretty sure that's what happened.

"We can only imagine what the Earth of the fortieth century is like, now that these *Krenegee* have been loose there for centuries. Perhaps the age of biologicals is past and the era of tools has returned there— magical tools beyond belief.

"I'd be glad of it, for the bioengineering did sound a bit questionable, ethically."

Dennis stood next to Linnora. She and Pix looked up at him and he

037

smiled. Dennis turned back to Brady and concluded, "Now, at last, the barriers to this world are dropping. For some reason a weird intertime path to twenty-first-century Earth was the first to open, perhaps because ours was the first zievatron of all.

"Soon other paths will open. And these people have got to be ready when they do. The Blecker are probably still out there, waiting for a chance to get in.

"That's why I think I'll hang around after we fix the return mechanism and send you back home."

Linnora took his hand. "At least that's one of the reasons," he amended.

Brady looked perplexed. "That's a pretty convincing story, Nuel. Except for one thing."

"What's that?"

"You still haven't told me what this *talent* is you're saying that nasty little thing has! What *was* this gift Earth supposedly sent through?"

Dennis looked surprised. "Oh! You mean nobody's explained that part of it to you yet?"

"No! And I'll tell you I can't take it much longer! Something's screwy about this world! Did you notice the strange juxtaposition of technologies these people have here? I can't figure out what's going on, and it's driving me crazy!"

Dennis remembered how many times he had sworn vengeance on Brady during his months on Tatir. Right now he had the fellow in his power, but all the malice he had felt before was gone. He decided to satisfy himself with one *little* bit of revenge.

"Oh, I'll let you figure it out for yourself, Brady. I'm sure a mind like yours can come up with the answer, if you practice it hard enough."

Bernald Brady sat there. He had no choice but to fume silently while Dennis Nuel laughed. As the woman, the little man, the alien creature from the future, and his onetime rival all grinned at him, Brady had the uneasy feeling that he wasn't going to enjoy the learning process much at all.

ABOUT THE AUTHOR

DAVID BRIN was born in 1950 in southern California. He has been an engineer with Hughes Aircraft Co., and attended Caltech and The University of California at San Diego, where he completed doctoral studies on comets and asteroids. He is presently a consultant with the California Space Institute, a unit of the University of California, San Diego, doing advanced studies concerning the Space Shuttle and space science. He also teaches university physics and occasionally creative writing.

A nominee for the Hugo and John W. Campbell awards, Brin is the author of two previous, highly praised novels, *Sundiver* and *Startide Rising*. He is currently secretary of the Science Fiction Writers of America and is at work on his next novel.